What critics have to say about *Changing The Past*:

"*Changing The Past* demonstrates again Berger's consistently witty, incisive vision. . . . This work confirms Berger's stature among America's finest writers.
— *San Francisco Chronicle*

"One of our most authentically American comic voices is back with another tale of social Darwinism among the hicks, rural and urban."
— *Fort Worth Star-Telegram*

"Berger has a wonderfully witty way of keeping us off-balance as he leads us through a maze constructed of the unlikeliest twists and turns."
— *The Sacramento Bee*

What critics have to say about Thomas Berger:

"An exquisitely subtle artist who can conjure character and emotion from the slightest verbal means"
— *The New Republic*

"A writer of enormous wit and incisive vision"
— *San Francisco Review of Books*

"[His] stylish fecundity, psychological insight, and social knowledge are seemingly inexhaustible."
— *Saturday Review*

CONTEMPORARY AMERICAN FICTION

CHANGING THE PAST

Thomas Berger is the author of fifteen novels, among which are *Little Big Man*, *Neighbors*, *The Feud*, and the quartet that comprises the Reinhart Series. He has been called, by *The Village Voice*, "America's wittiest, most elegant novelist," and, by *The Christian Science Monitor*, "an extraordinary prose stylist."

A NOVEL BY
Thomas Berger

CHANGING THE PAST

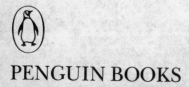

PENGUIN BOOKS

PENGUIN BOOKS
Published by the Penguin Group
Viking Penguin, a division of Penguin Books USA Inc.,
375 Hudson Street, New York, New York 10014, U.S.A.
Penguin Books Ltd, 27 Wrights Lane, London W8 5TZ, England
Penguin Books Australia Ltd, Ringwood, Victoria, Australia
Penguin Books Canada Ltd, 2801 John Street,
Markham, Ontario, Canada L3R 1B4
Penguin Books (N.Z.) Ltd, 182–190 Wairau Road,
Auckland 10, New Zealand

Penguin Books Ltd, Registered Offices:
Harmondsworth, Middlesex, England

First published in the United States of America by Little, Brown and Company 1989
Reprinted by arrangement with Little, Brown and Company
Published in Penguin Books 1991

10 9 8 7 6 5 4 3 2 1

The characters and events in this book are fictitious.
Any similarity to real persons, living or dead, is
coincidental and not intended by the author.

LIBRARY OF CONGRESS CATALOGING IN PUBLICATION DATA
Berger, Thomas, 1924–
Changing the past: a novel/ by Thomas Berger.
p.   cm. — (Contemporary American fiction)
"First published in the United States of America by Little, Brown
and Company 1989"—T.p. verso.
ISBN 0 14 01.3323 2
I. Title   II. Series.
[PS3552.E719C48   1991]
813'54—dc20   90–44963

Printed in the United States of America

To Ralph Ellison

Changing the Past

"**N**OT EVEN God can change the past," Walter Hunsicker had once read somewhere, and after living almost six decades in which virtually every other supposedly unassailable truth had been successfully challenged (how soon would the techniques of cloning make death obsolete?; tax evaders were legion; often it was better *not* to have loved . . . etc.), he assumed this adage was sound as ever and would surely persist in being so unto infinity.

Or anyway such was his assumption before meeting the man with whom he shared a doorway during a heavy city rainstorm. This fellow came only to Hunsicker's shoulder, and wore a battered felt hat and a shabby two-piece suit the cut of which was not enhanced by the water it had lately absorbed. His shirt collar was frayed at the points; his necktie had been knotted too often with unclean fingers. Hunsicker assessed him as belonging to a category somewhat above the derelict's — he did not stink, he asked for no money — but considerably below Hunsicker's own situation.

A careful viewer of television weather reports, Hunsicker had been prepared for the downpour. He now sought refuge only by reason of the failure of his equipment. The second gust of violent wind had instantly decommissioned his umbrella; his raincoat felt as though it were constructed of cheesecloth. Ordinarily he would not have spoken to even a well-dressed stranger, but at the moment he was in a state of indignation conditioned by discomfort, and the man was small and looked innocuous.

Hunsicker plucked at a wet lapel. "This is a brand-new coat, supposed to shed rain. Look at it."

The other shrugged inside his wilted jacket. "Then don't put up with it." His voice was dry and lacked depth, the kind that might easily become rasping.

"I've owned it too long now to take it back. Anyway, all it claimed to be was water-repellent: that would certainly be the store's argument. And this is, or was, a cloudburst." At the moment the rain was catching its breath for the next assault. Almost no water was falling, but standing in the air one felt as though immersed in liquidity.

"Could I interest you in a deal?" asked the other, eyes glittering under the brim of the felt hat.

Hunsicker groaned. "You're not about to offer me a genuine diamond ring for a bargain price? Or a luxury wristwatch at one-fifth what they're asking in the shop around the corner?"

The little man smirked now. "Look here, I'll give you a free sample."

"No thanks." Hunsicker was about to step out onto the sidewalk when it was as if the ceiling of heaven fell in great slabs of solid water, which pulverized when they struck the pavement near the doorway. He recoiled to the far limits of the niche.

"Oh, come on," said the little man, relentlessly indifferent to the weather. "You really can't lose. Examine that coat of yours now."

Hunsicker was very late in returning from lunch, and while he was in effect his own boss, he took some pains in not enjoying conspicuous privileges over the persons under him. Irrespective of the climate, he had to get going. Therefore he did deal with his coat, though not in response to the urging of the tiresome little man.

He examined the garment, to determine just how much water had penetrated to the lining, useless as such an inquiry might be, for it was obvious that he could not enter the deluge dressed only in his suit. . . . What he saw was another coat than that which he had lately removed from his shoulders. Not only was this one thoroughly dry as to its inside surface, but it had no lining. Rubber would seem foremost amongst the materials from which it had been fashioned, and a dark, rubbery cement was evident at all inside seams. He recognized the garment as what the English call a "riding mac," a raincoat designed primarily for persons on horseback, with an appropriate cut, lengthy vent, leg-straps, etc., but sometimes worn by those pedestrians determined to keep as dry as one could when not under a roof. It would be perfect for the weather at hand, though impractical if applied to any of the other functions of the vanished all-purpose trench coat.

But the fact was that he had entered the doorway wearing the latter, whereas he had never his life long owned a riding mac. This truth was so simple as to defy any effort to explain it simply.

"I don't know what's happening to me," he confessed to the shabby little man. "I may need an ambulance in a moment. Please call one. And take my wallet and phone my wife at the number on the identification card. Keep all of the money in the wallet, but, if you will, return all the papers, credit cards, et cetera, to her. God bless you." He was preparing to fall to the dirty concrete floor of the doorway.

"Stop this farce," said the little man. "You're not dying. You're in excellent health for a man of your age. Your blood pressure is actually a bit lower than normal. You're not overweight. You haven't smoked for twenty years, and you hardly drink at all."

Hunsicker shook his head. "I certainly don't feel well at the moment."

"It's just that you have had reason to look at things in a new way," said the stranger. "You've never before experienced the changing of the past."

Hunsicker tried to summon up some indignation, so as to resist the panic that continued to threaten him. "That can't be done!"

"Remember buying the raincoat last week. The salesman pressed you to purchase the trench coat, but you —"

Hunsicker eagerly broke in. "I've had such coats in the past: they *never* really shed water, no matter what the claims, and furthermore I have no need for the zip-in wool lining. I own a perfectly good topcoat that does the job. Therefore I insisted on the riding mac despite the salesman's opposition, which was odd since this coat, imported as it is, was priced higher, but then perhaps he got a higher commission on the other."

"Indeed," said the little man. "In any event, your memory is clear on this affair."

"Absolutely."

"And your wisdom has been confirmed by this rain: not a drop touched your body, and of course the cap has kept your head dry."

"Cap?" Hunsicker felt his scalp. Yes, what seemed to be a cap was there. Until this moment he had assumed he was bareheaded and his hair was wet from the water that had struck him between the discarding of the ruined umbrella and plunging into the doorway, but in the next instant of course he remembered the cap, which was made of a salt-and-pepper wool-like weave that despite its porous appearance was as resistant to falling water as a tin roof; perhaps it was treated with a wonder-chemical not available to those who made routine raincoats. In any event, with the cap and the riding mac, no umbrella was needed to keep dry in this gusty city.

"Is that acceptable proof?" asked his small companion in the doorway.

Hunsicker felt a warm sense of security, armored as he was against the weather, and in such a mood he was inclined towards generosity. He unsnapped one of the grommets of the coat and reached for his wallet.

"In fact, it worked so well," said the little man, "that you can't even remember what happened." He waved a scrawny finger. "Put your money away: I don't want it. Just attend to what I'm saying. A moment ago you were bareheaded and wearing a water-soaked outer garment, which you regretted having purchased. Can you remember that?"

Hunsicker lost his smile. "I'm trying not to think of that confusing moment. It can't have happened. It doesn't make any sense."

The little man groaned. "Ah, Walter, what a prisoner you are of a few simpleminded principles. Since when has 'making sense' had any serious reference to what happens in reality? Things rarely make sense except in the banalities of art. Reason is usually beside the point in anything but a product of the imagination."

"How do you know my first name?" Asking the question was therapeutic, distracting him from the little man's paradoxes, which though nonsense were nevertheless terrifying.

"Call me a private detective if it will make you feel better — and then I should assure you immediately I haven't been hired by your wife or your place of employment."

"You'll get no blackmail money from me. I've nothing to hide."

Now the little man smiled broadly. "Even the IRS would agree: you must be one of the few who ever emerged clean from a random audit. Fifteen years ago, you were sexually importuned by your wife's second cousin, at a wedding party at which she, like so many of the guests, excluding you, got drunk. You went so far as to let her kiss you and feel your behind before pushing her genially away and pretending it was a joke. Stranded because of bad weather at an airport hotel one night in Kansas City many years ago, you conversed at length with an unaccompanied young woman at the bar and for a few moments anyway considered the commercial proposal she put to you — she was your favorite type for erotic daydreams, with flaming red hair and very white skin — but naturally you returned to your room alone. You've never even brought home much loot from the office, save the odd pencil left forgotten in your pocket. You've never got a ticket for speeding, and only two for parking: once because of a faulty meter and another time when vandals defaced the sign and, late for a dental appointment of some consequence, you decided to take a chance."

Hearing the list reassured Hunsicker. Obviously this was still the world he knew, and it was only reasonable to expect that the unusual events of the last few minutes would soon be shown to make perfect sense when examined from a new perspective the existence of which, like that of an extra room in a house in a dream, he had not previously suspected might be available to him. He nonetheless was irritated by the report of the little man's surveillance, which seemed to go well beyond the kind of thing a private detective could be expected to discover, and though the accumulation of inconsequential data served to exonerate him from almost any kind of charge, he was not better off for the intrusion into his private life.

"Perhaps you'll be so good," he said frostily, "as to tell me for whom you made this investigation, and for what purpose?"

"You really should consider the power accessible to you if you so choose. Look at your new raincoat and cap. The past has been changed. This is not some sleight-of-hand: your credit-card receipts, which I know you keep carefully on file forever, will support the evidence of your eyes, as will your wife and office colleagues. Your purchase of the riding mac and cap is now a solid part of history."

Hunsicker did not want to ponder on this matter. "I'm sure you're right. Now, if you'll pardon me, I really must get back to work. I'm head of the department, you see, and though the people under me are mostly well intentioned, it goes without saying that they simply do not work as diligently when I'm not there."

"If you're concerned, then why not change the clock?" the little man asked, shrugging. "Return it to an acceptable time. You can always turn it back, but you cannot design what's to come." He grinned. "It would be futile to try that. But the past is infinitely malleable." He squinted at Hunsicker. "You still don't believe me."

"You'll have to admit that everything you say is awfully implausible," Hunsicker said. "I meet you by chance in a doorway during a cloudburst, and you know all about me and furthermore offer me, for no reason at all, the power to do something that is utterly impossible. Who in the world *are* you? And if you have this extraordinary power to give away to a stranger, why aren't you wearing a raincoat of your own? You're soaked."

"My style of dress helps me to maintain the inconspicuousness I favor. As to being a bit damp, I find it refreshing on a warmish day. Now, all you have to do in the case of the 'utterly impossible' is simply to try it. The time, as is, is two twenty-five. What would be more convenient?"

Hunsicker could not have said why he responded to this preposterous question, but he did. "An hour earlier. One-thirty should do it."

"Right you are," said the little man, pointing at Hunsicker's wrist. "Take a look."

The dial of the watch showed the time as precisely 1:30. Hunsicker began to tremble.

The little man was amused. "You might as well get used to it." He raised his thin eyebrows. "Unless you genuinely want no part of this. Opting out is usually the simplest thing to do in all human experiences, until of course the last one — at which time you however might well regret a long history of saying no in those situations in which you had a choice. . . . That's right: dying cannot be changed. You see why — it's never in the past. It's inevitably a thing of the future, is it not?"

Hunsicker sought refuge in banalities. For the first time he noticed the show windows of the shop whose doorway gave them shelter. Medical equipment was on display therein: bedpans, leg braces, trusses, all flyblown and dusty, the rubber tube of the enema gear looking brittle, the bulb half-deflated. The interior of the shop was unlighted and appeared deserted.

"Look," he forced himself to say at last, "I'm certain there is an explanation for what I hope is your sleight-of-hand and not some nervous ailment or even worse on my part. But what I'll have to get used to, if so, will be stark realism and not some supernatural nonsense. If I'm sick I'll have to get treatment. Now I *must* go. I won't ask again how you know my first name. I'm not even going to inquire into your own identity. I don't want to get in any deeper!" He stepped to the junction of doorway and sidewalk.

"All right, then," the little man said behind him. "I'll put things back where they were."

The garment which Hunsicker wore was once again the wet trench coat.

The little man was smiling at him. "It's your business, surely, but I don't see why you couldn't try it for a while. You can always go back, as I have just demonstrated — incidentally, it's two twenty-five again. You're just as late as you ever were, as well as being just as damp. Do you really think that's preferable?"

"What I would prefer," Hunsicker said in shaky resentment, "is being let alone. The normal sort of arrangement of things has always been good enough for me. I'm not the right sort of person to approach with an idea of this kind. You should get someone who lives an unsatisfactory life. This city must be full of them. Come to the office with me and choose almost anyone you see. But *I* can't do you much good. I've been happily married for almost thirty years to a woman who after discharging her responsibilities as a mother started her own business as a real-estate agent. I have a wonderful son. After a brilliant record at law school, he's now with a renowned firm of attorneys."

"I'm aware of those facts," said the little man. "They're not that remarkable nowadays, when almost everybody in your socioeconomic stratum could pretty well come up with the equivalent. Most middle-aged suburban wives sell real estate, don't they? And having intelligent and vigorous offspring is not unusual. Decadence is not as prevalent among the young as the journalists would have you think. Anyway, the other members of your family are not *you*. They have their own lives to deal with. As to yours, could it not stand some improvement? For example, what about your name? Is it really the one you'd want if you had your choice?"

As it happened, Walter Hunsicker had never much liked either of those names, and the middle, Grover, was no improvement. But he said now, defiantly, "It's a good name, a good strong solid three syllables, and it was my dad's, and I loved him."

"Very touching," said the little man, "but confess that if you could have changed it, no questions asked and no hard feelings, would you not have done so? What I'm talking about would be no betrayal of your forebears. Remember, it would be changing the past. Whatever new name you elected to take would thereupon *not* be new, but rather the one used by your family for generations. Now, what sounds good?"

It could do no harm to play this game, but, as he saw by his wristwatch, the time was now halfway to three. "Really, I must go."

"Remember that it could be changed back again," the little man said. "You've nothing to lose. Try some new names on for size!"

Hunsicker was shy. "I wouldn't know where to start. This is silly."

"That's why you can't get hurt."

"All right: Kellog. Channing Kellog the Third. No, that's pretentious. John Kellog, known except on formal documents as Jack."

The little man nodded soberly. "So be it. You may need a

whole new past to go with the name. Jack Kellog's not the name of someone your age who is chief copy-editor at a book-publishing firm, father of a son who has already gone beyond him in professional prestige."

Hunsicker grimaced. He had been foolish to dally here. "Well then," he said, "isn't it fortunate that I remain good old Walter Hunsicker?" He took the plunge into the rain.

Six blocks later, he reached his office, which was in a building that only from the exterior seemed a world of green glass. The receptionist was an amply proportioned young woman with auburn hair in an artificial friz, or so it seemed, for only last week it had been softly waved — unless the reverse was true and the tight little coils were natural, the waving manmade.

He nodded and said, "Judy." He was the head of a department of some consequence, for no book however exalted could go to the printer without being copy-edited, and yet he knew the name of this young kid, whereas after at least four months on the job she hadn't the foggiest knowledge of his. He realized that his wife was quite right, he shouldn't be irked over such inconsequentialities, but he *was*.

In silently acknowledging the nod, Judy displayed the progress she had made in recent weeks. For at least three weeks after assuming the post, she had continued to ask, on his return from lunch, whom he wanted to see and on what matter. On the wall behind her were recessed shelves, glass-fronted and conspicuously locked, showing the bright jackets of books recently published by the firm. The manuscript for each had passed through Hunsicker's department and, he liked to think, had been greatly improved thereby, perhaps even made publishable: it would be astonishing to the lay reader to know how careless many authors, even some of the most renowned, are not only about grammar and of course spelling, but also the accuracy of their facts. Or maybe just stupid, for one truth Hunsicker had learned in his years of wielding a blue pencil was that it takes less intelligence to write a book than to put together a Christmas toy that comes disassembled. He could admit there were exceptions, but his was scarcely the kind of work that tended to preserve the awe one had felt for story-tellers as a bookish, hypochondriacal child.

He passed through the vestibule into the inner reaches of Rodgers, Wirth & Maddox, known familiarly as RWM, none of whose founders was still alive, and went to his part of its world, an enclosure with walls and two doorways but without doors that could be closed. A certain separation from the rest of the office was useful, but for this kind of work there was no need for privacy — with a few exceptions during Hunsicker's long tenure: e.g., the memoirs of a former secretary of the treasury which, the publicity and advertising departments vulgarly hinted, were to reveal a lot of dirt on his former political colleagues. Access to this manuscript was restricted and Hunsicker himself had done all the copy-editing thereof, in the borrowed corner office of a vice-president (the promotional promise was exaggerated: most of the "revelations" had been known for ages and the rest were petty).

Three full-time copy-editors comprised Hunsicker's department, not counting him, and during the busy seasons when the manuscripts came in multitudes, he had to resort to a list of auxiliary free-lancers if the publishing schedule was to be met.

All three of his subordinates (though at least two of them would have rejected that term) were at work as he entered now. Myron Beckersmith, a tall, knobby young man with intense eyes under heavy brows, was poring over one of the tomes from the small but versatile reference library maintained by the copy-editing department on a wall of shelves not too far behind the desk of Carrie Janes, a pudgy young woman with a complexion of pearl, the newest member of the team and the most learned, having actually studied classical Greek. Carrie at the moment was exercising her most annoying habit, blowing the hanging hair away from her eyes rather than pinning it back in some fashion or, better yet — given a profession that kept her bending all day over a sheaf of paper — having a more practical coiffure. And worse than watching her fat lower lip extend, chimpanzee-style, to puff air upwards, was to check over a manuscript when her job was done (as head of department, Hunsicker always did this, for it was he who bore the official responsibility for any errors or oversights) and find stray hairs throughout: to Hunsicker this was almost as offensive as if he had found such in his lunchtime bowl of soup.

His return now was visibly marked only by the remaining member of the trio, Dorothy Kalergis, the eldest after him though at forty-one not all that old. She was also the only one other than he to have been married and have children, with the difference that Dorothy was a divorcée of some years and her children were still young enough to live with her.

She looked up now and winked sardonically at him. There was a possibility that she had formerly had some hopes he might wish to extend their professional association, which was amiable, into private life, and that her tendency to guy him in more recent times was founded in disappointment. The fact was that even if he had been free, he would not have been attracted sexually to Dorothy, who was of the type for which he had least physical taste, being thin to the point of gauntness, with nervous, darting eyes and a quick, shrill laugh, hearing which was like being poked in the nape with a sharp pencil.

"Hope the matinee was everything you hoped it would be," Dorothy said now. "Would we know the lady?"

To be a good sport, always advisable in a superior, Hunsicker had to play along with such japery though he found it tiresome.

"Can't keep a secret around here!" he complained in mock despair. He hung his damp trench coat on the hall tree in the corner: he had his own.

Dorothy moued in what suddenly did not seem good-natured irony. "Certainly not if your name is Jack Kellog."

"What's that?"

"What's what?"

"The name you called me."

Dorothy's nose became sharper. "Yes, your own."

At least Hunsicker now had a place to sit while dealing with the weird events that bedeviled him. He sank into the chair behind his desk.

Suddenly Dorothy became concerned. "Are you okay, Jack? You're awfully pale."

He tried to pull himself together. Dorothy was inclined to believe him excessively frail and older than he was. "I'm not ill," he said. "I'm preoccupied."

"What's that supposed to mean?"

Carrie Janes looked up. She had been distracted from her manuscript and was irritated. The expression caused her face to become a pinched bag. Her eyes were slightly glassy from contact lenses.

Hunsicker told Dorothy, "Don't worry about it."

She was miffed and turned away.

He briskly pulled the chair up to his desk, got his eyeglasses from the case in his left inside breast pocket, and having taken the wallet from the corresponding pocket on the right, examined the documents of identification he found there: several credit cards; a little plastic rectangle supplied by the head office of his health plan, with blood type, the address of next of kin, and a negative response to the question of possible allergies to medication; finally, a driver's license and a car-registration certificate.

Each of these documents identified a John A. Kellog, and the license bore a photograph of himself.

Myron Beckersmith closed, with a snap, the reference book he had taken from the shelves. "Say, Jack," said he, "aren't there such things as French slang dictionaries? If so, can't we get one? This is the third manuscript I've done in the past year that's had words and phrases that I can't find in here." He slapped the fat volume he was holding; Hunsicker recognized it as their French-English dictionary, published at least thirty years before. "I always have to query the authors. Couldn't we get something?"

Beckersmith often requested improvements in equipment and materials. The copy-editors asked questions of the authors on little gummed tags attached to the edge of a page. Hunsicker's department used the old-fashioned kind the glue of which must be moistened. Myron, perhaps not unreasonably, wanted the self-stick type, but it was not he who had to present this expensive plea to the managing editor, a tightfisted woman whose only apparent interest in books was to produce them as cheaply as possible. But no doubt she had her problems too and was probably oppressed by higher-placed executives. Hunsicker had a certain at least potential sympathy for most human beings.

But that had been Hunsicker. Kellog was another man. "Sure," he told Myron now. "I'll check the main public library and see what they have."

Carrie, more irritated than ever by the new intrusion into her consciousness, looked up and asked, "What word are you looking for?"

Myron obviously disliked her, as did Dorothy. He frowned and said, "It's a phrase: *faire minette*. 'Do a kitty'? 'Play with the pussycat'? That doesn't make sense in the context."

Carrie said coldly, "Oral sex." Myron took too long to understand. "Eating pussy," she added in impatience. He flushed.

Dorothy rolled her eyes and snickered.

Jack Kellog put away the documents that identified him. "With Carrie on hand, we don't *need* reference books," he said with superficial lightheartedness, rising from the chair. "But I'll go over to the library right now and see what I can find."

Dorothy curled her lip in disapproval. "You just got back. You could just look in *Books in Print* and save a trip."

"Ah," said Kellog, trying to preserve his counterfeit ebullience, "but there might be something published abroad." He seized his coat.

"But," Dorothy protested doggedly, "what about the Haseltine?" She was referring to the proofs over which she had been laboring for days: an exposé of the gynecological profession. The book had been on schedule, but now that a TV magazine-show had done its own provocative investigation in the same area, there was every reason to advance the publication date of the printed work. It had long since been copy-edited and set in type, but when the proofs were shown belatedly to the RWM lawyers, many pretexts for possible libel actions were discovered. Naming names could obviously help book sales, but these were rich and powerful doctors who would surely sue all concerned unless hard evidence of their malfeasance could be established. It was an arduous job of the kind Walter Hunsicker would not have entrusted to anybody but Dorothy. She had to verify with the author, a quondam muckraking tabloid reporter, each of the lawyer's hundreds of queries, and not only did this man prove to have been very careless in what he wrote, but he seemed to be thoroughly drunk at whichever time of day he was reached by telephone. In person, on the occasions on which he had visited the RWM offices, he appeared to be sober but was extremely obnoxious.

In any event, Dorothy had at last completed her job that morning, and all that remained was for Hunsicker to give it one more check-through and then his imprimatur: he was to have begun that perusal this afternoon.

Jack Kellog answered her question. "The world won't end if we take our time." He left the room and then the building, and returned, as rapidly as he could walk, to the doorway where he had encountered the little man. The rain having ended by now, he carried the damp trench coat over his arm.

Finding the doorway unoccupied was no surprise. It was merely a place to start the search, the only point of reference Kellog had with respect to the little man, who unfortunately did not seem to be a vagrant who spent his days on the streets, else he might be sought in similar crannies through- out the midtown area. The fact was, as Kellog stepped into the alcove to formulate a plan of action, he could have no serious hope of locating the person. It had been half an hour since he left him. The choice of directions in which the man could have moved, and the means of movement, foot, bus, etc., were in great variety. It was the kind of situation which Walter Hunsicker, a realist, would have had to accept with his habitual stoicism, as he had submitted, his life long, to the rulings of a Fate that kept him in his proper place in the grand scheme by which he was reasonably comfortable and relatively secure.

Jack Kellog on the other hand had a constitutional aver- sion to nay-saying, and his natural state of mind was defi- nitely sanguine in the face of a challenge. Knowing nothing whatever about the habits of the little man, he might as well suppose that chance would be on his side. He prepared to set out in an easterly direction.

But he was detained by a slight noise behind the door to

the shop. From its murky appearance through the dirty windows, he had assumed the place was closed. Who would buy medical appliances from such an unsanitary-looking establishment? Perhaps a burglary was in progress. With a like suspicion, Walter Hunsicker would promptly have moved on, though had he encountered a policeman in the ensuing block or two, he would not have remained silent.

Jack Kellog, however, not only stood his ground, but took a wide-legged stance should he have to defend himself. But when the door opened and a face peeped out, it was the little man for whom he had come searching!

Kellog cried, "I want to talk to you."

"I thought that might be likely," said the other. "Come in."

Kellog winced in puzzlement as he entered the shop, the interior of which was even drearier than it had looked from the street. There were bins full of crutches of assorted sizes, shelves stacked with bedpans, a parking area for wheelchairs, a table holding arm- and leg-braces, some formed of or covered with a pink plastic with a resemblance to real skin.

"Do you work here?" he asked the back of the little man, who was leading the way.

"As good a place as any," was the answer, given without turning. "I like privacy. Few people come to such a place as this unless they have serious business."

He maintained a brisk pace. Soon they had reached a small back office behind a flimsy-looking partition. An open roll-top desk was against one wall: it was a large piece, with a multitude of pigeonholes, all of them stuffed with papers. The little man sat down in the chair that went with the desk and swiveled it to face Kellog. "All right," he said with a sigh, "let's hear your complaint."

Kellog had been rudely left standing, but that situation suited him for the current purpose. He was really annoyed.

"I want to know what's going on! This switching of the coats and identification papers. The people at the office calling me Jack. You got to them somehow. Is this a practical joke? I could believe that of Dorothy and maybe Myron, but Carrie would never go along with it."

The little man pointed. "Better sit down while we get this straight."

Kellog found a loose-jointed straight-backed chair in a dark corner. He pulled it out and sat gingerly upon it.

The merchant of crutches resumed. "It's no joke. What it is, or was supposed to be, was a conclusive demonstration that the past can be changed. Naturally you were skeptical. That's all to the good. Someone who accepted it immediately would probably be demented. A nut or eccentric would not be acceptable, I assure you. What's needed is precisely the sort of fellow you were as Walter Hunsicker. By the way, don't you want to change a lot more than that name? Your job doesn't go with it."

Kellog would have liked to gesture, but he doubted that the chair would stand up to much motion. "I'll say one thing, though I can't explain it: my new name already feels natural."

The little man shrugged. "Of course. So will anything else you decide on."

"You really mean that I could choose to be —"

The other interrupted. "It's better to say 'have been,' which inevitably involves the present, to be sure, but we should always steer clear of implications of futurity."

Kellog was not certain that he understood this fully. He completed his question, "President of the United States?"

The little man leaned forward and asked, "But would you honestly want that?"

"No, certainly not. You're right. Then is that the criterion?

That it should be something I would rather have been or done?"

The little man replied with some heat. "Else it would be capricious, just trickery, a total waste of time, not worth doing!"

Kellog shook his head. "I still can't quite believe this conversation is taking place."

"Oh, that's understandable," said the little man in his first display of sympathy. "Initial faith is required. Remember when you first learned to swim? Or your first experience of sexual intercourse? Sure, everybody else can do it, but *you'll* never be able to. But this is only temporary cold feet — once you've become habituated you'll look back with amusement on the time of disbelief."

Kellog was still shaking his head. "The difference is that I've never heard of anyone's changing the past. I'd be the first, wouldn't I?"

The little man raised a twiglike finger. "You don't know that, and I'd advise you not to speculate on the matter. It might make a bad impression."

"On whom?"

The man smiled with his irregular front teeth. His expression was suddenly of the kind called boyish. "You never know."

"I'm afraid I *must* know more about this business," Kellog said. "It might be easy for you to make such a wild assertion — that my past can be changed just like that — and I'll admit I can't explain the things that have happened so far, but that doesn't mean I can blindly accept them, either, without some sense of who's behind the project." He threw a thumb at the doorway. "I'm assuming this medical equipment is a false front or cover. Who are you? Government? Ours, I hope."

The little man scowled. "If any government, anywhere, had anything to do with it, do you believe it would work?" He snorted. "The riding mac would have been three sizes too big and would have leaked!"

"No doubt," Kellog said, "but I really can't go along with you unless I know more. I want no part of a deal in which I take all the chances and am furthermore in the dark as to the larger picture."

"Yeah," the little man said wryly. "That's too much like life. But here's an opportunity to do that one all over again and get it right."

Kellog was shaking his head. "Whatever your aim, you're not going to give me something for nothing."

The little man made a rasping sound, politely covering his mouth, though not before Kellog could see several large silver fillings. "What a cynical fellow you are. That's still Hunsicker speaking. People who rise higher in life never lose their illusions."

"You took me for the kind of jerk who has lived such a dull life he would jump at the chance to change it."

"On the contrary, Walter — I mean Jack — you were chosen because you were seemingly satisfied with your life."

"You're giving me another chance to be unhappy?"

"Only if you perversely choose to be negative about the matter." The little man rubbed his wrinkled nose. "It's up to you, of course."

Kellog said levelly, "It's not worth my soul."

"You're being melodramatic. Look here, any time you want to change your past, you come here to the store — during business hours, of course, nine to six on weekdays only — and it will be arranged without delay. In answer to your question: this program is a scientific experiment, a study in human volition."

Kellog assumed he would have to sign a paper or at least shake hands, but the little man said merely, "Then let's get on with it. I gather the name Jack Kellog is satisfactory. If not, it can be changed again. Now what do you want by way of profession, home, wife, children . . . ?"

"I told you I was happily married, and my son is the best," Kellog said with asperity. "I certainly don't want to change anything about my family. They're really my sole accomplishment, if it comes to that, and even there most of the credit should go to my wife."

"You're still thinking like Hunsicker," the little man said, sneering. "If you don't believe you've done much of consequence, then *change your past!*"

But to what? The principle sounded fine; the trouble came with the particulars. "Let's see, when I was a kid, what did I want to grow up to be? Professional ballplayer, of course. . . . Soldier of fortune! Foreign correspondent. Counsel for the defense — but only with innocent clients. But that was the stuff of daydreams. In my early teens, believe it or not, I wanted the war to last long enough so that I could get into it, but it ended a month before my eighteenth birthday. My service was over and done with by the time of Korea: I guess I could have been recalled, but for some reason that never happened, and I didn't regret it, for by that time the moment had passed and I was in college."

"But," derisively asked the little man, "if you had it to do all over again, would you marry a woman who would cuckold you almost immediately after the ceremony? And would you want once again to be the father of a homosexual?"

For an instant Kellog lowered his head. Then he raised it and said calmly, "That was Hunsicker."

"Very good!" The little man spun around in the swivel chair and plucked a piece of paper from one of the cubbyholes of the rolltop desk. He scribbled on it with a pencil stub he found in the middle drawer. He turned back to Kellog.

"What kind of job do you have?"

"I inherited quite a bit of money from my father, who took what Grandpa left him and went on with it, not only expanding the laundry-and-cleaning business but also going in a big way into city real estate. Maybe you know the Kellog building? The firm for which Hunsicker worked occupied just one floor of it."

The little man was nodding eagerly as he took more notes. "Splendid, you're getting the idea now. A word of advice: if you change one thing, you've altered a lot, usually more than you might think. It's a chain reaction. If you have different children, then you've necessarily had a different wife."

Suddenly, Hunsicker had returned. "Look, I have the finest wife in the world. There's an explanation: he was an old boyfriend, down on his luck. Martha's the most compassionate person in the world. She simply couldn't reject him when he was in that situation. I know, it might sound implausible, but that's really the way she is. It wasn't easy for me to experience, I'll admit." He sighed before he might have to sob. How terrible that he should have to think of this matter again, after all those years. "As to my son, it's true that I was devastated when I first learned of it, which to his credit was from him, face-to-face. But that was long ago, more than a decade. He's a marvelous fellow. You know, he was a first-rate athlete in college. He might have realized my old dream to play professional ball. He had offers. His E.R.A. was one point eight. He batted three eighty-four in his senior year."

"Nevertheless, you'd never want to go through all that again," said the little man.

"Poor Hunsicker," said Kellog. "He had his limitations. I am myself separated from my third childless wife. It got into the tabloids when Mimi took a shot at me on the penthouse terrace. She came back from Barbados a day early and caught me in the sack with her best friend — female, I should add."

"It looks like you're on your way," the little man said, folding the piece of paper. He found a cubbyhole into which roughly to insert it. He rose. "If things are going well, there'll be no need to report in. But if you wish to make more changes of the past, come around and see me. But remember the office hours. I don't have a home phone."

Hunsicker would have wondered whether this odd person even had a home, but Kellog was too self-concerned for that. He was at the moment trying to recall his own address, which obviously would be in one of the better parts of town — but before it came to him, he reflected that if he was estranged from his current wife, he surely lived somewhere else at the moment, perhaps at a posh hotel.

When he reached the sidewalk, he remembered: of course, he had a suite at the Rudolf. The heavy rain had stopped now, but the air was still saturated and water stood in the gutters. It was a long walk to the hotel. En route there he might well get splashed by the frenzied cars of the rush hour that was just getting its earliest start. He walked towards the corner to look for a cab, although the time of day was not propitious.

But he had taken only a step or two before a car horn sounded behind him: hardly a novelty in the city, but there was an urgency about this one that demanded his attention. He turned and saw a uniformed chauffeur leave the pearl-gray Rolls-Royce that was parked in front of the medical-supply shop.

"Jack," asked this functionary, "do you want me to meet you somewhere? I'll have to go around the block. This is one-way."

So it was, in the wrong direction. "Just back it up, for God's sake," said Kellog, annoyed that the man had not done that on his own volition.

"Quite a bit of traffic," the chauffeur pointed out, "and there's a cop up there."

"Don't worry about him."

"You're the boss." The chauffeur opened the rear door of the limo, and Kellog stepped in. The interior was upholstered in a burgundy leather. Kellog sank into the deep seat. He found the remote-control unit and switched on the TV. Next to the television set was the bar. In the refrigerated section, among other bottles, was a demi of Ruinart, but he seldom drank champagne in daylight. A beer would be just right, if a baseball game was being broadcast. He began to roll through the channels.

Meanwhile, the chauffeur, as ordered, was backing up. When the vehicle reached the intersection the policeman at the corner came to the driver's window. He smiled and nodded through the glass partition at Kellog. He then said something pleasant to the chauffeur and went out and held back the traffic until the limousine could swing around to go north on the avenue.

Kellog slid the glass back electrically and asked, "No ball game this afternoon?"

"No," said the driver. "It's March. . . . Jack, you were sure right about the cop. He couldn't have been nicer."

"Remember that next time." This fellow was a new man at the job. His predecessor, himself an ex-cop, would not have had to be enlightened. The former policeman had retired to the west coast of Florida, where he bought a bar-and-grill with the handsome mustering-out payment given him by Kellog, always notably generous with employees who gave him personal service. Kellog's chauffeurs doubled as bodyguards: the current driver had been a professional football player of the third or fourth rank and had to leave the game because of injuries. Seen from behind, his head seemed to be of no greater diameter than his neck.

Kellog now asked, "Spring training's still in progress, I take it? Call somebody and find what games are scheduled for tonight. Then tell Ralph we're on our way to the airport." Ralph was his pilot.

"We're flying to Florida right now?" the chauffeur asked.

"I hope you took me seriously when I warned you I often act on short notice, Hal. After the game we'll jump over to St. Croix for the weekend." Kellog demanded efficiency, but he liked to provide pleasant surprises for those who worked for him.

"That's great," Hal said, though he still seemed dubious. "Are we going back to the hotel first?"

Now that he was asked, that seemed too banal a destination for Kellog in his current mood. He looked at the thin gold wafer of the watch that had replaced Hunsicker's mass-market digital. The time was 4:40 P.M.

"No. Go to the Kellog Building."

This was accomplished by two turns and a drive of four blocks. Kellog left the car and entered his building, where he was obsequiously saluted by the gray-suited functionary behind the desk in the lobby. Nowadays everybody entering at non-rush hours was scrutinized and, if suspicious-looking, detained until his identification could be established. This measure had been taken after a drug addict had murdered an executive in a washroom, and a woman had had a close escape from a would-be rapist. But it obviously was not possible to examine every arrival during the incoming tide of 8:30–9:30. Kellog was not overly concerned about such matters, because the building that bore his name was run by a company that did such things; but he had a way of noticing detail.

The man came out from behind the curved, chest-high counter and led him to an elevator. He leaned inside the car and was about to punch the button for the top floor when Kellog said, "I'm going to the sixth."

"Very good, Mr. Kellog."

"Please call me Jack." He saw that he had thrilled the man, whose name he did not know, nor could he remember whether he had ever seen him before.

The sixth floor was the home of Rodgers, Wirth & Maddox, where poor Hunsicker had worked for so many years. When the elevator's doors opened, Judy the receptionist was speaking to someone on the telephone. She gave him her brief, indifferent stare, then did the double-take of a comedienne and hung up the phone in midsentence.

"Gosh," she said. "Mr. Kellog!"

He smiled. "You're Judy, aren't you?" She was full-figured to the point just before plumpness. She had apple-cheeks and small pouting lips. Hunsicker had never been able to admit to himself that he lusted for her, but sleeping alongside his wife he had had at least one dream in which Judy said to him, "I know you might think this is crazy, but I find you an interesting man." Kellog himself could not quite see what her charms were. Her eye makeup tended towards the vulgar, and she was wearing huge earrings one of which must be removed for each phone call. But perhaps she'd be inventive in bed, and anyway he had this score to settle for his good old predecessor, who was more than a brother to him.

"Judy, I'm on my way to the airport, going to fly down to Florida for a spring-practice ball game, then hop over to the Virgins for a couple days or however long it takes for me to get bored. It occurred to me that maybe you might like to come along."

Judy leaned down to find an enormous purse somewhere below the desk, a big vinyl sack — large enough, indeed, to hold a week's essentials. She straightened up and said, expressionlessly, "We're outa here."

"Aren't you going to tell anybody you're leaving early?" Kellog disapproved of impulsiveness in others.

"It's near enough to closing time," said Judy, taking his arm. She had proved to be that rare person who addressed him as Jack without being asked. She did not appear to be impressed by the Rolls-Royce and, once inside, turned down champagne in favor of mineral water.

"I've always wanted to meet you," she said, settling into a leather corner. "I'm only working as a receptionist till I can get an opportunity to spread my wings."

It turned out she had ideas on urban planning and would love to get her hands on certain properties, of his ownership, in a transition neighborhood. "What we *don't* need is more high-priced housing."

When they reached the airport Hal the chauffeur, who had rolled his eyes when Kellog emerged from the office building with Judy, drove through a private gateway and right out to the side of the waiting Learjet.

"Now, Judy," Kellog said, patting the back of her near hand, "you go get into the airplane. The pilot's name is Ralph. I'll just have a word first with Hal, here."

"Okay," said she. "But if we're going to be friends, Jack, my name is Jodie, not Judy."

Kellog was about to ask her whether she was sure, but then realized that it was the error of Hunsicker, whose profession had been correcting the written mistakes of others.

When her plump round behind, a little too ample for his taste anyway, had disappeared into the aircraft, Kellog asked Hal to go over and tell Ralph to inform the lady that his boss had just remembered another appointment, but to offer to fly her alone to anywhere in the Caribbean she would like to visit, all expenses of course to be taken care of through the various agents a man of Kellog's means maintained in all places not under the control of Marxist-Leninist powers and in fact even some that were.

While Hal went to perform that task, Kellog suddenly had cold feet. Would Martha Hunsicker wait in vain for her husband to return from work this evening? Had she been widowed by this bizarre alteration of reality, which in spite of such phenomena as the Rolls-Royce, the Learjet, and the easy pickup of Judy-Jodie, he hardly believed himself? The simple fact was, he was still dressed in Hunsicker's clothing, the sensible suit, the stout shoes, the shirt with the inevitable button-down collar. There was a neatly folded handkerchief in the back right trousers pocket: this was never used. The sheaf of Kleenex in the inside breast pocket of the jacket served for all purposes, so that the square of white linen was preserved for emergencies in which someone else, perhaps bleeding, asked for a handkerchief. Hunsicker's socks and underclothes were changed seven times a week, and he bracketed the day between two showers, one on arising and the second when he returned from work.

Martha was not now awaiting Hunsicker's return: *there was no Hunsicker as such, and thus no Martha Hunsicker.* If the past had been changed, then Martha *née* Revere had married someone else, or stayed single, or never existed. If the past could be changed, anything was possible.

It was the absolute freedom of his situation that was so hard to get used to, but perhaps before he yielded to any more impulses he should do some stabilizing things such as acquiring clothes appropriate to Jack Kellog.

"Hal," he said when the chauffeur had returned, "do you think you can get back to town before the stores are all closed? I need new clothing."

"Excuse me, Jack," said Hal, "but didn't your tailor just yesterday deliver that whole new spring wardrobe?"

"Now, how could I have forgotten that? I'm getting old, Hal."

"I don't think the ladies would agree. The one I took home this morning looked like you wore her out."

Kellog smiled. That was certainly the kind of thing that made Hunsicker's memories fade and his own reality more credible. With such encouragement he forced himself to remember events that were germane to his new identity. The girl had leonine hair and green eyes that were much enlarged by means of liner and skillful shadowing. Her breasts were small as limes, and she had a pelvic girdle no wider than a boy's. She seemed to be semiprofessional: that is, asked for no money but was quite petulant in the morning until Kellog tucked bills into the slash pocket of her distressed-leather jacket.

She immediately pulled them out, counted them, and squealed. "God, are you serious? A thousand bucks? When can I move in?"

He wanted to make sure he was not chided for making her feel like a whore, which might have been the result had the sum been less: it had happened.

"What are you in the market for tonight?" Hal asked now.

Hal served as pimp, pulling to the curb when he sighted a female he liked the looks of, getting out, and propositioning her. The approach was fitted to the prey's attire, stride, and demeanor, and Hal could employ some finesse when warranted. There were relatively respectable young women who would at least accept a ride in a Rolls-Royce, and, once inside, a glass of champagne. But there was great variation. By no means did everyone acquiesce even in the idea of the limousine. What, one in twenty? And, to be sure, invitations were generally not extended to women who appeared excessively self-possessed — Jodie had been the exception, and of course the reason for her had been merely that fixation of

Hunsicker's. Kellog himself avoided the type. His interest was solely in the flesh. When he wanted spirit, he quarreled with whichever woman he was currently married to.

When Hal pulled up under the tinted-glass marquee of the Hotel Rudolf, Kellog saw the pickets: a dozen of them, one or two of whom were aged persons who limped in the slow march around an imaginary oval. Another was a wan little girl of six or seven, carrying too large a sign, which was being steadied by the two persons she walked between.

"What's this?" Kellog asked, instinctively out of sympathy with any cause of public display.

Hal flexed his shoulder muscles. "Sorry, boss, I guess it's the people from the Dickerson."

Now Kellog remembered that he owned a big old apartment building of that name, which because of local laws concerning rent-limitation was not as profitable as it had once been. The people he paid to advise him on such matters urged that the building be pulled down and a luxury high-rise be erected in its place. To realize this plan it was necessary that the tenants of the Dickerson be bought out. Some accepted the proffered terms, but most did not, despite the harassment of the rough types installed to pretend they were legitimately employed as service personnel. Kellog did not enjoy thinking of the people who went without heat in the winter and hot water at any time, nor of those who might be assaulted if they complained to the super and his assistants, though none of this would have happened but for their stubbornness.

He now asked Hal, "Would they recognize me?"

Hal had stopped the car. He said, "I don't think there's any question since that court hearing yesterday. God knows, you were all over the news."

That was true: the wretched tenants' association had started legal action against him. Of course this was grist to the mills of the local TV channels, and in fact he had even made at least one of the networks, owing to his having some years earlier given a large contribution to a presidential campaign and allegedly been promised the ambassadorship to a little Latin American country in which, on a visit once, an investigative reporter had charged, he had run afoul of the law against sexual knowledge of girls below the age of sixteen. Whether any of this could be proved, the candidate had lost the election, thus nullifying further public reference till now.

"Get me out of here," Kellog told Hal. "I'm not to blame for their troubles. I have people who dream up these projects. Hell, you know me, I just want to enjoy life. It's not my fault if my father built this empire and then died, foisting it onto me. Who needs it?" He was bitterly aware that Hal would feel no sympathy for him. No one ever did. The only emotion he evoked from the rest of the human race was envy. "God's sake," he repeated, "get out of here. Take me back to that medical-equipment shop, and hurry! It closes at six." He did not dare look at his watch.

Hal performed as asked through the now maximum midtown traffic, even at one point breaking gridlock by driving up over the curb and across a piece of sidewalk, all of it with the impunity peculiar to a limousine. Yet when they drew up before the crutch shop and Kellog finally permitted himself to glance at the time, it was 6:06. The little man had been emphatic about his office hours. Kellog did not expect to gain access to the shop a good six minutes after the scheduled closing, but by now he had become too desperate to remain in the car.

He leaped out and went to rap on the frame of the door and then to bang upon the glass so violently as to agitate the extended roller-shade behind it.

He was amazed to see that almost immediately the shade

was peeled back at one side and the little man looked out. When the latter recognized Kellog he scowled but opened the door.

"Aren't you fortunate that I had so little faith in you," said he. "I *knew* you'd be back." With disagreeable gestures he let Kellog in.

Kellog waited until they were back in the office to voice his indignation. "Goddammit, this was your idea, not mine. Do you know what you've made me? Apparently insofar as I have a profession I'm a slumlord among other things, all of them unsavory, and privately a demented lecher who drives about the streets with his pimp-chauffeur, importuning young women for sex. I must say I make my own flesh crawl. Why have you done this to me?"

"Now, hold on," the little man said, with an indignation of his own. "All I provided was your ability to change the past. I had nothing to do with *what* you changed it to. Why would I? That would negate the purpose of the experiment, which is concerned with free choice. Many human beings feel that what they are has been imposed upon them from without. Well, here's the chance to test the validity of that theory. You can go back and change whatever you don't like. I assumed that you had done so by making yourself rich with inherited wealth, so that you don't have to do any work at all, and by having a succession of women who can be considered only as pieces of flesh devoid of mind. If these are vulgar tastes, they are yours and freely chosen."

Kellog was chagrined to hear this argument. The little man had sought him out. But for that, Hunsicker would be half-way home by now, peacefully snoozing on the train. Reading was his work; after many years of it he seldom nowadays found off-duty recreation with a book. After a light dinner the menu of which did obeisance to the latest theories of diet, he watched whichever sports were in season on television, or even, after all those years of marriage, conversed with his wife.

"Well, I think it's unfair," he said now. "I wasn't really being serious, and you know it. It was just the kind of thing one thinks in an idle way from time to time: gosh, if I could just have unlimited money! The other, the satyriasis, must have come from my unconscious. I can't recall ever consciously desiring every woman I saw. I wasn't like that even as an adolescent. I now realize I probably could have gotten a lot more sex than I did in those days if I had not just accepted it when the girl said a preliminary *no*. But I was never assertive in that way. I guess I basically agreed with the girl that it was dirty and wrong. That was a long time ago, of course, before the great change of cultural climate regarding these matters."

"Obviously you want to make up for it, after all these years," said the little man. "And why not?"

"No, I *don't*," said Kellog. "It's ridiculous and degrading. But the sex thing is the least of it: I don't want to profit from human misery. A sick old man, who lived on canned dog food, died in one of my apartments last winter during a cold spell: the temperature of his bedroom was twenty-two Fahrenheit at the time. I was accused of *inviting* dope addicts to use the hallways as shooting galleries and to molest any tenant who passed by. It wasn't really me who did that, but the people who manage my affairs. Which makes me responsible, legally and morally. I didn't care what went on."

The little man shrugged. "It's pointless to whine to me about such matters. You got yourself into the situation. You could have chosen another past."

"Yes," said Kellog, "but you might have warned me of the possible pitfalls. . . . Look, just return me to the existence I had at the time I met you. I suspect I am stuck with Hunsicker's past."

"You want to give up the money? With their combined incomes, the Hunsickers haven't felt they could afford to have both the house painted and the roof reshingled this year."

"I don't need that much," said Hunsicker. "But I'm going to retire in a few years, and I don't have a lot put away. Sending Elliot to good schools, even with help from scholarships, pretty well kept me hand-to-mouth for a long time, and Martha hasn't always worked." He put his hand to his jaw. "Can't I just be well-to-do? Not so wealthy or powerful that I bully people, but just have enough to be secure?"

The little man grimaced. He was so nondescript-looking that one would have had great difficulty in describing him to — well, the police, if it came to that. But what kind of con man *provided* money to his victim? "Walter, I don't think you've yet got the right idea. Everything in existence is consequential. You should have learned that from briefly serving in the role which you so quickly discarded. What you must do is get a past of the kind to put you in the sort of situation you'd like today, but then you must accept what goes along with it."

"I don't think it's worth the risks. As I told you, I have had, and am still having, a good life, a happy life. Sure, you can maliciously point out some slight irregularities in its texture." He colored slightly. "I don't regret having risen above my wife's foibles — which is what they really were — so long ago that until you unkindly reminded me I had forgotten them. I'm sure she would have done as much for me. And Elliot, so he's homosexual, so what? At first I admit I was only ritualistically tolerant — barely that, but I'm proud to say I have never been a bigot. I lived to accept the situation genuinely. All right, so I won't be a grandfather. After him, Martha couldn't have more children. But to have such a regret would be awfully selfish."

The little man threw up his hands. "Okay, you've made your decision." He spun around and plucked from a cubby-hole what probably was that piece of notepaper on which he had made his earlier entries. He made a new notation on it.

"I'm sorry it didn't work out," said Hunsicker, leaving the rickety chair. "But then, I guess I still don't really believe it's possible to change the past. Or if it is, then it would be done at a university laboratory, beginning with frog embryos or whatnot, and take forever to get to human life."

MARTHA WAS waiting for him at the station as always except on the rare occasions when she made other arrangements by telephone. They lived only a mile from the railroad, and he could easily have walked it if not every day then twice or thrice a week in good weather, and no doubt should have done so for cardiovascular reasons, but Martha liked to provide the service. While she waited she read, and what she read was more often than not a book published by his firm, for he brought home many of the latest titles in advance of their appearance in the shops, which gave him a certain prestige amongst his neighbors if the book was one which got a lot of attention in the news media prior to its official publication date — say that former statesman's memoir from which he and the lawyers had worked so hard to eradicate pretexts for libel actions.

Today, as he approached the car, he could identify at quite a distance the volume she held against the steering wheel, for as she read a righthand page the front cover was at an angle to display the bold type thereupon. The book was the autobiography of a motion-picture actor who, though a has-been in the current professional context, was not only remembered by an over-fifty public but recognized by younger persons through film festivals, TV showings, and video cassettes, as being one sort of classic, the embodiment of a style no longer to be found even on celluloid: the felt hat, four-button double-breasted jacket, perhaps even white trousers, certainly an extremely widespread collar filled with the thick but neat triangle of "Windsor" knot, named for the ex-king of England who had married an American divorcée who was supposedly, uniquely, the cure for his impotence. Whatever the truth of this, the autobiographer at hand, Barry Howard, alluded to it as established fact in his prefatory remarks on the sex lives of the renowned, and then proceeded to characterize his own role as that of male Mrs. Simpson in satisfying the erotic needs of the wife of a president of the United States. Like the Windsors, both this woman and her husband were now deceased, needless to say, and thus without recourse to a suit for libel. Of the famous people of whom he had carnal knowledge and were yet alive to confirm or deny the tale, virtually all were professional performers and could be counted on not to make trouble: either, themselves faded or fading, they could use the publicity, or they were too successful to stoop to self-defense in such a context.

"Not to mention," said Mark Feld, the actor's acquisition editor at Rodgers, Wirth & Maddox, a movie addict thrilled to be in this situation, "that he's telling the truth."

"Even," Hunsicker had asked with a scowl, for he had voted with mild enthusiasm for the president in reference, "in the case of Mrs. —?"

"Who could doubt it?" Mark said loftily. Editors, as opposed to copy-editors like Hunsicker-Kellog, often fell under an author's enchantment and, like Madison Avenuers who believed their own ads, would give credence to all manner of twaddle. For example, Dan Gillespie, a professed atheist, accepted much of what Lilli-Ann Mulholland, whose manuscripts were barely literate, proclaimed as astrological truth.

And Susan Hillman, though to all appearances a stern rationalist, was a pushover for any book with a thesis opposed to any tradition whatever, and after reading the appropriate works believed, e.g., that General Custer was a full-blooded Negro, that Hitler was alive and living quietly in New South Wales, Australia, and that Sherlock Holmes had been not only a real person but also had royal blood.

Martha was engrossed at the moment and did not see her husband until he opened the door. "Oh, hi," she said then, hardly taking her eyes off the page. She slid to the passenger's side. She would have done the same without a book. Martha was unreconstructed in assigning roles according to sex. When they were together in a car, unless he was feeling very ill, Hunsicker drove, though he was not nearly so proficient behind the wheel as she, never having mastered the craft of parking next to a curb, for example.

"You're enjoying that?"

She lowered the book and moued. "I don't know." She leaned over and gave him a kiss.

"I told you, didn't I," Hunsicker asked, then waited till he had backed the car from the parking space and put it into forward motion, "that Howard insisted on writing it himself, refused to use even a collaborator. Naturally it was unpublishable in the form in which we received it. *We* had virtually to demolish it entirely and write what is really a new book. Dorothy did most of it. Everybody was afraid that in view of his original position, Howard would be enraged and never agree, but when the manuscript went to him for approval, he sent it back promptly and with much praise for our work in 'polishing it up.' I'm sure he didn't even look at it. In his egomaniacal way he assumed all we did was correct a misspelling here and there."

"He's not a likable person," Martha said in her calm but, to Hunsicker, definitive and sometimes even devastating way.

As usual, she had found the *mot juste*. Hunsicker himself would less eloquently have used the term "prick," which was also imprecise, Howard being well known for his apparently quite genuine efforts in raising financial aid for crippled children. All the same, on the evidence of this book, he was certainly not likable.

"The only thing is," Martha added, waiting until her husband got clear of the traffic at the station, for he was a nervous driver when at close quarters with other cars, "the dirt's fascinating."

Hunsicker was in the strangest of states. Ordinarily he was eager to share the events of his day with Martha. Now he had had what was obviously as remarkable an experience as a human being could have, whatever the little man's authenticity. That is to say, however his sleight of hand and/or hypnotic techniques were performed. Reason would have to rule him a charlatan in the absence of any evidence that such a shabby little person, operating out of a dusty bedpan shop, was an agent of divinity. Yet Hunsicker was unable to find a means by which even to introduce the subject to his wife, whom he had known for thirty years. Therefore, instead of taking the conversational initiative that would by tradition seem to be the responsibility of him who has only just returned from the big city, he remained silent for several blocks.

Finally Martha said, "I gather your day was not the greatest." She had been maternal to him, even as a young woman.

"No," he said quickly. "I'm just exhausted. I didn't catch my usual forty winks on the train. At my age I really need that little nap after the working day. But how about you? Did you sell the Workman place?" The reference was to an unimpressive colonial house for which the owner wanted an astronomical figure. Martha had assured him he would never get it and that she could not afford to do much to sell something that no one would consider on the proposed terms, but he said he was quite satisfied to wait passively amidst her other listings.

She smiled. "Not bloody likely, but I do think I've found a good prospect for the Horning." Martha was an excellent saleswoman, with a deceptively soft approach that often proved effective with initially resistant clients. Not only could she sell a huge house to someone who wanted a cottage, but such a buyer seldom displayed a subsequent regret. She was a large woman, not fat in the sense of ill-proportioned, but big. She was as tall as her husband, which meant taller in high heels, and looked as though she would weigh more, but that was an illusion, though in fact he was slender for his age. He had always found her a reassuring presence, yet now could not as yet find a way to tell her about the unsettling encounter with the strange little man.

"Great," he said now. "But we'd better not spend the commission before you collect it." He made the same comment with respect to every imminent sale. She agreed as always. Surely one of the reasons why they had been satisfactorily married so long was that they never quarreled about money. Both were conservatives in that area, having little taste for gloss and frippery, but shared an interest in providing Elliot with the best education and, when that had been accomplished, improving the house in which they were domiciled and the grounds around it. Last year the entire side yard had been resodded.

As always he let Martha out of the car at the top of the driveway and then continued on to the garage, before which he braked and, having found the gadget in the glove compartment, pressed the button that caused the garage door to rise. Inside, as he left the car, he reflected as usual on the need to take one whole Saturday and throw out the accumulation of useless material that filled most of the space which, had they owned one, would have been occupied by a second vehicle. Some of this — a snow tire, the frame of an old window screen, a rolled-up throw rug — constituted a fire hazard.

Before entering the house by the back door, he glanced towards the dogwoods at the bottom of the garden. He could never call a season spring until their blooming: they still had several weeks to go. It had been a dry winter. The heavy city rain would have been welcome, but as sometimes happened, none had fallen here, by the look of things.

The back door was still locked when he tried to turn the knob. Martha hadn't got there yet. He found the proper key amongst the several in the little leatherbound booklet he carried in the right trousers pocket, and let himself in. It had been the universal practice throughout the neighborhood, twenty years before, never to lock a door: of course that had changed.

Passing through the kitchen, where, judging from the aroma, something was simmering in the Crock Pot, he heard his wife's murmur from the top of the hallway. She had been detained there by a telephone call. Because he would have had to squeeze past her if he continued on that route, he took the circuitous one that went via the dining and living rooms, and emerged in the vestibule between the front door and the little desk at the beginning of the hall, where Martha stood, holding the phone at the level of her waist, neither speaking into it nor listening.

Her unusual expression alarmed him. "Not an obscene call?" he asked, remembering that Dorothy Kalergis, at work, had recently complained of receiving such, and had been militantly advised by her colleague Carrie Janes to keep a police whistle at phoneside to use on the next occasion: "Shatter his goddamn eardrums!"

"It's Elliot," Martha said at last, in a voice that went with her lusterless eyes.

"He's back?" Elliot had been abroad for a month and a half, taking a spring vacation to Paris — which went to show how well he was doing at the law firm, at which he had been employed less than three years. As it happened, Hunsicker himself had never been closer to Paris than the city of Québec. He had married young and soon thereafter had a child to bring up and educate. Since Elliot had been out on his own, domestic things — resodding lawns, conversions from oil to gas heat, etc. — had taken all the extra money. "If you're done," he said now to Martha, "let me talk to him." But the best time to hear Elliot's account of the trip — he was a marvelous raconteur — would be over a long dinner of the substantial kind: beef or leg of lamb. Elliot had in the last year taken up the practice of smoking an expensive cigar after such a meal. His father admired the elegance of all phases of the process in which his son, who had been fastidious even as a small child, pierced the chocolate-brown tube with a little vest-pocket tool of gold, then painstakingly applied to the cigar's end the intense blue flame of an engine-turned golden lighter, extending the snow-white cuffs of his shirt, discreetly exposing the small cuff links, also gold, exquisite in their simplicity. Everything about Elliot was classic. Hunsicker was wont sometimes to wonder where his son had acquired such style, which was unique on either side of the family.

"Well," he now said impatiently to Martha, who seemed frozen in position, "are you finished?"

"It's Elliot," she repeated stupidly, still not focusing her eyes.

"I *know* that, Martha," Hunsicker said, reaching. "I'd like to talk with him, if you don't mind."

"He's dying," Martha said.

"He's joking."

"He has AIDS," Martha said, in a tone of controlled reason. "That's why he was in Paris, you see: to try a new treatment."

"No," Hunsicker said firmly. "That's not possible. Elliot's too brilliant to contract a lethal disease. This can't be serious. I want to hear about Paris and the meals he ate there. Is he coming up for dinner on Saturday?"

Martha's expression was still more blank than anguished: that was what gave him such hope that all this was illusion. "We can't get to the hospital till tomorrow," she said. "Visiting hours would be over before we reached town." At last she hung up the telephone. "There's stew. You should eat something. I'm not hungry, and I can't sit down right now."

Hunsicker clutched at her. "Please believe me: this does not have to happen! I can get it changed."

"Walter," his wife said wearily, "try to get hold of yourself. I'm going to take a pill now and try to sleep."

"No, no that isn't —" But she had not stayed to listen, had instead gone upstairs and into the bathroom. He realized that there was no credible means by which the truth could be revealed to her at this point, if ever.

—————— **II**

NEXT MORNING, after a sleepless night behind the wheel of his car, Hunsicker drove to the city. From 8:50 on, he knocked at the door of the medical-equipment shop, but not until 9 sharp did the little man let him in.

In the back office he related the terrible news. "I'm sorry I didn't take you as seriously as I should have yesterday. I need your help." He leaned forward. "I'll do anything to save Elliot's life."

"Including changing the past so that he never existed?"

"It wouldn't be possible just to go back and change *him*?"

The little man gasped in disapproval. "My goodness, you can't exercise a line-item veto when it comes to these matters:

you have to take the package. If you'd like a heterosexual son, you've got to take what else comes with him. He could be mentally impaired, for example. Or he might have other carnal tastes that are abhorrent, even criminal. Also, if the past were changed in this respect, there would be consequences: if you replace Elliot with another son, you'll necessarily change your wife as well: flesh of her flesh, you see. That could not be changed."

This was not a shock to Hunsicker by now: it was one of the things that had kept him awake through the night — though to be sure he could not envision a life in which Martha had never been: something different from her suddenly dying.

"It's simply that I can't condemn him to a horrible death. *He's* not at fault: *we* made him. That was all our idea. Martha would do what I'm doing if she could. I know that. As it happens, only I have the power." He would have wept now, had he not felt the need to give his son a tribute. "Let me tell you about Elliot: he would stop me if he knew about this. That's the sort of man he is. If given the choice, he'd rather die this way than have the past changed so that his mother would never have existed for me. Elliot's the most generous person I have ever known. He was like that as a little child. For that matter, he might even prefer his current fate to never having existed. He so loves life! He has never slunk about in shame, nor did he ever make a spectacle of himself. He was what he was, a sweet man, an ethical man, a fine man." Now at last he let the tears come.

The medical-equipment dealer was embarrassed by this display, and spun round in the chair and fetched the spooled paper from the appropriate slot of the rolltop desk.

He turned back. "All right, what will it be?"

After a moment Hunsicker was able to speak again. "I'm

beginning to understand what a responsibility this can be. I'm scared of making a bad mistake. . . . Is there a rule against *your* choosing something for me?"

The little man scowled at the ceiling and shook his head.

"I won't blame you if it turns out badly," Hunsicker said earnestly. "It's just that this thing has really shattered my confidence. And by changing the past, I end up in effect killing my son anyway, don't I, as well as my wife? I'm saving them a lot of suffering, and therefore it must be done. But I'm giving up most of my own life, as I knew it, and stepping into the unknown. . . . I'm sorry. I'm being ungrateful. I'm aware that this is a unique privilege."

"Please," said the other, with a lifting of wrists. "Don't say such things. We're not doing you a favor. It's just an agreement, fair and square. You do your part, we do ours. There's no need to be grateful or humble."

"I've been thinking about this all night," said Hunsicker. "Changing my whole life! I don't know how or where to start."

"Loosen up a little. You're forgetting that the decision need not be permanent. This is not as solemn as you are making yourself believe."

"I've always taken life seriously," Hunsicker said. "I hope I've not been humorless, but existence has never seemed like a joke to me."

"Maybe you've been wrong," said the little man. "You might do worse than to try the lighter approach."

Hunsicker considered the matter. "Yes, that first brief experience as the rich slumlord and lecher wasn't exactly lighthearted, was it? It was too concerned with the ugly assertion of power. You might be right. But wouldn't it be mockery of my reason for being here? To flee tragedy into farce?"

"You really ought to free yourself from those old ways of looking at things," the little man said. "What other people have told you all your life might not be the whole truth but rather a version that will further their own ends with no regard whatever for yours. You are here being given the opportunity to arrange something on your own terms. You'll waste it if you insist on inconsequential considerations. Your object at the moment is to do away with your son's fatal illness. What difference would it make however you accomplished this end?"

Suddenly Hunsicker's burden seemed to have been lifted. "Okay, I'll try being Jack Kellog again, this time with a sense of humor."

The little man made a notation on the wretched scrap of paper and returned it to the cubbyhole. It was incomprehensible to Kellog that an organization with sufficient resources to develop a means of changing the past would have such a squalid office, but that was not his business. He could have no complaint as long as the process was working.

K ELLOG'S COMIC talents had appeared with his adolescence and a concomitant gain in weight that, by the middle of his freshman year in high school, had made him much chubbier than one could be and have much social success in the routine way. Not to mention that the morning came when he woke up with a face that was badly pimpled. (When his acne finally went away with the end of his pubescence, moonlike craters remained as a memory of the lesions.) He had no talents at sports, nor was he a good student. He masturbated four times a day, week in and week out, often into successive pairs of women's panties shoplifted from the lingerie department of a five-and-dime (he would have paid for these could he have done so gracefully). In any kind of competition with persons of his own age, he was at a loss; in any conflict he was likely to prove the coward. Yet, in spite of so many negative attributes, his determination to prevail remained undiminished — something he could not himself understand, and he was always careful to conceal it from others, with the exception of his parents, to whom he was wont to predict great personal success for himself when the time was ripe.

"I'm holding my breath," his father, a clerk, would say derisively, "so don't take too long." He had the dreariest parents of anybody he knew: no wonder that gaining distinction was a hard row to hoe.

Then one day, after a rain, he slipped on some wet leaves and performed an accidental pratfall to the asphalted surface of the schoolyard. At first it seemed unfortunate that he was at the time amidst many of his homeward-bound schoolmates, all of whom, having no other distraction at the moment, laughed uproariously. He was no stranger to the derision of a few persons at a time, but the response to what could be termed a real audience was unique to him, and far from being crushed by their laughter, he hungered for more of it. He proceeded to fall three more times before reaching the limits of school property, doing so now on purpose, and on each occasion making a more elaborate thing of it than he had on the last: throwing his books into the air, kicking off his loafers at the moment of impact, finally producing a shattering Bronx cheer that simulated a fart — the best effect of all, for though most of the girls professed to be disgusted by this, *everybody* made some kind of reaction, and Kellog, who had heretofore experienced far more disregard than condemnation, realized that he had stumbled upon a principle essential to him who seeks acclaim from his fellows: *viz.*, that even to inspire derision is to have made one's mark.

Now other people in groups no longer averted their heads on his approach, nor as individuals did they continue to find pressing engagements elsewhere. They stayed, often greeting him with an expectant smirk. After taking the pratfall to its limits without putting himself into the hospital — he did suffer a sprain, and was lucky it wasn't worse, when trying to add to one plunge a leap-twist that could only have been performed by a gymnast — he turned towards the verbal for his comedy. In this he exceeded himself. He had always been inarticulate in the written language, and writing themes and book reports was nightmarish. (*"Black Beauty* is the story of a horse. This horse is black, and real nice. Some people arnt so kind to horses, but luckily some people are.") Nor when called upon in class to respond vocally was he more eloquent, translating Caesar's dying words as "Brutus, you also are a brute," sniggering and blushing. But now he found that putting words in certain combinations could make people laugh. Of course there was more to it than the context. Some comedy (usually successful despite or because of the revulsion it evoked) was founded simply on bad taste: most schoolboy sex jokes were of this character ("The Reverend Fluff, a minister of the gospel, is putting it to the choirmaster's daughter in a parked car, when a policeman pokes a flashlight into the window. 'Officer,' indignantly says the preacher, 'I'll have you know I'm Pastor Fluff!' 'Buddy,' replies the cop, 'I don't care if you're all the way up her a-hole, you gotta move on.'") And sometimes there was virtually no point at all, nothing to laugh at whatever, except foul language ("'How can you tell if a girl will put out?' Joe the jerk asks Vic, the local authority on nooky, whose answer is, 'If she talks dirty.' So next time Joe sits on a couch next to a girl he asks her, 'What would you do if a bear came down that chimney there?' 'I'd shit,' says she. 'Let's fuck,' says Joe.")

Timing was crucial. The same joke, hilarious when told with the proper intervals between its elements, was lame when poorly timed (e.g., when one bum asks another, "Did you shit in your pants?" the question must be preceded by the visible and audible sniffing of the joke-teller, *pause;* and then a longer pause comes before the answer . . . "*Today?*"). And other acting skills were helpful: being able to suggest the bodily movements of a spastic; to produce accents ("Vot are you doink, children?" "Fucking, Mamma." "Dot's nice, just don't fight," or as Rastus addressing the blacksnake which crawled in a torn pocket and out his fly: "Ah knowed you was black, and ah knowed you was long, but ah *nevah* knowed you had eyes!"); to simulate the facial expressions of those with strabismus, harelips, and receding jaws.

You couldn't, however, use blue material with parents or teachers, or even, given the era, with "good" girls as opposed to those who were "bad," those, that is, who went beyond necking and engaged in mutual "petting" or even, in some cases, more. To entertain the respectable, Kellog therefore had to acquire a repertoire of hygienic jokes of the sort encountered in magazines in the dentist's waiting room or heard on the radio, but the trouble was *everybody* saw or heard those, and it was devastating to be beat to the punchline by your audience. That was the trouble with jokes as such: once uttered, they were available to all, and it was precisely the funniest ones that were most repeated, so you always ran the risk of either not getting a laugh or, getting one, being identified as not original. Kellog would have liked to be socially acceptable in the routine way, namely, without making an especial effort, but as that had proved impossible, what he craved now was to be unique, superior to the herd, a headliner, the one-and-only, and that could hardly come about with twice-told material.

But it was one thing to want to invent a joke, and another to do it. Where do you begin? If not restrained by prudery in the matter of sex and prudence with respect to your audience (not all of whose affiliations might be known to the comedian), a headstart could be gained by using real or implied foul language or bigot's epithets: "'Oh, how I love

Dick,' said Richard's girl." . . . "A nigger goes into a drugstore to buy rubbers. The druggist is this slick little sheeny . . ." But if obliged to keep a civil tongue in your head, you had to work much harder to arrive at something that was sufficiently biting to amuse but at which even the victim could not protest without attracting more derision. Fat people were God-given perfection, the ultimate; but eminently usable were the bald, the nearsighted, the bowlegged and the knock-kneed, those with impedimented speech, the effeminate male, and the unmarried female over forty.

Cruelty might not necessarily be funny, but nothing was funnier. This became clear to Kellog before he was out of his teens, but it was also evident to him that he had little gift for invention. He could tell jokes, even perform them with the vocal effects and bodily movements of a trained actor, but he could not cut one from the whole cloth. Soon he had to buy by mail, for twenty-five cents, a book entitled *The World's Hundred Best Jokes* and then its sequel, *100 More,* etc., and believed he could breathe easy for the moment with this stockpile behind it. But as ill luck would have it, one of the new acquaintances he had made through the exercise of wit plucked one of these volumes from the pocket of Jack's raincoat and held it high. "Hey, look where Kellog gets his jokes!"

But being so exposed had less effect on his other classmates than he at first had feared. In spite of the entertainment he had afforded them for months, most were indifferent to its sources. *He* was the one who got the laugh when he grabbed the other boy's right hand and thrust it aloft. "Hey, look where Riggins gets his lovin': Miss Rosie Palm!" He was helped by a blush of Riggins' that was so violent as to seem a prelude to hemorrhage, for by chance the straitlaced girl on whom Riggins had a crush was standing nearby at the time and though a reaction of disgust on her part would have been regrettable, her simper of amusement was disastrous: in the passion of self-pity Riggins upon the moment suspected her of not being the virgin he had supposed but rather a kind of slut, who would perhaps put out to anyone who applied, and took her to the movies and tried to feel her up. She made a scene in the theater, from which Riggins was thereupon banned for life, and next her father threatened to thrash him and subsequently almost came to blows with Gordon Riggins, Sr., after which the two families, friendly for a generation, became enemies.

And no one thought of blaming Jack Kellog, the only begetter of this calamitous sequence. Riggins in fact became, at least in his own mind, Kellog's best friend.

"I ain't any good with words, Jack. It don't matter with guys, but I just don't know how to talk to girls."

Ordinarily Kellog would have responded, callously, with the gag about the bear coming down the chimney, but Riggins had uniquely addressed him by his first name, and he was moved.

"Huh. That's tough, Gordo."

"See," Riggins said from his urinal, next to the one being used by Kellog, "what I was thinking, that's your specialty, talkin': you got a million of 'em. I don't care if they come from books, you know how to tell a joke. That one you told the other day, Jesus, it was real funny: the old coon seein' the snake crawlin' out of his pants and thinkin' it's his dick? I tried to tell that one to my old man, after supper that night, but you know what? I couldn't do it. I just can't get that nigger-talk right." He had finished peeing and was violently whipping his peter in the air, to dry it. "He slapped my face, anyway: he's the only one allowed to tell a dirty joke." Riggins punched his large fists together. "I tell you, I'm bigger'n him now. I could trim his ass any old day."

Kellog was on the last button of his fly; it was his other pair of pants that had the zipper. In a slightly superior tone, as befitted an expert, he said, "Whoever you're talking to, you got to act like you're in charge whether you are or not. You can't let them think you're uncertain. And don't let 'em rush you. And you have to get the words *exactly* right. For some reason, the same joke ain't funny if you stumble over just one word. They'll make fun of you for your mistake and won't laugh at the joke itself."

"I don't know," Riggins said dolefully. "I just get tongue-tied." He knew no need to wash his hands, even though Kellog was providing a good example. As the latter was reaching for a paper towel, Riggins said, "What I was wondering, maybe you could put in a word for me with Betty Jane Hopper. Know what I mean? Crack a few jokes — clean ones, nothing dirty. She goes to Sunday school every week. Then work in someplace that I like her, that Gordon Riggins thinks she's neat."

"Why the jokes?" asked Kellog. "I could just tell her, couldn't I?" Putting his talent to this sort of use would seem to demean it.

"Soften her up," Riggins said as they went through the swinging doors into the basement corridor. "Girls listen to guys who make 'em laugh."

Kellog had noticed this, to a degree, but he had not arrived at Riggins' theory of the so-called softening-up process. Being entertained was another thing than being manipulated . . . or was it? After classes he lingered at the corner of the schoolyard, where Riggins had assured him Betty Jane could be encountered on her way home, and when she came along he said, "Hey, Betty Jane, did you ever hear the one about the big fat lady who went into the department store and asked the floorwalker where she could buy talcum powder? Now, this guy was bowlegged, see, and he said, 'Walk this way.'" Kellog bowed his own legs and demonstrated. "So the lady said, 'If I walked that way, I wouldn't need the powder!'"

Betty Jane frowned. "That's pretty smutty."

"Are you kidding," Kellog asked in false indignation. "Talcum powder?"

She shook her head. "You know very well what I mean, Jack Kellog. You're getting quite a name for yourself with these off-color jokes."

"Come on, don't you have a sense of humor?" He was conscious of a newfound feeling of power. He had no memory of having addressed a girl to her face when he was alone with her, and though other homeward-bound students were nearby, he and Betty Jane were isolated from them at the moment.

"I certainly do, but I *don't* care for anything immoral. It just lowers a person."

Her prissy little mouth annoyed him, and he did not find her very attractive in the first place. He liked long blond straight hair with a sheen, and hers was short and dark. Her eyes seemed small, her complexion was too pale, and whereas his ideal was big jugs with an otherwise slender body, she was stocky, and her chest was thick; her tits were actually undersized, so far as he could tell from the Argyle sweater. Why Riggins was so stuck on her Kellog could not have explained. But he was irritated now by her criticism, and he remembered his mission.

"Look, I don't care what *you* think about me," he said to her petulant profile as they started up the sidewalk. "What I'm supposed to tell you is that Gordon Riggins likes you a lot."

She stopped and stared at him. "Is that supposed to be funny?"

"Well, dammit," Kellog said. "What's wrong with you? This

guy told me to say it, and I have, and that's that, as far as I'm concerned."

"You don't have to curse," Mary Jane told him. "I was just asking. Never, never have I given Gordon Riggins any reason whatsoever to think about me. I hardly know who he is. Is he that stupid jerk who is practically illiterate in class?"

This appealed to Kellog's natural malice. "That's pretty much on the head of the nail. I hear when he was born, the doctor lifted him up and slapped his face."

Betty Jane giggled at this, though she said, "Oh, you're so awful."

"He's so dumb," said Kellog, "he thinks Lincoln's Gettysburg Address is a post-office box."

Now Betty Jane shrieked. "See, you don't have to be dirty to be funny." She had the most grating laugh he had ever heard, though naturally he liked her better now.

"You know, he asked me to lend him a dime and said, 'I ain't had a bite all day.' . . . So I bit him!"

When her laughter was done, she asked, "Oh, my gosh, where do you get 'em?"

"Gordo went to the doctor to have a physical exam, and the doctor examined him and said, 'You're sick.' Gordo said, 'I feel fine. I want to get a second opinion.' 'Okay,' said the doc, 'you're ugly too.'"

Now Betty Jane laughed so hard that a breath went down the wrong way and she coughed and clasped her books to her chest. "If you don't stop you'll give me heart failure," said she when she was again able to speak.

"Okay, then," said Kellog, "I told you what I was supposed to: Riggins likes you. So long, then." They were coming to a corner, and he had run out of ready material. And even if he had not, he was aware of the need to leave the stage while they still wanted more instead of waiting till they began to long for relief.

"Where are you going now?" asked Betty Jane. "You live in this direction too, don't you?"

"Got to see a guy about a horse," he breezily answered, using a line he did not understand but had heard on the radio more than once.

"Well, say," said Betty Jane, a slight flush washing her freckles, "maybe we'll meet again I don't know where or when."

Kellog grunted. Now he had to pretend he really did have some important business elsewhere. He might go to the drugstore and buy some zinc oxide to put on his pimples (it was of little effect but you had to do something), but in recent weeks his acne had been clearing up, and the reason could not have been that he was beating his meat any less nowadays. Yet here he was, talking with a girl in the flesh, and sex was the last thing on his mind. Thick ankle-socks above dirty saddle oxfords and below a skirt of plaid wool was not a costume that evoked lust. His taste was for black lace underwear with long garters and high heels; tits upthrust and compressed to form a deep cleavage not far below the chin, in a brassiere strained to the breaking point; glistening scarlet lips; and a smoldering cigarette in a long holder of black onyx.

"I'm going to drink Canada Dry," said he, "starting in Toronto."

Betty Jane laughed dutifully at this, but she had been claimed by a new solemnity. She came closer to him and said, sotto voce though no one else was near enough to hear, "I don't approve of drinking myself, but my father's got some wine down cellar and there aren't any of them home right now."

"There's your chance, then," said he, "and next time anybody asks if you're drinking any more, tell 'em you're not drinking any less."

She failed even to smile at this, saying in a very small voice, "Come on, if you want."

So having really nothing else to do, he persisted awhile longer in her company. She lived behind a green lawn in a two-story house with a wide porch full of wicker furniture in good condition and not unraveling like his grandma's. This was one of the better streets in town. Kellog had not previously been aware that her family had more money than his, and learning this now, he felt he had still another reason to feel superior to her. He needed all the self-assurance he could muster, for if he had not even walked a girl home from school, he had assuredly never entered an unoccupied house with one. Nor, as he tried to keep from reminding himself, was he experienced at "drinking," though the word was so frequently to be heard in his jokes. He had had a sip of homemade grape wine from his father's glass before recent Thanksgiving and Christmas dinners. He loathed the filthy, sour smell of beer and had yet to taste any kind of spirits except blackberry cordial, which was not all bad but would have been better without the acrid alcohol content.

There they were in the Hopper basement, a very neat place as contrasted with the Kellog cellar, newspapers in tied stacks, no stink of damp, and a very modern, clean-looking furnace equipped with an automatic stoking device that fed coal into the fire when required. Jack noticed only the things that reminded him of his own chores at home, but it was spring now and no heat was on.

Betty Jane led him to a corner cupboard and opened the doors, saying, "There you go."

Inside were to be seen some pickles in Mason jars, strawberry jam with a disc of paraffin between the maroon contents and the metal lid, and a bottle of dark-brown glass bearing a label on which was printed: "Sherry."

His hostess snatched up the bottle and thrust it at him.

"C'mon," said she, "we'll pick up the corkscrew in the kitchen and go up to my room."

Kellog had to speak fast. He had never held a corkscrew in his hands, let alone used one to extract a cork, a process he had never paid much notice to when depicted in the movies except for the time that some comedian had pulled from a bottle a cork that kept coming and coming and when all the way out was magically longer than the bottle from which it had issued. To do that kind of stuff you had to have a lot more resources than were available to a high-school kid in a little hick town.

"Naw," he said now, sneering. "I hate sherry. Too weak." When, years later, he discovered that the cork in a fortified-wine bottle was topped by a knurled cap, requiring no extracting tool, he still did not regret having missed the drink, for had he taken it his reason might have been impaired for the succeeding forty-five minutes.

"I'm real sorry," said Betty Jane. "Because that's all there is." She smiled as if she knew something he didn't and closed the cupboard while taking his hand with her free one. "C'mon, I'll show you my room."

The route upstairs was a blur to him, and they arrived at their destination much too soon. Her hand was not even soft and smooth, and he withdrew from its clutch as soon as he could. Her room had some pink girl's stuff in its decor and a stuffed animal or two. Unlike him she apparently did not have to share it with anybody else (he had an older brother who appropriated the better of every alternative: position of bed, dresser-drawers, etc.) — except a tiger cat, who on seeing them leaped off the bed and slunk under it.

Kellog knew at least one joke that played on the two meanings of "pussy," but he could not bring it to mind at the moment, and perhaps just as well, for alone in the house as they were, any wrong move on his part might give Betty Jane grounds for a charge of rape. Such stories were always floating around, though it was never possible to confirm one.

Betty Jane sat down on the bed and asked brightly, "Well, what should we do? Look at movie magazines? I've got quite a few. My aunt brings them home from the beauty shop where she works. I don't know any card games but Old Maid. I've got a scrapbook, and also I collect autographs of the famous: so far I've got some baseball players' that my father gave me. I never heard of them but he says they're real well known. I have written to some of my favorite stars in Hollywood but that was just a few days ago, so they haven't had time to reply yet, but I am told they sure will."

"That's great," Kellog said without enthusiasm. He was just standing there.

She smiled at him. "You have a terrific sense of humor. My father says a person needs that above all to succeed in life."

"Uh-huh." His mind was barren. "I got to go now. My old man will give me a beating if I don't clean up a lotta junk in the garage."

"Are you serious?" she asked. "Your father beats you?"

"Well, not with a club. But he'll slap my face off if he feels like it. He split my lip once."

"That's too bad. My father is usually real swell to me. If anybody's lousy, it will be my mother, though mostly she's okay. My sister doesn't act right lots of times, but then later we make up."

Kellog looked around the room. "Where does she sleep?"

"She's got her own room." Betty Jane looked at the floor. "Do you really have to go?"

"I'm not lying," he said defiantly. "My old man beats hell out of me sometimes." He understood that he could get somewhere with her at this moment, but he did not know just where or how, and the fact remained that he had always hoped his first sexual association would be with a person he found attractive. On the other hand, he was aware that with his weight and skin problem he was not likely at this stage of life to get access to anybody of the sort he saw in the imagination as he masturbated. It might be either Betty or continued chastity for the forseeable future.

He sat down on the bed beside her, not yet ready to make the first move, but as luck would have it as soon as he was in place she fell heavily against him. He leaned back, and she descended into his lap, her elbow digging into his crotch. The effect was both painful and arousing. Soon he had the giant of boners, and as she erected her upper body she managed accidentally to press against it. No one except himself had ever touched his closest pal: he was now both jealous and excited to an even greater degree. She put her face to his, and he stopped breathing for fear of bad breath, either his or hers or even both, and did nothing whatever until she gave him a disappointingly light dry kiss, the first he had ever had that was not an element in a game like Spin the Bottle, but it was no more passionate than if it had been such.

"You meant that about my sense of humor?" he asked. "I really like to make people laugh." He did not say that though he momentarily loved them when they laughed, he never liked people in the mass. Furthermore, while he feared them when they did not laugh, he had a certain contempt for them when they did.

Betty Jane was looking at him with feeling. "I guess that's just about my favorite thing, a sense of humor. A lot of people don't have any, but I say if you can't smile at things, then there's not much —"

Kellog summoned up the nerve to put a hand on her forearm, at which touch, the first instituted by him, she fell silent. Her prominent sinews did not greatly suggest female flesh, and after an instant he took his hand away.

"All right," Betty Jane said submissively. "I'll do it." She proceeded gently but firmly to grasp his pecker, which had lost some of its recent tumidity, through the fabric of his pants, and simultaneously horrifying and thrilling him, it quickly became swollen once more. He made no sound, but his facial skin felt flammable. Far from being the Sunday school–goer of Riggins' innocent assumption, Betty Jane was a shameless whore. He wondered what the world would think of her were it to know that she would willfully misinterpret a guy's touch of an arm as a signal to play with his dick.

If she persisted, he would come in his pants, and then there'd be hell to pay at home, for nothing could be done discreetly in his house, being as he was always under the surveillance of his brother and father and mother, not to mention his grandmother, who lived with them and had little to do but snoop. Lucky he was allowed enough time to whack off in the bathroom while pretending to crap. He would never find the privacy in which to wash his underwear and sponge away such jizzum as penetrated to the fabric of his trousers.

Therefore he removed her hand. Frowning, she stared deep into his eyes. It took a moment for him to register that while doing so she had also gone deftly within her skirt and with two thumbs slipped her white underpants to her ankles.

"Now, Jack," she whispered, "take it easy. I don't have much experience." She lay back across the bed, the plaid skirt only as high as midthigh.

Kellog was not sure what was expected of him. Later on, he reflected that Betty Jane may have been inviting him only to some heavy petting — at least, that might be her own interpretation — but thus far in life he had done no more of that than he had fucked. So he smirked now, though with her eyes shut she could not see him, and pulled the pants over her heels so that he could get between her legs; and without removing any of his own clothes, he brought out his rigid member. Funny, though this first time he didn't even know precisely where the entryway was situated, and got no help from her, he was magically inside her instantly and no sooner there than he ejaculated. And no sooner had he come than he withdrew: in fact, he was still emitting fluid onto her motionless flesh, and so as not to wet his own clothing he eventually extinguished himself, as one might grind out a burning cigarette, onto, into her skirt, without really thinking of what he was doing, though he would have had no regrets if he had thought about it. He was here only by invitation. He found Betty Jane no more attractive than before. Then what obligation could he possibly have?

She finally opened her eyes to ask, with a certain awe, "Was that it?"

"Huh?"

"We went all the way?"

Already he had returned the horse to the stable. He removed himself from between her legs. "I guess so."

She looked down at the semen on her thigh. "I lost my *thing* a couple years ago, riding my bike, but I still thought it would hurt."

If what she was saying was true, he had got himself a cherry, that prize to which all menfolk aspired: you should shatter every maidenhead you could, and finally marry the girl who had resisted all comers and kept her own. That seemed to make sense. But he had little sense of accomplishment now.

"I really got to go," he said, standing. "I'll see you, Betty Jane."

"Well, Jack," said she, "I just hope you're ready to do the right thing if worse comes to worst."

For a few moments he assumed she meant: if her parents discovered that she had brought a boy home to an empty house. Of course she could count on him, if asked, to lie about what they had done together.

"I'll swear we were doin' homework," said he. To think of this brought back the normal world, and he felt better.

"I mean making it legal," said Betty Jane, in a wheedling tone that he hated to hear. She continued to lie there like a victim.

With a mixture of indignation and panic, Kellog almost howled. "Crysakes, it was all *your* idea!"

"Not to go all the way," she insisted. "I never did that before."

"I bet there's *nothin'* you never did before!" he shouted in outrage and got out of there as fast as he could, speeded up by her cries of placation and even her physical pursuit.

"Oh, don't go. I'm sorry. I'm not accusing you of —"

He was out the door and across the porch. Hardly had he reached the sidewalk when Gordon Riggins stepped out from behind a big tree at the edge of the Hopper yard. Kellog had forgotten about Riggins altogether. Gordon had been waiting all this while.

"So," Riggins said eagerly, "you did a great job, Jack. You've been talkin' me up for an hour. What did she say? She like me?"

"Hard to say, Gordo. There might be something wrong with her. I couldn't get far, frankly. Listen, she's not all that great-looking. A guy like you could do a lot better."

The sober truth was that Riggins, tall, broad-shouldered, and with curly hair and a square chin, was a handsome bastard, a far cry from Kellog with his dumpy figure and bad skin. It was reasonable that a girl would favor the former, but Jack was noticing for the first time what later on seemed to be a rule of human behavior in those days: that the attractive were drawn to those less so; this was true of both sexes. Kellog's brother, who had gone to college for one semester, assured him that the beauty queens all went steady with ugly guys with big noses, fan ears, or thick eyeglasses. But no doubt they all had great senses of humor.

Riggins stopped and scowled. "You done me a big favor, but I'm going to have to trim your ass if you talk like that about Betty Jane. She's an angel." He glowered at Kellog until he got an apology.

Jack added silently: *I just fucked your angel, Gordo, and left her beggin' for more, and I tell you she ain't much.* Furthermore, he continued doing so on and off for half a year more, and though neither of them took any precautions, being ignorant of how to do so (rubbers were only for protection from disease, as could be read on the wrappers), it was so long before Betty Jane got pregnant that she came to believe that losing her hymen on the bike had also affected her capacity to have children. During all this time, Riggins' love endured though never being requited, and he continued to urge Kellog to press his case with Betty Jane. In no other area of life was Riggins that dumb: in fact, he got better grades than Kellog, and in exchange for Jack's services as Cupid often helped him with the mathematical part of chemistry, which Kellog was taking because his father wanted him to go on to work his way through pharmacy school.

Then B.J. (as he called her, because except for sex he thought of her as a sort of boring guy) did miss a monthly, and despite Riggins' help he was flunking chemistry, and he had never had any intention of going on to any kind of formal education, and he feared that the next time his father struck him he might kill the old man with a butcher knife — so Jack Kellog, who had now turned seventeen, blew town.

JACK HAD never before been far from his hometown, a middle-sized place in the western provinces of the

East, but he knew how to thumb a car for a ride, and as it turned out he had good luck with the first vehicle to stop (after being passed up by all others for some time): it was occupied by a couple in their early fifties, the male member of which, and sole driver, intended to make it to Florida non-stop, with the aim of beating his brother-in-law's record for the same route. Jack slept from time to time in the rear seat, but when he was awake he maintained a repartee which kept the Bosemans in stitches, so the arrangement proved successful for all concerned. He told them he was in flight from the nasty woman whom his father had married on the death of his mother, and would seek refuge with a benevolent aunt in Hollywood, Fla., a name he had heard and remembered because of its incongruity with the idea of the California film capital. Mrs. Boseman maternally fed him from the carton of food she had brought along so that they might eat while continuing to roll, and when Hollywood was reached, the Mister wanted to deliver him to the door of his supposititious aunt, but Jack faked a gas-station phone call and pretended she had demanded to come and fetch him in place.

The season being April, he slept on the beach at night and managed, by prudent expenditure and starving himself, to live almost three weeks on the fourteen dollars that were his life savings, earned from caddying and mowing lawns, for in those days a hotdog could still be bought for a dime. At first he could not find employment, but finally was taken on as a busboy in a third-rate nightclub that was reputedly owned by mobsters, the floor show consisting of a glib emcee who began with a monologue of jokes and then introduced a series of strip acts. Except for this ringmaster, the performers were all female — so Jack assumed until once in the men's room, dutifully washing his hands as the regulations demanded, he saw the snake-dancer, who had the largest bosom of the entire company as well as the most elaborately made-up eyes, enter breezily and, lowering the sequined G-string, take a male organ in hand and pee into the wall-hung urinal.

This dancer used the stage name of Tanya. He had a real python, and in his act he lay on the floor and writhed with it, as a finale pressing its inscrutable wedge-head into his pumping groin and pretending to reach a female climax. After the performance he could sometimes be seen doing a spirited fox-trot with one of the patrons, all of whom were men. Whether in his case it went further than the dance floor, Jack could not say, but he was well aware that the sexual services of the female dancers were always for hire, though they were constrained from soliciting as such, owing to the local ordinances. Jack used to run errands for them, fetching cigarettes and drinks, and sometimes a paper bag containing some ready-made reefers from a guy who came into the kitchen through the alley door.

The girls were generous with Jack, whom they called Kid. If he had to go off the club's premises for some item, say to the drugstore for mascara, he was usually tipped if the transaction had been in cash, but Marie would run up a tab of three or four errands and then let him take it out in trade. Which is how he got his first blowjob as well as the first encouragement in his projected profession.

Marie and he sometimes had serious talks about their respective aims in life. She was saving up for a little house with a yard, where she and her daughter, now two and a half and being raised by her mother, could live until some clean-cut Christian would come along and marry them. For his part, Jack wanted someday to have a job like Buster Kline, the floorshow emcee. "Aw, gee, I bet you go a lot further than that loser," said Marie. "He's here because he couldn't never get nowhere better. But you're just a kid, Jack: you gotta whole life ahead of you. Kid like yourself, with a quick mind like yours, you could be a headliner someday. And when you get there, remember who tole ya so."

Meanwhile he studied how Buster did it, sometimes to the detriment of his job as busboy, and the waiters gave him a hard time. One even kicked his ass behind the partition between main room and bar. He might have been fired had the manager not been a faggot with a yen for young males and would settle if need be even for the likes of Jack Kellog, who was fat and sloppy though his skin was gradually clearing up. "Oh, come on, Jack," Vince would say when he had contrived to arrange a private encounter that he hoped would end in a discreet success (for he erroneously supposed he had kept his taste a secret from those of his subordinates whom he had not solicited). "You oughta learn that one hand washes the other in this world of ours. You be nice to me, I'll be real grateful to you. You could be a waiter, next opening." Jack was insulted by Vince's low assessment of his ambition, but he did not say so. Nor did he say yes. Instead he would look uneasy and mumble about his tender age, but the inclusion of "yet" in the rejection did not make it final.

Buster Kline, Jack's model, was a very thin, almost cadaverous man who was probably a good ten years older than his announced thirty-eight. He wore an inferior toupé and real sideburns that he dyed one or two degrees darker than the purchased hair on his scalp. His long upper lip was the kind that looked as though it had been, and perhaps should still be, the home of a mustache. His smile, crafted to accommodate a partial dental plate, could have been a sneer; his widest grin, a smirk. He chain-smoked, even when on stage. When performing he spoke in rapid-fire until he arrived at a punchline, then would pause for a moment and complete the joke as if he had all the time in the world. "These-two-colored-girls-go-to-a-photographer-and-have-their-picture-taken. Photographer-goes-back-of-the-camera-and-puts-the-black-hood-over-his-head. 'Whuh he gone do?' asks-one-girl-to-the-other. "The-other-says, 'Focus.' . . . So the first one says, '*Bofe* . . . of . . . us?'"

Buster had a lot of Negro jokes, as well as jokes about Jews, Irish-Catholics, Americans deriving from Latin America, Scandinavia, and China, and white-trash Southerners, all of which he performed with appropriate accents. Colored folks were invariably characterized as shiftless, sexually amoral, and likely to pocket anything of value while its owner was distracted, but this portrait, in intention anyway, was an affectionate one, as if its subject were a venerable family pet. Buster's Scandinavians were invariably dairy farmers and therefore owned milking machines which could be put to indecent purposes. The Irish jokes usually had a priest in a prominent role; the Chinese, a hand-laundryman; the Hispanic, a boy trying to sell a female relative to an American tourist. The Dogpatch rednecks were hilariously incestuous: "Billy Bob gets out of his sister's bed and says, 'Gee, Sis, you's better'n Maw.' 'That's jess what Pa always says,' she tells him."

Buster was himself a Jew, and his jokes that referred to this people often employed words or phrases in Yiddish, the mere sound of which was enough to send the Jews in the audience into paroxysms of laughter and applause. The terms were new to Jack, in whose hometown Jews were rare, but he soon acquired a vocabulary that was essential to the American comedian: *gonif, luftmensh, alter kocker, yenta,* and a multitude of words beginning with the *sh* sound, any of which when heard by a Jewish ear was guaranteed to produce hilarity: *shelp* and *shlock* and *shlemiel* and *shlimazl, shlub, shlump, shmalz, shmooz,* and *shmuck,* which represented just the tip of the iceberg. A pun on the Hebraic name for the ceremonial ram's horn was responsible for Buster's most successful joke with Jewish audiences (Gentiles laughed because it was filthy in its simple meaning): "Two old colored men were walking past a temple when they heard this sound: *Oooooo*. 'What dey doin' inside dere?' asked one. The other says, 'Dey blowin' de *shofar*.' 'Man,' says the first, 'them Jews sure know how to treat their help.'" One kind of joke that was for a long time not to be heard in Buster's routine, for obvious reasons, was any pertaining to Italians.

Vince was merely a salaried manager. The owners of the club stayed permanently in absentia, so far as the rest of the staff was aware. It was presumably off the premises somewhere that Vince handed over the week's take, including a hefty commission on the girls' supposedly private prostitution: sixty percent, according to Marie, who was bitter but too scared to misrepresent her tips by much. The john paid the fee directly to Vince. "They think of everything," she told Jack. "If you complain it oughta be at least fifty-fifty, they say, 'C'mon, you hold back your tips.'"

But Vince himself turned out to be the one who had been holding back money, at least in the opinion of the owners, and one morning his body was found in the back seat of his car, the throat slashed and his severed penis in its mouth. On the assumption that it was the murder of one pervert by another, which in those days was of little official interest, the cops worked over a few known queers and then shelved the inquiry. Not to mention that according to Marie as well as Max the bartender, Vince had also been stiffing the police on their weekly payoffs, which were supposed to be based on the club's income for the same period. Max shook his grizzled head. "Now, that's the way to score big in life. Try to fuck *both* the mob and the cops. Now, that makes sense."

The new manager was an impressive man named Mr. Charles. Unlike Vince he never wore a tuxedo, and he stayed mostly back of the closed door to his office, not even emerging on the occasions when there was trouble out front. It had been Vince's practice at such times to come out and first try to placate the drunken patron, and when that did not work, have a couple of the huskier waiters and bartenders throw him out. There had been no regular bouncer. But under the regime of Mr. Charles, the troublemaker was immediately bracketed by some efficient persons who had been posing as fellow customers, and it never failed that simultaneously the man passed out and was helped to his car and, unless he came to, even was driven home or to his hotel. Max explained this to Jack, who had assumed that Mr. Charles's men simply rubbed the guy out.

Not long after his arrival, Mr. Charles called Buster Kline into the office and told him it wasn't right that he never told Italian jokes: it made it seem like they either wasn't good enough or on the other hand was too good to be true, see? In either case, it lacked respect. "Only not the organ-grinder shit, you know?"

Buster told Jack, now his confidant, about this, and asked, "Say, kid, you know any Italian jokes? My mind suddenly went blank." Jack admitted with chagrin that he had never even known any Italians, "But maybe you could just substitute Italians for the people in the other jokes."

Buster set him straight. "Most gags if they're any good just apply to whoever's being kidded. You got to be *specific* to be funny: it's more than just switching spaghetti for matzoh balls. I would have to know Italian slang the way I know Yiddish. You gotta be real when it comes to yumah. Tragedy, you can make it up. But to get people to laugh you got to come up with the real McCoy."

All Buster could manage for the next show was: "Hey, what's the fastest thing in the world? Mussolini going through Harlem on a bike!" The war between Italy and

Ethiopia was a dim memory, if that, to the audience that evening at the Club Coronado, so Buster, who was nothing if not quick on his feet, immediately shouted; "Then what's the heaviest thing in the world? *Shit* — even an elephant can't hold it!" And got the boffola reaction he had been denied for the preceding. After the show Mr. Charles called him into the office once more and spoke in disappointment. Though no threats had been made, Buster retired to his one-room apartment, lowered the Murphy bed, and took to it with a nervous complaint.

He made it to the club the following evening and even began the first show, but when hardly into his monologue, he clutched his heart and staggered offstage. Marie came out sooner than she would have under normal conditions and did her act, always a crowd-pleaser, for she had terrific knockers, big but also firm and high with outsized nipples, and at the end she removed one G-string to uncover another, and finally that one was replaced by her hand, which was sufficient to conceal her snatch, so carefully was it trimmed of excess pubic hair. She strutted offstage, and with whistles and hoots and foot-stamping, the audience summoned her back. She smiled and bowed and brought both hands to her lips, then blew invisible kisses to the crowd. Suddenly, her mouth still in an *O*, her thin-penciled eyebrows climbed and she squeaked in fake dismay. Her naked pussy was on view! Quickly she grasped it with both hands and ran off, tits flopping, ass wiggling, to uproarious laughter and wild applause.

The next act was Elaine, a skinny-buttocked, pointy-nosed artificial redhead not in her earliest youth. Tonight, without Buster there to provide a lead-in — he and she would banter, he pleading lasciviously, she by turns hostile and teasing, with repeated bumps and grinds — she lacked conviction in her strip, not to mention that she had been unsuccessful in concealing with makeup the black eye given her by her current boyfriend when she had come home with too little money to defray his losses at the track that day.

"Buster didn't want an ambulance," Jack told Marie. "He just went home."

"He's had one foot inna grave for years," said she, indifferently. What worried her was the show, for Marie was a real trouper. And perhaps she too feared the reaction of Mr. Charles. She was staring dolefully from the wings, "After Elaine, there ain't nobody else tonight, so that's the show. Barbara's got the rag on, and Tanya got rolled and beat up by a sailor he took home, the stupid little bitch, he gets so hard up: it ain't the money." She cracked her gum. "Ordinarily you could count on Buster to stretch with somepin, you know, dig deep down for some old material from the Year One, take on a heckler, or whatever . . ."

Elaine was doing her finish, pumping her crotch into the edge of the curtain while the drummer in the three-man band (piano and sax) made accompanying rim-shots on his snare and, after an exceptional hump, adding a crash of the high-hat.

Without a conscious thought Jack strode onto the stage in his busboy's red mess jacket. The lights were brighter than he anticipated, but that only added to an atmosphere which was both that of make-believe and heightened reality. He felt the master of himself and all he surveyed.

"Thank you, thank you," he said to Elaine in a new, piercingly clear voice that he produced by instinct. "Let's give the little lady a hand, oh yeah, oh yeah." He grasped his groin. "Hey, Elaine, I got a big hand for yuh!" The audience guffawed. "Now, I don't want any of you comin' up here, smellin' that curtain. That won't leave *me* with anything to do after the show!" He sniffed audibly. "'Hi, you-a girls,' said the blind Italian as he passed the fish store." Next, Jack shouted, "Why is a police station like a men's room? . . . It's where the dicks hang out!" Without being signaled, the drummer began to hit a rim-shot after each punchline, just as he did for the strippers' bumps-and-grinds.

He got off a dozen jokes in rapid-fire, hitting them with the next before they had recovered from the previous gag, understanding instinctively that handling an audience has much to do with rhythm and pace, and of course confidence, which he had had from the first, perhaps because he despised these men who had nothing better to do than swill drinks and leer at women they couldn't have except for a fee, and many of them were servicemen, some with colored ribbons over the breast pocket, for the war had not been over long. Whereas he was just a punk kid, manipulating all the people in the room.

Mr. Charles called him in when he left the stage. "Kid, I got ta hand it to yuh: you got balls. And you ain't bad, you ain't bad."

Still swollen with a sense of triumph, Jack said, "I think I did great!"

The saturnine manager pointed a finger at him. "Don't get too fresh too soon. I said not bad: I didn't fuckin' say great. I liked the Eyetalian gag; it was comical yet respectful." He pointed again. "So you do the rest of the shows tonight. Tomorrow, I'll think about it. I don't know about Buster. He might be ready for the pasture." Mr. Charles had never been seen to smile. Now he added dolefully, "Listen, anybody come up and ast how old you are, you say twenty-one. If we keep you on as a comic, we'll fix you up with I.D. You ran away from home, right? You ain't registered for the draft, are ya?"

Jack was settling down now, ready to deal with reality, and therefore he answered with simulated submissiveness. "No, sir."

"Okay, kid, keep it up." Mr. Charles lowered his head and began to examine a ledger that lay open before him.

"Sir," said Jack, "I'm only getting a busboy's money."

Mr. Charles looked up lugubriously. "So? You're a busboy."

Jack was making fifteen a week in wages and came in for a minuscule share of the tips of the three waiters whose tables he cleared, but he was dependent on the figures they gave him and assumed these were on the minimizing side, for his income from that source was only about three bucks per week. He did get most of his meals gratis in the club kitchen, which meant he lived on hamburgers, for the cuisine was exclusively short-order and the chef was hardly going to give him the so-called sirloin steak sandwich that led the menu and was priced at a whopping dollar and a half. (There was a cover charge of $2.50 at the Club Coronado, a minimum of two bucks. Mixed drinks cost a dollar per, and beer was fifty cents for a short glass. Customers paid through the nose, but there were few complaints: they came to see the naked girls, in a time when smutty movies could only be seen at Legion smokers.)

"Maybe if this works out," he asked Mr. Charles, "you would —"

"I don't like being hustled for money," the manager said, staring with lusterless eyes. "It shows a lack of respect."

Jack continued to grow as an audience favorite throughout the subsequent months, though in a place the commercial purpose of which was to create drunks, troublemakers would appear from time to time, usually harmless hecklers whom he found it easy to demolish ("Hey, when I come where *you* work, do I bother *you*? Do I kick the toilet-brush outa your hand?"), but infrequently someone would pose a genuine menace. Once a man hurled a glass at the stage, and another time a husky crewcut fellow in a sailor's uniform stood up and shouted in a drunken Southern voice that he would whip Jack's ass for not making him laugh even once. Though fearing no man's verbal assault, Jack was physically a total coward, and he would have been seriously upset on such occasions had not the bouncers introduced by Mr. Charles not soon materialized and escorted the offenders off the premises, after having in both cases done something discreet and effective to bring about a violent bending at the waist and the immediate disappearance of all aggressive display.

Jack had the sense never again to bring up the subject of money with Mr. Charles, whom even Marie was scared to cross, whereas she had taken liberties with Vince, faggot that he was, and had been wont to skim from the tips she was supposed to split with the club. She admitted she would never try as much with Mr. Charles. "They burned a girl's nipple up in Jersey for doin' that," said she, in an almost inaudible undertone, for she insisted that all areas of the club were wired. "They're mean, Jackie, real mean. You oughta get out of this business and do something clean like join the army."

But the fact remained that Jack was in his element. He saw Mr. Charles & Co. as his protectors and, doing what he enjoyed, in those early days he did not see money as the supreme good. Anyway, after he had proved himself for a couple of months, Mr. Charles called him in and said, "Move outa that fleabag room of yours, Jackie. It don't make the right impression for one of the featured performers at the Coronado Club. Get over the Mountford Hotel, they'll fix you up. You can afford it: you're making fifty a week."

This seemed a fortune to Jackie, who was now called by his stage name and not Kid. The latest posters mounted on either side of the main doors to the club showed an elaborately retouched life-sized photograph of a showgirl in tassled bra and sequined G-string and identified as "fresh from the Follies Berger in Gay Paree, the glamorous MARIE BONJOUR, heading a bevy of exotic, erotic beauties for your delectation." Diagonaled across a lower corner of the poster on the right ran a yellow band on which was printed: "Fresh from the Great White Way, the sidesplitting comic JACKIE KELLOG!"

But after six-eight months it had become clear to Jackie that he could never become a headliner at such a club, which was essentially a whorehouse with added attractions. However, he lacked the nerve to speak of his ambitions to Mr. Charles, who might well find him ungrateful. But once again the heavenly powers came to his aid without being asked. Mr. Charles called him in.

"Here's how it goes, Jackie. Me and my associates are wrapping it up here. But I got a soft spot in my heart for you, maybe because it was me gave you your start and you're like a son to me. We got some interests in Havana, a lot nicer than this shithole which I don't mind telling you we just kept open for sentimental reasons, you know? You can come along over to Cuba, or I'll give ya a good send-off for someplace else, your choice."

Someplace else turned out to be Atlantic City, and Jackie took that choice, for Havana was farther from the Big Time to which he aspired. The Atlantic City club proved to be much like the Coronado, with the difference that it maintained no resident performers but every few weeks changed all the personnel of one show for an entirely new group. Owing to Mr. Charles's recommendation, Jackie was given an opportunity to go on for ten minutes of standup for a few nights, but the reception was lukewarm at best, and soon the arrogance he had so quickly attained by hearing laughter degenerated to what in a weaker character might well have become true self-pity, which is never funny, as opposed to the simulated kind that is so successful for comics who pretend to be victims of their associates, especially the women to whom they are hypothetically married.

But Jackie Kellog was too tough a nut to be cracked by disregard, he who after all had risen above his lack of superficially attractive attributes to win the respect of his high-school classmates and even the unwelcome devotion of a Betty Jane Hopper (whom he realized, looking back, not only Gordon Riggins but most of the other boys believed both sexually and socially desirable). Far from being discouraged, he acquired strength by hating the people whom he could not make laugh, but he had far too much self-command to display resentment, always the trait of a loser.

It was at this time that Jackie first formulated what was to become his trademark style: abuse of individual members of the audience, which made the others hilarious and caused the victim him- or herself to laugh even more vigorously or seem that most shameful of Americans, the creature who could not take a joke, *viz.*, the Poor Sport. It began one night when Jackie could not evoke an audible snicker with his first five, the strongest, jokes. If *they* didn't make it, he faced stark disaster, for the material went downhill from there. He found himself praying for a heckler, for an audience is invariably sympathetic to a performer who is being harassed. Had he thought of it, he might have found someone to hire for the role, but it was too late now, and in fact this was the last of his scheduled shows, after which the efficacy of Mr. Charles's recommendation ran out.

Jackie stared malevolently at the tables nearest the stage, and of the persons sitting at them chose a man with a huge belly and several chins. "Hey, buddy," he cried, "didn't you come in with a whole party? Where'd they go? You *eat* 'em? . . . Where's the wife tonight?" He put his hand to his ear, pretending to listen for an answer. The fat man remained silent though he was grinning widely. "Dog-training class? What kind of dog does she have? . . . Oh, you don't have a pet? But the wife can now bring your slippers and newspaper?"

People had begun to laugh now. "I know your wife, sir," Jackie continued, rolling his eyes. "I don't want to hurt your feelings, but I think she made a pass at me the other day: at least she mounted my leg and started to hump it." He was on a roll now, the audience in his pocket, and this audience, unlike that of the Coronado, included both sexes. Some of the women were even married to their escorts, while others were the spouses of men not present; the point was that wives, like Italian-Americans, fat people, et al., were *obliged* to enjoy jokes about their own kind, their natural self-interest permitting no choice in the matter. The only wrong was to be ignored. In the case at hand, if anybody failed to make the maximum response she would probably be a single woman, the girlfriend of a married man.

Jackie finally let the first victim sink back into eternal oblivion and seized another, a relatively young woman with prominent incisors, and proceeded to deliver a series of gibes in which squirrels, chipmunks, and other rodents figured. She colored though of course was constrained to laugh at least as heartily as anyone else, but her escort, a man with a sinewy jaw, had begun to glower loyally. The answer was to turn the attack on *him*. "Look at this guy," Jackie said, pointing, "When his girl says, 'Tell me sweet nothings,' he belches in a higher key. He just sent back his salad; they put garlic in it, and he refuses to eat anything flavored with his favorite underarm deodorant." The man had already been conquered. He was laughing behind a cupped hand, which probably meant he had ugly front teeth, but Jackie had already done the dental material, so he passed up this opportunity and chose a new target, a middle-aged woman who wore too much costume jewelry and looked Jewish. His hypothesis was easily confirmed. "Hey, lady," he shouted, "so you wanted your son to become a physician? Congratulations, he's thirty-two and still plays doctor with little girls." The woman produced shrieks of mirth, her outsized earrings swinging wildly, and slapped her husband's outstretched forearm.

A man named Gus Sebastian managed the Harlequin Club. He called Jackie in after the show and commended him on the change of act, predicting that he was onto something which might take him a long way if used correctly. However, now that he had discharged the obligation to Mr. Charles, Sebastian himself had no more openings in his schedule for the next half year unless someone got sick, in which case if Jackie were then available, he would get hold of him through his agent.

From a fellow comic who was not as competitive as some, Jackie got the name of an agent named Marty Trenier and went to New York for the first time in his life, and after meeting some resistance from Marty, who contrary to expectation was dressed in black suit and white shirt, phoned the number in Havana given him by Mr. Charles, who was pleased to hear from his protégé. "Gimme the bum's name again? . . . Don't worry about it. He'll ask *you* next time. So when you comin' down to see us, Jackie? We got a real nice set-up here: you know, tables, blackjack and the rest. All legal. Good-looking young girls, too. No cows, ya know. Okay, Jackie, glad to help out. Any time."

An hour later, Marty Trenier called at the hotel and apologized. At his office, Marty said, "You got friends, Jackie. How come you need me?" He raised a pair of white hands. "Not that I'm prying!"

"I'm not long in the business," Jackie said. "I just came up from Florida."

"I can book you in the mountains. Don't expect a top place: I take what I can get. Got to make a living like the next man." Marty was a whiner. He sent Jackie to a small Catskill resort called Rudner's where the pay was small but included full room and board. Jackie performed at two shows per night, with Fridays off, and used his new insult style on the exclusively Jewish audiences, with even greater success, Jews being even more anxious than Gentile Americans to prove themselves able to laugh when abused, and all the more so in the years immediately following the war, an event of which Jackie had scarcely been aware except as it was depicted in the blood-and-guts movies in which the Yanks whipped Japs, and Jews, except for the obligatory G.I. from Brooklyn, who often had fair hair and freckles, were seldom mentioned.

"You're not Jewish?" asked Natalie. "Kellog's your real name?"

"My mother was Irish," said Jackie.

"Close enough," Natalie replied, winking. Jackie found her attractive, with her deep cleavage and drenched as she was in pungent perfume. In those days his taste was for women older than himself, with ample figures. It was only later on that he was principally attracted to young stuff, firm and trim. But Natalie never gave a sign of a like yen for him, and since she was the boss he certainly made no move towards her.

He did not want for cooze: women liked men who made them laugh, and his pudgy body and short height were not deterrents to romance. He found, to his initial amazement, that the kind of girl he had desired in vain while in high school, namely the leggy, high-breasted sort, preferably honey-blond (though the fairhaired at Rudner's were usually artificially so, with dark eyes: close enough), was no longer inaccessible to Jackie Kellog the featured performer, who had added cachet owing to his current lack of erotic interest in the type: the liaison with Marie in what was still his formative time had given him not only a leaning towards mature sexual partners but also a predilection for whores, with whom, uniquely amongst womankind, lust is decisively distinguished from love. Marie could service him on application, yet they remained friends; indeed, it was because they were friends that she could do him such favors, as one neighbor gives a ride to another whose car is in the shop, or lends him the lawnmower. This was not true of either the single or the married women at Rudner's, each of whom invariably found it necessary to excuse herself, after the first session in bed, as having first lost her heart to him before yielding her virtue — or insisting she had got helplessly drunk. This was still the era for that kind of female thinking.

Jackie was such a success at Rudner's that Natalie rebooked him for the rest of the summer, and though the resort was one of the more modest establishments in the area, the word somehow got out, and by the end of the season even Marty, a melancholy man by nature, was predicting better money for the summer to follow. But Jackie had to survive the intervening winter, nor was he by now inclined to limit his ambition to seasonal resorts, certainly not those on the next level above Rudner's, at which Marty assured him he could likely get a shot. The fact was that he had been approached by a big talent agency which booked acts for clubs in Las Vegas, Reno, and California, places beyond Marty's purview and at which he stupidly scoffed, unable to foresee the spectacular future of Nevada and Tahoe.

Jackie's career in that part of the world was in its own way as successful as that of the mobsters who came to flourish in Vegas in the years after the war. A hit in the lounges from the first, before long he was being hired to "open" for the headliners, perform as a prefatory act to that of the star, in the big nightclub rooms of the major hotels. He thus became

83

a subordinate colleague of the most successful entertainers of that place and time, and discovered that people in the top ranks of show business are the most generous on the face of the earth. Tony Gamble was the greatest of them. He was then at the height of his career as singer, movie actor, pal of international statesmen, and had the nice habit of giving expensive presents to those around him at the end of every week of an engagement: gemmed cuff links, engraved cigarette cases, belts made from rare snakeskins, etc. And were he to hear of the medical problems of anyone in his entourage or crew, or finally anyone so much as employed anywhere in the hotel during his gig, Tony would insist on sending the unfortunates to his personal physicians and picking up the tab, including those for hospitalization and surgery.

That Tony was considered a living saint by the recipients of his generosity went without saying. But he was also notorious for abusing the women with whom he was intimate — in certain moods, always unpredictable, striking them so savagely in the face with a fist bearing many rings as to require reconstructive work by the finest practitioners, which of course was paid for by Tony as his apology. Were the ex-wives and mistresses and even, as time went on, the one-night stands not to accept this act of contrition, they were henceforth shunned absolutely. And if they had recourse to the law or, worse, to journalists inimical to Tony, they might well be subjects of a baleful interest on the part of certain thugs who sentimentally considered an attack on him as one on themselves.

Among Tony's virtues was a splendid record in giving encouragement to newcoming performers. He regularly made a tour of the lounges and the shows on lower levels than his own, and he loved Jackie Kellog's act as soon as he saw it, sending backstage to Jackie, that very night, a case of the limited-stock sour-mash bourbon specially bottled for himself, his caricature and signature on the label, and a gilt-edged pass to his own show and subsequent admission to his dressing room.

"I like what I see in you, kid," Tony said when Jackie had used the privilege last-named. "All I know is you make me laugh my ass off — and hey, I'm not all that great an audience." It was between shows, and Tony was drinking Coke and chain-smoking king-sized cigarettes. There were three of his people with him in the dressing room, two men and one woman, and others came and went incessantly. "Get him what he wants," he told the woman, a motherly sort in middle age, and to Jackie, "What do you want?"

At this time Jackie still drank little, did not smoke, and took no pills but an occasional aspirin. He was brought a Coke of his own.

"I got friends," Tony said, his clip-on bow tie unfastened and dangling down the ruffled front of his shirt. One of his helpers had removed the tuxedo jacket. There were great circles of damp under his armpits. Glancing at himself in the mirror, Tony saw these and saying, "I can't stand sweat!" ripped the shirt off himself, buttons flying. The woman brought him a new shirt. As Jackie was to learn, Tony never had any item of apparel laundered or dry-cleaned: he wore brand-new garments every time he performed; it was his fetish.

"I gotta lotta friends," he went on as the woman was buttoning the new shirt on him. "That's my only religion: friends. If you're a friend of mine, you share all my other friends. We all love one another. Wanna be my friend? . . . Good, I like that. You want a sandwich or anything?"

Jackie was not hungry at the moment, and he was too heavy anyway (190 with a height of 5′5″), but neither did he wish to offend against Tony's legendary hospitality, and therefore when Tony recommended the tuna-fish sandwich (made to the great man's own specifications: the fish minced and mixed with raw egg yolk, chopped scallions, horseradish, and mayo and served with Bibb lettuce and tomato on one of the onion rolls specially flown in from New York to wherever Tony was performing), Jackie believed it politic to order one of his own.

"Jackie," Tony said, "I make quick decisions. I want you to open for me tomorrow night. Comic I got now — what's his fuckin' name? — uh, Joey: he's a bum. He ain't ever been funny, and he's a lush besides." From the side of his mouth he spoke to the larger of his two male assistants, "Get rid of him, Sid." "Sure, Tony," said this man and started briskly to leave the room. "Hey, Sid," Tony added. "Pay him for the whole gig and add an extra five big ones for his trouble. That's for his family — he gets his fuckin' legs broke if he plays it on the tables." "Sure, Tony," said Sid, departing.

"It's just," said Jackie, "that I had to sign a contract where I am now," which was the lounge of another hotel than the one at which Tony Gamble was currently engaged.

"Dint I say I got friends everyplace?" asked Tony. "Dint I just say that?" He addressed the remaining male in his entourage. "Billy, call up Jerry and tell him I need the kid as of yesterday. Be nice. Send him a nice present, a case of something — no, wait a minute, he don't drink any more. He can always use cooze. Call up Minxie, tell her to do me a personal favor and fly up here."

The man frowned behind his tinted glasses. "She's on location in New Mexico, Tony."

Tony stuck a pugnacious jaw towards him. "Did I ask you for that information, asshole?"

"No, Tony."

"Then call her." The man left in haste. Jackie remembered reading in the gossip columns that Minxie Morrow, then one of the most promising of the latest crop of starlets, was a pal of Tony Gamble's.

"So that's taken care of," Tony told Jackie. "I want you to start next show, which is . . . ?" He snapped his fingers at his female helper, the woman wearing octagonal eyeglasses. She said, "The midnight."

"You forget my name?" asked Tony. "Sorry, Tony," said she. Tony addressed Jackie, "The midnight."

"Tonight?"

"When do you think, you shmuck, next Groundhog Day?" Tony cried jovially. Then he frowned. "Do what you been doin', only nastier. Draw blood, you know? People love that. Be a good contrast for when I come on with the ballads. People like to laugh, and they like to cry. That's what we do, kid, get the feelings out of them. You might say we're kinda doctors." He threw back his head and chortled. "Or whores!"

The tuna sandwiches arrived. Tony took a sharklike bite out of his and chewed briefly, then grimaced at the woman, who automatically put out her hand, and he spat the mouthful into her palm. In view of this incident, Jackie assumed he was correct in not touching his own sandwich, which he hadn't wanted in the first place, and now he was sick with anxiety about going into a big room to open for the major attraction in Vegas, for that was the era when Tony Gamble had no peer as a popular performer. Going in without preparation, furthermore, and the place was enormous. Whereas his current act was proportioned to much more intimate dimensions, and while space is not quite so important to comedy as timing (which is of the essence, never more than a millisecond separating success from failure), it could be crucial with a style of the kind that Jackie had been developing in recent months. He had nearly eliminated the telling of set jokes in favor of insulting ad libs directed to individuals in the audience that he wandered through after a brief time on stage. This was ideally suited to the lounges. It seemed to him that you might easily get lost in a big main room, not to mention that, for optimum effect, the victim must be close enough to the other patrons so that they can see the butt of the derision. Obviously that could not be the case with many people in a large audience.

And Jackie was by now sufficiently experienced in the ways of the world to be sure that though this was all Tony Gamble's idea, it would not be like Tony to take any responsibility if he failed. Tony might in fact be offended, and take some ugly vengeance: he had heard such stories. Therefore when Tony dismissed him now, Jackie went to his new hotel room (arranged for him by Gladys, Tony's gray-haired aide, and she had also had his clothes transferred from the other place), and he spent an hour and a half drinking black coffee and vomiting into the toilet bowl. When he went downstairs to perform, his eyes were red, his complexion was ashen; his voice had been roughened by the puking; his guts were wracked with gas pains; his nerves hummed with caffeine; his ankles had turned elastic and could not bear his weight. He ran with sweat and yet his spine was a column of ice. In the wings he all but pissed his pants despite having urinated thrice within the previous quarter hour, and he had double vision.

All he heard of the introduction was the second syllable of his last name, but it was enough not only to restore his faculties but to raise them to a higher plane. For years afterward people bragged of being present at Jackie Kellog's premier performance in the big time.

It was true he could not roam through the audience in such a large room. What he could do was pick targets for his scorn from the stage — and if need be, these could be altogether imaginary. You could assume that in any large assemblage there would be overweight people; persons with large noses, mouths, ears; husbands with unattractive wives; wives whose husbands belched at the dinner table and farted in bed and wore underwear yellowed at the crotch; women who were frigid or pretended to be; men over fifty who desired girls under twenty; and those of either sex who were addicted to unhealthy and/or immoral pleasures (with the exception of gambling, which for obvious reasons could not be derided), and even the unnatural.

When it came to the last-named, you could not of course have focused on individuals in any event, and thus Jackie's act on stage had an advantage over the more intimate performances, for at such a distance he could pretend to notice a sexy dress or spectacular piece of jewelry and commend the wearer: "You have perfect taste, *sir*."

But his boldest stroke, a product of the inspiration which was his when in the heat of a performance, owing nothing to reason, was to poke fun at, of all people, Tony Gamble. Looking at his watch, "Tony's gonna be out here in a few minutes — that means he's only got enough time left to *shtup* three more starlets. . . . J'ever notice those guys who hang around Tony — you know, the ones whose hands hang down to their knees? He's worked out a good deal with them: he pays 'em as high as they can count: which means they all make ten bucks a week — except the guy who shot off a pinky while cleaning his gun, he gets nine. . . . But Tony's big-hearted. He gives a lot of wine to his friends. He sent a bottle the other day to the vet who takes care of his dog. The vet returned it with a note that said, 'Your horse has diabetes.'"

Tony could be sent into homicidal rage by the mildest criticism from a newspaper columnist, and he had once actually kicked the rump of a maître d' who grinned at him when he was himself scowling. But he was so delighted by Jackie that he brought the comic out on stage during his own show, hugged him, and said to the audience, "How about this guy, ladies and gentlemen? You listen to Tony: this young man's going to the top. And would old Tony lie to you?" The phrase drew extra applause, echoing as it did a line from the lyrics of his current No. 1 single, "Too Many Lies, Too Little Love." Then he seized Jackie and kissed him on the lips, a Tony Gamble trademark when publicly saluting his male friends and, given his notorious heterosexual activity, unassailable though provocative. Jackie seized the microphone at this point, and asked, "Does this mean you'll only have your pals break *one* of my arms?" Tony guffawed, flashing the teeth that were blindingly white in a face that was kept tanned to the brink of negritude. He was darker than the most prominent of the black girl singers of the day, when their fashion was to be pale — a fact that was more grist to Jackie's mill in future performances.

Jackie remained Tony's protégé for some five years, during which time he was able to establish his identity with the public, or rather several of the various publics for show business, for there are many such, some overlapping with others, like that of television, and one that was distinct and limited though with a great influence peculiar to itself, namely, Broadway, which was yet to come for him, but he was by now long since a star in his own right in Vegas, Tahoe, and Miami Beach, with lesser performers opening for him now, and had done hygienic though no less outrageous versions of his act many times on the leading television variety programs. TV people had talked with him about possible shows of his own, and at any given moment there was at least one movie project under discussion. His career was in good shape by the time that Tony cooled towards him — a change that he had learned was inevitable.

As IT turned out, Jackie moved away from Tony at just the right time. Another philosophy of popular music than Tony's was gaining ground everywhere, one which furthermore had Leftist connotations, whereas Tony was, when not entire apolitical, of the old-fashioned school of sentimental patriotism, singing the national anthem at World Series openers and occasionally visiting army bases, sometimes at nearby overseas installations. And his drug was alcohol, not herbs or powders, nor was he unbarbered and dirty and epicene and publicly foulmouthed, and he made no bones about preferring leaders who were stuffed shirts to those who were terrorists (besides, having served as their pimp, he had seen the former with their hair down, and they were regular guys).

Television at last came up with the right part for Jackie: the tyrannical mess sergeant in a situation comedy that derided the U.S. Army. The kitchen of the character played by Jackie prepared shit-on-a-shingle for every meal (called "Ess-Oh-Ess" in the dialogue, causing the laugh track to respond with hilarity), but now and again his Negro assistant, who in contrast to Jackie spoke an impeccable English, distracted him by some ruse and served thick sirloins to the troops, followed by apple pie à la mode rather than the canned fruit that was the orthodox dessert. This unit was on peacetime duty in Germany, where wicked but comic Fascists were still plentiful, and while the Jackie character would seem superficially to operate on their principles, his basic American decency would manifest itself sooner or later, and it was sometimes he who frustrated the neo-Nazis or anyway did not obstruct his black helper from so doing.

After becoming famous, Jackie was invited to appear at the White House by a series of presidents of various persuasions, he remained pure entertainer and, if called upon to perform, would jovially insult the reigning Chief Executive, along with the rest of the First Family and cabinet, though of course not as raunchily as when in a show-biz venue: no sex stuff ever, and no booze material unless the target was virtually a teetotaller, and very little of an ethnic nature. So deprived of the resources on which he drew for his nightclub act, Jackie was however not at the least disadvantage: one president had cracked a tooth on a fragment of shell in his maple-walnut ice cream; another had stepped in dog poop while exercising a pet at Camp David. That sort of thing: minor human frailties, which we all find amusing. To laugh at these was to share in the ultimate state of democracy and classlessness. Nothing could have been more appropriate under that roof.

When his sitcom came to an end after four seasons, Jackie made three movies, of which two were bombs and one a feeble success, enough to prove that when performing someone else's material, your fate was in the writer's hands. Therefore when he subsequently received a startling invitation to come to Broadway, he had the courage to accept, for the dialogue anyway would be tops: W. Shakespeare had written it.

Cartwright Law, the noted director, had asked Jackie Kellog to play Falstaff in a new production of *The Merry Wives of Windsor.* Law made a specialty of offbeat casting, along with innovations in many another area. He had staged a *Lear* with an entire cast of midgets; had done an *Othello* in which the Moor was a white actor in blackface and Iago a black actor in a white ski mask. His Hamlet was a Lesbian, while the remainder of the roles were cast and performed in the orthodox mode — and, as a powerful critic said, *it made perfect sense!*

The reviewers adored Jackie's Falstaff, which he was by now sufficiently fat to perform with little padding. During the previews and throughout the first night, he adhered to the letter of Shakespeare's dialogue insofar as he had memorized it from the script as edited by Cartwright Law, which deleted a good deal of the language in favor of clownish stage business by the stout Knight, including obscene self-gropings as he spoke of being ogled lasciviously by Mistress Page: "O! she did so course o'er my exteriors with such a greedy intention, that the appetite of her eye did seem to scorch me up like a burning-glass." He did bumps and grinds whenever he addressed a female character, and belches, farts, and crotch-scratching at any time. "An idiosyncratic interpretation, perhaps," said one critic in a Sunday supplement thinkpiece, "but well justified."

Years of performing in smoke-filled rooms, in a style of comedy that, despite the more than adequate sound systems of the day, seemed to require sustained shouting, plus the liquor of which his daily intake now was copious, along with the huge cigars that he had first used as props but finally began to smoke incessantly on- and offstage, had roughened Jackie's voice until its timbre was that of a Hollywood version of a gangster, and as any attempt on his part to simulate an English accent would have been pathetic, he used his own unrefined Standard American — and was praised for that too by reviewers scornful of the now outmoded Broadway-British voices of the pretentious local thespians who usually essayed the Bard.

Jackie was now at the summit of a phase of show business of which he had no prior experience. Indeed, he had never seen anything on a stage that was not a musical. He was getting highbrow praise while being paid for doing what came naturally. He understood that most of those people to whom the show was sold out for a solid six months were coming to see *him* and not Shakespeare, and gradually Falstaff became a Catskill-Vegas-Miami comic, updating his lines to include "Bullshit!" and adding "-hole" to the terminal word in "I do begin to perceive that I am made an ass." His bawdy gestures became more extreme. Leering at a female character, he would fuck his fist with an index finger. Next he began to go to the footlights and perform a similar gesture while winking at attractive women in the first few rows of the audience, regardless of their escorts.

He was usually drunk nowadays, coming to the theater with a buzz on and then, onstage as Falstaff, drinking the prop grape juice that he laced with vodka. Between the acts he drank more, and he sometimes had a girl, a pro, blow him in the dressing room, a form of midshow tension-reliever much used, and urged on his friends, by Tony Gamble. Once, while waiting to make his entrance and having urgently to piss, Jackie did so in the wings. He had regularly been rude and at times even abusive to the other members of the cast, who, though many were respected American Shakespeareans and all were Broadway professionals, were of course not known to Jackie Kellog's vast share of the public, but he had remained at least civil to the crew, for no show, however successful, could survive without their cooperation. By the distribution of hundred-dollar bills, his personal manager, Harold Opel, was able to put the lid on the pissing incident, but hardly had that been done when Jackie, stumbling drunkenly backstage, tripped on a cable and swore at an electrician, who said, "Listen, I don't have to take that," to which Jackie responded, "You have to take anything I hand out, because you're a piece of shit, and I'm a star."

The crew thereupon walked out. The theater was dark for two evenings and one matinee thereafter, and no sooner had this dispute been settled (by more bribes, the featherbed hiring of several more crew members who had no duties whatever, and a maudlin apology by Jackie to the man he had insulted: "I love people, Richie, I think I've proved that in everything I've ever done . . .") than the husband of a woman to whom Jackie had made especially obscene gestures from the stage waylaid the star as Jackie left the theater that night, bruised his face and broke his nose. (The publicists represented this attack as an attempted mugging, and obviously Jackie could not sue his assailant.) Trouper that he was, he missed not a single performance, going on with a bandaged skull and extra-heavy makeup, drunker than ever owing to the pain.

But next the actress who played Mistress Quickly, an arrogant bitch who had in the past won two Tonys, made a formal complaint to Equity, accusing Jackie of taking liberties with her onstage and off, ignoring her protests. Jackie's response was to write an abusive, semiliterate letter to the board attacking not only the offending colleague but all highbrow Broadway snobs who thought they were better than the combat troops of show business, namely, those who had served their time out where a lush could hit you with a bottle for not making him laugh, and concluding with kiss-my-ass-you-no-talent-bums.

All persons and institutions concerned, except the fearful producers of the play, leaked this communication to the press. Jackie did so because he was proud of himself, speaking as he thought he had for the Common Man of entertainment, but in fact not even his fellow standup comics were in sympathy with him in the case at hand: he had willfully ruined what at first had been seen as a victory for their craft, a demonstration that he who could do standup, the most demanding job in show biz, could outdo the snobs at their own game. But now he had played into the hands of the disdainful and also probably destroyed forever any chance that the experiment would be tried again.

His best friends in the business and previously generous media people publicly turned against him: e.g., Roz Wilshire, the gossip columnist and an old pal, called him "a disgusting slob" on TV, and Tony Gamble, who now let his hair grow shoulder-length, sang protest songs, and embraced Leftist causes in a desperate effort to regain popularity with American youth, said, when asked about his old protégé, "I love the cat's talent, but it was this hangup of his about abusing the ladies. I just couldn't dig it and told him so, and he told me to stuff it. Hey, what can you do?"

When militant women's groups picketed the theater, Jackie walked out of the show. Who needed that shit? He could make five times the money, back in the big hotel rooms of which he was now reigning king, for in an age when rock-and-roll and country-and-western were successfully invading every medium, and the take-my-wife one-liner comics were becoming superannuated, when Tony Gamble, once the favorite entertainer of the American Legion, performed at counterculture rallies, Jackie Kellog could be relied on to maintain the old standards.

His private style vis-à-vis the opposite sex had not changed since high school. He certainly was not queer. He had no sexual taste for his fellow man, but he had no other use for women. He was bored by anything a woman said unless it was dirty. To suffer a woman's company when engaged in recreational pursuits, such as the racetrack, the fights, crap tables, and drinking to insensibility, tended to ruin these sources of the only pleasure Jackie knew in his offstage time, and sex was never fun for him but rather a necessity of nature like moving his bowels. He fucked showgirls but as always preferred whores, who did what they were paid for and left promptly thereafter.

At one point in his early forties, however, after a physical examination at which the doctor had warned him about an ever-rising blood pressure, Jackie suddenly became aware that he was in effect all alone in the world. Since leaving home he had never communicated in any way with the members of his family, who had not appreciated him when he lived amidst them and nowadays would surely want to borrow money, and in fact his brother did try twice to reach him by phone, and his mother wrote once, on the occasion of his father's death, with her hand out, she who had always conspicuously favored his brother, now bankrupted by a small-business flop. "Never but *never* take any calls from any cocksuckers pretending to be my relatives!" Jackie told his people. "They're all phonies. I was an orphan from birth on."

Becoming aware of his mortality with the news of the high blood pressure, Jackie decided he would be less vulnerable under the aspect of eternity if he produced offspring, and he therefore chose as a potential mother one of the robust Vegas showgirls, at five-eleven taller than he by almost half a foot, and underneath her thick makeup a prime piece of Swedish flesh. Their marriage was a show-biz event, held in the main room of the casino-hotel, and attended by a U.S. senator and other political notables, most of the big-name performers then appearing elsewhere in town (not Tony Gamble, who shared the bill at an outdoor rock concert that weekend with a roster of bisexual, junky degenerates, two of whom were to overdose and die before the gig was over), and even a representation of the mobsters who owned most of the Strip but were rarely seen on such an occasion: Joey "the Jockey" Marino, Fat Sal Testarossa, and Mel Lapidus, called "the Hebe" but not to his face.

Sandy was two months pregnant at the time of the ceremony. Half a year later a dead child was produced by cesarean section. The mother thereafter went into a melancholy from which she never emerged till she and Jackie were divorced a few months later, soon after which she married a Texas high-roller, went to live with him in Houston, and bore a series of healthy blond offspring.

Jackie's second wife was an almost plain-looking girl from the cashier's department of the hotel at which he often appeared in Miami Beach. By now he was sick of elaborate hairdos, heavy makeup, and showgirl flesh. Cecilia wore neat white blouses and black string ties. Though she had lived in southern Florida all her life, she rarely exposed any part of herself to the sunshine, and her skin remained almost blue-white. She went to confession every Saturday and on Sunday morning to the eight o'clock mass. She drank nothing that contained alcohol. At the age of twenty-seven she lived with her widowed mother. She was genuinely offended by Jackie's sexual overtures and soon stated that unless he desisted from them — though she liked him a lot otherwise — she would not date him again.

Perhaps it was the insanity of this — a little plain-Jane nobody like her, rejecting a star of his magnitude — that caused him to fall in love for the first time in his life. He doted on her. They held hands at sentimental movies, in one of which Minxie Morrow, Tony Gamble's friend, played an ingenuous high-schooler, one of the vivacious gang at the malt shop; when with Cecilia, Jackie could not really believe that he had once drunkenly gone down on a stoned Minxie in front of a private audience at one of Tony's parties. Afterwards, Ceil would make burned fudge in her mother's modest kitchen, unfortunately her only culinary talent. But her mom was by Jackie's standards a great cook, with her emphasis on abundant meat and potatoes and heavy desserts, menus by which she had kept her late husband, a salesman of soda-fountain equipment, for twenty years until his untimely demise from lung cancer (he had smoked three and a half packs of cigarettes a day since the age of nineteen).

Jackie married Cecilia at some provincial redneck courthouse where nobody recognized him, and installed her and her mother in a triplex apartment on the oceanfront, intending from now on to perform only in Florida. But once Ceil had quit her job, her finagling with the hotel's books came to light. As the months had gone by, the head cashier had given her more and more responsibility, freeing himself for the golf course and thereby enabling her to embezzle $78,000, all of which she had subsequently lost to the horses. Now, the peculiarly outrageous thing about this was that among the vices from which Jackie had been liberated by his association with Cecilia was the track: he hadn't placed a bet in months, just as he had not had a drink.

Despite her criminality, the press, who now hated Jackie, championed Ceil throughout the subsequent mess. He repaid the hotel for what she stole in return for their agreement not to file charges. He was taken to the cleaner's in the divorce settlement, for though he had hired the most expensive lawyer in the state, a nationally renowned civil-rights attorney from New York offered to take Cecilia's case for nothing, with the obvious purpose of adding persecuted women to the roster of victims, real or supposed, on which he had made his reputation. This resulted in the maximum in adverse publicity, and Jackie was transformed from the maker of jokes into the butt of many. Hardly a night went by that he was not the subject of a derisive reference on the TV talk show on which he had in better days so often been a favorite guest. He was named as a characteristic male villain by professional feminists, and next a band of militant women set up a picket line outside the hotel at which he performed.

What with his many reverses, Jackie began to drink heavily again. One day when, returning from the racetrack, where he had lost a bundle, he found his limo surrounded by screeching harpies. He lost control and threatened to punch "you cunts inna tit." Unfortunately for him, a local TV news team happened to be there on a slow-news day elsewhere. With the obscenities bleeped though perfectly understandable, all three national networks showed the tape that evening.

Despite his subsequent public apology, Jackie lost most of his bookings when the contractual clauses designed to meet such emergencies were invoked. He thereupon sued the offending hotels — against the advice of the people he employed to manage his career, all of whom insisted that he could not possibly profit from such litigation. Win or lose in court, he could never afterward perform in any top room. But when he eventually dropped the suits, the result was the same.

Jackie arrived at middle age with a career on the skids, no wife, no children, no money, and not even a home of his own. Soon the only gigs he could get were in provincial dinner theaters, playing roles in comedies of the past before audiences the youngest members of which were his own age. No one wanted the standup act. The kind of women who offered themselves now were well-upholstered old broads whose prime was in the mists of the past, whose husbands went to bed with them only to sleep. He rejected these people as rudely as he could. Once again he was always drunk as he performed, in which state he could usually get by when playing such parts as Sheridan Whiteside in *The Man Who Came to Dinner,* which permitted extravagant movements and shouting, and even the forgetting of lines and loud demands to the prompter, but he had at least to remain conscious, even when in some Nowheresville where anything else would be accepted. But the fact was he passed out cold one night in Little Rock, coming to, however, before the curtain was closed and completing the play without further incident.

Then a month later, in Oklahoma City, he tripped on his first entrance, fell to the stage, and had to be carried into the wings.

His heart attack made mostly local news, aside from one brief reference in a New York gossip column, by a woman who hated his guts to the degree that simply this report, without comment, could be considered gloating.

He survived, but his blood pressure remained impossibly high, his weight outlandish, his cholesterol count out of sight, not to mention that his liver was morbid, and he was assured that unless he immediately cold-turkeyed the cigarette habit, he could say good-bye to his lungs. Before they discovered that he could not pay their fees, the doctors were gravely concerned.

Ironically enough, this was just the impetus he needed for a comeback. Seeking a more compassionate image, a nighttime talk-show host invited Jackie to use his program as a ten-minute forum for the story of his victimization by certain members of the medical profession. This was at a time when people in general were turning against physicians, who were regularly depicted in films, cartoons, and jokes as mercenary incompetents who drove costly German cars and spent their prime time on the golf course, popping briefly into operating rooms to cut off the wrong organ from some poor bastard whom they bankrupted with their fees.

The network subsequently received thousands of letters in support of Jackie Kellog, and his star began to rise once again. He was in demand for guest shots on television, and he was signed for a movie satire on practitioners of internal medicine, provisionally entitled *Guts*. Gradually he paid off his creditors, but not the doctors, whom he countersued for malpractice, but he did take their previous advice and cleaned up his physical act, stopped smoking, drinking, and gorging on the greasy, salty, sweet foods he preferred, and began to consume fiber, even worked out every morning on the portable rowing machine that accompanied him on his tours. He had always stayed too old-fashioned to do much of drugs, which he identified with rock music, clown's clothing, shrill do-gooder politics, and a limp-wristed style that was the antithesis of the classic two-fisted show-biz culture, from the comics like himself, who started in gangsters' clubs, all the way up to the tough guys on the screen in his favorite movie era of George Raft and Edward G.

E N R O U T E to a local morning TV show at the moment, Jackie was sixty pounds below his maximum weight and still losing. His blood pressure had been lowered to an acceptable level. He no longer panted when climbing a slight grade. Not only could he now see his toes, he could even touch them. He had all but forgotten what a hangover felt like, or how it tasted to wake up in the morning after smoking forty cigarettes in the sixteen hours of the previous day. He was on his fourth wardrobe since beginning to lose weight, and for an appearance of this kind, he brought along a pair of the tent-sized trousers he had worn at his largest.

"I still can't *believe* it," screeched Sara Neil, the female half of the morning show's pair of hosts, when Jackie held the garment up for inspection by the camera. "*How* much did you weigh then?"

"I stopped counting after three-forty."

Sara was in her middle twenties and of the lean and sinewy build of those to whom the sensuous appetites are never a problem, are likely even a bore.

She asked, "But you didn't lose all this weight on an ordinary diet, did you, Jackie? There's something more to the story."

"A lot more," Jackie said, seeing in his peripheral vision that an enormous close-up of his face filled the screen of the monitor that was sunk in a depression in the desk at which he sat with Sara — that was the distinctive style of this show: when being interviewed, you temporarily occupied the seat of one of the co-hosts. He had of course been made up for such close-ups, his nose-hairs trimmed, etc., and for many years now he had been using chemical means to keep his real hair dark. On his crown he wore the best toupé money could buy: he was told by all that it was undetectable. But his skin was lined and leathery with the loss of fat. To some degree he was now like a deflating balloon.

"There's a whole nother spiritual dimension," he went on. "This might sound corny, comin' from a guy like me, but . . ." His voice trailed away, and he shrugged.

"No," Sara said quickly. Young as she was, she was a real professional. If she hadn't been, she would never have got where she was. Girls couldn't fuck their way to the top of the business as things stood today. "No, not at all, Jackie. I think there's a lot of people who are going to want to hear this just because it comes from somebody like yourself."

Jackie nodded. "Ya know, people think, well, those guys in the public eye — and gals too — with their inflated egos, they got great ideas of themselves, they don't have any of the problems of we working stiffs. Not true!"

In her straight-man role, Sara groaned assent, though surely she was being hypocritical. What problems could she have ever had? The little snot got this job at the ripe old age of twenty-one, after less than a year's experience with some nothing channel in the New Mexican boondocks.

"People think," Jackie continued, "that you must have all the confidence in the world to get up here and make a fool of yourself, but that is far from true — with some of us, anyway."

Sara looked bored. "Are you saying your weight problem came from a *poor* self-image, Jackie? *You*?"

He hung his head briefly before bringing it up with a sheepish grin. "That's just what I am saying. It wasn't easy to understand. It took a lot of work. And that was only the first phase."

"Which means?"

Jackie lowered his eyelids momentarily. Then he stared

boldly at Sara. He had nothing to be ashamed of. "I finally realized that God loves me."

Sara, likely an atheist, might have been embarrassed by this confession, had she not been armed with a book that bore his name on the jacket. She raised this volume so that the camera could see it. "And you've told all about it right here."

"It's all my ideas," Jackie said. "I'm a talker, not a writer. I'm a high-school dropout, I'm sorry to say. I talked to Dick Trout and he wrote it all down. He's a terrific author, with a string of best-sellers on his belt."

Sara pursed her lips and opened the book as if arbitrarily, but in fact the book had been inconspicuously taped so it would be exposed by such means. "What makes this unique," said she, "at least among the ones I've seen, and a lot of these sorts of things are coming out nowadays — are we looking for a faith, identifiable values, some evidence of love, of caring? Your book is the only one I know that gives recipes along with the spiritual, uh —"

"That's right," Jackie broke in. "And there's nothing sacrilegious about it. God made us and He made the food we eat, too. We'd all be a lot healthier if we kept that in mind when we sit down to dinner, and not violate our systems." He lifted his hands. "I'm not being holier-than-thou, the way I used to abuse myself."

"This certainly looks tasty," Sara said, pretending to be interested in the page she had opened. "'Shrimp Body and Soul.'"

"For the whole person," said Jackie. The recipes had been supplied by a nutritionist hired by the publisher. Jackie had never boiled water, making coffee in the early days with water from the hot tap.

"We'll be back to cook up a storm with Jackie Kellog," Sara said to the camera with the red light. A commercial came on.

CHANGING THE PAST

Sara ignored Jackie to speak intensely with one of the production assistants, then got up and took a sip of coffee brought her by a flunky, then had her makeup dabbed at by a young woman whose own style was aggressively punk.

Someone conducted Jackie to an area set up as a kitchen, fitted an apron to his body, and told him where to stand. Jackie had briefly studied the shrimp recipe before going on the air, but in case he forgot, all of it was written in large letters on prompt cards held up behind the cameras by a functionary.

Sara joined him two seconds before they came back on. "Pick up the pace a little, huh?" she asked in the last possible instant, and then smiled into the camera. "We're back with Jackie Kellog, who's been busy these last few years. He's been undergoing a change of pace. The insult comic we once knew, and yes, loved, because there was never any real malice in his humor, however hard-hitting, and I think everybody realized that . . . the old Jackie has become a man of deep religious convictions. He tells about them in his new book." She had brought it along with her and displayed it once more. "He's also become an authority on healthy eating, as I think you can see from his present figure — if you remember the old Jackie." She smiled at him. "Show us how to make Shrimp Body and Soul, Jackie."

All the ingredients had been trimmed, cleaned, and pre-measured, the skillet put in place, the stove turned on. All he had to do was dump the olive oil in, and the shrimps, minced garlic and shallots, and chopped lemon rind, all of these waiting in little glass bowls. The dish was presumably done in seconds, in any event Sara pretended it was, for the show was ending and she had to announce tomorrow's guests and say good-bye to the home audience.

Jackie had had his makeup removed and was on his way to the dressing room when Sara Neil caught up with him. He had not expected this courtesy, but it turned out not to be such.

"Look," she said, "can I talk to you? This religious stuff is a bunch of shit, right? Say so, and I won't bother you."

"No, it's real. It might sound phony, but it's real. I ran away from home when I was just a young kid. Everything I know I had to learn from life, most of it in gin mills full of lowlifes, I guess. But, hell, we're all human. They can't take that away."

"I mean what's beyond that. We're talking about God, right?"

He was embarrassed. "I guess so." But it didn't seem serious, in this studio corridor, people rushing by. Nor did she, with her bright hair and pale complexion.

She cocked an ironic eye. "This is crap, isn't it? Some comeback shtick?"

He was stung. "What do you take me for? Who are you? I was a headliner when you were loading your diapers. Fuck you."

Sara touched his arm. "Wait a minute. I'm sorry. I apologize. Could we go someplace and talk? I'm being canceled."

He was immediately sympathetic. "I know how that feels. Sure."

They went to her apartment, on an upper floor with quite a view of the city from the terrace. He had to turn down every form of refreshment offered until she got to the mineral water advertised on the program and thus provided, by the case, for free.

Sara sat down next to him on a satin-striped couch. Her cat, whose hair was long and pure white, leaped into her lap. "My life is all fucked up," said she, combing the cat's fur with her fingers. "I'm pretty tough, Jackie, but I've been taking it on the chin for a couple of months. Then my previous cat got out the door when my stupid shit of a housekeeper left it open, and he disappeared. I was going through hell at the time, on sick leave, just back from the clinic, on cold turkey — we won't go into that. This is confidential, it never got out, well, only a few rumors. Swear?"

Jackie raised a hand of affirmation. "Not that it would matter nowadays, you know?"

"My parents live in the middle of Iowa," Sara said. "I'm a small-town kid."

"So am I," said Jackie. "I've had plenty of my own ups and downs, mostly downs, and yet I'm still kicking. You're young: there'll be other shows. Christ, you're not even thirty yet, are you? Everybody knows and loves you."

"That hasn't saved the show," she said mournfully. "The ratings are in the cellar."

"It's probably that no-talent shmuck Basehart," Jackie said, referring to her co-host. "He brings the show down. He don't have any sense of humor, and it's real pathetic when he interviews some politician and tries to act like he knows current affairs."

She smiled at him. "You're sweet, Jackie."

"It's true, isn't it? Nobody likes that guy."

"If so, he's fucked me." She raised her brow. "I don't mean literally."

"They should of given you the serious stuff, the foreign-policy guests and so on, and let Doug do the light crap — like me." He laughed, but then added solemnly, "It's because you're a woman."

"Gee," Sara said, "people'd never know from your act just how sensitive you can be when you're not on — though I always did hear you were a nice guy when you're not on. Of course, that can mean nothing: I've heard 'em say the same thing about that mean motherfucker Tony Gamble. You know he slapped my face once and walked off the show? Fortunately, we were on a commercial at the time."

"Yeah, I heard that. You were questioning his credibility in claiming to be a Buddhist, weren't you? Tony and me go back a long ways. We used to be real close, I admit. He really gave me one of my first breaks. I can't dump on him now — but I tell you, I haven't liked him for a long time." He leaned forward. "I'll go so far as to say, just to you alone, I never did like him. But you got to be loyal to those who helped."

They never did get around to talking about God. Which was just as well, for other than the obvious ethical issues, which were more or less the same for everybody with or without a formal faith, Jackie would not have known what to say on the subject. God really was that which could not be talked about. On the other hand, there was nobody who knew more about show business, of which he had been from one extremity to the other. He had even made a cameo appearance in a video with an Irish rock group, who as it turned out had been, as children, fans of his old TV sitcom, which in its day had played in a number of foreign markets.

He could, and did, advise Sara Neil how to handle herself. It was essential that she suggest in no way that the canceling of this local show was a setback, or to have anything but public praise for her co-host Bill Basehart. But in private she should lose no opportunity to discredit him with the gossip-mongers, some of whom were professionals with their own regular spots on TV news programs and/or columns. "In the old days, you coulda called him a fag, but then for a while they got more sympathy. Then came AIDS and a turn against them, but nowadays there's sympathy again with so many dying. You better stick with just straight professional grounds. The ladies are always eager to get some chauvinist thing to pin on any man, so your line should be that Basehart took all the hard news for himself while giving you the frilly stuff like couturier clothes for dogs, fad diets, et cetera."

"Which he did, the little faggot," snarled Sara.

"Then you oughta get speaking gigs: you know, colleges, women's groups: you build up a grass-roots following. You got a great delivery, but being on so early in the morning, and then just in this area, even though it's metropolitan, a lot of people haven't got a chance to seeya. But don't *ask* to get on talk shows: do the shitjob on Basehart. When that gets around, you'll be invited, and when you do, deny all the rumors that you and him never got along and give it to the people who like to make that sort of shit known for their own scummy motives. That way you do a lot more than kill two birds, and even Basehart probably won't hold a grudge. How could he, when it's you who will go someplace? He'll think maybe you'll throw him a fish someday. Main thing, the insiders will see you're a real pro, along with being smart."

Between such sessions of advice, they sent out for Chinese and later on watched the issue-oriented shows of late afternoon, with their audience of females whom Jackie considered more pushy than intelligent, though he was careful not to reveal as much to Sara while assuring her that she could do a much better job in such a format than the current practitioners. In fact, he might suggest as much to Syd Stanger, a producer of such shows, with whom Jackie claimed to be close friends since Borscht Belt days.

After some more TV, interspersed with many phone calls to and from professional colleagues — like him, she seemed to have no actual friends; she had been married at eighteen and divorced six months later — Sara yawned. Jackie saw the time was only nine P.M. but remembered that she got up before dawn to begin her show.

"I'm outa here," said he, standing up. He had nothing better to look forward to now but more television and then a night's sleep in a hotel bed, no thick red steak and oven fries and afterwards a nightful of booze, ending up with a half hour with a hooker and finally a sleep till midday. Now that he didn't drink any more, he had lost his sexual urge too, which was more depressing than losing it temporarily through a surfeit of alcohol: in that case, at least you knew what you wanted when you were next able to handle it. Now he had been sitting all day in the proximity of a good-looking young chick and had felt only avuncular.

"Jackie," Sara said, "it really helped, talking with you. You understand me like nobody else I have ever known." She touched his arm. "No, I mean it. But after you leave I know I'll be as blue as ever. This thing has really hit me, I'm sorry. I gave my all to the show, and then to have shit thrown in my face this way." She spoke as if she might weep, but she did not follow through; she was a tough little cookie. Jackie liked that.

"You know what the English say: Keep your pecker up, kid. I did a command performance at the London Palladium once. Met the Boss Lady herself backstage. Told her, 'Hey, you're the only queen I ever met over here who was female!'" He winked at Sara, in the unlikely case she would have believed him.

She took his hand. "Mister Show Business," said she. "You can't buy that kind of experience. You've got to pay for it with your life."

She understood him better than anyone ever had. He not only stayed the night; a couple of weeks later, they got married, astonishing everybody and giving much material to other comedians, Jackie being thirty-three years older than his bride and at least two inches shorter. The fact was that they never had sexual relations. They tried twice, but Jackie was simply incapable, and Sara seemed to have almost no urge, being passionate only about her profession, an emotion Jackie could understand and sympathize with — to the degree that, in the succeeding months, he performed less and less though the offers came in more frequently than they had during his decline, and the consensus was that his comeback had been successful. But he had begun to prefer Sara's career to his own, which had always been a thing of chance, helplessly subject to every wind of trend and whim of fate. But guiding her, he could exert a control of the kind he never could have taken over himself as a performer. For it's the person in the spotlight who is vulnerable. If he scores, then all around him share in the triumph. But if he flops, he flops alone.

Before long, Jackie ceased altogether to perform and became Sara's manager full-time, a move that not only kept a lot of commissions in the family but also employed faculties of his that he had never known he possessed. He had always simply assumed he was no good at business — without ever trying it. He had left that to the people who were paid to work for him, and he now realized what a bad job they had done. From the many millions he had earned his own share had been pathetically small. It was quite possible that he had been criminally cheated, could probably have sent people to prison, had he only been aware.

His most gratifying success came in those quarters where comics were ordinarily disdained: the news departments of the networks, the high-and-mighties who concerned themselves not with entertainment but with what they saw as their sacred obligation to inform and enlighten the public. Jackie the performer would have been scared of these pompous shits, but, representing Sara, he was fearless. Here was a young woman at the cutting edge of her generation, and therefore of the era, and at the same time her personal style had almost universal appeal. Polls (by an organization that guaranteed Jackie would get the results he wished) showed that she was also popular among the over-fifties, that segment of the society whose numbers were always increasing because of the advances made by medical science. When one network executive noted good-humoredly that these pollsters were the best money could buy, Jackie boldly said, "Aren't they all?"

Unlike many managers and agents, he never sucked up to the boys with the power. He performed as arrogantly as he had ever done onstage. In truth, he began to use the style that had characterized his act. "You're not really gonna wear that tie all day?" he asked the head of the news division at NBS, and at Continental he pulled an oldie on Ron Ferguson, the very young man whose revamping of their seven o'clock newscast had brought it, in six months, from a distant third in the ratings to a tie for the lead, asking Ron, who was currently dating top model Liza Welch, if he had any pornographic photos of her. "No," said Ferguson, laughing already. "Wanna buy some?" Jackie punchlined, and though Ferguson's flunkies blanched, the boy wonder cracked up.

Now, Jackie never pretended that material from his old act was instrumental in Sara's subsequent rise to the top of her profession, the first woman ever to be sole anchorperson of an evening network news program, but he did believe his handling of her had made the difference. After all, when they first met, her local show was being canceled. Sara sneeringly rejected this theory, even more disdainfully in public than in private, and her lawyer did a much better job on the divorce than did his own.

Again he was on his ass both emotionally and financially, and this time he lacked all incentive to attempt another comeback. Some years earlier, when he was still performing, he had received, in care of the TV talk show on which he had lately appeared, a letter from Betty Jane *née* Hopper, of his high-school days, who had now, for decades, been married to another name from those far-off times.

I don't know if you recall me, we had a thing way back in the mists of the past, but Gordon Riggins — remember him? — and I got married not long after and we've now been together 32 years in April, had three kids, all out in the world now, and last year Gordon took an early retirement due to health problems. He sold his real estate and insurance business and stays home nowadays, watching baseball and so on, underfoot when I want to clean and so on but I'm glad to have him still. Sometime ago, you came to the Fair, which if you remember isn't far from here, and we were thinking of coming to see you perform and then maybe sending a note if we could see you backstage or something, just shake hands maybe, but lost our nerve.

Well, anyway, Jack — as we still always call you — we just wanted to let you know we always remember you with a real warm feeling, because I hope you haven't forgotten it was you who brought us together in the old days.

Your old friends from school,
Betty Jane (Hopper) and Gordon Riggins

Looking through some personal papers, Jackie came upon this letter, which he had never answered but had saved perhaps for some future sentimental use. After all, he was the father of the Riggins' first child. How rottenly ironic life was! Sporadically he wanted a kid, and there was the one he had already created and run away from, to become what he was . . . and whatever else he was, he was now about to check out of it all, without ever having seen so much as a picture of his offspring or knowing its name.

He got the Riggins number from Information in his hometown and called it.

"Betty Jane, believe it or not, this is Jack Kellog." He wait-ed a long moment for her scream, but it did not come. "Jack Kellog," he repeated. "Your old high-school pal."

"Funny you would call just now," Betty Jane said at last in a solemn voice he did not remember. "Yesterday I buried Gordon."

"God," said Jackie. "I'm sorry. I'm really sorry." This was true. He felt as though his heart would break, though he had cared nothing for Riggins even as a boy. "He was a good man."

"No, he wasn't," Betty Jane said. "He died in bed with an-other woman. Sudden heart attack, though he had had a condition for years. I was the last to know. I hate his dirty guts for that. I'm glad the son-of-a-bitch is dead." Her voice was steely; she was nowhere near tears.

He didn't know what to say. What a mistake it had been to call!

"*You're* the only good man I ever knew," Betty Jane said with a sudden intensity, "and I had to ruin that deal. I cer-tainly had cause to regret what I did, even before this latest stunt which makes a mockery of my whole life."

"What deal was that?"

"Oh," said Betty Jane, "I guess you could of figured it out if you had been a little older, but we were both such young kids then, Jack. . . . You probably never thought about it later on, what with becoming such a big star like you did, but I once told you I was pregnant and you acted like you really believed me. Oh, I hope you didn't! Tell me you didn't. Tell me, *please*. I'd rather you dropped me for some other reason. I couldn't reproach myself in that case."

Jackie hung up. So even his kid had been taken from him. There could be no dealing with the matter of Jackie Kellog except total annihilation.

III

THE LITTLE MAN looked grubbier than ever in the squalid office lighted only by the bare bulb at the end of the wire that hung from the ceiling.

"I should have known better," said Walter Hunsicker. "I've copy-edited a number of show-business books, autobiographies, tell-all memoirs. Other type of performers tend to name-drop, boast of their sexual conquests, give some political platitudes, but now and again at least, the reader might get a glimpse of something that might be called a human being underneath it all. But comedians can never stop performing, in whichever medium. It's always jokes. While amusing to everyone else, that must be a sad state of affairs for them. Imagine never being able to be serious."

The little man grimaced. "Jackie Kellog wasn't sad: he was a nasty son-of-a-bitch. That those whose business is comedy are compensating for some profound personal sorrow is crap: it's only a self-serving excuse for being cruel. If they weren't telling jokes they might be torturing their loved ones. The fact is that human beings are amused by seeing their fellows in pain —" Hunsicker tried to protest here, but was forestalled by a raised hand. "Of course, there is a point at which, if the cruelty is too vulgar, the amusement lessens — unless the torturers are political or religious or sexual fanatics, but there's no paucity of those, as history or in fact the daily paper will prove."

Hunsicker did not altogether disagree with this savage commentary on his breed, but he was annoyed at the man's self-righteousness: either this character was himself human, and thus the same fundamental sadist as the rest of us, or he partook in some way in divinity, in which case he might well be asked why his crowd had made us as we were, when, starting from scratch, they could presumably have turned out anything they wanted.

But what he said was, "Jackie Kellog was as unlikely a role for me as the slumlord. In choosing those lives, maybe I was getting something out of my system: I'd like to think it was my loathing for their most prominent traits."

"I'm sure it was," said the little man, but he was being obviously sardonic.

"All right," Hunsicker said, "I'll admit it really was nice when Jackie would come out on stage and receive an ovation — mind you, from those whom he was going to insult for the next hour! And look how cops and other functionaries sucked up to Kellog-the-tycoon: that wasn't hard to take. I think it could be said of Jackie as comic that he didn't have much success with persons, but he was, at the height of his career anyway, loved by people. They'd line up to touch his hand!"

"Would you say there's something monstrous about any performer?" asked the little man. "It's more obvious with a standup comic, but it's just as true of an actor who plays only in the classical theater, no?"

But being familiar now with the other side of the fence, Hunsicker wanted to make a different point. "Listen here," said he. "Even with the applause, when you're up there in front of *them* you're always scared."

"Of what?"

"That they'll turn on you at any moment. You're right, it *is* an unnatural situation. But it requires a good deal of courage."

"Or desperation," the little man said. "And I think you'll agree that the audience turning on you is not the ultimate fear. No, the worst is that they'll turn *away*. Then you'd be alone again, all by yourself. That's the real horror."

The odd thing is that the man did not for once seem to speak derisively: there was a suggestion of genuine feeling here.

"Are you speaking from experience?"

The other returned immediately to his usual style and said, with a disagreeable smirk, "All the world's a stage . . ."

Hunsicker felt a sudden pang. "My son was active in prep-school and college dramatics. I always thought he had a real talent, enough to have a professional try anyhow, and was willing to underwrite him, at least to the limits of my modest resources. But it's Elliot who's always been the conservative when it comes to financial matters. He wouldn't hear of such a thing. Elliot has always been the fogy in our family."

"Then you're back again to stay? You're Walter Hunsicker, and you accept your lot in life."

But Hunsicker, on a surge of defiance, cried, "No! Certainly not. I'm going to beat this: I *have* to. But the next time I must be somebody I can be proud of — someone Martha and Elliot would have been proud of, had they known, though they can't ever know. . . . It's complicated. They will never have lived, but as of this moment they are back in existence, suffering . . ."

The little man stirred impatiently. "So what will it be?"

"I suppose it would make sense to go back to my earlier life for an idea," Hunsicker said. "Maybe a bit later than when I wanted to ride the range with Hoot Gibson, though it too was probably partly influenced by the movies. I did read a lot as a kid and at some point began to think I might like to be a writer, but I also have memories of films I saw in which authors wore ascots and smoked pipes and holed up in quaint little cottages in Connecticut and wrote novels or plays —"

The little man sniffed and asked, "Given your opportunity to choose any role in all of existence, your choice is one that does not act but rather *represents?*" He sniffed again. "Interesting."

"As a young chap I thought I might wait till I had some experiences and then write about them. But I was in the service between wars, at camps in the U.S., didn't have any combat or foreign *mise en scènes* to write about. Then I got married, became a father, and had to make a living. My job has involved me with the other side of writing: they don't mix, generally speaking. The way I have to read a manuscript is not conducive to creativity. Some of the most noted authors spell badly, make grammatical errors, real howlers, you wouldn't believe it. In my job one doesn't always have the respect for writers that one probably should have, that one started with. But many of them are so awful! Of course, they all think they're Tolstoys and sometimes go so far as to insist that some incorrect usage is right because it's theirs: that correct usage becomes so through being that of great writers." Kellog cleared his throat, thickened with indignation. "Well, it does. But there's a question as to who's great."

He might have continued with another audience, but the little man, bored, said, "What you *are* is your business. Mine is concerned with what you'd rather be."

Kellog had to add, "My job doesn't bring me as close to authors as if I were an acquisition editor. And just as well! The average writer is a self-pitying neurotic with some kind of addiction, most often alcohol though it can be anything else as well, drugs, sex, sometimes all of them at once, he's usually in debt, a monster of vanity, wracked with envy. . ."

"It sounds as though you've just about talked yourself into it," said the little man.

"The fact remains that without them there'd be nothing to edit or print. Even if what they produce is drivel, it didn't exist before they produced it."

"That doesn't sound especially valuable to me," said the other. "The same thing could be said of excrement."

It might well have been the Philistinism of that remark that stung Kellog into making his decision. There was an ongoing need for all persons of culture to make common cause against barbarism.

THE COLLEGE magazine, *The Owl*, had printed Kellog's first fiction, the characters in which were soldiers in the war just ended. In response he received a note of commendation from the man who taught the creative-writing course which in fact John had not taken: one Brock Forrester, a professor of English but also a genuine author in that he had published several short stories in national magazines. John had seen one once in his dentist's waiting room but hadn't had time to read it before being called to the chair.

Forrester wore a brushy mustache that concealed most of his mouth. His salt-and-pepper hair was wiry and abundant. He removed his horn-rimmed glasses when Kellog entered the office.

"Yes," said he, "I found much to praise in the story, but the reason I asked you to come see me was that you also made a lot of errors, which I didn't like to mention in the note because I like to always accentuate the positive, like the song says." He stuck a pipe under his mustache. It already had tobacco in it, for he proceeded to light it and puff smoke. "I'll make an exception and let you join my class at midterm, if you want." He took the pipe from his mouth, pointed the stem at John, and said jovially, "Now there's an offer to conjure with."

Forrester's class met at the same hour as the section of Spanish that John had been pressured into signing up for by his faculty adviser, who assured him that the language, unlike the two years of French with which he had already satisfied the requirement, would be invaluable now that the war was over, "with our increasing business with the up-and-coming nations south of the border, down Mexico way, like the song says." Having no interest in Spanish, John was not reluctant to switch to Forrester's course, which he had scarcely noticed heretofore, for he had not thought of writing as a subject to be studied. If it were, then Forrester, a professor of it, ought to be a celebrity in the field, like . . . actually, no names of living writers came to mind, all of John's favorites being practitioners of the past like Edgar Allan Poe and Mark Twain. Surely Poe never made a formal study of writing. And perhaps was the worse for it, according to Forrester's theory, which held that there was no worker in words, however exalted, whose text could not have been improved by extensive editing and rewriting in response to suggestions by such teachers as himself.

John was thrilled, on the first day he attended the class, to hear Forrester read his college-magazine story aloud. It was astonishing to learn how one's words might be improved by the human voice, and Forrester was a gifted actor, changing tones for each of the characters and sometimes even adding regional accents of which the author had made only slight indications if any. He was certainly being hospitable, to do this before a group of students all of whom, unlike John, had been with him for the preceding semester.

But when the reading was done Forrester said, "There you have our new arrival. Now, who wants to be the first to assault him?"

Assuming that this remark was facetious, Kellog looked eagerly from his seat in the back row to see who responded. Three or four hands were in the air, including that of a girl in a tight sweater of robin's egg blue. She also had bright blond hair, worn in front in bangs that came just to her eyebrows. But it was not she whom Forrester chose.

"Mr. Backlin?"

Backlin was a stocky fellow with a low forehead and, at twenty, a five o'clock shadow. "Well," said he, "it really doesn't work in so many ways I don't know just where to start. One, the characterization is poor; these are cardboard figures. You can't tell one from the other."

But that was the idea, said John to himself. He tried to keep his expression from betraying the feeling he had against Backlin.

A guy named Ross spoke next. He derided the story for its use of dashes for foul language. "Either we use the words and let the chips fall where they may," said he, "or use other words that convey the sense of obscenity without being obscene. Oh, that may not always be easy, but then writing is supposed to require some effort. This is just laziness."

Next a skinny brunette named Kleemeyer said, "There are some very good things in it —"

A general groan was heard, and somebody said, "Name one!"

"Come on now," said Miss Kleemeyer. "The sergeant from Brooklyn, he's not a badly drawn character."

"He's out of every second-rate war movie Hollywood ever made!" jeered Backlin.

"I didn't say he was original," noted Miss Kleemeyer. "I just said he has something."

"Anyone else, before I get my two cents in?" Forrester asked. He was ignoring the blonde's hand, to Kellog the most conspicuous signal that had been made. "I'm surprised nobody has mentioned the obvious." Ross put up his hand, but Forrester cried, "Too late now, sir!" He assumed a wide smirk and cried, "Structure!" He strolled to and fro. "Situation established, then conflict enters to threaten the status quo, and finally the resolution creates a new situation. In this story we just have these guys cowering in a foxhole. They are the same people at the end as they were on page one. Therefore nothing has happened. The story makes no point." He lowered his head and plucked up another sheaf of papers from the desktop. "Now here we have another piece of work from the prolific Miss Daphne Kleemeyer."

"Excuse me," said Kellog from the back row, redundantly raising and waving his hand. "Do I get to answer?"

Forrester raised his head very slowly. "Answer what?"

"These attacks?"

Forrester sighed. "These aren't *attacks,* Mr. Kellog. This is constructive criticism, to get which is presumably why you begged to be allowed to join this class in midstream, which ordinarily I wouldn't permit."

John made no response to the outrageous lie, but he said with spirit, "The *point* is the deadly boredom of war. Yes, the situation stays the same, because the war is not over. The characters are all soldiers of the same age, so naturally they'd be a lot like one another. However, I did try to a certain extent to give them different voices. I admit I wasn't being too original in the case of 'Brooklyn.' I guess I wrote that without thinking. As for rough language, I don't know how to deal with it except as I did. I just don't have the experience as a writer as yet to think up ways to make it seem dirty when it actually isn't."

"This is not the debating team, Mr. Kellog," acerbly said Mr. Forrester. He picked up the Kleemeyer manuscript and began to read from it. He managed to finish the story just as the period ended, but any discussion would have to be postponed for the next class.

Still smarting, John decided to quit the writing course and return to Spanish. He waited outside the classroom door for Forrester to get free of the many students who clustered around him to claim manuscripts he had read and marked and leave others for his future consideration. One of these persons was the blonde, and another was Miss Kleemeyer, who now came out into the corridor, holding a burden of books as though it were a baby.

"Hi! I just wanted to say I really liked your story."

Having no physical interest in her, he would probably not even have recognized her as a fellow member of the class had she not distinguished herself by being the only voice with anything positive to say about the story.

"Thanks. I liked yours too." It was fortunate he could so much as remember it was hers that Forrester had just read:

preoccupied as he had been with his injuries, he had not heard a word of it.

Staring earnestly through her glasses, Daphne Kleemeyer said, "Once in a while somebody says something useful, but mostly the criticism is worthless, just sounding off by people who think they're impressing Forrester."

"He seems like a jerk to me," said John.

She hesitated. "Actually, he's got some talent himself, but he's been writing at the same novel for years and just can't finish it. Frustration makes him peevish. If you've got a minute and want to talk more about him, we ought to go somewhere else, because he'll be coming out here in a moment."

"All right," Kellog said. She was, after all, his favorite reader; he owed her something, and perhaps he was being overhasty in wanting to leave the class.

They went to the cafeteria in the basement of the Student Union building, where she had a mug of tea and he sipped from a tall glass filled with a ton of ice and a tot of Coke yet costing a nickel all the same.

"My name's John Kellog."

Daphne reached across the table and shook his hand, like a man. Her hand was delicate of bone. She brought it back to grasp the little tab of the teabag, which she removed to the tabletop, where it immediately exuded a good deal of brown liquid into the folded paper napkin she quickly brought into play. She asked him to use her first name.

"You really liked my story?"

"I did indeed," she said. "But are you professional enough at this point to accept the fact that a lot of what Forrester said about it was right?"

He did not welcome this turn, but she had proved her good will and was entitled to courteous treatment. "I know I have a long way to go."

"That's true of everybody," said she. "But generalities are

pretty useless when applied to writing, where it's particulars that matter. As for your story, I listened to your remarks and I think I know what you're trying to accomplish, and you certainly did succeed in part, but Forrester *was* right in saying it lacked structure. You shouldn't automatically reject what others say just because they are sometimes wrong — which I think you tend to do."

John was both irritated and flattered. He did not like to be criticized by a girl, but he was gratified to be the focus of her attention all the same. Changing the subject was his move to claim the initiative. "Who's Blondie? Forrester ignored her."

"She's his wife now," Daphne answered. "She was his mistress first term, but he knocked her up (if you'll pardon the language) and would have lost his job through the moral-turpitude clause, so they got married during winter vacation just ended."

The Kellog of those days was shocked. "God, how much older is he?"

Daphne nodded with her firm chin. "She's twenty and he just turned forty-two."

John chewed a piece of cracked ice as his sense of normality reeled. He had not himself known a female carnally. That a girl of twenty would copulate voluntarily with an old man was not acceptable to his reason.

Slush in his mouth, he asked, "Why?"

"Well, he *is* a published writer."

At the next meeting of the writing class, Daphne was awaiting his arrival. "Here," she said, gesturing, "sit right here." She indicated the chair to her left.

"Doesn't that belong to somebody?"

She shook her head, her dark hair moving and calling attention to how short it was: now that he thought about it, she looked rather like a flapper of bygone times. He had seen pictures of his aunt with such a haircut, but he did not find it especially feminine. "Ross used to sit here, but I told him to take off."

Though annoyed, John stayed, setting a precedent with Daphne.

She leaned close and whispered, "Remember, today's the discussion of my story. Since you liked it, I hope you'll make your opinion known."

When Forrester asked for comments on the Kleemeyer story, Jack raised his hand. He had not listened to a word of it when it was being read, but expected, as the newest member of the class, not to be called on first. By listening carefully to the remarks of his predecessors, he could surely learn enough to fake a comment of his own. For example, if Backlin attacked the characterization, he could defend it in a general way.

The trouble was, neither Backlin nor anyone else competed with him for the teacher's attention. His was the only hand aloft.

"Good for you, Mr. Kellog," Forrester commended him. "To accept the challenge singlehandedly that so many others have run away from. Now at long last we'll perhaps have an interpretation of Miss Kleemeyer's work, which I don't mind telling you baffled everyone else, including your humble servant, last term."

There was no escape. John had to measure up. "What I thought was especially successful was the characterization."

People laughed. By the sound of it, most of the class. Forrester snorted and asked him to give some examples.

"I liked them all," said John. "I thought all the characters were well drawn."

More laughter, this time with a derisive aftertone.

"Oh," Forrester said, his mustache quivering, "Name just one of the characters that you admire so much."

John looked at Daphne, sending the unspoken complaint: see what you got me into? Now, if it had been Blondie, he might have been capable of some superhuman effort . . .

It was at this point that the miraculous event occurred. The blonde herself, Mrs. Forrester, suddenly and unexpectedly, came to his defense. "Oh, come on," she said with righteous emotion, "don't give him a hard time. At least he's *trying*. He shouldn't be laughed at, just because nobody else knows what she's trying to do. Maybe she's doing something no one ever did before, and we just can't recognize it. Maybe it *is* a lot of different characters. Maybe he's got something." She turned and spoke in Daphne's direction. "This has been said before, but you know, *you* might help. I still can't see what harm it would do if you provided some interpretation of your own writing."

Daphne agitated her hair with a negative movement. "And I've said before that my work has to stand on its own. If it doesn't mean anything to others, so be it. To explain it would be to announce its failure, in my opinion."

Forrester was seething. "Remember me?" he asked the ceiling. "I believe I'm the professional in this part of the forest." He picked up a manuscript from the stack on the desk and began to read. "'Whether only because the chrysanthemums were crystallizing and the daisies were lackadaisical, or because the roses arose too early, the waters waited to subside or subvert, to preside or pervert, while down in the deep dusky dell the deer dashed, his mossy bossy horns akimbo like the spread legs of a bimbo.'" Forrester raised his head and stared at Kellog. "Now, are those your idea of characters? The bimbo, or the deer? Or both?"

John loathed Daphne for getting him into this mess, and he despised himself. Her writing was pretentious twaddle. His hatred of Forrester was now long-standing — and as if these feelings were not enough, he was absolutely in love with Mrs. Forrester.

But it was here that he discovered that violent and clashing feelings may awaken, or create from scratch, a kind of eloquence.

"That's right!" He laughed recklessly. "When you've got comedy. Read humorlessly, of course it doesn't have any sense. That's what's so good about it: it separates the sheep from the goats. The joke's on the readers without a sense of humor."

Forrester narrowed his eyes. No doubt he was considering which way to go with the least damage to his amour propre. He quickly decided. "All right, that's one of the possible interpretations — one, I might add, that was my own on seeing the very first example of Miss Kleemeyer's work last fall, but I've been reluctant to mention it because beginning writers are sometimes terribly thin-skinned about being called funny. Sometimes people are, as Hemingway says, solemn as bloody owls."

"Golly, you know you might have hit it, you just might," the glorious Mrs. Forrester said to John, and she along with the rest of the class turned to stare expectantly at Daphne Kleemeyer.

But John now began to lose his nerve. It was a foolish thing to say: there was not a shred of wit in Daphne, who was all intensity and no doubt now preparing to embarrass him for an egregious misrepresentation.

But when she spoke, it was to commend him for critical acumen. "How gratifying," said she, gazing worshipfully at him, "to be understood for once! I can go it alone if I have to, but how much more comfortable it is to be heard."

Forrester was huffy. It was beneath his dignity to insist, against all the evidence, that he had genuinely from the first assessed Daphne's work as comic, and therefore he took another tack. "All right, all right," he said with a superior smile, "now that we've got that settled, let's consider some of the less than successful features. Mr. Styles?"

Styles was young enough still to be suffering from facial skin problems. He rarely spoke in class, and being publicly identified now caused a blush to flood his already discolored, swollen cheeks. "Uh, I don't have any criticism," said he.

Nor did anyone else. Eventually Forrester had to supply his own. He said the piece was too long and too self-conscious; if that sort of writing was to be effective it should be brief and, of course, reveal as little as possible of its author's self-satisfaction.

Kellog's emotions were complex at this point, but he was able to understand that what Forrester said was right — as Daphne had seen the sense in the teacher's criticism of John's own story. Unfortunately she was not sufficiently large of soul to see the justice in these comments. Her white face became even paler within its frame of dark hair, and when the period was over she clasped her books to her skinny chest and marched indignantly from the room. John was greatly relieved by her prompt departure, for he wished to linger and take advantage of Forrester's distraction by talking to his wife, who remained in her seat, looking at some papers, while her husband dealt with the clustered students.

John went to her and said, to the thick strand of gold which swept, on that side, behind the pink shell of an ear, "I want to thank you for giving me moral support."

She looked up. "It wasn't anything."

"Oh, it was to me," said John. He added, pathetically, "I'm new here and don't know anybody."

Mrs. Forrester was that rare person who could look delectable when frowning. "Listen," she said after a moment,

"Brock and I just got married. We haven't had time yet to have anyone over, but I just decided to give a little party Friday night. Can you come? Bring somebody if you want."

"Okay if I come alone? I don't really know anybody."

"Sure," said she. "Seven P.M., after supper. We live in an apartment over Knowland's Shoes, next to the bakery, you know?" Her giggle was a wondrous thing. "It was Brock's. I had been living at the Chi O house. Gee, I guess I'm a faculty wife now."

He was brought back to stark reality when Daphne seized him as he emerged from the building. "God," said she. "Until I met you I was ready to leave school. There's nobody else around here with any capacity whatever for understanding my work. Did you hear that simpleminded jerk Forrester?"

John wished to put some moral distance between them. He sensed that the best way would be to make negative implications with respect to her writing. "Well," said he, "didn't you just tell me the other day that he was right about my own story?"

She clutched at his arm. "I was wrong! Sorry about that." She swung to face him, which of course impeded him in his plan to escape. "Will you forgive me?"

"Maybe he was right in both cases," John ruthlessly suggested. "He *is* a professional, after all."

"He's a cheap hack." Daphne sneered with her narrow nose and thin lips. She was more unappealing than ever now that he had actually spoken to and even got an invitation from Mrs. Forrester, whose own nose was retroussé and whose lips, especially the lower one, were full.

"I wonder what kind of husband he is?"

"Just the kind that stupid chippie deserves," Daphne replied venomously. But her expression quickly became amiable, and she asked, "Listen, what should we do on the weekend? Here's my vote for Friday night: the French Club's arranged a screening of *La Femme du Boulanger*, with Raimu. It's got English subtitles if you need them."

John was revolted by her proprietary tone. If he had earlier been in her debt for the lukewarm defense she made of his story, he had more than balanced the account by the desperately concocted rubbish he had produced on the subject of her own story, than which he could think of nothing less humorous.

He said coldly, "I'm busy on Friday."

She was undeterred by the announcement. "I hope you'll save Saturday and Sunday for us, anyway. I want you to read more of my novel and tell me what you think. That excerpt was only a small portion of it."

For God's sake. "Look, Daphne, we'd better get something straight. I can't see you outside of class, because my girlfriend is a jealous type. Sorry, but that's just the way it is." He left before she could react.

On Friday evening he made his way to the business district of the college town. For an author of published magazine stories, Forrester lived in a very modest place. Perhaps he had another, permanent home somewhere, maybe New York City, where it was assumed the domiciles of most writers were, though they might be temporarily in Hollywood, selling out, or even on such a campus as this.

The door to the second story was to the left of the shoe store. Inside, it turned out that the Forresters' apartment did not even have exclusive use of their floor: another button was alongside theirs and labeled "2-B/Miraglia." John pushed the one for 2-A. From the fact that it gave his finger no resistance he suspected it was inoperative, but the inner, glass door was anyway unlocked, and he pushed through and ascended a stairway several degrees steeper than any but cellar steps. It was lighted with one bulb of weak wattage, in the ceiling of the remote landing above.

Having completed the climb, he searched the jamb of the door to 2-A but could find no bell-push. He knocked. No party sounds came from within; he must be an early arrival.

The door opened at last and an impatient Forrester, dressed in a plaid shirt with the tails out, asked, 'Yes?"

"Mr. Forrester?"

"What are you doing here, Kellog?"

"I came for the party."

"Party?" asked Forrester. "It's news to me." Without moving off the threshold, he turned his head and shouted. "Hey!" A frumpy-looking Mrs. Forrester came into view. She was wearing a sweatshirt with the name and seal of the university printed on it. The garment was of a size to fit the largest tackle on the football team. On her it hung almost to the knees. Aside from a pair of puffball slippers, badly run over, she apparently wore nothing else, but was decently attired as to sexual modesty, displaying no figure whatever.

Her husband asked her, "Do you know of any party?"

He was blocking most of John, so she could not identify her contemporary. "Naw," she muttered sullenly.

Waving, John did a bit of footwork to be seen. "Hi! Did I get the wrong night?"

"Oh." The arms of the sweatshirt hung slack; her own were inside, against her body, and not inserted into the sleeves. She seemed to be hugging herself as she came forward. Forrester stubbornly maintained his position, so she had to look around him. "Oh, hi. Gee, I think I did say Friday, but to tell you the truth I forgot all about it."

"Oh, sure," John said. "That's all right."

"But it isn't really," said she. "Why don't you come in anyhow?" She wiggled violently inside the sweatshirt and brought her hands out of the cuffs.

As Forrester showed no intention of permitting him to make entry, John believed the graceful thing was to decline.

But then the writer did something unexpected. "No, Kellog, come in," said Forrester, stepping out of his way. "If you were invited, then you were invited. There's to be no turning away of a guest" — he turned to glare at his wife — "even if the host was not aware there was to be a guest."

"My fault, my fault," said she with a wailing inflection, raising her shoulders as high as her ears, which brought the hem of the sweatshirt to midthigh, disclosing half of her lush thighs.

Forrester led John into the nearest room, which proved to be the entire apartment except for the sanitary facilities, which were presumably kept private behind the only door that was shut, for that which was wide open held too much clothing to allow its door to be closed. An unmade bed extended from the middle of a wall in which two flanking windows looked down on the street. Mrs. Forrester loped to it, caught a purchase under the front of the mattress, and with one vigorous motion caused the whole works to fold up on itself and sink into a base that became, with the addition of two pillows from the floor, a couch.

At the rear of the room, wide-flung latticework doors framed a kind of abstract kitchen: perfunctory two-burner stove above quarter-sized refrigerator; doll's house sink; open shelves holding a can of soup, condiments, and a saltine box with a crushed end. Mrs. Forrester skipped there with her flawless bare calves and brought the folding doors together, but the catch wouldn't hold, and the two halves slowly yawned apart during the succeeding five minutes.

"Take a pew," said Forrester, throwing an elbow at a shabbily upholstered chair.

His wife continued around the premises, collecting what looked like discarded underwear and dirty towels and stockings from the furniture, floor, and doorknobs. A hangered man's shirt, which looked clean enough, hung from a lighting sconce on the wall. A little desk, its top concealed beneath a portable typewriter and reams of disorderly papers that rose on either side of the machine, stood in the far front corner of the room, its accompanying camp chair a scant foot from the arm of the couch.

"I was just taking a nap," said Mrs. Forrester, stretching and yawning felinely to support her assertion. "Brock was working on the Great American —"

"Don't ever use that vulgar expression, please!" cried Forrester.

"Why not?" whined the girl. "It's not dirty."

"'Vulgar' doesn't mean 'dirty.' How many times must I tell you that?"

She grinned at Kellog and shrugged again, the sweatshirt rising even higher this time. John had never before seen her in such squalid attire, and it was even more exciting than her routine campus costume. But he was embarrassed by it and hoped she did not sit down directly across from him and with arrangements of thigh give him glimpses of the underpants she had to be wearing under the sweatshirt.

He was therefore much relieved when she chose an end of the sofa that was nearest him and therefore almost at a right angle.

Forrester remained standing. "That's right," said he. "I was working. But as it happens I don't mind being interrupted. I'm not one of those prima donnas."

"When Brock gets cooking," Mrs. Forrester said, with a smile that was as snowy as ever though she was otherwise in a somewhat soiled condition, "he types through hell and high water."

Forrester closed his eyes and shuddered. He opened them and said to Kellog, "Now, if you'll forgive me, I'll get back to work. You're not *my* guest, after all."

John got up. But his teacher waved him down imperiously,

then took a seat at the littered desk, inserted a sheet of paper into the little machine, and began furiously to type, making sufficient noise so that his wife had to shout at the guest.

"So what have you been doing since I last saw you?"

John grimaced and tried to remember. *"Oh, just classes, I guess."*

"Are you married?"

He thought this just might be a joke, but apparently it was not, given her solemn mien.

Forrester suddenly stopped typing and ripped the paper from a screaming platen, crumpled it into a ball, and hurled it into the kitchenette, the doors to which had by now opened themselves all the way.

It would seem some crisis was at hand, and John wished he were elsewhere but feared that any attempt to exit would offend Forrester with its negative implications.

Mrs. F. chose this moment to raise her heels to the edge of the couch, which put her knees under her chin. He tried to keep his eyes up, but got the definite impression that she was *not* wearing lower underwear.

Forrester stood up. He stared at the wall facing his desk, which was unadorned except for a lone pushpin. "Substance," said he to the wall, "seeking a form."

John was wondering whether he should make some polite response when Mrs. Forrester lowered her thighs violently, slapped their top surfaces, and said, chortling, "Did you see 'L'il Abner' today?" She simpered at her husband. "Brock thinks I'm just like Daisy Mae. That's what brought us together, you know: that strip."

Forrester made an incoherent cry and lowered his face into his hands.

John stared at the girl in alarm and bent forward to ask, sotto voce, "Is he all right?"

She too bent, bringing her face almost to touch his. Her

skin looked somewhat oily but it was flawless of texture. She whispered, "He's creating. Don't pay any attention: he'll just think you're making fun of him." In a normal voice she said, "You know Doyle's? They stopped including cole slaw on the cheeseburger platter. If you want it, you've got to pay extra."

One of the college hangouts was in reference. John seldom went there because he had little money with which to snack and lived exclusively on the prepaid meals at the dormitory dining room. But he said, "That's too bad."

She shrugged. "That's the way it goes."

Forrester turned around, chin high. He spoke as if to himself. "I simply must come to grips with this thing." He went to the closet and put on a capacious coat and a slouch hat with a very wide brim turned down all the way around. He found a pipe in the pocket of the coat, filled it with tobacco from an accompanying pouch, and strode to the kitchenette, where he claimed and ignited a wooden match and fired up the pipe.

He buttoned the outermost fastening of the coat collar, a crescent-shaped strap, and saying, "Carry on" to the young people, swept himself with a flourish into the hallway.

When the door was closed Mrs. Forrester scowled at Kellog and said, "He supposedly takes long walks to meditate."

John nodded.

"He hasn't written anything since we got married," she continued. "I suppose I'll get blamed for that."

John was suddenly afraid to be alone with her. He rose. "I've had a nice time, but I have to go now."

She stared up at him with her pale blue eyes and pouted. "Don't you leave too! What do I have, B.O. or something?" Of course he sat down. "I want somebody to tell my troubles to," said she, leaning towards him. "I don't trust other females."

"I wasn't leaving because of you," said John.

Mrs. Forrester sighed. "It seems like years since I was single and playing the field. But it's only a couple weeks. We didn't have any honeymoon or anything! We just went to a courthouse in the city. I haven't got up the nerve to tell the news to my folks yet. My mother's heart will break when she hears she won't be coming to a wedding. I was with the finalists last year for Homecoming Queen. I had my poetry published in my hometown paper on several occasions. I took his course because he's supposedly got a name as a writer. I guess you could say he just turned my head. I didn't realize he hasn't got any money at all and he can't seem to write anything more than those little short stories and lives in this crummy dump." She wriggled her arms out of the sleeves and returned to the perhaps naked self-embrace under the huge sweatshirt. "I'm always cold here. The landlord is some stingy Wop who keeps the heat turned as low as possible."

Kellog felt no desire for her in her current condition, but his love for her was enriched by the information that, despite her beauty, she was a victim, an underaged waif kept in bondage by a wretched old man. But there was little he could do about it other than say, "That's just awful."

She scowled. "I guess everybody's talking about me, aren't they?"

He shrugged. "I wouldn't say that."

"Okay, so be it, then. I don't have anything to be ashamed of. I guess it was stupid, but could have happened to anybody." She jumped up. "I'm starving. We didn't have any supper."

John was shocked. "He doesn't even feed you?"

"I just didn't feel like opening cans," said she. "Hey, you want to go to Doyle's and get something to eat?"

It was a degrading thing to have to do, but he had no

choice. "I'm sorry. I don't have a cent. My salary, working at the library, isn't due till tomorrow, and my parents haven't been able to send me any money for a long time."

She flounced to the closet. "Don't worry about it. I know Doyle. He'll put us on the cuff if I ask him pretty please."

It was true that she was on good terms with the fat middle-aged proprietor: Doyle chucked her familiarly under the chin on their entrance, and before they had finished their club sandwiches, came to their booth, bent ponderously over, and whispered into her ear, continuing to ignore Kellog. She responded with a low-pitched giggle and, when Doyle wheezingly straightened up, a wink.

After the fat man had waddled away, Jack, warmed by the food and sugared coffee, said, "I guess he's a pretty good friend of yours?"

"I used to wait tables here," said she. "I've got to keep an in with Doyle: I might be back any time." She swallowed some coffee and pouted. "I might have made a mistake with Forrester. But I got panicky, you know. I'm not going to spell it out, but it looked like I had a good reason to get married at the time. And then only a couple hours after we went and tied the knot, the reason went away. I think you know what I mean. What I'm wondering now is if I could get an annulment? It's only been a couple weeks, and I don't see what *he* gets from it: I'm just somebody around to watch him create. He could get a window dummy for that."

John was overcome by an intense feeling that elevated him to another level of being. "Oh yes!" he cried. "You must get it annulled. You don't want to get stuck in this situation, a fantastic girl like you? He's old and selfish, and he's probably a phony as a writer, if he can't get anywhere with his book. Mark my words," he added, as though he were seasoned in the ways of life, "it won't get better; it can only get worse."

She gave him a wink. "I'll think about it."

CHANGING THE PAST

He was besotted with her, adored the way she drank coffee, her white teeth at the lip of the thick beige beanery-mug, could have watched her masticate food all day. She had gone into the home bathroom to comb her hair and use mascara and lipstick, not to dress for the outside world: she had done that with him in the room, deftly and not immodestly, pulling the slacks on, the waistband going high up under the big sweatshirt, over which she drew a still larger felted jacket in the colors of the school, green and gold, and with an athletic letter, S, over the left breast. She had completed the ensemble with a baseball cap, a pair of fuzzy white mittens, and penny loafers. John felt drab in an ancient plaid jacket that had once belonged to his father.

He now made a rash, indeed a demented offer. "Look, if I can help in any way . . . Do you need money?"

"You got some?"

"I can get some."

Her smile had never looked so glorious. "You mean, rob a bank?"

"I've got sources," he said, though he could not have named one if challenged: he was at college by means of a combination of scholarships and the earnings from summer and part-time jobs.

She lifted her mug. "It would sure be nice if . . ." She drank some coffee and never finished the sentence, but it was clear to John that he had been given his mission.

"What amount do you estimate will be needed?"

Her blue eyes widened. "Gosh, I don't have the foggiest." She pressed a paper napkin against her lips and then stared at the red oval there imprinted. "I've got to talk to Doyle about something. If you don't mind — I told you I might come back to work here."

"Sure," John said, though he was disappointed.

"You better go on. I'll be a while. See you in class next

week." She gave him one more gorgeous smile and slid to an exit from the booth.

John said, "Just hang on. I'll think of something." But she was already out of earshot. He had forgotten to thank her for the sandwich and coffee.

The woman behind the cash register smiled wryly when he explained that the check was supposed to be taken care of by the proprietor.

"That's a new one. Mr. Doyle's now giving food away?"

John looked down towards the end of the bar, where when last seen his recent companion, the love of his life, had joined Doyle. Neither was there now, nor anywhere else in view.

"You see," John said, "I was with Mrs. Forrester, who comes in here all the time and is a friend of Mr. Doyle's. Our orders were on the house."

The cashier stopped smiling. "I don't know what you're trying to pull, sonny boy, but you've got to pay the check."

John told her what he had had. "I didn't get a check. Isn't that proof of what I'm saying?"

"Okay," the cashier said. "If you want to do it the hard way." She lifted the handpiece of the telephone at her elbow. "I'll call the police and you can tell them your story."

"Wait a minute," someone said in a female voice behind John. Daphne Kleemeyer stepped up beside him and gave the cashier a check and a dollar bill. "Put it with mine."

The woman at the cash register shook her head and asked John, "You went through all of that for fifty cents?"

Daphne got her change and pursued John out of the restaurant. "Thanks," said he. "There was a misunderstanding. It would have been worked out but meanwhile it was an embarrassing moment. I'll pay you back tomorrow."

"No hurry," said she. "What puzzles me is how you'd happen to be here without bringing money, or was your pocket picked?"

Apparently then she had heard only the very end of his remarks to the cashier and not the prior explanation. "Turned out I forgot to bring my wallet along." He smiled falsely. "No harm done."

"I decided not to go to see Raimu, since you were busy," said she. "I stayed home and read Thomas Mann. I'm on the second volume of *Joseph and His Brothers: Young Joseph*. But the heat in the dorm is so high, my throat got terribly parched, so I came here for a Coke and some ice cream."

What a bore she was. If she expected a full explanation of his own presence, she would be disappointed. "Well, thanks again," said he, when they had emerged from the restaurant. "I'll give you the money tomorrow, if you want to come into the library after one." He turned away but neglected to walk fast enough to make it clear that he was leaving her.

She kept pace with him. "Hey, you know who I saw in there? I went to the ladies' room, and there was Cissy, big as life, going out the back door with that big lard Doyle who owns the greasy spoon."

"Cissy?"

"Who married Forrester. Remember I told you the other day? The blonde in our class."

The odd thing about this was that not until Jack heard her name for the first time did it occur to him that he had not previously known it.

"Do you suppose," Daphne asked, "she's carrying on with Doyle, of all people? *Already?*"

"She *works* there," said John.

"She does?"

He looked at Daphne under the last streetlamp in the business district, before they entered the tree-lined, now leafless lane that was a shortcut to the campus, and asked, "You wouldn't know how I could make some money quickly?"

Her pale face was framed within a knitted cap of green wool. Her breath steaming, she asked, "How much money?"

"Maybe a hundred dollars." In those days, this to him was the first figure that came to mind as being impressive.

"The quickest way to get that much," said Daphne, "would be to borrow it from me. I've got a savings account right here in town. I'll get the cash and bring it to the library tomorrow at one."

He walked her home. "Goodnight, then," said she in front of her dormitory, and took his hand and shook it.

Next day, more prompt than he, she was waiting for him at the big central desk where the books were checked out.

"Thanks," he said, taking the envelope she extended, and, to ease his conscience, "Do you have a rich father?"

She snorted. "Nope. I worked for it. But I can earn more. Don't worry about it."

"I'm not taking it as a gift," he said for pride's sake. "I'll get it back as soon as I can."

"Sure." She smirked and heel-and-toed out of the building in a funny, mannered stride he had not seen before. At least she had not tried to use the loan as leverage in arranging a date.

Now that he had the money, he could not find Cissy. He could scarcely phone her at home on the subject of providing the necessary funds for her departure from said residence. He had no idea of which other courses were on her schedule or which routes to frequent in hopes of encountering her as a pedestrian between classes. And he had very little free time, what with his own four courses and the library job.

When Wednesday came, and Cissy appeared at the writing class, it was, appropriately but damnably enough, in the company of her husband. The two-hour session was endless on this day, what with the reading of a long story which John was far too preoccupied to hear and would surely not have liked anyway, for it seemed to be a "sensitive" childhood reminiscence and was by a fat-faced girl who had sat in the back and looked inscrutable when his own story was under discussion, followed by Forrester's effusive and probably defiant praise, sensing as the teacher did, correctly, that it would be attacked by its writer's classmates.

The critics included John's creditor Daphne Kleemeyer, whom he had managed to evade throughout the weekend by obsessively staying in his single room and pretending not to be therein when, at Sunday noontime, someone pounded on his door and shoutingly informed him he had a call on the hallway phone.

"What's wrong with fake feeling is that it reflects on and degenerates genuine emotion," she was saying now. "The narrator of this story wants us to believe she loves staying with her aunt and uncle while her mother and father go to the fancy-dress ball but what I for one would like to hear is her resentment and envy, which is really what all human beings feel when they're left behind when other people are going out to enjoy themselves. This is especially true of children."

Forrester was annoyed. "Oh, come now, Miss Kleemeyer. *Now* who's being sentimental?"

John had to endure an entire hour of this before the period came to an end and, while Forrester was occupied with the students who converged on him, Cissy could be approached.

John spoke in a discreet voice, for people were moving nearby. Luckily Daphne had something to ask of Forrester and had gone up there.

"I had a wonderful time the other night," said he, and not waiting for a response, whispered, "I've got some money for you."

She winced and said, "Huh?"

"I've got a hundred dollars for you."

Her smile was radiant. "Hey," she said, "that's all right!"

"It might not be enough, but I'll see what else I can dig up."

"No," she said, touching his forearm. "That's fine. Come over tonight if you want. He's going to the city for some writers' get-together."

"Give me your notebook," said John.

"Why?" But she relinquished it, and deftly, while looking elsewhere to delude any possible observers, he slipped the envelope full of money between the pages.

But the point of this maneuver was nullified when she proceeded to remove the envelope from concealment and poke her forefinger within it.

"Gosh," she cried, "you're as good as your word!" She might have said more had he not seen Daphne, the business with Forrester now concluded, staring their way. So he interrupted Cissy with a clearing of the throat.

"Tonight. I can't wait." Clutching his books, he headed doggedly towards the door, but Daphne had a shorter route there than his and caught him.

She waved a manuscript. "Take a look at his comments!" It was the story Forrester had read aloud at the previous class. He had now returned it with marginal criticisms in red pencil.

John's fears that Daphne would see her money being transferred to Cissy were groundless. Daphne was a monomaniac about her writing. He could in fact use that obsession to distract her from her plans for a personal connection with him. He took the manuscript and scanned the red-penciled commentary.

"He likes *this*." He read the underlined sentence adjacent to Forrester's "Well done!": "Having toiled in the toilet, Tillie made her toilette." "Well done" seemed an inappropriate re-mark, but at least it was positive, whereas the other notes on this page were disapproving, e.g., "Poor imagery! . . . An-thropomorphism . . . Doesn't work." John didn't really have the energy to connect these with their textual referents and then console Daphne with particularity. He settled for the catch-all: "Hell, what does he know? If he was such a great authority he would write a book."

"Think so?" Daphne asked, softly bumping against him as they walked along the hallway. "It galls me to read such su-perficial responses to things I labored over for days. Mind you, I'm no Flaubert, but I really do take enormous pains with my sentences."

Professing to be late for a dental appointment, John made his escape.

Cissy had not specified a time at which he should appear, but he assumed seven, the hour at which he had come on the previous week, would be satisfactory, and was in the street outside the apartment at six-thirty, clutching the dozen roses purchased with most of his week's pay from the library. At the echo of the seventh chime from the campanile, he mounted the staircase and climbed to her door, as if ascend-ing an enchanted mountain.

While knocking, he had the awful premonition that, as on his first visit, Forrester would again be the one who opened the door. But it was Cissy who answered. She was nicely dressed in skirt and blouse and even high-heeled shoes, and wearing more makeup than in class as well as more jewelry. She irradiated a rich scent.

"Hi there." She turned and walked rapidly towards the open closet, letting him deal with the door, and found a green coat with a hairy fur collar and, plunging one arm into a sleeve, had virtually donned it before John could drop the roses and get there to help. When he did, grasping the long hair of the collar, he was deliciously almost asphyxiated by the fumes of her scent.

"Listen," Cissy said, buttoning the coat over her exquisite bosom, "something's come up. I have to go see my grandma, who's in the hospital in the city."

"I'm really sorry," said John. "Anything I can do?"

"I'm getting a ride," Cissy told him. She had not seen the flowers, and it would have been bad taste for him to point them out now.

But he had to make some impression, even if she was understandably distracted. "I realize the money I gave you won't go far: you'll need a place to live and so on. I'll get more, I promise."

She frowned. "We'll talk about that next time. You take care."

As they were descending the stairs, John offered to wait with her till her ride showed up.

"That wouldn't look good," said Cissy. "You know?"

Momentarily he had forgotten she was married. "Sure," he agreed. "I'll make myself scarce. I hope your grandmother recovers soon."

"Oh, yeah, that's right. Now, you take care."

Not even the main library of a large state university takes in a fortune in fines, and John had direct access only to those paid by the students who returned late books while he was on duty: the entire take of one shift in those days might not amount to a dollar. Clearly this was no source of serious money. Selling books might be a better means. On Saturday he hitchhiked to the city and found a used-book store. The man behind the littered desk had a cast in one eye and the knot of his tie was darker than the shaft. He and his shop were of a like squalor, but even so his hypothetical offer was much lower than John had expected.

"*Britannica*?" the man asked, sneering with only one side of his face. "Depending on condition, *maybe* twenty cents per volume, but only if it's a whole set."

"Costs more than a hundred now, doesn't it?"

"But we're talkin' used. Anyway, what you got in mind is selling somebody else's property, am I right? Probably belongs to your father. You wouldn't be so dumb as to peddle one you swiped from a school, I hope. It would be stamped with the name of the place, or maybe even perforated."

John was obsessed with the intention of furnishing Cissy with enough money so that she could escape from her imprisonment. Though he had, to this point in life, been of an exemplary honesty (once even, as a child of eleven, having found in the street a wallet containing almost fifty dollars in cash, he went to some pains to track down its owner and return it to him), he had now, through love, become utterly amoral and might have robbed a bank if he had had the requisite armament.

As the situation stood, when assessed with reason, his sole hope for funds in significant quantity remained Daphne Kleemeyer. Nor did he have to beg. In consequence, he knew little guilt and less responsibility.

He had only to look lugubrious.

"Why so melancholy?" Daphne was returning some of the many books she found time to read in addition to what was required in her courses: today they were *The Bohemian Life*, by Henri Murger; Xenophon's *Memorabilia*; and a bilingual edition of Petrarch. John respected the great writers of the past, but considered an inordinate questing after them as probably phony.

He sighed and stamped the books in. Daphne was not the sort ever to pay a fine.

She leaned forward across the counter, even though he was

momentarily alone at the big desk. "If you need more help of a financial nature, just say the word."

"Only if I thought you were some rich man's daughter." He placed the books in a rolling bin, which another employee would push away and lower into the stacks on a dumbwaiter.

"I told you I've saved some."

"You have time for all the course work and all this reading too?"

Daphne smiled. She had unusually small teeth behind her pale lips. She would never have been a beauty, God knew, but could have done more with herself than she did. "I just make efficient use of the time at my disposal. Also I don't sleep a whole lot." She grew sober. "I'm embarrassed at having to read some things not in their original languages, but it's either that or go without it, sometimes. I have a fair reading knowledge of French, for example, but it would have taken me too long to read Murger in the original if I were to do it carefully. And I got a late start on Greek, so tackling a classic text at the moment would be foolhardy."

"You're taking Greek?" He was not really interested, the idea of a scholarly female being only slightly less dreary than that of a girl-athlete, when one's criterion was Cissy Forrester.

"Dumb me," she exclaimed. "I took a lot of Latin and *only then* got to Greek."

He leaned across the counter. "I don't like to do this, but since it was you yourself who mentioned it, I —"

She put against his lips a finger encased in a woolen glove. It was an unpleasant sensation. "Please," said she. "What's mine is yours."

That evening he took a walk with her in the snow that had been falling all day. It was her idea. John hated winter in all its manifestations. Daphne loved the clean crisp air. He was there only because she brought him another hundred dollars.

She stomped along in floppy galoshes. The campus walks had been shoveled more than once by maintenance workers, but the snow continued to descend, and John, whose distaste for cold weather inhibited him from taking serious measures against it, was shod in thin-soled oxfords and the cheap lisle socks given him at Christmas by the aunt and uncle who were supposed to have more money than the rest of the family and perhaps proved it by spending so little.

The money had already been surrendered to him, and therefore his preoccupation was how to separate himself from Daphne by the quickest means that would not be conspicuously rude. He tarried under one of the globed lamps along the walk between the Natural Sciences building and the campanile and stamped his feet, wondering how long he must stay out to a make a reasonable claim of incipient frostbite.

Daphne had been bumping against him as they walked, and now she gingerly asserted her claim on him with a hand between his arm and chest, though she had as yet not closed her fingers.

"I suppose this is our first date," said she, "in the sense of arranging a time and place and meeting there."

Such a definition made him as morally uneasy as he was physically uncomfortable in the cold.

He said quickly, "Listen, if I sell a short story one of these days, I'm not going to forget what I owe you." This promise was not intentionally hypocritical. Brooding about Forrester, John had desperately decided that the story of his printed in the college magazine was of professional quality and had mailed it only that afternoon to *Collier's*, a well-known periodical of the day, to which Forrester might well himself have contributed. If its editors bought his story, he would remember his promise to Daphne, if only after turning over the entire fee to Cissy. He was not a cruel or unfeeling person; he had made no overtures to Daphne Kleemeyer and thus was conscious of no great obligation to her. And he *was* in the grip of a passion for another woman, furthermore the first such he had ever experienced.

He finally got away from Daphne now, using the authentic plea of being chilled to the marrow.

On the strength of another sum of money, John took the courage to call the Forrester apartment, and was rewarded by fate for his unprecedented boldness: it was Cissy who answered.

He spoke rapidly. "I know you can't talk now, but if you could come to the library tomorrow, main desk, I can give you some more help."

"*Who* is this?" Cissy asked, in a happy squeal.

"John Kellog. *Can* you talk?"

"I don't know why not," said she, though it seemed as if her voice had lost some of its verve.

"How's your grandmother?"

"Fine, I guess."

"She's still in the hospital?"

"Oh, that. Uh, no . . . she's out. False alarm. Hey, look, I know I owe you —"

"No!" he cried. "No, you don't!"

"You're a funny guy," said Cissy. "You're certainly different. But nobody ever can call me a crook. I come through! If you wanna drop over here now, I'm available."

John had a test next day on the Civil War, in an American history course he had elected to take for its promise of examples of hopeless gallantry such as Pickett's Charge, flamboyant personalities like Jeb Stuart and Custer the boy-general, and the glistening brown faces of liberated slaves.

Instead a bulbous professor with dandruff on his shoulders lectured monotonously on economics. Also he was already one period late with the paper assigned by the white-haired woman who taught the course in Victorian poetry, another regrettable choice of John's at registration time (for Browning was often impenetrable even with so-called elucidation, while Tennyson was either too sentimental or simply a stuffed shirt).

But in his current madness he would have betrayed much greater causes than those, and of course he responded to Cissy's summons with all haste.

Once again she was wearing the oversized sweatshirt. Her legs were encased in thick knee-socks of bright green throughout but red at the heel and across the toes. She wore no shoes.

As soon as the door was closed behind him, John gave her the latest envelope.

She poked at it with a red-nailed forefinger. "What is it with you?" she asked, with a quizzical little nose.

"It's little enough," John said, gazing at her in adoration.

She proceeded to ask him the same question he had put to Daphne: was his father rich?

"I've got a job."

"You don't make this kind of money at the library. I can't take this from you. You're just a college kid."

"No," said he, desperately pushing the extended envelope back towards her breasts. "You've got to get out of this hell."

"Oh, come on, it's not as bad as that. It's all we could afford until just lately, but we're doing better now, and we're going to move soon."

"You're not getting a divorce?"

She smiled easily. "Not so's you could notice. Why do you ask that?"

. . . He had made a fool of himself. "Oh," he said at last.

"Oh. I guess I got it wrong. I'm sorry."

"Everybody has their ups and downs," Cissy said. "It's generally about money when we've had our troubles, but I've got enough now, really. You take this back. You already gave me that other last week."

"No," John cried. "To take it back now would make it worse for me. I'm in love with you! I'll continue to love you with all my heart even if you stay married. I can't help it. Please keep the money. I have to *do* something, you see. I just can't stand by. And maybe this isn't the place to say it, but can this old guy be right for you? He's not even a very successful writer, is he? If so, why is he teaching in this hick college?"

"Johnny," Cissy said, taking both his hands. "You don't know what you're saying. You're all worked up."

He did not quite burst into tears, but he made more of a spectacle of himself than he could bear to remember in detail throughout the remainder of his life. The similar scene in his first novel, *The Life and Death of Jerry Claggett*, probably put more fiction into the mix than fact: e.g., "Jerry" does weep and is joined by "Cindy," who embraces him and, weeping, leads him to the sofa, which in a graceful gesture she converts to a bed. In a transition of the sort that marked Kellog's early procedures, next they are in bed and nude, without any squalid business of undressing, and they make love for the first and last time before parting forever: indeed Jerry believes it will be the last time he will make it with anybody.

Of the reality as he recalled it (though it was eventually much less believable than the fantasy) the essentials were that to console him Cissy pulled him to the sofa bed, already open and rather sordidly unmade, lifted but did not take off the sweatshirt — at last it was definite: she was not wearing any underwear — got his trousers down but not off, and screwed him or anyway would have, had he been able to perform which he however could not, even though, shocking him into greater enervation, she made strenuous efforts with two strong hands.

But the meaningful differences between the novel and life were moral: "Cindy" stays with her husband, "Stephen," for motives of compassion and has become a whore through a combination of need (while on one of his nighttime walks, distracted by his writer's block, Stephen is run down by a car operated by an uninsured driver and is confined thereafter to a wheelchair) and the evil machinations of "Teddy Boyle," restaurateur and pimp. In the version that actually took place, Cissy was no doubt simply greedy: the obese Ed Doyle first paid for her favors and then conceived the idea that other older unattractive men might do the same for the unique opportunity to taste the flesh of a curvaceous blonde coed. Doyle's error was in offering Cissy's services to one J. Donald Hillerman, the local druggist, who he correctly supposed to be lascivious, but when Hillerman came to Doyle's eatery it was rather to eye the young men who accompanied the girls, and therefore he was self-righteously outraged at the proposal and notified the authorities.

When apprised, the president of the university persuaded the chief of police (most of whose force, had it not been for the state-supported institution that dominated the little town, would be back behind the plow) to do nothing that would result in negative publicity, and as a result Doyle was permitted to sell the college hangout to Hillerman and leave town uncharged with lawbreaking. The matter of Cissy was concluded to all local intents and purposes when she left Forrester and was never seen again on campus or in town. Forrester's contract was not renewed the following year.

John had been due to become a senior by the end of the

term, but having dropped both the writing course and that on the Civil War had insufficient credits and should have done summer school if he wished to graduate the following year. Daphne Kleemeyer, though of his own age a year ahead of him in college, graduated with high honors in June and went to New York City, where she house-sat the apartment of a traveling relative and paid no rent.

"I hope it doesn't shock you," she wrote, four days after her arrival in the big town,

> but I'm going to suggest that you come to the city for the summer. It should be decorous enough: there's an extra bedroom here, and it's equipped with a desk and even an upright typewriter, which I don't myself require, having brought along my portable Remington-Rand. As I'm not paying rent, you would pay none. We could split the costs of food and whatever else we share, and you could certainly put your part on credit, for I have some savings and my plan is to apply immediately for secretarial work: obviously I type, but I can also do Gregg shorthand (which I learned in high school against such an eventuality as this). I don't have to point out to you the advantages of being here if you wish to publish what you write, not to mention the special services I may well be able to provide, such as typing manuscripts in a professional style.

Certainly the invitation did have its shocking aspect, which however, given the circumstances, was superficial. John had not yet so much as kissed Daphne. If he accepted, he would most assuredly not be doing so for carnal purposes. He had now had one sexual encounter, and the experience had discouraged him from anxiously awaiting the next, even if one were likely with a girl more to his physical taste than Daphne could ever be.

Not to mention that he still owed Daphne two hundred

dollars, which she had thus far been good enough never to refer to, not even by indirection, but nobody was likely to forget a sum of such magnitude in a time when it might have been a month's salary. Though he had had little previous experience with indebtedness, he instinctively began to understand that unless a loan is canceled by simply repaying what is owed, the next best emotional strategy is to borrow more, as the worst is to do nothing and thus in effect deny the creditor's existence.

John went to New York and moved into the extra room in the apartment on East 17th Street. It was much shabbier than he had supposed, though after he had lived in the city for a while and learned the ropes, his standards were necessarily lowered and he understood that the flat was locally considered not only handsome but generously proportioned and, having as it did, a fireplace, could even qualify as luxurious, even if no fire could be made in the grate, the flue having long since been cemented shut.

He immediately assured Daphne he would get a summer job and not only begin to repay the loan but also provide what he could towards the cost of such food as they ate in common, but when she begged him not to worry about *that,* he as quickly put the obligation out of his mind, and while she was out during the day, looking, as promised, for work as a secretary, John sat at the typewriter for perhaps a quarter hour in the aggregate, in increments of two or three minutes during which first the chair was too low for the desk, then too hard, next the machine's keys required a distracting amount of energy to strike home, and the supply of paper, only a few sheets, was soon exhausted and he hated to use the little money he had for such a thing when he was always ravenously hungry and needed funds to pay for snacks at the lunch counter at the Third Avenue corner, visiting which was also research, for many of his fellow customers were exotic, e.g., the Chinaman from the nearby hand laundry, who could be seen through the window, working the steam iron no matter how late at night one passed, or how early in the morning, but habitually breakfasted, lunched, and dined on the same diet, *viz.*, a fried-egg sandwich on untoasted white bread (the cheapest item on the menu-board) and a mug of tea. A conspicuously effeminate white man was another regular customer and made animated conversation with the short-order cooks and countermen about events of the day and prissily used his paper napkin overfrequently. Everybody snickered on his departure.

Once a Negro entered and ordered a hamburger, but when it was not served as promptly as he wished, he loudly denounced the establishment as being prejudiced against his color and forthwith departed. John initially believed this to be probably an unfair charge, for his own order had seemingly taken quite as long to come, but when Lou, the baldheaded guy who manned the far right end of the counter at midday winked at him and said, "Smells better in here now," he wondered whether the colored man might not have had a point. He had previously believed the city flawless in these matters, perhaps because in his hometown, as at college, Negroes were rareties and thus none was normally seen in a restaurant or movie theater, whereas in New York they were commonplace everywhere, a state of affairs that pleased him, and he would have liked to assure some dark-skinned person that he thought this was as it should be, but when he tried to meet a Negro's eye he was usually ignored, though once, on the subway, a perhaps drunken colored man interpreted his smile as being derisive and threatened him. The only occasion on which he was the recipient of a friendly approach was on lower Third Avenue once, at night, and then it was a black prostitute who made it.

He wandered around the city almost every evening after dinner, partly because he was fascinated by Manhattan after dark and partly because he liked to avoid Daphne as much as possible. He took little pleasure in her company in the best of times, but now, when she was really supporting him, buying *all* the food, while he stayed home during daylight, listening to radio soap operas, sleeping for hours, and having waking dreams of sex with fanciful Negresses, he dreaded the sight of her. He had ceased even to sit at the desk. And then when she came back every evening from her job as secretary in an apartment-rental agency, what she wanted to talk about was his writing: how it had gone that day and when she might read some of it. The sole current nonsexual use of his imagination was in inventing plausible progress reports and being firm about withholding his manuscripts until the work had taken on a shape that would sustain it against disintegration when exposed to the eyes of others.

"Well," Daphne would say, in affectionate reproach, "I'm not exactly the outside world, I hope." But she never displayed the slightest doubt of him nor issued the least challenge. He wished she would have made demands; then he might have had the courage to admit he was making a fool of her and squandering his summer. He could have gone home then and made a few dollars filling in for those on vacation at the local canning factory, perhaps even have repaid Daphne some of the outstanding loan, which she persisted in never mentioning, which persistence made him resent her all the more. He had never before been aware that benevolence could be so obnoxious to its recipient. New York was the appropriate place in which to learn such disagreeable truths, for quotidian life there was made up of such.

Deflected from the subject of his writing, Daphne would tell of the daily swindles perpetrated by her boss on the defenseless seekers of apartments, of which there had apparently been a grievous shortage since the time of Peter Stuyvesant. Not only did he take a commission of two months' rent, but he often demanded the purchase of furniture supposedly the possessions of the last tenant but actually stuff bought by the landlords from used-furniture stores at a fraction of what was now being asked for them. Most of the man's income came from such schemes, in which he represented the owners' interests, never that of the unfortunates who sought dwellingplaces. Stern laws forbade such practices, but he simply *shmeered* those who were supposed to enforce them. That was the New York way.

In their own borrowed apartment house, the janitor, called locally "duh soopuh," an embittered, potbellied, middle-aged man named Stan Mainboch, according to the only other tenant with whom they had an acquaintance, a genteel sort of widow named Mrs. Feltring, had a habit of doing meaningless favors, such as promptly delivering to one's door junk mail from the lobby (first grinning, then glaring until a tip was surrendered, then sneering if he considered it insufficient), but delaying cruelly with plumbing problems. Daphne said that scarcely had she arrived when Mainboch, after a perfunctory, almost inaudible knock, let himself in with his master key and told her it was a violation of her cousins' lease to sublet, but that for a consideration the landlord would not be notified. When she informed him that the apartment was simply on loan to her, Mainboch said that was even worse, for the insurance would not cover the premises under such conditions, but that, again, the absentee owner, a big impersonal company, need never know, and after looking her over, elucidated that by "consideration" he did not necessarily mean money: he was aware that cash might be in short supply for a young kid.

When she told him she would have to check with her relatives on these matters, the super made a bitter exit and had since not so much as responded to her nod in the hallway. She just had to pray that nothing broke down in the apartment during her term there, for it seemed obvious that Mainboch would not help.

John was relieved that Daphne apparently did not expect anything of him. He was of little practical use in a household, perhaps because his father had been so handy, and he was depressed to hear about the disagreeable janitor. Too much of the life he had yet known in New York consisted exclusively of the squalid. It seemed as though he was farther from the grand and glittering than when at a provincial college, and going to midtown to watch the limousines pull up at luxury hotels and restaurants made it worse. But worst of all was to enter a bookstore and inspect the novels that were being published currently — looking at the jacket-portraits of authors was usually enough to turn the stomach: brushy mustaches with pipes, the occasional pale pansy, the smug females with heavy eyebrows and pursed lips. John was especially crushed by discovering that most of the war novels had been written by those who had actually served in the wartime armed forces, and he cursed the fate that had made him too young for that great adventure.

When he finally confessed to Daphne not that he had yet to write a word, but rather that he was having trouble with his work owing to a lack of experience, she said, "But that's not insuperable. Remember Stephen Crane, who wrote *The Red Badge of Courage* before he had ever been anywhere near a battle. Fiction isn't history. What's important in it is what's invented, because even if you write about something you've actually done, the telling about it is different, isn't it?, because it's in words."

She loved to talk in this theoretical way, citing examples from her preposterously wide range of reading, which he suspected of being superficial, whereas he read and reread the same works and believed he knew them in depth: *Of Human Bondage, A Farewell to Arms, Of Mice and Men,* and a play entitled *The Petrified Forest,* in which one of the characters was a poet who didn't care whether he died or not: he seemed to speak peculiarly for John, when the latter was in a state of melancholy, which was most of the time since the matter of Cissy Forrester, which had very likely ruined his life.

Daphne not only brought home the food but cooked it as well, and did such housecleaning as was required, along with taking the laundry to the Chinese and other chores. The little pleasure John had these days was in reflecting, masochistically, on how thoroughly worthless he was, even to the degree of overeating, claiming, with Daphne's maternal encouragement, most of each meal she prepared, three-quarters of the meatballs in the can of spaghetti sauce, most of the melted Velveeta from the top of the tuna casserole. Without thinking, he might easily put away the entire contents of a newly opened box of those things in which raisins were squashed between two tasteless strips of unsalted soda-cracker dough or whatever, which he hated, and told Daphne as much, for she did the shopping as well.

No doubt it was her fear of loneliness in the big city that made her put up with him for so long and without complaint. In his current state he could not bear to entertain the thought that she might genuinely believe him capable of writing something of merit. As to any physical interest on her part, that subject was too repugnant to consider. In the morning he stayed in bed behind a closed door until she had completed the preparation of his breakfast; if he continued to sleep, she left the scrambled eggs or French toast covered, in an oven turned to minimum heat and with its door partially opened — until he complained that it made the kitchen too warm on a summer morning and also pointed out the possible danger if the flame went out. At night he was seldom there when she retired at the early hour of eleven and thus never saw her dressed for bed. He was usually himself out till midnight, walking the city streets. It was something to do that cost nothing, and not too dangerous in those days. The muggings that did occur usually happened to those who were dressed in clothes more prosperous-looking than the old work shirt and chinos worn by him.

A merciless heat wave claimed the city in late July. Airconditioning was unknown to private domiciles of the nonwealthy in that era, and very unlikely in smaller offices. Of course Daphne's had none, nor was her boss quick to repair the ailing wall-hung electric fan high above her desk. In the apartment John lay on a cotton blanket on the floor, clad only in his underdrawers, which were none too clean, for he was sensitive about including them with the laundry Daphne took to the Chinaman, and he usually forgot to wash them for himself. One of these days when he got some funds he would simply buy new ones. He would also get his own apartment on a more fashionable street, perhaps a duplex in the Sixties just off Fifth Avenue, and keep a convertible in a nearby garage, and on Friday drive in it, with a nonsluttish Cissy Forrester, to a weekend at his charming country place in Connecticut, there to canoe on the pond, drink Pimm's Cup Number Whichever (the one stirred with a raw cucumber stick), and have a picnic using an English-made wicker basket from Abercrombie & Fitch, fitted with china plates, silverware, and even salt and pepper shakers, a corkscrew, and a little board for the cutting of cheese. In the evening there'd be a dinner party at the nearby estate of rich and grand people, worshipful admirers of John Kellog's novels, fellow guests to include prominent painters, ballerinas, celebrated actors from the Broadway stage, philanthropic bankers with Harvard accents, and perhaps a tabloid columnist with inside knowledge of mob crime.

At such moments, there on the floor, staring towards the cracked ceiling and seeing instead images of a glamorous future, the pity was that to acquire it anything more was needed: that his extraordinary powers of fantasy were not enough in themselves to bring about their own realization; they were quite as vivid as the movies he took them from. . . .

The truth was, he had no usable imagination nowadays and could entertain nothing in his head except the most simpleminded wish-fulfillment and even that was plagiarized. The cure for this, had he possessed the stomach for it, was probably to pore over some author renowned for his gloomy profundity, Herman Melville perhaps, or maybe Dostoevski, of whom Daphne was wont to babble and whom she found time to read amidst her other activities, along with the many other classic writers John had thus far not got around to, if he had heard of them at all, for some were poets, and he had never his life long looked at a poem unless it was assigned in class. There were two authors to whom Daphne referred so often that John made them into one: Henry James Joyce, but lacked the energy to read him/them, or indeed the courage to try. "*Ulysses* isn't even written in English, is it?" "You're thinking of *Finnegans Wake*," Daphne explained in her annoyingly patient way. "*Ulysses* is really pretty comprehensible, if you don't get all anxious and just read it calmly. It's very funny, too. You'd really enjoy it, John, with *your* sense of humor."

She had the oddest idea of him: of course he wasn't humorless, but if he had ever displayed any wit to her, of all people, he was unaware of it. He had been consistently melancholy since meeting her, and though of course she could hardly be blamed, still it was inevitable that he should make at least a subliminal connection between her and being in a state of depression.

When it was time for Daphne to return from work on this suffocating summer day, John resentfully put on his clothes and prepared to share the electric fan. He had long since been aware that doing something for the sake of simple justice was no guarantee that it would make you feel at all better, but undoubtedly it was rotten that she had to work all day in this weather, she who, he could admit in such a mood, was smarter than he and more gifted: faint praise, for anyone's talent exceeded his; and as to intelligence, such as he had had to start with had dwindled to the point that, choosing a sentence at random in Daphne's copy of *The Golden Bowl,* another work by that compound author, he could not make head nor tail of it ("He found it convenient, oddly, for his relation with himself — though not unmindful that there might not still, as time went on, be others, including a more intimate degree of *that* one that would seek, possibly with violence, the larger of the finer issue — which was it? — of the vernacular.")

He really ought to leave. New York had done nothing for him. If he went home now, he could still get in a month's work at the factory and pick up a few dollars towards the expenses of what, with some extra effort to make up the missing credits, would be his last year of college. Then, with a B.A. in English from a provincial university, he could . . . get a permanent job at the factory, but rather in the office than the plant. Or return to New York, find employment even less attractive than Daphne's, for he would not be equipped with touch-typing and shorthand, unless of course one of the big magazines or major publishing houses demanded that he take over their operation as editor-in-chief.

He said as much, bitterly, to Daphne that evening as they sat in the living-dining room, eating the Chinese food she had brought home in several paper cartons.

"I know," she said in her unfailingly sympathetic way, "it can seem discouraging, but I'm convinced that there's no answer but 'in the destructive element, immerse.' Speaking for myself, if I were to take the kind of job that requires the exercise of a certain kind of intellectual energy, say editing books, I'd never have enough left for my own writing."

"But how much do you write now?" John asked indignantly, perhaps unkindly.

She winced and speared a few squiggly vegetable things with her fork. "I will, though. I'm reading a lot, and at least in my mind I'm looking for a new style. It would be pointless to do any more of that naïve, derivative stuff I did in Forrester's class. That's what is so impressive about your work, John: it doesn't read like juvenilia."

He hated Chinese food, at least this kind, in which only by chance could you ever locate a fragment of protein, and in the extended intervals during which the slow-oscillating fan did not play upon him, he was unbearably hot.

"*My* work?" he asked angrily. "Where is it? It doesn't exist! Do you hear me, Daphne? Don't keep talking as if I'm a writer. I haven't written a word since coming to New York. Not a *word*. I've been living off you, and *I haven't written a single word in all this time*."

This to him most dramatic statement had no visible effect on her. She drank some of the weak iced tea of her making, which was further diluted with ice cubes. She carefully dried her lips with the paper napkin, a gesture that irritated him in the best of times if indeed there had ever been any with her.

"But you will," said she. "You will."

She was so infuriatingly smug about this that he found it

simple to blame her for not only the wasting of his summer but the withering of his dream. Without her, he would never have had to recognize his utter lack of capacity to be a writer. He might have endured in the sticks forever on the never to be realized intention of moving to New York.

"Where do you get your arrogant certainty?" he asked now. "How do you know better about me than I do?" In addition to all else, he was ravenously hungry, the oriental fake food having only served to increase his appetite for genuine nourishment, but to get any he would have to ask her for money, continue to be a disgusting beggar, whereas if she had let him alone he would be peacefully working in the canning factory (probably again this summer on the machines in the labeling department), putting some money aside but spending some too on beer and hamburgers and inexpensive dates with the factory girls, whom as a college boy he could easily impress. This summer he might even have got into someone's pants, given his experience with Cissy; he knew the ropes now. Whereas in New York he had been utterly sexless. Unaccompanied girls never came to the lunch counter when he could afford to eat there, and he had no idea of where to go to meet them. You probably had to be born locally, to Jewish or Italian parents.

Daphne's answer to his angry question was first merely to stare at him for a long time, and for good reason: it was unanswerable. He was sorry if he had hurt her feelings, but no doubt it was to everybody's advantage for the truth to be so aired. Hitherto he had avoided coming to such a focus.

But finally she said, "I knew you hadn't written anything —" She caught herself. "I mean, I suspected that you hadn't probably been able to write yet, but I *know* you will. I believe in you. I'll continue to believe in you if it takes all year."

"Look, Daphne, the only thing I've ever written that had any substance was that war story *The Owl* published last winter. That's how I got into Forrester's class, where I really never did anything but little unfinished sketches. And the other day I reread, or tried to, my story. It's all corny sentimentality, and it's not even original: I wasn't thinking consciously at the time, but remembered when rereading it that the big scene had pretty obviously been lifted from the end of a movie about World War One in which James Cagney falls on a hand grenade to save his comrades."

She laughed. "What's good enough for Shakespeare should not be denied you. He never invented the plot of a single one of his plays."

That kind of thing made John feel worse. "The point is, I really haven't demonstrated any talent at all, so far as I'm concerned. I always liked to read as a young kid. I'd stay indoors and immerse myself in make-believe when the others were outside with baseballs and fishing poles. So later on when having to think of what I wanted to do in life, nothing appealed to me. I'm a lazy guy, and so many things bore me. The studying necessary to become a doctor or lawyer doesn't even bear thinking about. That's why I majored in English, after all. One day I got the bright idea that maybe I could make a living, maybe even a pretty big one, staying home and writing stuff I made up in my imagination — journalism is too hard work! But I have now discovered that my imagination just doesn't work on demand. I have to live more, experience more, so as to have something to write about, but I can't do much of that without any money."

Daphne said, "All right. Then wait awhile. Just don't give up the idea, get tired of thinking about it, and quit altogether. Don't let the pilot light go out, in other words. Because whatever you say about that story of yours, it displayed the real thing, believe me."

For the first time, sitting there staring into the detritus of the chow mein, he began to take her seriously, or rather take seriously her interest in him. Until that moment he had tried to think about her as little as possible, for she had always been a potential embarrassment to him. He had found her neither attractive nor interesting, yet somehow had become closely associated with and even dependent on her. But the situation was not absurd if there was a point to it. Now one had been identified: she believed in him, and this was of crucial significance, for he did not believe in himself. Therefore, if he were to achieve anything, she was a necessity to him.

Transformed by this recognition, and in an odd physical state owing to the heat of the day, which grew even warmer as the evening came and such little breeze as there had been was as it were stilled by the waning of the light — being excessively warmed both enervated and aroused him — he began to look at Daphne in a new way. Where she had previously seemed bony, she now could be seen as sculptured. Her dark hair and almost black eyes might be more exotic than run-of-the-mill. Her lips were rather fine than thin. On this hot night she was wearing a lighter blouse than usual, and it looked as though she might have some breasts after all. When she rose to clear the table, her skirt adhered to a certain roundness of posterior. It was possible that in form-fitting garb she might be both elegant and sexually desirable, a combination that hitherto he had assumed was peculiar to figures on the silver screen of an earlier era, or in advertisements in magazines for the well-to-do.

"If I ever make some money," said he, "I'm going to buy you a silver lamé evening gown, and we'll dine at the Rainbow Room."

Daphne dropped the empty carton into the pedal can. "Just write good prose."

"I'll try," John said. "But I want to do something in return for what you've done for me."

"Don't worry. You will." She was being conspicuously matter-of-fact, scraping the plates and then washing them, one by one, in running water, mounting them in the rack to drain. Bits of dried food might well be found on them to-morrow; she was not his mother's match as a housekeeper.

When she had finished with the cleanup, she made instant iced coffee for them both. She brought him his glass. "Dessert's ice cream, but I'm afraid it began to melt on the way home and that old refrigerator doesn't get cold enough to refreeze it. Sorry."

"That's okay," John said. "You take good care of me." It was the most affectionate thing he had ever said to her, and she was moved by it. As in fact was he, learning as he did for the first time that in life one occasionally comes across certain matters that seem consistent with the textbook theories: in this case, that words sometimes create emotions, rather than vice versa, so that speaking of anger might make one angry: he remembered that from a course in Psych. But he had no intention of betraying a firm fidelity to his doomed love for Cissy Forrester, which had changed in character but remained as passionate as ever and by now had little to do with the real Cissy.

Years later, when he had become weary of reflecting generally on the relations between the sexes and decided that there was no sexual truth that was not particular, he believed that what he had felt that night was simply lust: any other female who was not physically repulsive could have been substituted for Daphne — a sad realization, but then what was not?

After living under the same roof for a month without touching each other, he and she went to bed together on that hot night not long after finishing their melted ice cream. Despite her vast knowledge of literary love, Daphne was a virgin in life, which thrust the role of expert on John, who had had but the one encounter with Cissy, which Cissy had directed, with perhaps too much authority. But now that he was obliged to be master, he was notably successful, and in a much more sensitive situation.

They did it a lot on succeeding days, and Daphne was never again to menstruate in that borrowed apartment. Being ignorant of contraceptive means more subtle than abstention, she was pregnant within a couple of weeks. They got married before the end of August and had to find their own place immediately thereafter. The one-room studio apartment to which they moved caused John to remember the Forresters' college-town abode as spacious and luxurious. Its rent was twice the wages Daphne earned weekly.

She had found the place through her own office, and her boss behaved more generously than expected: as wedding gift he waived half his usual commission of two months' rent, which left the young couple to pay only the remainder, plus a month's rent in advance, plus rent for the final month of the two-year lease, plus still another month's rent as so-called security against excessive damage, as well as, by the landlord's demand, the outright purchase of the wall-to-wall carpeting, everywhere faded, worn through to the backing just inside the front door and stained, near the kitchenette area, with grease and other substances.

The sum of these charges was very near the balance of Daph's lifetime savings, even when supplemented with a nice wedding-present check from her parents (John had postponed informing his parents of his new status; anyway, they had no extra money), and as modest ordinary living already consumed her entire income, how the expenses of having a baby could be met was an unanswerable question in the current arrangement. Not to mention that in time she would not be able to hold a job at all.

Despite John's belief that regular and frequent sexual intercourse would liberate his sensibility for writing, it had not done so. Perhaps if anything his literary imagination was less effective now than when he had been a virgin — though his sexual imaginings were much more vivid than of old, now that he knew what was possible. Unfortunately, marriage and the idea of a pregnant wife soon began to vitiate his appetite for Daphne. Though the doctor assured her it was far too soon to curtail her sexual activities, John could not disregard an uneasy sense that screwing so to speak in the presence of a third being, namely one's own growing offspring, was not only unsavory but, no matter what the authorities said, unhealthy for the tiny blob of protoplasm. He therefore began to lust for others.

First he trafficked with them only in fantasy (some of the most compelling examples of which came to him while he made love with Daph) but soon enough this trick of mind no longer sufficed. He became especially lascivious whenever he tried to write — another reason for avoiding the desk. But as soon as his organ of lust (which was nowhere near his genitals) reacted to a change of venue, as it quickly did, the same urge interfered with whatever he tried as distraction. Reading one of the novels recommended by Daphne, he could not restrain himself from plucking through the pages to the sex scenes, which in the classic sort of work were none too carnal in detail: there are few particulars when Julien Sorel at last invades the bedroom of Mme de Rênal and nothing but abstractions when Alec d'Urberville takes the sleeping Tess.

If he carried the garbage down to the communal cans in the subterranean areaway (his sole household chore) he would see, amongst the passing parade on the adjacent sidewalk, at least three female persons, per five minutes, whom he found desirable, from quite young but buxom teens to women of comparative middle age (which to him in those days would have been thirty). Not one stranger returned his gaze, but it was otherwise with certain fellow tenants: there were at least two he was sure he could have for the asking. Unfortunately so, for he absolutely would not commit adultery under the same roof shared by his faithful, impeccable wife.

Which meant he was constantly in a state of dissatisfaction, unable to think of anything but illicit sex. Surely that was not healthy for a man of his age. The fact was, he had married too young, and why? Merely to do the right thing. But it was Daph's fault she got pregnant; she should have known how to avoid it. It had been she who lured him to New York, she whose relatives had decided to stay in California and give up the lease on the Manhattan apartment, forcing the newlyweds to find this dump; she who did not earn enough to sustain them. But far worse than any of these malefactions was her major crime of insisting he could become a writer.

He owed her nothing. In truth, she had robbed him of the final years of his youth, had probably ruined his life beyond reclamation. When the baby came, he would have to take some wretched New York job, riding the subways every day and on weekends, wheeling a stroller over phlegm-spattered, dog-beshat pavements, past doorways from which sprawling winos shouted importunities while pissing their pants.

He began to quarrel with Daphne, using such pretexts as the encrusted cap on the ketchup bottle and going on to accuse her of sexual association with her loathsome boss. Eventually he became sufficiently exercised to question whether the embryo in her belly was his own. This was finally sufficient to overtax even Daphne's stamina, and in her counterattack she charged him with being more or less what he had for some time believed himself despite the reassurances she had previously provided: she wondered whether she might have been wrong in her assessment of his talent.

Now, the extraordinary thing was that though when she

had encouraged and made sacrifices for him he could not write at all, now he was given formidable psychic energy by her contempt. He did not speak to her for two days following that row, and during this period was able to write effectively for the first time since arriving in New York — really since the shattering love affair with Cissy. On the third day Daphne apologized to *him*, and by the following morning the muse had vanished behind a barrier of guilt and shame, which were succeeded by the debilitating kind of resentment as opposed to the sort that generated power. He went so far in degradation as to take their one set of bed linen to the laundromat, a day before Daph was scheduled to do that chore, and sit waiting for the machines to finish, there amongst the collection of persons to be found in such a place: slatternly housewives, old men with spotted pates, young mothers with children in attendant vehicles — Daphne's situation by next summer: the repulsive image could not be endured.

When she came home that evening they quarreled again, and again she was driven finally to make the cruel charge. John slept on the sofa that night, and the next day did the best writing ever. In one sustained burst of force lasting six hours, with interruptions only to make more coffee and to urinate, he completed the story he had begun during the previous interval of creativity. That evening he showed it to Daph as a peace offering, and with tears of joy she pronounced it an extraordinary success, not unworthy of inclusion in a collection of her favorites such as D. H. Lawrence's "Rocking-Horse Winner," Mérimée's "Vénus d'Ille," and Kafka's "In der Strafkolonie."

John enjoyed her praise less than he detested her pretentions at such a time. What he needed at his moment of triumph was not the cloying touch of a submissive, pregnant wife but something coarser, even unsavory, so he helped himself to the wages she had only just brought home, scarcely sufficient in sum to cover the expenses of the next two weeks, went to a midtown bar and drank enough courage to follow a streetwalker to a hotbed hotel: she seemed to be a Puerto Rican, reeked of liquor herself and, most thrilling of all, displayed emaciated arms with conspicuous needle tracks. It was appalling, revolting, disgusting in the extreme, and all in all the most exciting sexual experience he had yet experienced except in fantasy.

While he was having a postcoital pee in the corner washbasin, the whore, having dressed speedily, took a hasty leave with his wallet and watch, which had been prudently deposited on the bedside table.

He despised Daphne even more for sympathetically accepting his story of having been robbed at knifepoint, but most of all, for he was still drunk, he hated himself for lacking the courage to make an outrageous full confession. He and his wife were always circumspect about sex in conversation. Even when they had gone at it hot and heavy, it was "making love," and as to reaching a climax, the polite question, "Did you finish?" When John's organ had actually been overused in the course of one of their early weekends, he had confessed, "I'm sore," and not mentioned the name of where. Daphne's menses were called by her "Les anglais," the short form of "what the French say: *Les anglais sont debarqué.*" "Huh?" "'The redcoats have landed'!" "Oh."

Within three days the story had been mailed to that magazine to which all stories were sent first, presumably read by someone there, and returned in the stamped envelope he had provided, with a rejection note that had been printed in fixed type.

"Let's face it," said Daphne that evening. "It's unreasonable to expect victory the first time out. We should probably prepare ourselves for more rejections."

"Why do you say that?" he asked in fury.

"Remember *Moby-Dick*'s bad reviews." she said. "And Stendhal never sold more than a couple of thousand copies of anything."

This defeatism caused John to storm out of the apartment, not this time to look for sex, for indeed he felt utterly sexless when meeting the resistance of the world, but to march vast distances of sidewalk in a military stride, head erect, chin projected, energetically alone in the passive urban mob. Walking proved to be as if winding up his motor, and he came back to sit down at the portable typewriter that nowadays permanently occupied the former dining table in the living room (they ate their meals from their laps, seated on the couch) and by morning had written most of another short story. He went to a warm bed just as Daphne was arising, she who had soon fallen asleep despite the sound of the typewriter.

That evening he had another manuscript for her to read. She admired this story even more than the previous one: its emotions were richer, its characterization more trenchant, its style — well, style was of course always so subtle a thing to assess, but his was becoming more of a fine-tooled instrument as he proceeded. As it happened, this was the most extraordinarily appropriate response she could have made at this moment, for he was especially pleased with his style, having given much conscious effort to it, alternating long sentences of many dependent clauses with those short and curt, which if read aloud might even sound staccato.

However, Daphne had to ruin it all by pointing out a solecism: "scarcely" was properly followed by "when," not "than." He was too exhausted to walk the streets that night, but he slept alone on the couch. Eventually he was able to admit to himself that she was right, but he simply could not confess it to her face, for the reason that while he recognized that

Daphne was more learned than he, and of course generous and kind and admirable in so many ways, it galled him to be dependent on her for all forms of support, financial, moral, and sexual.

The second story quickly came back from the same publication that had so speedily rejected the first. The first, meanwhile, had been sent to another magazine, one that took a week longer to return it, the first few days of which John found so encouraging that he was already planning the celebratory dinner at a grand French restaurant that he had read, in *Life* magazine, was the most expensive in America, at which a full-course meal cost more than twenty dollars per person. But that manuscript too came back, accompanied only by a printed comment.

John produced seven such stories in rapid succession. Each took slightly longer to write, for each was a little longer than its predecessor though no more complex. Looking back from years later, he remembered them as having been mood pieces, their subject a sensitive young man a-wander across an urban terrain, tarrying now and again for superficially simple yet profoundly eloquent exchanges with dirty-faced urchins, spunky oldsters, Negroes with their dignified wisdom and vivid language. . . . It embarrassed the older Kellog to think of these pathetic efforts, all evidence of which he eventually burned.

He had hoped to skip over the "little" literary journals and begin at the top, where the fees were said to be as much as a thousand dollars for a short story. By contrast, the "little" magazines might pay as little as twenty-five. But in fact his first appearance was in a publication that paid nothing at all in money: a contributor's promised reward was but ten copies of the issue in which his work appeared. As it happened, John received only one. His importunate notes to the editor-in-chief, whose address was a P.O. box in Boston, went unanswered. John felt that the copy he had might be the only one in the world, so forlorn-looking was it, not even printed in letterpress but rather typed and mimeographed and bound in a pink-colored paper not much heavier than that which carried the text. Sending the story to this wretched thing had been Daphne's idea. "Better to get in print somewhere than not at all" — one of her many fallacious theories. He was beginning to doubt that back of the façade of high-brow references there was much practical intelligence.

He had better initial luck with the story that was accepted (after eighteen rejections elsewhere) by a quarterly called *Budding*, a copy of which Daphne had found in the cultish bookshop she frequented, conveniently near her place of work, at the edge of the Village. This time John received a letter of acceptance within only a fortnight of the mailing of the story. Once again there was no immediate money, but a twenty-five-dollar fee was to be paid on publication. This would be the first money he had ever earned with his pen. Daphne was ecstatic. She went right out again after coming home to hear the news, and bought a steak, a package of frozen potato puffs, and a bottle of Liebfraumilch (their favorite wine, because of the name, along with Lacrima Christi). Now that this had happened John tried to maintain his composure, but it was impossible not to be gratified by hearing a stranger's promise to pay money for the right to make public the product of one's private imagination. Even though it wasn't much money, and deferred at that, and the magazine was awfully obscure.

In the letter of acceptance, the editor asked to meet John, a request easily complied with, for the quarterly was published locally, down in the Village. John as yet knew nobody literary, unless Daphne qualified, and while he liked to think that talent is recognized for its own sake, he agreed with his wife that it doesn't exactly hurt to have friends with influence. So he went to see this Ross Philbin.

After wandering for some time, he at last found the street and number for which he had been searching, but obviously one or both were wrong, for this was a stooped brownstone residential building and not the office sort of edifice that would have been appropriate, but perhaps simply to confirm and prolong his chagrin he mounted the steps and glanced over the rank of mailboxes in the entryway, finding no *Budding,* but there *was* a "Philbin" in the farthermost nameslot.

John pressed the button. After a moment he heard a shout from above. He went out of the entryway, onto the top step, and looked up to see a face in an open window on the top floor.

He waited until it was clear that the face would not speak until he did. "My name is John Kellog," he shouted up. "You wanted to see me?"

"Why?"

"You're publishing a story of mine in *Budding* —?"

The presumable answer to this question was provided by a buzzing at the lock of the inner door. John scrambled to get inside and catch the knob before the noise stopped. He climbed until there were no more stairs and arrived on the top floor out of breath. Philbin, if indeed it was he, waited for him in an open door.

"You're better-looking than I thought you would be. Those *sensitive* little stories are so often written by small toadlike people."

John followed him into the apartment, breathing heavily. Philbin, a tall, thin, fairhaired man of an indeterminate age, flopped onto a couch upholstered in a charcoal-gray fabric, scattering a pile of vividly colored pillows. He wore a loose shirt but very tight dungarees, and his feet were bare and a bit dirty.

Apparently no invitation to be seated could be expected. At length John took one of those modernist butterfly chairs he had seen depicted in slick magazines. Its body-bearing part was constructed of sleek black leather but proved none too comfortable to the behind. Everything in the room looked quite fashionable, in either black or white except for the accessories and the paintings on the walls. The latter were all originals and not the reproductions of nonobjectivist pictures Daphne clipped from the pages of *Life* and attached, with masking tape, to the walls of the short hallway that led to the bathroom. Philbin's pictures too were essentially just messes of bright colors.

"So," Philbin said, crossing his long legs. Slumped on the couch as he was, with John necessarily in a similar posture in the sling chair, the editor seemed all knees for a moment, until he parted them and showed a long chin with a smile. His eyebrows were darker than his hair, and his eyes were pale. "We liked your story a *lot*. You are a talented man. We foresee quite a future for you."

John was thrilled to hear these words, but he believed he should not make a naïve show of his pleasure. "I realize I still have a way to go."

Philbin's stare was piercing. "I'd say you've arrived, if you've been recognized by *Budding*." He crossed his legs the other way and pointed, with an oddly curved finger. "Pour yourself something." There was a low, glossy black cabinet in the corner indicated, atop which was a trayful of bottles.

"No, thanks," said John. He would have been embarrassed to struggle up out of the chair and, under his host's gaze, walk to the cabinet and make a choice among drinks he probably wouldn't recognize. Knowing nothing of life on this level — which was not exactly luxurious but it *was* sophisticated —

he believed he should remain cautious lest he be dismissed as a hopeless bumpkin.

Philbin continued to stare. Suddenly he showed a glorious grin and brought his long hands together. "We should celebrate! Make me a drink, too."

When the request was put that way, John could hardly fail to honor it. He rose with the anticipated gracelessness and went to the cabinet. As expected, several of the bottles bore labels that signified nothing to him.

He turned to Philbin. "What would you like?"

"Pernod," said his host, then, with an impatient movement of his knobbed wrist, "the green bottle . . . that's it. Now pour about an inch and a half into one of those tumblers. Then add some ice water from that jug — just till it turns milky. . . . Good. Now taste it."

The flavor was reminiscent of licorice, but strange and unpleasant. Having sipped of this one, however, he kept it for himself and made another for Philbin.

The editor smiled up at him when he delivered the glass. "May I call you — uh, what?"

"John."

"Yes, you did say that when you shouted up, didn't you?" He sipped at the Pernod. "I'm Jamie."

John had returned to the uncomfortable chair. "Uh," he asked cautiously, "is that a nickname?"

"No."

Tired of feeling so awkward in every way, John came right out and asked, "Aren't you Ross Philbin?"

"Ross had another appointment," said Jamie. "Anyway, I'm the fiction editor. He likes your story, of course, or we wouldn't have accepted it. But he takes my word for what's good in fiction."

After a few more sips, John began to get the point of Pernod. He hoisted the glass. "This isn't bad."

"In a more civilized place and time," said Jamie, gesturing with his own tumbler, "it would be real absinthe, wormwood and all."

John nodded. "I've written some other stories as well. I don't want to ruin my welcome, but if you'd like to see them . . ."

"As soon as we put this one in shape," said Jamie, who rose abruptly and left the room in a swift glide. He returned more slowly, wearing a pair of hornrimmed glasses and peering at the manuscript in his uplifted hands. "I've taken the liberty of deleting the first two pages and beginning in the middle of things."

He extended the sheaf of paper towards John, but stayed so far away that the latter, fearful that the butterfly chair would tip over if he leaned so far to the side, felt obliged to rise and take two steps.

John sat down and examined his story, the first two pages of which bore each a vast X in blue pencil, touching each corner of the sheet. Page 3 had not been excised in toto but looked radically rewritten, the interlinear spaces filled with blue handscript. He turned to page 4, of which an entire paragraph had been marked for deletion. He looked no further, but put his glass on the floor and stood up.

"I'm sorry," he said as coldly as he could. "I'm going to withdraw the story. If you want to publish your own work, why not just write something from scratch? You don't need a manuscript of mine."

Jamie made a sly smile. "I was just trying to help. You've got talent, but you lack discipline. All writers worth their salt begin that way and need the help of people like me. That's professionalism. If you reject all assistance, you will remain a tourist."

"No thanks," said John, going to the door.

Jamie came after him. "I hope you reconsider. I'm really eager to work with you!"

John again declined with thanks and turned to seize the doorknob. Jamie's hand swooped around his hip and closed gently on the lump of his genitalia.

John literally had to struggle for freedom against a man who was stronger than he looked.

He complained bitterly to Daphne that evening. "*You* got me into that."

"Well," said Daphne, "I could hardly have known."

"You ought to have been able to tell from reading the magazine."

She frowned. "I did read a couple of issues. I didn't see anything suspicious."

John sawed off and forked up a segment of rubbery frankfurter. He gestured with it before dipping it into the ketchup he preferred over the local mustard. "That's because all your favorites are fairies: Proust and Gide and so on."

What he really couldn't stand about her was that she suddenly wouldn't fight back, but rose above such mean matters, preserving herself for better things: putting in a full day's work, preparing to be a mother, and thinking about highbrow literature.

"This pansy wasn't even the editor-in-chief. I guess he's his boyfriend. Jesus."

Daphne contritely served him more cole slaw from the container in which it came from the delicatessen. She herself had quite a small appetite for someone who was pregnant: he thought such women were supposed to eat more than usual, but what he then assumed was his pride (and only in time to come understood was rather vanity) kept him from inquiring.

Two days later he got a letter from Ross Philbin.

Dear Mr. Kellog,

Will you please accept my apology for the unfortunate experience you were obliged to endure on Tuesday? Jamie
Quill, I'm afraid, while being a superb fiction editor, has a
nervous problem. Be assured we would be pleased to publish
your fine story exactly as you have written it, and in view of
the inconvenience you have suffered, raise the fee to $50, pay-
able on publication. This is twice our usual rate and at a time
when we are hard-pressed financially, but it should be taken
to represent our sincere apologies to you.

Furthermore, I hope I can persuade you to be my guest at
lunch on Tuesday next. If you agree, simply meet me at 12:30
at Yolanda's on Cornelia Street. Afraid I don't know the number, but it's in the book.

John was conquered by the note, and when the day came
he found the restaurant and entered it some twenty minutes
early. He waited at the bar while one by one all the tables
were claimed by other customers. Apparently there was only
one room in the establishment, and a modestly proportioned
one at that. The bar was only about eight feet long, with no
seating facilities whatever. Soon it too was fully occupied, and
next a second rank had formed behind the first. By one
o'clock Philbin still had not arrived, and as the bartender assumed a surly expression, John could nurse his glass of Pernod no further. He paid the tab: seventy-five cents, for God's
sake. He had brought along only two dollars. It was a good
thing he had not taken a table and eaten any food.

When he had maneuvered himself through the people
standing at the bar and was about to leave the restaurant, he
collided with the entering Jamie Quill, who poked an index
finger at him.

"John Kellog."

John acknowledged him with a cool nod. "I was supposed

to meet Ross Philbin here for lunch. I'm sure it's the right day, but he hasn't shown up."

"Ah," Quill said excitedly, "that's why I came! Ross alas is all tied up and can't get away. He sent me instead, with his apologies."

John could not help showing his disappointment, but Quill proceeded strenuously to seek his favor, using the most effective means.

"I thought we might talk seriously about your future. You know, you're such an exciting discovery that we're thinking of exploiting our opportunity: maybe devoting an entire issue of *Budding* to your work, several stories, along with assessments of your talent by some well-known critics, Maxwell Wholey, Louis T. Klein, people of that caliber."

John had never heard of these persons, but necessarily believed them to be renowned, and Quill was making sense today. Furthermore, he was not likely to make sexual importunities in a crowded restaurant.

"It looks like we'll have a long wait."

"Oh, not here," petulantly said Quill. "We never eat in this dump!"

John followed him out the door. Today Jamie wore a sweater under which was no shirt. The tips of both his elbows could be seen through the holes that had been perforated by long use. His feet were naked in strap sandals. Moving rapidly, he led John for several blocks and around more than one corner, eventually plunging into the doorway of another little restaurant of similar size to that of Yolanda's, as crowded, and with much the same aroma, though judging from the name, Au Milieu De, it was French.

Quill went to the bar, at which two places were suddenly made available by a pair of persons who departed for a table in the dining area.

"I'm on the wagon," said he. "But you get what you want."

John ordered a Pernod. Quill turned up his nose at it when it was delivered. "I'm on aitch two oh," said he, gulping at a tall iced tumbler. "Now," slapping his free hand on the bar-top, "let's get to work. I trust you know your story as well as I do: page eight, second paragraph, I really insist on deleting in its entirety. Paragraph three can get by with extensive re-writing." He thirstily consumed, in one long swallow, the remainder of his glass. "But I'm getting ahead of myself. The first two pages, really, should be moved from the beginning to the very *end* of the story! Just think, and you'll realize I am spectacularly right about this."

John had hardly touched his Pernod. Eventually he said, quietly, "Aren't you aware that Ross Philbin wrote me a letter promising to print my story without any changes whatever?"

Jamie Quill nodded judiciously. "I changed his mind."

John retained a calm exterior. "Why are you doing this to my story?"

The bartender had brought Quill a new glass of water, of which Jamie had already drunk a third. "Because I want to make it better!" he cried. "I want to display your talent in the best light possible. That's the point of *Budding*, to find and launch new people in the best possible way. And, believe me, Ross and I are authorities on that process. Look at Maynard Means, Harvey Speck, Timothy James Wine." He smiled angelically. "Timmy's work was a real mess. You had to dig to find the diamonds."

John had decided at least to pose as being more patient this time. He asked who Timothy Wine was, and Quill identified him as the winner of some literary prize that was presumably of great prestige.

"And it's not just the work," Jamie added. "Far from it! It's how it is presented. For example, we've decided to print your story as a prose poem, in stanzas of no more than three sentences each, separated by white spaces of varying widths." He gulped more water and almost screamed, causing some other people at the bar to glance their way in the mirror and the bartender to shrug. "No, I've got it! We'll do another marvelous story, by someone else, in the same way, in the spaces between the segments of yours: Willi Mülhausen's. They'll be perfect complements to each other. Willi's a young German protégé of Ross's."

John was very hungry by now, but he decided he was being so badly dealt with that he must forgo a free lunch. He was somewhat tipsy from the two Pernods, though certainly not sufficiently drunk to lose his temper in public.

"Sorry," said he, leaving the bar stool. "I really don't see much point in continuing this discussion."

Quill seized his wrist, and for a moment John believed he must once again fight for his freedom. But he was soon released.

"All right," Jamie said, showing a wide though somewhat asymetrical smile. "I thought I'd try. I know I'm right, but a deal's a deal. I'll print your story as written, every jot and tittle of it." He finished off his current glass of water. "Now, if you'll pay the tab here, we'll go and eat."

The bartender went to work with a pencil. "Okay," said he, "that's one Pernod and three double vodkas . . ."

It was now John who seized the retreating Quill. "I don't have the money for anything but my own drink," said he. But he was really more bitter about the hoax. "You told me you were drinking water!" He slammed his only remaining dollar onto the bartop and left the establishment: if it wasn't enough to cover his own part of the bill, let them call the police.

Quill overtook him several blocks later, and then only by having sprinted so strenuously that he could speak only in interstices between gasps.

"Please . . . I forgot . . . wallet . . . in other pants." He was sweating, and one dirty-blond lock of hair hung across his right eye. "So I left my Patek Philippe. Ross gave it to me for my last birthday. . . . Please don't be angry with me. I've had the most atrocious morning. At the moment I'm playing hooky from my analyst. I really need someone to talk to. Please come and break bread with me."

"Neither of us has any money."

"Home, I mean. The fridge is loaded with food. Really! It's right around the corner."

"All right," John said with conspicuous reluctance, "but I don't —"

"Oh, *please*!" Quill lifted his long-wristed hands towards the sky and started off at his usual rapid pace.

By this time John was so starved he had no alternative but to follow. At the apartment Jamie invited him into the kitchen, which was very generously proportioned when compared with the niches of both the places John and Daphne had called home in Manhattan, and handsomely furnished with a table the top of which looked like one large chopping block. Copper vessels hung from an overhead rack of ornamental ironwork. A honeycombed arrangement held countless bottles of wine, all properly on their sides, as John had once read fine vintages should be maintained.

Quill took a frosted bottle from the refrigerator and poured them each a glass. It was delicious stuff. John decided that it would be gauche for him to examine the label, so he did not do so. Jamie opened an unusually shaped tin, a kind of long wedge, of what he called just *foie gras*, without the "pâté": John was taking careful mental notes of everything new to him, should he need material for his future stories, even though by now he was feeling the effects of the alcohol.

Quill delivered a basketful of chunks of French bread. "Excuse me while I make the omelettes, which will be *fines herbes,* if that's okay with you. We're out of cheese, et cetera."

Of omelettes John had had experience only of "Spanish," so-called, covered with an acid tomato sauce, and the Western, containing diced ingredients difficult to identify, both dry and brown as leather, as prepared at New York lunch counters. Jamie Quill's product was lemon yellow, light and moist, and exotically though subtly flavored.

That was about it for the menu. No dessert was forthcoming, unless the array of brandies and liqueurs offered by Quill was intended to serve that function. Nor was coffee mentioned. Still, it had been one of the most interesting meals John had ever eaten.

And Quill was behaving impeccably, though by now he had drunk a great deal more than John, who was himself woozy. It was Jamie who brought up the matter of the previous visit.

"You deserve an explanation," said he, swirling cognac in one of those balloon glasses seen in the movies. "Obviously, from your story, I am aware that you are sophisticated in psychopathology. Well then! I am that type of heterosexual who has a need, under certain special conditions, to shock and disgust myself by entertaining fantasies of deviate activity."

What an extraordinary confession for a man to make! John had no idea of how to respond. He could hardly take offense: Quill wasn't making a pass at him. He shook his head and sipped some of the Grand Marnier he had requested purely because of its name. "That sounds like a real problem."

"I think it's probably due to my unusual powers of empathy," Quill said. "I'm quite a lecher, you know." He winked roguishly. "I do so enjoy mounting a wench and having at her with vigor. But no doubt all the while in some cranny of my consciousness I am putting myself in *her* situation." He made a startled, wide-eyed grin.

John found the grin somewhat disquieting, but as they were still seated at the kitchen table, he could hardly be in danger. He nodded and said, "Uh-huh. . . . Do you suppose I'll ever get the chance to meet Ross Philbin?"

Jamie Quill's smile turned ugly. "You would be sorry if you did! He's as queer as a three-dollar bill. He's not *our* kind of man. Don't think he'll want to talk about literature: he'll just see you as somebody to go down on."

"I thought you were friends."

"Actually," said Quill in a solemn voice, "we're enemies. I don't know why I still talk to him — yes I do: it's because he's got the money, whereas like you I have never been given anything. We're fighters, you and I." His stare was now fixed on John's nose. "Oh, *please*. I *must* have you!"

As the appeal was accompanied by no physical movement, John stayed seated. "I thought you just insisted you were not —"

Quill looked desperate. "I can't believe that came out of me! I must have a demon dwelling inside my head." He leaped to his feet. "I swear that men disgust me. Now be fair. Let me prove that conclusively." He loped out of the kitchen at high speed.

John sat there for a long time, though his internal clock was somewhat out of order owing to the alcohol he had ingested, and it may have been only a few moments. But Quill persisted in not returning, and at last John struggled to his feet and went to look for his host, if only to bid him a mannerly good-bye.

He tracked him to a bedroom. Quill had stripped. He was scrawny and seemed even taller when naked.

"Get your clothes off," he said levelly to John, "and I'll prove that the sight of your nude body will revolt me. I'm so confident that I'll make you a guarantee: if I become the least bit excited, I'll pay you a forfeit. Say that fifty dollars right now, instead of on publication of the story."

John suddenly received a magical insight, perhaps simply through having become unbearably bored with his own naïveté. "The fact is," he told Quill, "*you* are Ross Philbin, aren't you? . . . Thanks for lunch. Let's drop the idea of publishing my story, if you ever had any serious intention of doing it."

"Just a moment." Philbin (if it was he) seized a dingy pair of underpants from the chair where he had hurled them. He snorted. "I might have said don't go off half-cocked, had I not feared that you would misinterpret *that* too! You love to think the worst of me. Well so be it!" He dressed as swiftly as he had doffed his clothes, but then there were only three items of such. He went up the hall and into the front room, sat down at the glossy black table that only now John identified as a desk, and withdrew from a shallow drawer a checkbook the size of a magazine.

He wrote a check and gave it to John. The amount was twenty-five dollars, and the signature was "Ross Philbin."

"In a word," said Philbin, "I've bought the story. Now please leave. And kindly don't go about town saying I'm queer, because I'm anything but, as I think I've proved conclusively."

In the succeeding months Kellog wrote more stories but, having had enough of Philbin, sent them all elsewhere and sold none. Daphne began to swell and had to leave her employment, for in those days women whose pregnancies were showing did not work at jobs dealing with the public. In consequence, the Kellogs were running low on money. At length Daphne made a decision, though it was heartrending, to go home and live with her parents in upstate New York while she had the baby, and of course be prepared to return as soon as John was successful, for she insisted that he stay where most books and magazines were published. Though she could not help him as much as she had formerly done, she hoped to persuade her father to advance her a few dollars, of which she would send what she could to John. Her father had given her sister and brother-in-law the down payment on a house, but he was not a rich man; nor did he, she admitted, like what he had heard of John, whom he had not met.

Kellog had begun to regret that he ever became intimate with Daphne. And he simply could not entertain the idea of being a father. Yet he felt sorry for himself when he was left alone in a New York that had yet to grant him recognition. Getting a job was unthinkable: he could never write again if he had to squander the best hours of the day on earning a salary.

Then Philbin sent him the issue of *Budding* in which his story was printed. Though the worst of the assaults upon it contemplated by "Jamie Quill" had not been carried out, the text had been considerably altered: e.g., the first two paragraphs of the original were gone and rewriting had taken place throughout, usually for no discernible reason, "little" might well be changed in favor of "small," or vice versa, and "raised" to "elevated," and here and there John found the gratuitous use of words which were not part of his vocabulary, such as "sapient," "droll," "glabrous," and "canescent."

He was at work on a furious letter to Philbin when the phone rang. Speak of the devil.

Philbin said, "I've got sensational news. Someone very influential is crazy about your story and wants to meet you. We're booked for lunch tomorrow at Soulange. Twelve-thirty. Jacket and tie." He rang off.

John had seen the façade of the restaurant on his nighttime walks: it was a fancy place of which simply the name had aroused his hate and envy, but immediately his feelings changed. He belonged there, if invited. And he was ready to suspend judgment on Philbin's editing of his story.

Philbin, well dressed in suit and clean shirt and tie, was already at the table when John arrived. His companion was a slender, angular, dark-haired woman who looked well into her thirties.

"Meet Elaine Kis*sell*," Philbin said.

"Hi, John," said Elaine, giving him a sinewy handshake and, owing to her elongated jaw, a somewhat vulpine smile. She took one more deep drag of the cigarette currently in play, extinguished it in the ashtray, and lighted another with a nervous match.

"Elaine," Philbin said, "happens to be the best literary agent in town. She's very impressed by your story."

Elaine's hair was pulled tightly into a bun at her nape, so tight it made John feel even more uncomfortable than he would have been made by her face alone: to him a bony countenance, especially on a woman, signified severity, and when one was encountered on a character of his creation, its possessor tended to lack warmth, reflecting his bias in life. Despite what Philbin had said, he was wary of this person and suspected she would be critical of his work.

How astonished he was when after exhaling a great deal of smoke she said solemnly, "I want to see everything you've written to date. If it is anywhere near as good as this story, mister, you've got yourself an agent" — she brought her thick eyebrows together — "that is, if you want one."

He did.

Elaine urged him to be more ambitious and abandon those little ten-page stories, really sketches, that came so fluently from his typewriter: none went beyond the piece published by Philbin. It was time now for longer and more complex narratives, of which the subject would be not the lone sensibility but rather the social interplay of several and varied characters. When John confessed that at twenty-one he had not yet known enough real people on whom to base fictional characters, Elaine pointed out that he obviously came from a family made up of persons, he had gone to school at several successive levels, and he had surely had some experience with the opposite sex (she was not aware he was married, that being a state too unsophisticated to reveal at this point, if ever).

Without her encouragement he might have remained too squeamish to use intimates, relatives, and close associates as sources for his work. His father's little appliance-repair business had failed during the Depression, the poor guy had gone bankrupt and had never recovered emotionally or financially. An uncle was the town drunk, and his daughter was commonly known as the local bad girl with whom most young males had had their sexual initiation. His mother had a way of babbling foolishly and was notoriously stingy; he knew people laughed behind her back. But it was precisely that sort of dirty linen that Elaine urged him to wash in public. When he protested against what he assumed, given her commercial role, was vulgar sensationalism designed solely to make a buck, she asked him to reflect on the work of the masters of fiction, the Balzacs, Dostoevskis, and Stendhals, whose candid portraitures must have drawn on their families and friends.

He would have preferred Elaine not to be so cultured literarily (having had too much of that with Daphne) and to have been instead a procuress for mercenary hacks, for money was what he needed now, not mere assessments of his promise, but he had no other option, and anyway when she learned of his want, she was willing to extend him a series of loans that were modest each by each but in the aggregate reached about four hundred dollars before his next sale: to one of the better literary quarterlies, published at a university with a recognizable name and printed on thick, book-paper stock. The fee was less than a quarter of what he owed Elaine, but she was good enough to take only the agent's ten percent and let the loan ride for the moment, believing in his future as she did. And not only that. She took him to an expensive dinner to celebrate and then back to her apartment for Irish coffee.

"I told you," she said. "Strike blood."

The story was a portrait of his paternal aunt, Connie, who for literary purposes he called Marie and who was persistently unlucky in love. Even as a young girl, according to his mother, Connie was always being dumped by a guy for whom she had done everything. But in John's story Marie finally rebels against her own character, and it is she who hurts the boyfriend badly. Of course he proves to be the only decent man she has ever known — as she realizes once he is irretrievably gone.

"You've learned to penetrate where it hurts," Elaine said, her eyes slightly glassy. "That's good writing."

She had put at least as much whiskey in the drink as coffee; John had as yet never developed much taste for either. Nor did he smoke. Elaine lighted one cigarette from the butt of the last, and he came slowly to understand that though she was speaking as rationally as ever, she was physically somewhat drunk and showing a lack of coordination in her movements. Finally, lowering the glass cup with an intention of meeting the coffee table, she missed it entirely. Though the vessel did not break, the rug was drenched.

John lent moral support from above as she brought some dampened paper towels and knelt to deal with the mess. The whipped cream was especially troublesome, with more of it forced into the pile of the rug than was removed.

"I'd better wait till tomorrow," Elaine said at last. "I'm too woozy now." She put up a hand from the floor.

After a moment John realized he was supposed to take it. But he did not like to touch his agent, and furthermore the hand was probably sticky with coffee and cream. Yet she had been generous with him, and in fact the ending of this latest story had been suggested by Elaine, the fact being that he had found himself unable to go beyond a fairly literal account of his aunt's career in love.

He helped her up. It was the least he could do. But somehow it became the most. She lost her balance, to recover which she embraced him fiercely, thrust her tongue deep into his mouth, and moaned. The tobacco residue on her lips burned his, and he had never found her attractive anyway, not to mention that she was surely a decade and a half older than he, but he had not had any sexual activity since Daphne went home — and perversely enough, now that he was free to be as promiscuous as he had been in his fantasies of freedom, he had forgotten his desires — and almost immediately he responded now to Elaine.

That he was for the first time in a superior role, or anyway what he considered a situation of dominance (as it was she who had applied to him and he who mounted her), whereas she had had the upper hand in his career, a certain brutality characterized the fucking, for it was certainly that and not true lovemaking — as in fact it had been with Daphne as well. When he had been in love, with Cissy Forrester, he was impotent. From the perspective of later years, he was to recognize how characteristic had been that early equation.

Next morning he was embarrassed to wake up and identify his agent as the sharer of his bed — actually, *her* bed, and he was her guest. Elaine looked no younger in the morning light. He tried to come to terms with their now personal arrangement, and had just about decided discreetly to slip out of the sheets and into his clothing and steal from the apartment. But before he could act on this plan, Elaine's fingers stole over his thigh and into his groin, and he had no alternative but to relieve the resulting pressure.

They stayed in bed till well after noon, because it was Sunday, the only day as luck would have it that sex, love it though she did, could keep Elaine from her work. Between couplings he heard an account of her history of men. Elaine had been married twice but divorced only once. Though long separated from him, she was still legally attached to her second husband and in fact emotionally connected as well, in a complex way: as many of his attributes were objectionable to her as were to be admired.

Too exhausted in mind and body to listen carefully to this, yet not able to resist her hunger for him, which was even more desperate than that of Daphne, John remained, and only after some time did he understand that Elaine's second and still current husband was Ross Philbin.

"He's not all queer," said she, propped up on one elbow. "Far from it. But he does have that side, definitely. Imagine my shock when I found that out."

"Look," John said in some concern. "I didn't have —"

She waved her finger at him. "I know. He tells me everything, now that we don't live together any more. He always did keep a secret second place for his other life."

"As Jamie Quill?"

"That actually makes sense," said Elaine, whose position enlarged her nearer breast, though not enough. John really liked fleshy fair women of a vulgar culture, but invariably ended up with skinny brunettes who were brainy though emotionally vulnerable. "Ross's family would disown him if they ever found out. He picks up the most awful people sometimes. Imagine if they knew his background."

"Rich family?"

"Godamighty, yes." Elaine's voice tended to be husky, especially when she spoke with emphasis. "There's a skyscraper in midtown named the Philbin Building." Since their latest screw she had smoked an entire cigarette and now turned to fetch another from the bedside table. John's throat was sore from smoke.

"He certainly doesn't seem to spend much."

In what was intended as a considerate gesture, Elaine blew a blast of smoke over John's head, showing him the prominent cords in her neck. "He's horribly stingy. Do you know, I supported *him* for an entire year? I actually thought he was a starving poet."

What interested John most here was her obvious proclivity for supporting men. He had not been aware that such women existed until he met Daphne. Already in life he had met two such. He really didn't like the type; they made him feel uncomfortable though never inadequate. But he seemed to have no choice.

While Elaine was knocking the ash off her cigarette into a saucer on the bedside table on her side, he slipped out of bed.

She groaned. "You're going?"

"It's twelve-thirty."

She pouted. "But it's Sunday. I'll make us breakfast."

"I've got to work."

She fluttered her lashes at him, which called attention to her crow's-feet. "That's commendable, darling. But oh all right, come over here and let me kiss you good-bye."

When he arrived, she was sitting on the edge of the bed. Before he could bend down, she had leaned forward and taken his member into her mouth.

After a while she removed it to say, "My oh my, there's nothing like youth!"

He did not get back home until Monday morning. Scarcely had he finally forced himself to sit down at the typewriter when the telephone rang. Certain it was Elaine, and furious about the invasion of his privacy, he answered in sullen humor.

But it was Daphne, and she was overwrought. "Thank God! Are you all right?" It appeared that she had been trying to reach him for two days and by Sunday had attempted to get the aid of the New York police in determining whether he was still alive, but had been sidestepped. Knowing no one else to ask — in true New York style she had not met their neighbors — she had been about ready to fly in, swollen belly and all, to make a personal search.

"Oh, come on," John chided her. "I'm hardly the suicidal kind. Besides, my work is really going well." He told her of his latest sale.

"I guess you were out walking a lot."

"That's right. And Philbin took me to dinner to celebrate. He's settled down. He's really been a good friend to my work."

Daphne was silent for a moment, and then she said in a voice that seemed to be under restraint, "Look, John, I think you should come back here till the baby's born. I'm sorry, I can't send any more money. And then I really need your presence. My parents just don't understand. Nobody does. The neighbors think it's illegitimate!" She was growing more emotional.

"I can't," John said firmly. "I just can't. I'm about ready to break through. I've got influential contacts now. You don't have to send money. I'm getting regular advances from my agent. One of these days I'll send something to the slicks. Then maybe I'll be able to send something to *you* for a change —"

Suddenly his wife cried, "You're disgusting! You're being kept by that fairy, aren't you? You've become a male prostitute!"

He had heard that pregnant women easily become hysterical and made the mistake of defending himself on the charge, which was so outlandish that he could not believe she was being sincere in making it, not to mention that it could be said he actually was, in effect, being kept by Philbin's estranged wife, who as it turned out was not exactly estranged but was in some other category that obviously he could not define to Daphne without disclosing his association with Elaine.

Without warning, a disagreeable male voice came on the line. "You little pansy, I'll give you a good horsewhipping! Mother and I have always hated everything our girl has told us about you, but you're even a worse skunk than we thought."

John had yet to meet Daphne's father, who in snapshots was bald and pudgy. It was an outrage that such an ugly old mediocrity would have the nerve to speak in such a manner to one of the foremost talents in the latest generation of American writers, and he gave as good as he got.

"Go to hell, you illiterate slob." And hung up. He felt bad about Daphne, but then he always had.

In the ensuing months John wrote some more stories, and finally Elaine placed one of them with a slick magazine, the fiction editor of which rewrote every third sentence and provided another ending than the original version. John was angry about this, but Elaine took the editor's part and effectively made the point that the fee, fifteen hundred dollars, gave the payer thereof a certain authority in matters of style and form. Looking at the situation realistically, John had to agree, though with Elaine's extraction of her commission, what he got was really thirteen hundred and fifty dollars. Of course by now he probably owed her a goodly portion of the remainder as well, but he left it to her to keep an account of those things and do what she would about them. As it happened, she did nothing, but in view of the sexual service he rendered her, he was not notably grateful. The fact is that by now he had begun to assume that the monetary debt would be forgotten, as more or less had been the case with the money he owed Daphne, at least on his part.

He proceeded to write three more stories of the same sort as the one purchased by the magazine, and yet each was turned down by the man who had been so enthusiastic about the first.

"That's the way they are," said Elaine, shrugging. "It's hopeless to try to understand an editor's taste." She grinned self-indulgently. "God knows, I can't, and I used to be one!"

John was getting awfully tired of her, even in professional matters. It turned out that she hadn't told him that several book editors had written him in response to his story, but as the letters were sent him in care of her, Elaine had intercepted them.

"How dare you open my mail?"

"Come now, darling, that's my job. Yours is creating."

"What did they say?"

"They want a novel. That's always what they want. But you're not ready yet. Keep going with the stories. It won't take many more, maybe only two or three in good magazines, enough to show you're no flash in the pan. By then their tongues will be hanging out. We'll be able to make a nice deal on a novel."

"If anybody else gets in touch," John said coldly, "I want you to show me the letters. And I'd like to meet somebody for a change. I don't know anyone connected with writing or publishing, except you and Ross."

Elaine chuckled and said patronizingly, "How lucky you are!"

John was tired of writing stories. Continuing to produce them until several more were sold seemed an interminable labor. Why not put the effort into a novel? He had always seen that as likely at some time in the future, but if people were already clamoring for one . . . He needed a plot, a pretext. Forrester had once said in class that first novels were invariably autobiographical. In writing short stories John had avoided the one subject of intense personal reference, whatever it was he had felt for Cissy. He had now got far enough beyond it to consider whether it might have been rather a form of erotic enchantment than love — and of course the irony was that he had proved incapable at the moment the ideal became carnal. Then there was Daphne, whom he did not love and whom he had never desired. Were these the makings of a novel?

As soon was proved, indeed they were, and he was writing well when Daphne phoned with the news that she had had a miscarriage. Overwrought as she was, she was in no mood to hear his warning that negative intrusions from the real world might throw him into the celebrated writer's block, with disastrous results for the ambitious work on which he was at last successfully under way. When she hysterically threatened to divorce him, his only feeling was relief.

Elaine had now begun to take John along to publishing parties, at which she introduced him to certain specially selected persons amongst the crowd that always included a good many people of no utility, lesser writers and other inconsequential types, some of whom came for the free drinks and an illusion of literary fellowship, and if they deigned to learn for whom the party was being held, derided him or her and not even, if they drank enough, that quietly.

It was by such means that John met Calvin Cavanaugh of Foley & Nash, who was to be his first book editor; Gilligan Hurst, the best-known daily reviewer in the U.S.A., who, starting as a friend of his work, eventually became its most virulent enemy; and several other writers now or formerly represented by Elaine, among them George Binson, whose latest, assumed by his publishers to be another in his lengthy list of cult-novels, had proved to be a surprise best-seller; Molly Dye, who looked too beautiful to be a writer; and an English poet, now teaching at a local university, Peregrine Vole.

Binson had an unfriendly manner at the outset, telling John he had read the story in *Budding* and thought it pretty dull except for certain sentences that were plagiarized from his own novels. But when John innocently insisted that could hardly have been the case, for he had never read a line of Binson's, George's scowl became a grin.

"Good for you," said he. "In fact, I've never opened a copy of that fucking thing. Who wants to see who's up-and-coming? I'll go further: the wise writer never reads any of his contemporaries: either they're better or worse than oneself. If worse, why read them? If better, you'd only be envious, so why read them?"

Binson was at every party to which John ever went in those days, and they became the sort of friends who meet only at such gatherings and have no other sense of each other. What Binson got from John was a listener who would laugh at his cynicisms, which bored those who had known him for years, and all the more so now that he was making a lot of money. For John's part, he assumed, for a while anyway, that Binson dispensed a unique wisdom, e.g., claiming his recent novel had sold so well only because it was viciously attacked by Gilligan Hurst.

"But I'm out of luck for my next," he added, "given his practice of saying something good about the book that comes just after the one he's savaged."

When Hurst later wandered by, with his pasty complexion and baggy suit, Binson said, in a genial tone, "Fuck you, Gil."

To which the critic answered, "Come on, George, you know it's nothing personal." "Fuck you." Hurst shrugged and plodded on. Binson told John, "I don't want him to like me. It's the kiss of death."

Vole, the British poet, spoke in a voice with extreme rises and falls, he giggled while raising and compressing his already narrow shoulders, and when seated he often tucked one leg under a buttock in a quaint way. But when John mentioned as much to Binson, he was told, "Perry's not queer. In fact, he's quite a swordsman. He screws all his pretty students and gets away with it because he's a literary star. He's got the administration and the parents bluffed. If some young girl's mother complains, he quiets her with a fuck for herself."

When Elaine introduced John to Vole, the poet scarcely brushed his hand before turning away with no facial response apart from the twitching of a nostril. But later on, when the party had thinned out, and most of the guests who remained, including John, were at least partially drunk, Vole was not, or if he was, he didn't show it. And he was the only other person at the gathering who remembered John's name.

"Lookyeah, Kellog," said he, "Russ Philbin tells me you're a *damned* fine writer, and I'll take his wud for it. As it happens I cahn't read narrative prase — just cahn't fahsten my mind to it if it has characters who are suppased to be recognizable as *human* beins and things happen to them within some sort of plut."

John considered whether Vole was making fun of him. "Funny," he answered, "I haven't been able to read much poetry precisely because it *doesn't* usually have characters or a plot."

Vole nodded solemnly. His sandy hair needed a trim, and the points of his collar were bent upwards. "I'm familiar with that sort of thing, though it's always seemed so *curious*. Why is make-believe understandable while *reality* is nut?" He shrugged in the seemingly pansy style, his shoulders virtually touching his earlobes.

At first John believed that such a question was of a piece with virility masquerading as effeminacy — *viz.*, bogus — but when he got to know Vole better and not only respect but like him, he understood that the Englishman, as befitted a poet, was more theoretically minded than he. Kellog could admit to himself, though he was shrewd enough never to tell anyone else, not even Elaine, that his own primary motive was to become a celebrity in a wider culture than the restrictively literary stratum in which Vole was a known name though movie stars and statesmen would never have heard of him.

Not a hack of course, whose books were seized by the herd and devoured like some salty snack, but rather that sort of writer who is read for his penetrating depictions of society and the implications thereof, which will perhaps be of influence on public policy, e.g., as would pertain to the Negro, who was still relegated to the back of the bus in that day. American Puritanism with regard to sex was another such issue. Babbittry was everywhere still regnant, despite victory in another world war. John was embarrassed to have an Englishman like Vole hear President Ike's disjointed syntax. Stevenson, with his felicitous verbal style, got only the votes of superior people, which meant an overwhelming defeat. Sociopolitical interest was new to John but a concomitant of literary life in the city. In the first draft of *The Life and Death of Jerry Claggett,* the hero suddenly became a Negro at about the midpoint of the story. The idea worked perfectly, and the preceding chapters would be easy to fix, the differences between Negroes and whites being, after all, accidental and not of the human essence, and it really gave Jerry's hopeless love for Cindy another dimension, as well as removing it even further from the narrowly autobiographical.

He continued to keep the novel a secret from Elaine, but he found himself finally in need of someone else's reaction to the work-in-progress — with which he had to admit he was himself pleased to the point of ecstasy. All the same, it seemed too good to be true.

He showed his manuscript to Peregrine Vole, which he felt was not so presumptuous as it would have been had Vole not been a foreigner. He also disregarded Perry's announced disdain for fiction, but was furious all the same when the poet's response was less than enthusiastic. "With all respect, old fellow, this is twaddle. What would a sensible nigguh see in such a *silly* tart — unless of course he was a ponce!" The Englishman emitted his high-pitched giggle.

John was now certain Vole was queer. He slammed the phone down.

A few moments later the poet rang back. "Bloody tellyphone! I was all at once speaking into the *void*. As I was about to say, Jerry doesn't seem at all *Negro* except for being so identified *à propos de rien*. He seems to have had no experiences of whites-only facilities. Would there be no color bar in this small provincial university town? Would nobody even *scowl* at Cindy and him eating together in the restaurant? Then it would differ markedly from those I've known. Do you know I was sacked once, in Ohio, for having a bloody *drink* in public with one of my female students? Good job I wasn't colored into the bargain!"

By now John had cooled down, but he did say sullenly, "I forgot you don't care for fiction."

"Because whenever I read any, I am *invariably* distracted by such foolish questions as this. I'm much too literal. Forgive me! *Ectually,* it's quite an interesting story, and you've told it rather well."

He awoke next morning with the conviction that Vole was right about Jerry Claggett. Were he to make him Negro, he must return to the first paragraph and begin another book, furthermore, one that was not about himself.

Nowadays he slept at home as often as possible and not with Elaine, with whom he was subtly trying if not to break it off, then to tone down their personal association without threatening the professional. He needed Elaine for his career, but as time went on, her sexual appeal, never great, diminished to the degree that he feared soon he would find her downright repulsive, fascinated as he was by Molly Dye, the established novelist, another of Elaine's clients.

In age Molly was about midway between him and their agent. She had straight auburn hair that framed a faultless face. Her limpid eyes were remarkable: knowing, but generous all the same; and though she invariably wore loose clothing, her figure was probably the lush sort John favored. He did not even mind a certain plumpness. Elaine currently was looking more skinny than slender, perhaps even somewhat withered. It was more and more unpleasant to see her on first waking up in the morning, before her eyes were on but not before she had lighted the first cigarette of what would be the two-and-a-half packs she would inhale that day.

The problem with Molly Dye was that she was married and, to all appearances, happily enough, to Joseph P. Foley, who with M. Robert Nash owned the publishing firm that bore their names. Indeed it was the very house that John hoped would publish his novel, for he had observed that Foley & Nash books tended to get respectful reviews, and while he wished to become conspicuously successful, thus offering a target to all, he had a horror of being abused in print — as much as he enjoyed the hatchet jobs done by the critics on other writers: even, or perhaps especially on his friends, e.g., George Binson's current surprise critical and commercial success demonstrated that not everybody could be pleased simultaneously by any given novel: at the dentist's office John read, with a frank, involuntary smirk, an unattributed review in a newsweekly that called Binson's work in general that of a spoiled child, and in the example at hand, one that had furthermore noisomely soiled his diapers.

But Molly was younger, taller, and more robust than the powerful publisher who was her husband, a slight, short, and bald man in late middle age: she could hardly be satisfied by him in bed. Whereas amongst the other things done for John by Elaine Kissell was to train him to be an inexhaustible sexual performer. Simply being young was not, of course, sufficient, though it did supply the necessary physical capacity. But much instruction by Elaine (always gently and generously provided, so as not to shrivel that resolve which she would hearten) was needed before he could refrain from climaxing as soon as he could, always his practice heretofore in life. Nowadays it was routine for him to astonish himself with his endurance.

On the other hand he did not want Molly to see him as no more than a potential lover. In fact he was a better writer than she, who was greatly overrated. Her view was parochial, her characters being invariably educated married people living in either cities or in the immediate suburbs thereof and reading books, going to the theater, picnicking on wine and cheese, and having genteel illicit love affairs. John had actually forced himself to read one of Molly's novels, in preparation for his seduction of her, and its style tended towards preciousness, with its frequent resort to the subjunctive, "were she" and "should we," references to oloroso sherry and Pont l'Évêque cheese, and men who spoke in exactly the same idiom as the females and wore such clothing as espadrilles and hacking jackets.

Unfortunately, Molly persisted in ignoring him so thoroughly on at least three meetings, at two of which he was introduced to her as the most promising of up-and-comers, that it was likely she had not so much as heard his name. "I don't think she likes me," he told Elaine. "Molly's like that with everybody," Elaine replied. "Whenever she wins a prize, she just says 'Thank you' and sits down."

Two of Molly's novels had won literary honors; all three had sold well. These facts must be added to her eyes and full breasts as aphrodisiac to John, whose best access to Molly was provided by an invitation to dine, without Elaine (who was not as miffed as he had expected, for she could seldom be hurt by a lucrative client), at the handsome apartment belonging to Millicent Clegg, a wealthy young woman with whom George Binson was having an affair, and who in literarily social matters accepted his direction.

The meal was brought, course by course, by servitors and included several things John had never tasted before — e.g., an appetizer of poached eggs sealed in aspic, which when cut into exuded a still molten though cold yolk. He was seated between Molly Dye and a young woman whose name he had not heard and in whom, given the person on his left, he had no interest whatever.

"I've read your books," he said to Molly, as soon as he could, having been delayed by the arrival of filled plates and then the pouring of the wine, and added, "I like them a lot."

She put her glass down, said "Thank you," and turned to the man seated to her left.

But John patiently waited for his next opportunity and when it came said, "The names you give your characters: they're very striking. Xenia Smith, for example, and Russell Footling, Harvey Wilson Pucket, Glendora Green." He had consciously memorized the list. In truth such names annoyed him, he who in his own fiction preferred simplicity in this area, so as not to distract from the important issues.

Molly said levelly, "You have to call them something." Again she spoke to the person on her left, who responded with a murmur that rose and fell.

Obviously John was not getting anywhere. Next time Molly reached for her wineglass, he said, in a mixture of truth and falsehood, "I admire your novels, even if what I'm trying to say about them might not be the right thing."

Molly finally looked at him with those luminous eyes. "I'm afraid I don't respond well to compliments. I never know what to say about my work. After all, I write fiction so I won't *have* to say anything. My commenting on my own work would therefore suggest that it had failed." When she produced more than a polite mumble, the words came too rapidly, and she breathed as though having made some strenuous physical effort.

John was thrilled to believe that he had broken the ice, but when he was ready to respond, Molly again turned away to make what would seem animated chatter with the person on her left, a sallow, craggy-faced man wearing a plaid necktie. She spent most of the meal so occupied, and when dinner was over she rose quickly and, joining her little old husband, the powerful publisher, bade goodnight to the hosts and left the party.

John found the experience sufficiently chagrining as to make an early departure himself, without having spoken to anyone aside from Millicent Clegg, whom he thanked en route to the door.

"Oh," said she, "can't you wait till George is off the phone? Those Hollywood producers call at all hours, and usually for silly reasons."

"I really have to go." It seemed better to leave it at that: at the moment he was incapable of inventing some glamorous excuse. Millicent was young and rich and exquisite, with pale gold hair, a perfect nose, and a flawless complexion. She was obviously devoted to Binson, who had just published a critically successful best-selling novel that had been bought by the movies.

John was taken by surprise a week later when, at a reception for a visiting French man-of-letters to which Elaine took him, he was chided by Binson. "I seat you next to a lovely girl who has read your quarter-inch shelf of collected works and for some reason thinks you've got talent — and you didn't look at her!"

To apply "girl" to Molly was to alter its meaning. "I tried to strike up a conversation, but she had to rush home with that little bald-headed husband of hers."

"I'm talking about Lucinda Houghton," said Binson. "She's an actress, currently playing in Strindberg. She actually wanted to meet you." He snorted. "It must have been a waste of time to speak with Molly, who's an egomaniac as well as a raving bull dyke, and if you think you can get her old man to publish you by flattering her, you're in error. She uses her influence only for scribblers with pussies." He gestured with his empty glass. "C'mon, let's get a refill before somebody tries to introduce us to the visiting Froggy, who I'll bet can't wait to go back home and write maliciously of the land of the fee and the home of the knave."

Finding it unbearable to be without any money but that which he borrowed from his agent, John turned on the heat, writing all day and even some evenings, and completed his novel within only another few weeks. It had been his original intention immediately to show the finished product to Elaine. He was aware that she would be offended by his having written it in secret, but counted on the book itself soon to distract her from such considerations of vanity: it was a marvelous piece of work, about which he could be completely objective, for he reread it as though it had been written by someone else. The characters had a vivid existence of their own, and the emotions, always rich and authentic, at times were truly shattering.

It was really too exciting a triumph to take to Elaine and have corrupted by some selfish reaction of hers. He decided therefore to send out the manuscript on his own. Then he could confront her armed with a publisher's acceptance. She was much too professional to make trouble at that stage, at which point she could take over the monetary negotiations and earn her commission.

Because he had met Calvin Cavanaugh, a senior editor at Foley & Nash, at several parties, John's pride was such that he found it unpalatable to put himself at the mercy of the man. Therefore he got the name of another editor from Peregrine Vole. He had never met nor heard of this fellow, who worked at Turnbull & Sons, a firm not one of whose recent books he had seen though he had a vague sense that some classic practitioners with three names (perhaps William Cullen Bryant and/or Oliver Wendell Holmes) had started out under the imprint.

The letter he received from this editor was so vicious as to remove John's scruples against applying to Cavanaugh, who was at least a gracious man.

Dear Mr. Kellog:
    I'm afraid *The Life and Death of Jerry Claggett* needs more editorial work than we are equipped to do, given the problems of fundamental structure as well as those of character and in fact style. But thanks for letting us see it, and my respects to Perry Vole.

Yours faithfully,
Ralph Brandywine

Blaming Vole for causing him to be so humiliated, John henceforth avoided the Englishman.

Brandywine's rejection made it all the more advisable that Elaine be kept in the dark. John therefore took the courage to send the manuscript directly to Cavanaugh, with a brief note saying only, with fake modesty, that he had met him a time or two at big parties but did not expect to be remembered for *that*.

It was a good month before he heard from the editor. During this time John found he could not write at all, having (temporarily, he hoped) burned himself out on the marathon of his first novel. Not daring to run into Cavanaugh at this point, he stayed away from parties, but having nothing else with which to occupy himself, he began to drink heavily in private, sometimes in the now established squalor of his own womanless apartment, but more often at Elaine's, to which he had a key and where he would go when he knew she was elsewhere. The latter practice led to bitter quarrels, for while she did not begrudge him the booze, she greatly resented his finding her home attractive only when she was absent from it. John's efforts at discretion went for naught, for the doorman was her spy.

When for purposes of mollification he took Elaine to bed, the alcohol in his system suppressed his ability to perform. This kind of delinquency was the only one amongst the human frailties that Elaine, the soul of generosity in every other area, found truly unforgivable. He had not suspected what a harpy she could be, and when she impugned his virility, he could not forbear from telling her that his failure might rather be due to her advanced age.

Therefore by the time Cavanaugh at last reported on the novel, John was no longer represented by Elaine Kissell, but he owed her fifteen hundred dollars, three times the advance offered him by the editor and then only on the condition that he was willing to do extensive work on the manuscript under Cavanaugh's direction.

Calvin Cavanaugh was the most famous editor of his day, having first published a number of the writers who were celebrities to persons who read books. George Binson had started out with him but left after the first novel, when he was approached by another house with a more generous contract. According to Binson, F&N's tightfistedness was notorious: "Cavanaugh will pretend it's Foley's doing — that if Cal had the money it'd be a different story. But they have a conspiracy going, each blaming the other while in perfect agreement underneath it all. When you finally catch on to that, they'll both blame Nash, whom nobody's ever seen and may be supposititious. Cal's never forgiven me for leaving them, but amusingly enough, Foley's been cultivating me since I hit it big with a book published elsewhere. That's the only fundamental distinction between the ed-in-chief and the publisher at any firm: the latter owns the company and thus has more respect for money, and therefore is the one worth cultivating."

Cavanaugh's desk held a lot of papers in no arrangement that was apparent to the visitor. An open window not far away kept these things agitated, but the editor provided nothing by way of anchor until, having shaken Kellog's hand, he lowered a buttock onto the stack at the nearest corner.

"I thought it funny that you sent the book directly to me rather than through Elaine," said he, gesturing towards a chair. "Because I had just seen you with her at a party. Usually there's a break-up before that happens. But I understand this time the row happened afterward."

"You know about it?"

"Elaine loves to whine about such matters."

Then it had happened before with her clients. Kellog felt

at once disgusted and also relieved that he now had no great moral reason to be quick about repaying what he owed her.

"Don't feel bad," Cavanaugh added ungallantly. "I too have had my moment with Elaine. There was a time when she cultivated editors, but that was eons ago, when we were all so young."

Therefore Kellog already disliked Cavanaugh before the editor even mentioned the novel. When he heard Cavanaugh's plans for *The Life and Death of Jerry Claggett,* he could have pushed him out the window.

The version of *Jerry Claggett* published two years hence was a collaborative product. During this time Kellog got no financial aid beyond the niggardly advance from Foley & Nash and maintained himself precariously by occasionally selling a story; taking a series of male roommates, with each of which he soon quarreled; and sponging off Binson, who was opposed to lending money and therefore extracted some service for every penny: typing, running errands, and once even the writing of a preface to a collection of short stories by past masters (Anatole France's "Our Lady's Juggler," Robert Louis Stevenson's "The Sire de Malétroit's Door," and others) for which Binson, with his new prestige, had been commissioned; it amused him to sign Kellog's text and give half the fee to its author, who in its composition had paraphrased generously from the standard authorities available at the Public Library.

Cavanaugh's assaults on the original manuscript — perhaps as much as forty percent of the text was discarded outright, with the rest extensively rewritten — were justified when the novel became a blockbuster in sales, the main selection of a book club, and a favorite of the popular reviewers. Soon several motion-picture companies were bidding against one another for the screen rights.

Kellog had hated the book after its violent molestation at the hands of Cavanaugh, but when the favorable notices began to appear he felt proprietary about the work and murderous towards the few critics who disparaged it while adoring those who wrote praise, chief amongst whom was Gilligan Hurst, whose opinions appeared three mornings per week locally and were syndicated nationwide. There were those who believed that Hurst could singlehandedly make or break a novel though perhaps he was not quite so influential with nonfiction, for owing to personal impatience he regularly damned all biographies of more than four hundred pages, which meant most of them, but some sold well regardless. When *Jerry* reached the best-seller list its author forgot that Cavanaugh had done much more than correct a few misspellings, and when the book arrived at No. 1 and remained there for fifteen weeks, Kellog believed it a classic, in the creation of which he received no human aid.

Though he had been tendered only a five-hundred-dollar advance, Foley & Nash at first resisted his efforts to get his hands on any of the money accumulating from club fee, hardback sales, and now a paperback deal for an enormous sum, insisting that legally none of it was due until the first royalty period, a year hence. George Binson recommended that Kellog use the services of the noted literary lawyer, C. Paul Kleinsinger, his own counsel, who in fact also acted as Binson's agent now, replacing Elaine Kissell.

On Kleinsinger's application Foley & Nash released a sum of money for Kellog's use, but they did impose a 4 percent interest on the sum, contractually premature as it was, and the lawyer himself extracted a large fee. Nevertheless, Kellog liked being represented by Kleinsinger, a waistcoated dandy who drove a vintage Rolls-Royce, and decided to use him as his literary agent, an appointment to which the lawyer agreed, having set his commission at 25 percent of all earnings.

As advance on Kellog's next novel, Kleinsinger demanded more than the president of the United States was paid at that time, asserting that he could get still more from any other publisher in New York. F&N countered with an offer of less than half as much, and pointed out that in the contract for *Jerry Claggett* they had been granted first refusal rights for its successor. This was where Kleinsinger came into his own and earned the gluttonous commission: he found so many clauses in that contract which were of dubious legality that F&N's own lawyers predicted possible litigation that might well go on for years, given Kleinsinger's appetite for such, and they recommended that some accommodation be made, subsequently rewriting the standard form.

Kleinsinger eventually settled for a sum that was three-quarters of the original demand, half payable on Kellog's submitting an outline of his second novel, and in addition there was to be a higher royalty rate and a greater proportion of the paperback fee than the standard one-half. *Jerry Claggett* was still selling well as this contract was signed, but Joseph Foley was bitter about the deal, from which he had stayed physically away, Cal Cavanaugh serving as front man. At dinner that evening, at home in the country, he denounced John Kellog as an insolent puppy too big for his breeches, and Molly Dye, looking at him with her heavy-lidded violet eyes, asked, "Who?"

Kleinsinger also dealt with the lawsuits brought against Kellog by Daphne; Elaine; and a man named Helmut Krantz, of Hershey, Pennsylvania, for allegedly using Krantz as model for the husband in *The Life and Death of Jerry Claggett*.

"How can he do that?" Kellog asked his attorney. "I've never met nor heard of this guy, and never even gone through his town."

"Justice is blind," Kleinsinger murmured with satisfaction, his silver hair looking so perfect it might have been sprayed on.

"But it's *fiction*. It didn't happen. I mean, I'm not being sued by the real guy I was thinking of."

"Real guy?" Kleinsinger asked, not without pleasure.

John told him for the first time about Forrester and Cissy.

The attorney made a series of rapid, happy nods. "We don't have to worry about the girl: she's obviously an illiterate trollop, who could be easily dealt with in any event. As for Forrester, you say he's a writer. Who's his publisher?"

"I guess he didn't have one," said John. "When I knew him, a few years back, he hadn't ever been able to finish a novel, and I'll bet things haven't changed since."

Kleinsinger brought his manicured fingers together and smiled.

Since Foley & Nash would be co-defendants with Kellog in any libel suit, Cavanaugh agreed to track Forrester down and, pretending to have admired his published stories, offer him a modest option on a novel. But poor Forrester, as it turned out, had been accidentally killed, down at the little college in West Virginia at which he had lately been teaching (hit-and-run driver), whereas Cissy was not only alive and well but lived in southern California, where on reading the novel she found a celebrated attorney who was eager to take her case. A jury agreed that her prospective career in the motion pictures had been adversely affected by the degrading portrayal in Kellog's book and awarded her a sum in damages that even when subsequently reduced by two-thirds remained substantial, and this time Foley & Nash's lawyers outmaneuvered a Kleinsinger suddenly on the decline (he was about to be disbarred and sent to jail for his part in a real-estate scandal on Staten Island), and Kellog had to foot most of the bill alone. Scarcely had he begun to make money when much of it was taken from him.

For the next several years he could write only incoherently or not at all. He began to drink heavily beginning at noon and continued drunk until he went to bed fourteen or fifteen hours later. On publication of *Jerry Claggett* he had taken an expensive apartment on the Upper East Side and had it decorated by a demonstrative man with a penchant for swagged lamps. Kellog was never comfortable there when alone, yet remained desperately lonely even when he threw parties, as a result of which the place was soon in tatters, the rugs and chairs stained. The neighbors complained about the noise of these events and sometimes called the police, who after a few such visits threatened (as they could in those days) to kick his faggot ass if they were summoned again, and having only just smoked his first joint at the time, he lacked the moral certitude to protest effectively, though he was anything but queer, nor were his guests, who were always in the bedrooms, fucking the sort of girls who were attracted to the literary life of the day.

Eventually these pleasures came to an end, for at last his publishers lost patience and threatened to take him to court unless he submitted a complete manuscript of the novel for which they had extended him an advance so many years before.

Under such pressure Kellog managed to keep away from the bottle for the first half of each day and, blanched of face and with shaking fingers, write a second novel. Once begun, this narrative proceeded so smoothly as to lead him to wonder why he had taken so long to get down to work. Again his life provided the situation and characters, with the difference that this time he would not draw so naïvely and literally on himself but rather make his hero a playwright. The supporting roles were all neat equivalents, a director having rather the moral weight of an editor; producer — publisher, and so on. He dropped the deserted wife and the importunate female agent: "Charles Koenig" was an unmarried satyr and was represented professionally by a hairy-nostriled, aggressive man named Sy. And "Sally Day," the prominent actress and wife of producer "William B. Dolan" was rather a nymphomaniac than homosexual, and Cal Cavanaugh was at least partly concealed in the character of director "Stan Stanley," a tasteless man when it came to stagecraft and in life a brute to women as well as an anti-Semitic bigot (Koenig and he quarreled incessantly and once came to blows in Sardi's men's room, a fight that the playwright won, as he prevailed in putting his own version of the play on the boards against Stanley's vicious opposition).

The novel was necessarily rejected by Foley & Nash, freeing Kellog to go elsewhere, though he must refund the advance before another publisher could bring out the book. Beyond that, Cavanaugh warned him that Foley might well consider bringing a libel suit if the book reached print with the same characters that appeared in the manuscript.

By now Kleinsinger was himself being tried, with his associates in the real-estate scheme, for conspiracy to defraud, and Kellog was acting as his own agent. His second novel, *Koenig's Ordeal*, was turned down by all the major publishers, and when it was finally accepted, by a small house named Karney Byrne & Co., the advance was no more than a fifth of what was owed Foley & Nash. Kellog was convinced that once in print it would sell at least as well as had *Jerry Claggett*, having more explicit-sex scenes (with the particulars that were now coming into vogue as censorship was on the wane) and a lot of authentic inside dirt on Broadway, furnished him by Lucinda Houghton, the actress he had ignored at the dinner when Molly Dye sat on his left. (Kellog provided the pretext for one of Lucy Houghton's simulated attempts at suicide, which luckily by then he had learned were routine in every one of her frequent love affairs and invariably brought on when her current companion failed to be as ardent as she in political passions.)

But *Koenig's Ordeal* was loathed by the reviewers. Some deplored its style. ("Kellog seems to have written this with a pen stuck between his toes. Characters are usually given two adjectives, no more no less, by way of description: e.g., 'short fat Paul Wayne'; 'slender, grim Mona Bingley'; a policeman is 'robust and ruddy'; one actor is 'unshaven and haggard,' another, 'trim and rangy,' and on and on. But occasionally he assigns only one attribute to a personage and refers to it exclusively and incessantly. Jenny Langsam's red hair is never forgotten for more than a paragraph, though we're never told another thing about this woman, not even an approximation of her age.")

Other critics found the novel morally offensive. ("Is *everyone* in the Broadway theater a greedy, unscrupulous sexual degenerate? Kellog's insufferable hero is the sole exception, and after some exposure to him, you long to be back with the scoundrels"), and there were some who attacked the book as a catastrophe in both substance and form. Gilligan Hurst, the most extravagant of the admirers of *Jerry Claggett*, was this time the most vicious of detractors, libelously (in Kellog's view, though not in the opinion of any of the attorneys to whom he applied) questioning the sanity of the publisher who would put such a piece of trash in print and in effect calling the author downright depraved. George Binson found it hilarious that Kellog was not aware that Hurst's wife had been a Broadway actress in an earlier era of genteel drawing-room comedies, when those of the legitimate theater, perhaps to differentiate themselves from tarty movie stars, at least kept up a decorous front.

Koenig's Ordeal sold nowhere nearly as many copies as its predecessor. During the ensuing decade, those who admired Kellog's work were ever more difficult to find, and after his third book, a short novel about divorcing a lesbian wife, which was more or less ignored by the reviewers and purchased by few readers, he found himself for a long time unable to complete a fourth. The project to make a movie of *The Life and Death of Jerry Claggett* had long since been abandoned.

Kellog now taught "creative writing" at a suburban college, a job he had been given on the recommendation of Peregrine Vole, who after returning such good for the evil things John had said about him, finally went back to Britain, where he published a collection of lyrics that was lavishly admired throughout the English-speaking world, and some said he was a likely candidate for the next Nobel Prize. Kellog still had not read more than one or two examples of Perry's verse, which made no sense to him, and he assumed that Vole's high reputation was due almost solely to the Englishman's skill at literary politics.

Cal Cavanaugh retired and wrote a widely praised memoir of his many years as editor, in which all his writers were named, including a number who had never distinguished themselves either critically or in sales. With one exception: John Kellog went unmentioned.

After scanning the index twice again, Kellog threw the book into the wastecan beneath his desk, that receptacle into which so much of what he had written in recent years had been discarded hot from the typewriter, and spoke in the direction of Candy Budge, the student who was currently living with him out of wedlock, in a more enlightened time than his own era as undergraduate, for all the real good it did him: had he married Candy it might have been easier to get rid of her. As it was, this spoiled daughter of a prosperous family paid her share of the rent and food and thus felt licensed to bring other male friends to the apartment, often while he was in one room, writing, and go to bed with them in another. Not to mention that she was a godawful slob who clogged the washstand with her hair and the toilet with tampons and almost immediately on moving in had exchanged her previously sunny disposition for a sullenness occasionally relieved by tantrums. She was also given to belching loudly, something he had never known another woman to do, and scratching her crotch like a baseball player, which was appropriate enough given her style in bed, as manifested during the short period during which they had screwed, or tried to, for though sex with an eighteen-year-old was aphrodisiac in the mind, the physical experience of it failed to stimulate Kellog's genitals when Candy immediately insisted on his remaining supine while she vigorously entertained the illusion that it was she who penetrated him. Her odd idea of arousing him was to fend off his attempts to caress her and then painfully claw at his testicles.

And as elsewhere, so in bed: no matter what he did, however obsequious, it was by her assessment "degrading to women," then a new nonce-phrase. When it got to the point that Candy blamed *him* for her "rape" at the hands of a husky football player she had brought home to copulate with in her own style, Kellog began to pack his possessions into the liquor cartons he had procured for that function.

Having no formal credentials or even a basic degree, he had never throughout the years acquired tenure in his job, but rather was hired by biennial contract, which meant he ever skated on the thin ice of academic politics and found it necessary to ingratiate himself with whoever served as chairman of the Department of English except at those times when a cabal of professors was working clandestinely for the ouster of a particular chairman disliked by his colleagues for espousing critical theories repugnant to them: in such cases Kellog had to choose the side which would emerge victorious though secretly despising all, and this constant drain on his faculties left him with insufficient resources for his own writing.

Therefore it proved to be a blessing, though not at first apparent as such, when after some years of correct choices, he at last put his money on a losing nag, and when T. Barton Spahn, a middle-aged Freudian, was outmaneuvered by a clutch of younger people who dressed as farmhands and called for a literature between which and social studies there was to be no distinction, Kellog's contract was not renewed for the following academic year.

But finally he had another usable theme for a novel: an affair between a college teacher of a certain age and a student two decades his junior. The time proved precisely right for such a narrative, youth being on a national rampage; adults, especially when male, either cowered in dread of denunciation by enraged striplings or seethed with resentment against parasites who had never earned a paycheck, who indeed had been reared and were still supported by those they attacked. In the original version "Martin Canning," a widely respected novelist who, because of an instinctive attraction towards youth with its hope and vivacity and artistic potential, takes a post as a creative-writing instructor at Eastern State College and not long thereafter falls ardently in love with Clarissa St. James, a very young woman, gorgeous, statuesque, and superficially charming but, as Canning is eventually to discover, fundamentally of mean spirit and no feeling that is not ruthlessly self-concerned.

Though publicly successful, Canning in private has been the victim of more than one female in the past. Owing to his persistent need for love (and an enormous capacity for returning it) and learning nothing from his past mistakes, he puts himself at Clarissa's callow mercy and inexorably (what with rock concerts, *au courant* wardrobe and hairstyle, "demonstrations" that were sometimes tear-gassed) becomes an object of scorn by persons of all generations but more poignantly by the "kids" with whom he had thrown his lot. He begins to think of suicide . . .

The dénouement was subject to alteration. After all these years away from publishing, he could no longer trust his own judgment, and anyway his only success, as he could now admit, had been the novel so extensively edited by Cal Cavanaugh. Therefore when he submitted the current MS to Trudy Bolger, a current senior editor at Karney Byrne, whose name he had found in *Literary Marketplace*, he felt it necessary not only to explain that he had been a KB author back in the Dark Ages when she (who he imagined was slender, winsome, and poetic) was probably a toddler, but he would welcome any suggestions for revision of any part of the narrative, including the ending.

Six weeks later, Trudy invited him to come into the city, though not for lunch, just to the office. In person she proved to be not as young as he had assumed, oriented to students as he had been for so many years. Trudy was stocky and unusually short (perhaps not even five feet tall). Her graying hair was curly and cut very close to reveal large ears.

"Here's the situation," said she, in the melodious voice that on the telephone had given him the impression of quite another person. "You got a story to tell all right, but the characters are all wrong for today's reader. She doesn't want to empathize with the problems of this Marvin."

"Martin."

Trudy shook her square face. "The whole point of view must be changed . . ."

Kellog went through many emotions before the issue was settled, but over the course of the next year, living in a furnished room on unemployment insurance and wretched fees for hackery, including book reviews in which he disparaged contemporary novels, he gradually with many rewritings transformed Martin Canning into the villain of the story: a monster of vanity whose predominant emotion towards himself was pity; to others, envy or contempt. Clarissa emerged as a sympathetic personage, a young woman of vivacious intelligence, generous to those deserving compassion, defiant towards misusers, even witty without a touch of malice. And, as Candy Budge hardly provided such a model, this was a triumph of original characterization all of which was Kellog's achievement, for Trudy had no hand in the creation of a woman she still considered as being far too passive.

When published, the novel received all manner of notices. Some, more or less favorable, were by persons who had never read his books of years before but pretended, welcoming him back, to have missed his presence on the scene. As always there were critics who had not actually read the one at hand and rather reviewed outlandish fantasies of their own making, finding in the novel only that which was everywhere in creation their respective exclusive concerns: e.g., the identification of transsexualism, the smelling out of crypto-fascist sympathies, the denunciation of the culture of television. But there were gratifying reviews as well, written by spiritual soulmates of whose existence he had been hitherto ignorant, including even one, from a New England paper and signed "Nancy Parkman," making virtually every point he had made to himself in private reflection.

He wrote a note of seductive thanks to Nancy Parkman, with whom he was already in love, and received an answer from his ex-wife. It took him a while to digest her letter and then the review, reread in the light of this new information.

Dear John:

I so much enjoyed using a WASP name that I might keep it as my permanent nom de guerre. The review of *Canceled Male* was its first appearance. Believe it or not, I had delicate feelings about revealing my identity to you, though I welcomed the opportunity to distinguish formally between the author and his work. My admiration for the latter, which was evoked by that first story of yours in Forrester's class so many years ago, has never failed, though it was sorely tried by *Koenig's Ordeal* and then even more by Number Three, which I despised so heartily for the sloppiness of its writing and its provincial schoolboy's version of "sophistication," that I can't remember the title — only that it was taken, God help us, from some awful line of Carl Sandburg's.

After much deliberation on the matter, I have decided that you probably don't really know what you're doing, but that when you speak literally, candidly, of your honest emotions, you have a natural eloquence that at its best is superior to most, if not all, artifice, but even more important, when you retain a sense of proportion and don't try to achieve effects beyond your reach, your literary voice can be called mellifluous.

> Sincerely,
> Daphne Kleemeyer

In the ensuing years, his ex-wife quickly rose from reviewer for the local paper in the college town where she lived (and had become a tenured professor of English) to a contributor to national periodicals and finally to write a tendentious, influential book of the feminist persuasion. Kellog never met her again nor exchanged another letter, but Daphne was frequently to be seen on television panel shows. She was better-looking now than she had ever been, at least to him, as a young woman, her features handsomely defined, the touch of gray just right for her somewhat wiry hair. As Daphne had never remarried, John found it easy to suppose that she was Sapphic — until she published an account, obviously autobiographical, of how a middle-aged woman can live successfully with a male lover half her age. This work sold extraordinarily well and was nationally praised for its "courage," which Kellog bitterly recognized as the code-word used when something essentially obscene was meant.

Not only did he have his private motive in this judgment, but in general age had gradually turned his nose blue. He whose second novel had so reveled in graphic accounts of cunnilingus and fellatio now was revolted by movies in which those activities were so much as given their vulgar names, and when deviate sexuality became commonplace in TV discussions, and was not only sanctioned but even, except by illiterate fundamentalist Christians, admired, Kellog was first outraged and next, all of a sudden, rendered devoid of any energy whatever.

The culture had simply become alien to him. He had no place in it, and with *Canceled Male*, the sales of which, despite the several good notices, were meager, he had exhausted his supply of subjects. Trudy Bolger was no longer prompt to return his calls and when she did respond, it was often in the form of a noncommittal note. He had no friends both extant and usable. Perry Vole was dead (without the Nobel Prize), having been rather older than he had looked, and George Binson had married a wealthy woman and taken up the pursuits of her milieu, racehorses and entertaining America's Cup competitors, and was now too cynical, or genuinely too pompous, to remember he had once been a writer: in any event, he failed to answer Kellog's appeal.

After all the years that had gone by, Kellog believed it was likely that his caricature of Elaine Kissell in *Koenig's Ordeal* was no longer any more vivid to her than it was to its author, and he wrote her an affectionate old-times'-sake message, which he intended to be a prelude to returning to her as client. But her memory was long-lived and of an unwarranted bitterness. How, over the years, could she fail to see any humor in his depiction of her strenuous efforts to achieve vaginal orgasm or in quoting her literally on an uncomfortable interuterine device?

Finally he was so desperate as to contemplate offering himself belatedly to Jamie Quill, but no longer as young as he once had been, he could not have borne, at this stage of the game, to add that kind of rejection to the others he had accumulated.

He recognized, with a certain reluctance but little true regret, that the time had come when he should, in all decency, be expunged.

──── IV

"**H**EAVENS," said the little man with mock dismay, "could it have happened that your life as an author wasn't to your satisfaction?"

Hunsicker was sheepish. "It's easy, once out of it, to see how awful Kellog was, how badly he treated Daphne. He couldn't be blamed for finding her unattractive, but it was contemptible of him, in view of that, to accept her help. Yet, having said as much, I must admit I find more embarrassing his addiction to Cissy Forrester." He hesitated for a moment, and then added, "Maybe it's not to my credit, but I find it more humiliating to be the victim."

"What an odd thing to be apologetic about," the little man said. "I hope you're being hypocritical." He rubbed his nose.

"In any event, you have nothing to worry about: it never happened."

"As a boy I had a crush on the first girl in class to develop visible breasts: that was in the later years of grade school. Like Cissy, she was blonde, but that was the only resemblance. She dropped out of high school as soon as she was sixteen, got married, and had many children in quick succession. By the time she was twenty, those to me famous breasts, once so high and firm, had fallen, her teeth were discolored, and the once golden hair was — well, it's cruel even to remember, especially since by then she had long since ceased to mean anything to me — if she ever did: I don't think I exchanged ten words with her in school. It was a big class, and anyway I was too shy. . . . I never knew anybody who could have been Daphne. I met Martha in college. She was really beautiful, with those big brown eyes and that hair, but at five feet ten and a half she scared off most guys. In heels she towered over the boys of that day. Even in flat shoes she was half an inch taller than I, but it never bothered me. She always made me feel like a man."

"You had doubts?"

Hunsicker smiled. "No. I always liked girls. It was just that so many of them in those days were somewhat disagreeable in manner: snippy, if I might use an outmoded word. Maybe it was the style of the time. You can see it in old movies: at first the female acts as if she's offended by the most decent, respectful attention on the part of the man, and is positively nasty to him. Presumably this was part of a technique by which she could eventually lure or trick him into marriage — speaking from the man's point of view. On the woman's side — or so I'm told — the male's sole interest seemed to be in getting her into bed by any means, without assuming any obligation whatever. I always hated that game or war, and never played or waged it. And neither did Martha. I never made an actual pass at her, and for her part, after we had dated most of one whole term and I was a Thanksgiving-weekend guest at her parents' home, she crawled into bed with me one night — after all, I *was* sleeping in her room."

"Very tender," said the little man. "But it hasn't ended happily."

Hunsicker cried, "Not because we did anything wrong! Not because we haven't cared for each other." It was not something that should be argued about, though, whatever the provocation. It was clear enough why he had to do what he was doing. "But it's really hard to manage without her. I haven't been on my own for three decades. I have to be a man now without her help. That's why it's gone bad every time: I become a weakling in the absence of the right woman."

"You're not accusing yourself of uxoriousness, I see," the little man said. "Your phrasing is nicely done." He leaned back in his complaining chair and shrugged. "It's your life, to make of it what you will."

"But it really is life, once I begin to live it, and what I want to make of it is not a thing of my will: I can't create to order the people with whom I come in contact. They're all excruciatingly real, and therefore independent, pursuing their own destinies. They're not the marionettes of wish-fulfillment fantasies."

"You've had such?"

"I'm still capable of them at this late date, and they're easier to manage nowadays, in the degree to which they have become unlikely of achievement, in fact, impossible. . . . My idea of a desirable girl has not changed in forty years, though the girls certainly have. So what I lust for I suppose is still Ruthie Breese, that little blonde from my adolescence, just as she was then, just as I was then."

The little man spun his chair around and fetched the piece

of paper from the cubbyhole. With the stub of a pencil he blackened out the words that presumably had sanctioned John Kellog's authorial career.

"I take it you want to try again?"

"If I haven't been morally acceptable as yet, at least I have acquired experience as what not to be and do. Jack, Jackie, and John were so horribly selfish. I hope I've got that out of the way by now. I want an opportunity to redress the balance."

The other sighed.

"All right," Hunsicker said. "I know that sounds facile. But I'm serious."

"What is it to be, then? Doctor?" The little man grinned. "Don't tell me clergyman!"

"I'm scared that I'd be one of those clerical frauds, shaking down his congregation to buy whores. Or the kind of doctor whose specialty is annually exchanging last year's Bentley for a new one, while fending off dying paupers."

"You're becoming cynical."

"For good reason," said Hunsicker. "There is some perversity to this process that I can't quite figure out. The best of intentions get twisted . . . as I suppose they always are in danger of doing in life." He raised his chin. "Nevertheless I am convinced that I can do better."

"In doing good," said the little man in his flattest voice, and prepared to scrawl a notation on the paper.

THE CALLS that came in to the radio station were first "screened" by the producer, a young woman who took the first name and a statement of intent from each caller and sent the information along to Kellog's computer terminal, with the number of the button he must push on the telephone console to bring the person's voice into his headset and also onto the air.

He now activated Line 3 and spoke into the little mouthpiece that curved around from the earphone. "Jonathan Kellog. Good morning, Harriet. How may I help you?"

"Oh, Doctor . . ." Harriet wept awhile in a muffled way that seemed authentic. After years of experience, the phonies, the jokers, making too much of their bogus distress, could usually be recognized for what they were and terminated. But it sounded as though Harriet was genuine.

"Now, Harriet," said he in the deeper-pitched, more deliberate voice he had developed for radio use, "nobody's listening but me, and you know I'm sympathetic. . . . Harriet?"

"Yes, Doctor." She cleared her throat. "Okay, my daughter always was a fine, moral girl, a fine student. We couldn't of been closer all the while she was growing up. Doctor, we never even argued about anything!"

"What's wrong now?"

"Two years ago she married out of our faith. Well, I didn't like that exactly but didn't make any trouble about it even when the wedding was held in this other place of worship, you see, with everything so different than how I was brought up, and my daughter too. Next I'm told the children have to be brought up in this other religion. Well, I didn't like that much, either, but what could I —"

Time being always of the essence of radio, as was maintaining the listeners' interest, Kellog interrupted here. "So these things that hurt you continued to accumulate?"

"Yes they did, Doctor, on and on, but not a word of complaint came from me."

"What was the straw that broke the camel's back?"

"Now she wants me to —" Harriet's voice broke before she could complete the incredulous expression — "*convert!*" She wept again.

"Harriet," Kellog asked. "Tell me this: you're a devoutly religious person?"

After a moment she replied, in a low voice, "Not exactly."

"You make some observance at major holidays?"

"I guess you could say that."

"But you still want to call yourself a member of the faith into which you were born. It's the way most people are. But zealots find it hard to understand, especially those who have themselves recently converted, and all the more so when they're young. You'll just have to talk turkey to your daughter. Put the case to her as you've put it to me: you've never criticized her for what she did. Now it's her turn to be fair. Maybe relations between the two of you will be strained for a while. But eventually, I'm sure, she'll see you're right. What does your husband think?"

"He passed away nine years ago."

"Standing up for what's right can be a lonely thing, but in the end it's always worth it."

"He'd turn over in his grave if I ever became a dirty Catholic!" cried Harriet.

The program as aired was broadcast from tape played seven seconds after the recording of the live conversation: sufficient time in which to delete indecencies and other unacceptable expressions such as Harriet's. So far as the listeners knew now, the current colloquy ended with Kellog's homily on the inevitable success of moral courage, in delivering which he was by no means being hypocritical. One of his strengths as a broadcaster in a cynical era was that he actually believed in most of what he told those who applied for his advice. He personally embraced no organized faith but generally approved of all religions that did not call for the destruction of nonbelievers. With obvious exceptions — to spare pain, to save lives — he disapproved of mendacity and celebrated the telling of literal truth, encouraged the exercise of forgiveness, urged people to be kind and generous and try at least, hard as it was, to rise above envy and to resist

the spiteful impulses to which all human beings are sometimes given. To the young he advocated respect for elders,
but ever counseled the latter to be receptive to the energy
and yea-saying of youth. As to sex he could be either bluenosed or permissive, according to the caller. If a mother was
in anguish over the possibility that her college-aged daughter
intended to sleep with the boy invited as weekend house-
guest, Kellog disparaged her fears, reminding her of prevailing mores, pointing out that the girl would do better at
home than in a motel or, worse, the rear of a van. But if it
was rather the daughter who phoned him, he would take the
avuncular opposition: "Put yourself in *her* place. Even if she
accepts the fact you sleep with him somewhere else, that's
quite different from having it go on under her own roof.
There are all sorts of rights. As you say, if you're old enough
to vote, you're old enough to choose to go to bed with someone: that's your right. But your mother has a right to say
what goes on in her home."

There was no scientific means of gauging how often his
counsel was taken. He regularly received many letters of
thanks, and often a caller with a new problem praised the
successful solution Kellog had provided for the previous one.
Much less frequent were complaints, and though all, except
those made by obvious cranks, were politely acknowledged,
if only by a form letter, none was allowed to reach the air and
so vitiate the public's trust in Dr. Jonathan Kellog, who had
no such degree whether in medicine or philosophy. His only
formal education in psychology consisted of a basic introduc-
tory course, taken decades earlier and in an accelerated summer semester at that. He had been lucky to sneak through
with a C, in a season of record temperatures, pitchers of cold
beer on humid evenings, and a girlfriend who with a naked
tan torso wore a brassiere of white skin: but for a long time
that display and a restricted bit of fondling were all the sex

he got, though he and she were in love and inseparable. Which was normal enough for that place and time, even though contemporaneously, in other places and milieus, people of the same age were screwing lustily.

He married the same girl, when just out of college with a B.S. in business and no prospects to speak of, given his lackluster university, less than average grades, and a suddenly stagnant economy. His wife at the same time took her degree in fine arts, having majored in music, specifically the pipe organ, an impractical instrument examples of which were to be found in the college chapel and again in the suburban church where they were married and to which his wife belonged, but was not the sort of thing that could be played at home — and that fact was what Kellog saw as uniquely instrumental in the breakup of the marriage that came within three years. Though otherwise a housewife to whom no exception could be taken, whose windows sparkled and whose pastry was so light a fork could hardly hold it down, June insisted on keeping up with her music, which meant she played the Episcopal organ at Sunday and holiday services and practiced midweek. Kellog was himself not a churchgoer and for him the organ was most naturally used in a ballpark or as it had slowly risen into view on the stages of the grander movie theaters of his childhood, but he thought it an excellent hobby for June, especially when he was on the road as a salesman of wholesale hardware. They were waiting to have children as soon as he did better, and buy a house as well. Meanwhile June was alone a lot in the little apartment with outmoded appliances. She spent ever more time at the church, even when Kellog was in town.

When he finally confronted her with his suspicions, she admitted immediately that she was having an affair with the choirmaster, and felt no guilt about it, having been for some time aware, from a scrawled name and phone number on a matchbook cover found in one of her husband's shirts when she was about to launder it, that he took care of his own needs when on the road. Though her confession of course ended the marriage for him — June had been a virgin when he married her — he patiently tried to explain, if only for the principle of the thing, the difference between his fooling with a girl from a distant bar and her committing adultery with some sissy in a house of worship, but she self-righteously rejected the argument.

Kellog did not remarry until he was in his mid-thirties. He had done well as a salesman and been hired away, at a substantial raise, by a competitor company and then, at a younger age than most, was elevated to a lower executive position. He would surely have continued to rise had he not at this point begun an impolitic affair with the daughter of the president of the firm. At twenty she was legally still a minor in those days. Karen was a college dropout who drank heavily and drove her red convertible at dangerous speeds, her long black hair in the wind. Kellog had never known a girl of this breed and he was immediately entranced. Certainly taking up with her did not advance his career, not even when they returned from having run away, on an impulse of Karen's, to be married. Her father fired him instantly and arranged for a quick Mexican divorce.

Kellog decided he had had enough of wholesale hardware and went into retail sales in television and stereos, doing quite well in several branches of a large metropolitan chain. Eventually he took a position of importance in its advertising department, specializing in the commercials broadcast on the radio, a medium which, despite what might seem, to the layman, the absolute rule of TV, had done even better throughout the years in its mercantile function. Kellog had the knack for what appealed to the potential buyer by way of words — unlike television commercials, those on radio had to do the job with nothing but language. At least that was true of those that he demanded from the ad agency, whose people, when he started out, were addicted to the use of music, first in the form of ear-catching jingles, and then as background to the copy being read aloud.

But it was his theory that there was a danger in the employment of jingles: true, they stayed in the memory, but did they sell the product? He could recall several such ditties, melodious, clever, cute, but could not have said, without effort, which products they spoke for. Others, the lyrics of which consisted of little more than the repetition of the product's name, still might not induce a consumer to make the appropriate purchase. Again he went by personal taste. For example, on seeing a loaf of bread labeled "Buckminster," he felt a slight distaste owing to the radio jingle in which "Buck, Buckminster Bread" was repeated again and again to the tune of "Over the Waves." Being himself of the nature never to purchase a product of which any connotations were unpleasant, he was unmoved by the theory of some professionals in the field to the effect that fixing an identification in the consciousness of the potential customer, and not charming him, was the foremost aim of advertising.

Kellog eschewed the employment of anything irritating, loud, vulgar, or incantatory, and constructed radio ads to be read in a level tone by a male voice that would seem to belong to a reasonable human being, for example, "If you're like me, and not somebody with years of training in electronics, going into an enormous store to look through hundreds of television sets to find the best one for your particular needs is not a great way of spending time on the weekend. Not to mention the job of sorting through stereo components! That's why I go to the nearest Harrigan's, where all the salesmen *are* experts in electronics — and also the nicest, most considerate people you'll find anywhere. They'll be just as nice if you want to just look as if you buy out the place. . . . Well, that's *one* of the reasons I go to the nearest Harrigan's — and there *is* a Harrigan's near you, wherever you live. I'm not even going to talk about prices. I want you to do that yourself, after a visit to Harrigan's."

The Harrigan management had to be persuaded to replace their long-running commercials — always introduced with blaring Sousa marches, which gave way to a man shouting with lunatic intensity, and ended with an adult actress simulating a child's voice to ask, "Daddy, can we go to Harrigan's today?" But sales throughout their branches had declined slightly during the past year, and whether that had anything to do with their radio advertisements or rather owed to new competition from another chain lately established in the region could not be said, for the Harrigan people were too reactionary, and tightfisted, to pay for demographic studies. Eventually it was agreed that Kellog's sort of commercials be given a limited try.

Listeners liked them, proof of which were the letters and phone calls to the station and, more credibly, to Harrigan's itself, whose executives, not being in broadcasting, would not have been impressed with such evidence, but in fact overall sales did increase during the ensuing weeks, though that may well have happened because the rival chain had got some bad publicity when a man suddenly burst into one of their branches and blew out a series of TV screens with fire from an automatic shotgun. He proved to be not a disgruntled customer with a grudge against the store but rather someone with a long history of emotional problems of undisclosed origin. As these things go, not only this branch but all those in the chain suffered undeservedly: for an indeterminate time, though no human being had been scratched, their name would connote mayhem to potential customers, and people stayed away.

Though lonely in his private life, Kellog was cautious about taking a third spouse. He saw that the next one, should there be another, must be chosen for her qualities as, in effect, a business associate rather than simply a bed partner. Meanwhile he dated only divorced or widowed women, who, having lived with men, were less importunate than the single girls who were looking, often without patience, for someone to marry, for those were the days before it became fashionable to deplore that quest.

Kellog went through various changes of job. From Harrigan's he went to the advertising agency with which he had done business, and next, taking a cut in salary in exchange for a field the possibilities of which were to him more promising, to the local radio station, and eventually to the flagship station of the network, in New York. Always he remained far from the microphone, back in the executive offices, where the money was made for the firm. He was proficient in this work, and who knows how far he could have gone in management had he remained there, had he not by accident found himself in a superficially related but fundamentally quite different profession.

The most popular programs on the weekend schedule of station WKEG (days were mostly recorded Broadway show tunes, interspersed with news reports on the half hour and baseball games in the summer) was that of Dr. Paul Pomerantz, a consulting psychologist. Dr. Pomerantz had been one of the first radio personalities to take on-the-air telephone calls from listeners with personal problems: fellow workers with whom they could not get along, children without gratitude, obnoxious in-laws, fiancés impatient for premarriage intimacies, spendthrift wives, crude husbands, and so on.

Pomerantz was a legitimate professional, having a weekday practice from which he earned a comfortable income, and did the Sunday-evening gig (as in fact he called it) for fun, though he did receive a fee, which was increased regularly as his audience grew and attracted more commercials at higher costs to the advertisers — the normal progression of a successful show, to the greater profits of all concerned. He was a favorite of the station's executives, for previous to his arrival Sunday evening had been a dead zone. Soon they were trying to persuade the good doctor to offer a similar show every evening of the week and had sweetened his potential earnings to the point beyond which he could not sustain a resistance.

His agents had only just concluded the oral deal — the lawyers had not yet had time to draw up the printed contract — when Dr. Pomerantz suffered a lethal heart attack.

The calamity occurred early on a Sunday morning. Kellog, the executive who had been most closely concerned with Pomerantz' program, had only a few hours in which to find a replacement for the evening show. He had no success. The alternatives were either two hours of musical-comedy hits or a rebroadcast of an earlier program. The latter would be even more unsatisfactory than the former, for it had been determined that at least part of what devoted listeners responded to so favorably was the spontaneity of the show. Last week's would surely not do, not to mention a repeat of something older. These case histories were remembered: each had evoked its share of calls and letters from persons similarly troubled. Radio listeners could be fickle and, once disappointed, might forget where the offending station could be found on the dial.

Kellog made a desperate decision. As the concerned executive, he had listened to most of Pomerantz' broadcasts. While it was true that the commercials were his own area of focus, after three years he was sufficiently familiar with the questions put to the psychologist and the responses thereto that he could give a reasonably accurate imitation of such interchanges for the amusement of the women he dated. "Hello, *Doctuh?* Moy name is *Estelle?* From *Bwooklyn?*" "Yes, Estelle." "Doctuh, oym having a *lot* of trouble with my *daugh-tuh-rin-lor* and huh mothuh *ralso*." Pomerantz was himself not a local, stemming rather from the West Coast, his pronunciation standard American, his style crisp, almost cool, vaguely sympathetic but never identifiably involved. He seemed less compassionate the greater the apparent distress of the caller. His style was perfect for the job: surely it was just what was wanted by the kind of persons who were eager to reveal their problems to a stranger. However, after his own experience, and having listened to a succession of the imitators, on rival stations, of Pomerantz' original format but with a variety of different broadcasting styles — maudlin, solipsistic, abusive, etc. — Kellog arrived at the belief that in this area many people would put up with anything. For all concerned, both this sort of "patients" and this kind of "doctor" were essentially performers.

When he substituted himself for the deceased Pomerantz on that first show, Kellog of course had no intention of giving even one encore. With an entire week at his disposal, it went without saying that a permanent replacement would be on the air the following Sunday. Meanwhile it seemed advisable that Dr. Pomerantz' death be given no gratuitous advertisement, lest the listeners see the free counsel offered by WKEG as less than godlike. Nor could an unqualified practitioner do even one program. Thus was born Dr. Jonathan Kellog — the legal department having advised that it was not against the law to call oneself, generally, "doctor," so long as one did not seek to practice medicine or lay claim to a particular degree.

The program on that historic Sunday evening began with a staff announcer's mellow tones. "Good evening. Filling in for Dr. Pomerantz tonight is Dr. Jonathan Kellog. Those who would like to call Dr. Kellog with questions about personal problems are invited to do so." He gave the telephone number. "Now, here's Dr. Kellog."

"Good evening," said the *ad hoc* psychologist, his voice as yet unsteady despite his remarkable feeling of basic confidence for no reason at all. He had never before addressed an anonymous public, had never even acted or debated at any level of school. He now hit the button that killed his microphone, cleared his throat quickly, and returned to the air. "I *am* Dr. Jonathan Kellog, and I'll welcome your calls."

The lights on the telephone console were already glowing: there were those who put in calls before airtime, sometimes more than an hour early, so as to get prompt access to Pomerantz. These were the callers who now awaited Kellog. It remained to be seen whether listeners would continue to phone after the substitution had been announced. Unless calls came in there could be no show.

"Yes. You're on the air."

"My name is Bobby. Actually, it's Robert, but I've always been called Bobby, maybe because I've always been small for my age. I look younger than I really am, and people always treat me like a kid, though I'm forty-seven years of age by now. My mother still tells me what to eat, what to wear!"

"You still live at home, Robert?"

"Not at my mother's home. I'm married. My mother lives with us."

"She orders your wife around, too?"

"Actually, the two of them team up against me. Now they're getting my daughter into the act. She's twelve."

Kellog's self-confidence dissolved. He had no idea whatever of how Pomerantz might have dealt with this man, and the home in which he himself grew up, with a vain, assertive father and a quiet mother whose strength was subterranean, provided no precedent. He knew nothing of what it was to be bossed around by women.

He sought to delay. "Well, Robert . . ."

"Actually, I prefer Bobby."

Kellog had a flash of inspiration. This man was very likely born to be a toady to someone: better with his own females than criminal elements, ideological or religious fanatics, or, for that matter, sexual deviates. What Bobby might want from the doctor was simply reassurance.

"Let me ask this, Bobby: are your mother and wife good women?"

Bobby answered almost shyly. "If you mean like morally, I don't know anything against them."

"And your daughter is a nice girl?"

"A-student, very popular."

"You should thank your lucky stars," said Dr. Kellog, "that you have three such good people who love you. The usual complaint about a wife and mother is that they're jealous of each other and seldom get along, that a daughter has too little respect for her dad."

"I guess I *should* look at it that way," Bobby said in his weak voice. "Thank you, Doctor."

During the ensuing break for recorded commercials, Kellog had the opportunity to take several draughts of lukewarm coffee. All the phone lights stayed on; a new caller was already on Bobby's late line. But no sooner had his rush of relief come and gone than the bogus psychologist fell back into self-doubt. He hadn't given any answer at all to Bobby's problem! Perhaps Bobby would go on for a while, maintaining his obsequious status quo, then crack suddenly and murder the women in his house. . . . It now occurred to him, as it had not at the appropriate time, that Pomerantz would have urged Bobby to seek marriage-counseling, which indeed was the late doctor's standard response to most callers enmired in domestic conflict.

The caller on Line 2 was named Vivian. "Let me say first, Dr. Kellog, how much better you are than Pomerantz — I know your ethics forbid you from commenting on this, but I wanted to say it. You've got so much more common sense! You don't talk that headshrinker junk — and you're not always telling people to get professional help! If they did that, then why would they need to call a radio station?" She chuckled righteously.

"What's your problem, Vivian?" Kellog hated her for taking away the first advantage he had identified, he who had foreseen getting through the rest of the program by urging callers to see real specialists in their troubles. Thus he was inclined to be malicious when Vivian told him her problem. Her neighbors, otherwise the kindest, most considerate persons on earth, had a to-them-beloved cat that lurked all day in her yard and killed many of the songbirds that visited the feeders she kept filled with seed even in summer. Or was this rather a question for a veterinarian?

"What's more important to you, Vivian? Good friends or strange birds?" He bitterly switched her off and went to the next caller, who though having the voice of a little girl was a married woman.

". . . I think he's doing something else with the money. The thing is, should I just come out and ask, or should I tell him he just doesn't give me enough to run the house and see what he says?"

"If he's spending it on other women," Kellog said, remembering his own experience, "he's not going to volunteer any information. On the other hand, if you ask him outright, he might walk out the door, with real or fake indignation, it wouldn't matter. How about serving him dinner that consists only of something like boiled cabbage and dry rice, and when he protests, say you didn't have enough money for anything else."

"He might punch me in the face."

"Is he capable of that sort of thing?"

"Done it more than once."

Kellog had now got over his lingering pique with Vivian. "Look, Dolores, this is a much more serious matter than whatever he does with his money. If he strikes you . . . these are serious blows?"

"I got a black eye right now."

"That's criminal behavior on his part," said Kellog. "It should not be tolerated by you! You should go to the police."

"I did," Dolores said. "They say they can't do anything in family squabbles."

"Leave him."

"I got two young kids and no other source of income. I never finished high school. I couldn't get much of a job, and if I did, who would watch the kids all day?"

Once again Kellog was nonplussed: neither he nor anyone else, including the late Pomerantz, would have been able to resolve Dolores' problem by a suggestion that would be acceptable if made public. But he had to say something now.

"Dolores, I'm afraid there are times in life when we all have to make choices, though both alternatives are unattractive. You'll just have to choose. If you stay with this man, you're going to be mistreated. If you leave him, you're not going to have any income. You have to weigh each choice carefully, you have to —"

"You phony," said Dolores. "I thought you were supposed to really help people."

Of course this did not reach the air, but it had its effect on Dr. Kellog, who shakily completed his remarks as if Dolores had not interrupted. "No one else can make certain decisions for you. That's what being an adult means."

In self-loathing he went to a commercial. Dolores was absolutely right. He alternated between wishing he could somehow, off the air anyway, have told her so and detesting her for presenting him with such a dilemma so early in his radio career.

He decided to institute a policy that would apply to any subsequent calls of Dolores' kind, that is, those to which an ambiguous answer must be given.

In response to persons in search of particular information, e.g., the names of psychotherapeutic practitioners — mention of which, because it constituted free advertising, was forbidden by the peculiar ethics of broadcasting — Pomerantz would ask the caller to stay on the line and speak off the air to the producer, who kept available a list of such professionals, as well as local clinics, appropriate agencies of local, state, and federal governments, and other potential sources of help. The needs of the radio show took precedence over all others, and to meet them it was necessary *to have something positive to say at all times when broadcasting*. Pomerantz could be extraordinarily negative in private phone calls, especially those to his wife and his secretary, but his public voice never faltered in its optimism. Kellog now began to understand that it was possible to do this consistently only by deflecting those callers with unanswerable problems — and not with truisms easily recognizable as such, as he had done in the case of Dolores. Yet, to maintain the distinction between himself and the late psychologist, for which he had been publicly commended by Vivian, neither could he gracefully advise a succession of those seeking his free help to report to the kind of counseling for which a fee was charged.

What he could do was what he did with the next caller whose predicament was certainly too complex to be dealt with on the radio. A man who gave his name as Norman told Dr. Kellog he was sure his wife would make an attempt to poison him — in fact, she had promised as much — but he had no idea of when and how. He could not go to the police, for she might be bluffing, plus he would be embarrassed, and anyway, feeling thus far physically tiptop, he could confidently assert that she had not yet carried out her threat. But how to keep her from doing so without causing a scandal and while preserving the marriage?

"You believe the woman is trying to murder you, yet you want to stay married?"

"I don't think that affects my basic love for her. She really has done a good job as a wife."

"Norman, I think this is too delicate a matter to discuss further on the air. Stay on the line and give your number to Pat, my producer. I'll get back just after the show."

Kellog kept his promise, but when he phoned the number obtained from Pat, just after the close of the program, the man who answered insisted his name was not Norman and that he had no knowledge of the matter: he was himself unmarried. Pat had either inaccurately taken down the number or Norman, if such was his real name, had been perpetrating a hoax.

After dealing on the air with Norman in a manner that had seemed successful at the moment, he had given a similar response to two other callers — Marilyn, who had a speech defect that was surely painful to hear on the radio, and a man named Sal, who professed to suffer from priapism, i.e., had an eternal erection, which was not even reduced by ejaculation. These were the days before candor in sexual matters was routine on the airwaves, before people boasted, to the frenetic vulgarians who hosted mass-market TV shows, of merrily practicing an assortment of erotic bizarreries with their parents, children, and pets and being none the worse for it, which era was eventually succeeded by that of the next category of guests, whose lives had professedly been ruined by the deviates of the previous generation. Kellog would not let Sal's complaint reach the air, but he did have Pat get the man's number. He was scarcely qualified to make a professional comment, but it was of interest to him as a man.

After the fruitless call to Norman, however, Kellog was in an irritated mood. He phoned Marilyn and tried to understand her sputter, then told her as kindly as he could that what she needed was a speech therapist. However, she had been to several and not been helped: what she required now was advice on how socially to survive her affliction, find friends, meet men.

"Marilyn," said he, "you'll just have to keep your courage up and keep trying, tough as it is. Fortunately you live in one of the most highly populated areas of the country: there are millions of chances for you to find people with whom you'll get on. It's not as if you're in some rural area. I'm sure there are organized groups of people who share your affliction. You should be able to get in touch with them through one of the speech therapists with whom you've been in contact."

Marilyn hung up without a word, not helping Kellog's state of mind. He placed the call to Sal.

"Who?" Sal asked. "Oh, yeah, Doc Kellog. Are we on the air? Okay. Like I said, I am hung real big to begin with, and most of the time I got a boner besides. But what gets me is it don't go down even after I come. Now, I been to see a regular doctor, but he says he can't do nothing about it. It's just that way. I guess it don't mean you're sick or anything, really don't do any harm. When I was a young kid, I was always being embarrassed to have that bulge showing in my pants, though I tell you there was a married lady who lived on the next floor up who used to lick her lips when she saw it, but that was a time when I was too young and dumb to do anything about it. Anyway, Doc, what I wanted to get from you was the names and addresses of some of the companies that make stag films. I've seen some with guys whose schlongs were nowhere near as long as mine. I got nine and a half inches! Why should I slave away behind the wheel of a cab when I could make good money fucking, getting blown, and all. You nut-doctors know how to get in touch with these movies, I bet."

"You degenerate," said Kellog, and hung up. Immediately he regretted doing so. He should not have blamed Sal for the desolating effect Marilyn had had on him. And why should the taxi driver not make the most of his natural endowments? But a more important concern was this tendency of his own to lose control of his emotions. He was the worst replacement imaginable for Pomerantz. It was absolutely essential to hire a genuine practitioner during the ensuing week.

He did interview several professionals, but found none of them suitable. One had an extremely unpleasant-sounding, raspy voice. Another was very arrogant and demanded more than twice what Pomerantz had received. The third assured Kellog that he would take the job only if he could broadcast from his office, at hours when he had no other appointments.

Meanwhile a considerable amount of mail had come into the station on the subject of Pomerantz' replacement. There were those who missed the late psychologist (some of them unaware of his death) and found Kellog a miserable substitute. But many more preferred Dr. Kellog by far — and if a reason was given it was likely to be that he was down-to-earth, not some intellectual snob but rather the kind of guy you could talk to, not afraid to admit he could not help when he couldn't, sometimes almost inarticulate but always in a human way, always *warm* (the word then in vogue, later to be replaced, when participles came into fashion, by "caring").

What he had seen as his glaring inadequacies — inexperience, ignorance, lack of emotional stability — were taken as rather his strengths.

So there he was behind the microphone again on the following Sunday evening. It began much better this time, with a series of callers whose problems could be answered with platitudes that, owing to Kellog's growing fluency in this mode of expression (harking back to his salesman days), did not seem, to him or the callers, as stale as they were. But then, was anything new ever to be said in the area of human affairs?

Only ten minutes remained of the two-hour show when Kellog punched the button that brought him the voice of a man who said, pleasantly, "Doctor, I've had enough of your vicious attempts to ruin me. I'm afraid I'm going to have to kill you."

Kellog did of course have the capacity either to hang up or to go to commercial and talk to the man off the air. Pomerantz had made it a practice instantly to use the advantage of the seven-second delay and cut off any caller who expressed the slightest criticism of him. He would have disposed of this one at the word "vicious" and thus never would have heard the threat.

But Kellog, though so frightened he could hardly speak, made a bold decision that changed his life. He permitted the caller to go on the air and, after some deep breathing, managed to speak coherently with him.

"What attempts could I have made to ruin you?"

"You told the FBI that I was a pervert."

"Are you a pervert?"

"You know better than that."

"No, I don't," said Kellog. "I don't know you at all. But I wish I did, because I'm sure I could help you. I think your trouble is that people don't take you seriously, so you have to call up someone on the radio, who is just some voice, somebody so remote that it seems they don't really exist, and you can make threats against them without doing anybody harm, because it's all make-believe, isn't it, uh, what's your name?"

"Warren."

"I'm right about you, Warren, am I not?" Warren remained silent. "I'll tell you how right I am: I'm willing to meet you someplace, unarmed and alone. You're not going to do me any harm, because if you do, then you have eliminated what well may be your last chance in life to be listened to, really listened to, by someone who respects you."

Now Warren was sobbing. Kellog allowed his weeping acquiescence to be heard by the public, but took Warren's address off the air, passed it to the producer, who phoned it in to the police. Warren was taken into custody. The store of deadly weapons found at his home in the far northern Bronx suggested that his threat had not been empty. Next it was determined that he had twice been institutionalized for mental problems but subsequently released as being harmless.

The publicity department of WKEG made the event known to the other media, and next day it was mentioned on several local TV newscasts and in two papers. For the most part, Kellog was seen by the public as having performed admirably, though some professionals in the field of psychotherapy pointed out enviously that he had no credentials for the job and criticized him for what was really a breach of ethics, *viz.,* betraying Warren. But in fact when Kellog visited Warren shortly after the latter's arrest, Warren, a small, gaunt man with a disarming smile, insisted that Dr. Kellog had provided just the right medicine. "I was really crying out for help," he told a TV reporter, "and only he heard me, God bless him."

Thereafter it became fashionable for other madmen and then even wanted criminals, more or less rational, to telephone Dr. Kellog on the air and offer to surrender to him. At the height of this rage, his ratings were not only higher than those of any other show in the long history of WKEG (which had been founded in the 1920s by a brewer), but they also set a record for New York radio. But finally the practice palled on listeners, especially when the crimes in reference were no worse than the evasion of three hundred traffic summonses and when too many of the lunatics were proved to be but mischievous high-school students.

But by now Dr. Jonathan Kellog was an established feature of New York radio, and he had long since ceased to look for a replacement. He made the move to weekdays that had been planned for Dr. Pomerantz and tried various time slots, all of them successfully, before audience surveys indicated that the hour just before noon was likely to reach most listeners, for Kellog's appeal was wide and came to include the self-employed, housewives, adolescents of either sex, the drivers of cars, retirees, persons of all races. He was exceptionally courteous to people with accents, but if they were too hard to understand, he spoke to them off the air, for the needs of the audience could not be forgotten. This was never less than a performance, though he liked to think it was sometimes a good deal more. In time, return calls from those who had taken his counsel and prospered were routine. "Doctor, you were so right! That mistake my husband made was less important than the continuation of the marriage." . . . "Just as you predicted, my son soon came home, his tail between his legs. He's settled down now. Thank God for your help."

Perhaps it did even more for his reputation as sage when someone praised him for providing correct advice which, through cowardice, vanity, or sloth, they had failed to act upon. "I'll never forgive myself. I just couldn't bring myself to apologize to her, and now she's dead." . . . "I didn't have the nerve to turn him down. So I gave him the money and he poured it down another one of his rat-holes and went bankrupt anyway."

As the prevailing culture began to undergo what was soon called the sexual revolution, the problems presented to Dr. Kellog pertained more and more to the erotic. Old men, who had not had an erection since before impotence could be confessed to over the airwaves, now phoned to ask Dr. Kellog, in the hearing of the world, whether there was still hope. Mothers inquired whether it could lead to incest when toddler twins, one male, one female, caressed each other's genitals. A teenager wanted to know if the unrequited oral gratification she gave her boyfriend would result in his despising her. A homosexual husband insisted that liberation had made things much worse for him: now his boyfriends wanted to identify themselves to the world, ruining him, whose old-fashioned principles of polite discretion were shared by his wife and straight associates.

Kellog had got cold feet when he heard the first of the sexually explicit questions and killed the earliest calls, but by now he had acquired some local rivals in broadcast psychotherapy, and the nearest to him in popularity had made sex a specialty and was thereby gaining in the ratings. When the executives at WKEG urged him to be bolder, Kellog took the plunge. Thus began the era in which the program became almost exclusively devoted to Eros.

"He puts on my bra stuffed full of socks and tucks his organ back between his legs so you can see only a triangle of pubic hair that looks like a woman's. Would you say that's homosexual?"

"No, not at all, if that's all he does. It wouldn't be even if he dressed completely in female clothes and went out in public. He would be gay only if he had sexual relations with others of his own sex."

"He makes love to me okay. Maybe I'm worrying over nothing. Thanks, Doctor. You've set my mind at ease."

At the outset of his new profession Kellog considered himself reasonably sophisticated in sexual matters — over the course of the adult decades he had been to bed with a variety of women — but it soon appeared that he had had little preparation for many of the questions that were put to him.

What could be said to the man who confessed to being his daughter's lover since she had reached the age of seventeen?

"I'm no child molester," boasted the man. "I never touched her earlier though I've been a lonely widower for some years."

"Of course you are aware that that's against the law," was the best Kellog could produce on such short notice.

"So was sitting in the front of the bus if you were black, not long ago! So was just living if you were a Jew in Nazi Germany."

Kellog rallied. "Be that as it may, what you're doing is not right."

"Then why did Lot do it?"

"Who?"

"Lot, in the Bible, whose wife turned to a pillar of salt. He got both his daughters pregnant, and that was fine with God. Go read it and see."

"Sir, if I have to explain what's wrong with incest . . . The morality aside, isn't it genetically dangerous if a child is produced?"

"We're not thinking of having children. We're just satisfying each other's needs."

"It would be much better if you both got other lovers,"

Kellog said wearily. The only meaningful response to certain propositions — e.g., that coldblooded murder of another human being could be justified, that torture was permissible, that having sexual relations with a blood relative could be sanctioned — was simply to call them wrong. Proof, as such, could not be furnished, and if it could be, it would only vitiate the clear and obvious truth. Unless a human being could see that, there was nothing to talk about. But this man could not simply be turned away. Whatever his defiance of the natural law, he had called for help.

Kellog spoke gently. "The situation must not be as satisfactory as you make it sound. If you're calling me, you must have some doubts."

"I have none at all," said the man. "I'm calling to help others who may be in similar straits. You see, both my daughter and I were badly disfigured in the fire in which my wife died. We're not attractive to anyone else."

Even in a society that had at one seemingly arbitrary point instantaneously exchanged the Puritanism that had been basic since its importers deboarded at Plymouth Rock for the licentiousness of the Roman baths (only yesterday the movies were so bluenosed that husband and wife could not be shown as occupying the same bed; now yesterday's shameful parts were everywhere on obligatory display and polymorphous perversity was lauded, and often practiced, by clergymen), even in a place and time where in peep-show films one could watch a German shepherd copulating with a human female, a male in ardent erotic sport with an underaged girl represented as being of his own flesh and blood, there was amongst the callers to Dr. Kellog no paucity of those who disapproved of simple sex education in the schools, any manifestation of sexual inversion including that discreetly practiced in private, any heterosexual connection not sanctioned by marriage, and in fact, with some, any sex whatever including the solitary: there actually still were parents who tried to discourage their offspring from masturbating.

But some complaints eventually revealed more than first met the eye.

"Surely that's harmless," Dr. Kellog said. "Would you rather he impregnate a young girl or get a disease from a streetwalker?"

"But isn't he doing it too much? He stays in the bathroom for hours."

"I wouldn't worry about it. It's normal enough, including the borrowed underwear. How old is the boy?"

"Doctor," said the woman, "I wasn't telling the exact truth. He's my husband."

Kellog recommended professional counseling.

Another wife and mother said her thirty-year-old son had separated from his spouse and come back to live at home. "I think something's going on between him and his stepsister. She's only twelve: that's the thing."

"Have you tried confronting him about the matter? Simply telling him of your concern. Discreetly, nonconfrontationally, of course."

"I don't know," said the mother. "He tends to fly off the handle at any hint of criticism. He was always like that as a young kid. And that's why his marriage broke up. He says his wife was always needling him. He just couldn't take it."

"It doesn't sound like a healthy situation, Phyllis."

"It's not his fault, see," said Phyllis. "The girl is quite a tease. She'll sometimes run around in scanty attire, and she's already getting to be, uh, you know, developed. She'll sit on his lap and scrootch around, or she'll suddenly dig him in the ribs or grab something of his, like his pen while he's trying to write a check, and run to some corner of the house, and he's supposed to chase her."

"Does he?"

"Yeah, and they're gone a long while, sometimes."

"You'll really have to discuss the matter with him. And speak to the girl too, separately, privately. It may all still be relatively innocent, at least in deed, but it could go too far." He saw a commercial was due. "Try that, Phyllis, and good luck. Now —"

"Please, doctor," said Phyllis. "I can't get on any worse terms with my stepdaughter. She hates me already for marrying her father. And the fact is, I haven't been getting along lately with my husband. If he finds out about this, I don't know what he'll do. He's never liked my son."

Kellog put some severity into his voice. "I *am* sorry, Phyllis, but we are simply out of time —"

"She's just a little chippy, Doctor, is what she is. I made a bad mistake marrying this man. He's run up all kinds of debts and last week he just went and sold my car. I'll tell you what I think, awful as it is. I think he might even be instigating the girl to do this to my son, to get something to blackmail him with."

"Phyllis —"

"Could I just please stay on the line until after the commercial?"

Kellog never usually permitted this sort of thing, which could too easily be abused, for every caller's predicament was desperate according to him- or herself, and it was unfair to those waiting in the telephonic queue to allow one person to monopolize the doctor's attention — but, more important, the professional broadcaster's assumption was that the audience, many of whom were, at any given hour, in cars, had necessary limits to its attention.

But he now granted Phyllis' wish, and when he returned to the air after recorded commercials had been played, he said, "Tell your husband candidly about the girl and your son, but don't mention your suspicions about *his* own motives. I leave it up to you to decide whether you want to stay married to this man."

"I'm afraid I signed over most of my property to him, so I couldn't afford a breakup now."

Phyllis' problem was then essentially one of irresponsible naïveté. This must be apparent to all, and Kellog felt that to maintain the respect of his listeners he had to make note of it. "How did you let this man gain such power over you?"

"Sex," Phyllis said. "I never had been made love to by anybody else like that. I never even had an orgasm with my first husband. With this guy, every single time. I have a whole series with the clitoris and then there it comes, the big vaginal bang. I didn't believe in that until the first time I had one." She chuckled. "And you know, his penis isn't all that big. It's just a little bitty thing, in fact. It's the way he uses it, and his fantastic hands, and also his incredible ability to stimulate me orally."

Kellog could well remember that not too many years earlier "damn" and "hell" were taboo on radio and that he himself had not known the proper name for the clitoris during his first marriage, and that wife returned the favor by never even, unless guided physically, touching him below the waist. And yet at the time he had thought they were satisfactorily compatible as to sex, and so apparently had she, whose complaint against him was that his business kept him too much on the road, whereas the choirmaster was always nearby. Now there were ordinary laypersons who not only were possessed of clinical information about sex and routinely practiced refinements and embellishments of an act that was basically so stark as practiced by all other mammals, but also boasted to an audience of countless invisible strangers. Certainly it was something that Kellog himself could not have considered doing, and no doubt it was his disdain for such callers that gave him sufficient authority to be respected by them.

He now told Phyllis that the choices before her were simple: she had only to assemble the respective arguments, one, two, three, on either side, and then count up the points of each. Such enumeration was soon institutionalized by him as the Count, and it became a kind of Kellogian trademark. Before long the callers anticipated it and by the time they reached him already had made their counts and wanted them assessed.

"Made two columns on a sheet of paper like you said, listed everything in either Column A or B. What I get from my girlfriend in A, as opposed to the disadvantages in B. Like she's real pretty, A. But she's unfaithful, B. B, her father hates me. A, I get along real well with her mom. She claims she's really in love with me: that's A. But so far I can't get her to engage in any real sex, B. It's not like she won't ever do it, according to her: she's just waiting for the right time. I guess that would be A, because it's not turning me down. But suppose it's just teasing: that would definitely be in Column B."

"All right, Tim. I get the point."

"Then what should I do?"

"I can't make your mind up for you. That's what you're supposed to do with the help of the Count."

"Trouble is," Tim said, "I know she's having some kind of sex with other guys, which isn't good, but if it's nothing more than she does with me, then it's not *all* that bad. I guess I could live with it, if all she's doing is hand jobs."

"That's what she does for you?"

"That's right."

"Well, it's something, then, isn't it? But maybe you should

consider playing the field as she does. Try dating some other girls and see what happens."

"I *knew* you'd come up with the perfect solution," Tim said fervently. "*Thank* you, Doctor."

Male homosexual callers tended to be more romantic and less coarse or clinical than many of the heterosexuals who applied to Dr. Kellog. Their sort of conjunction was invariably called "making love" and references to it were sans details — to Kellog's great relief, for any show of distaste for any sexual variant could get one in trouble in contemporary New York, yet he still found certain images uncomfortable, e.g., any that featured the rectum of any living thing (of whichever sex) as an erotic part. And if they were almost never merry or even light of heart while calling themselves "gay" (a term he eventually identified as a kind of whistling in the dark, a self-courage builder), they were unfailingly civil in the purest sense of the word, commonly amongst the best citizens, unless of course some individual went too far, but that could happen with zealots of any persuasion.

"My lover and I have gotten into a complex situation," said a caller named David, "and I can't talk directly to him about it. He's — I'll call him Martin — Martin's a good deal older than I. He's middle-aged, married, and with a family. His children, a boy and a girl, are of my generation. Now what happened was by accident, really. I got to know his son, who is absolutely straight. This son, I'll call him Rob, and I in fact work together at the same firm. He hasn't any idea I know his father, let alone have an affair going with him. Now, Rob keeps wanting to introduce me to his sister, in fact to double-date with him and his fiancée. I have kept putting him off, but unfortunately he knows that I don't have a regular girl. He really cares for me as a friend, and I am touched, because I don't think ever in my life I've had any male friends with whom I wasn't also involved sexually, except maybe when I was just a little kid."

"Has he ever mentioned you by name to his father?"

"He and his father have had nothing to do with one another for several years. What's more, I don't know but strongly suspect from little hints that their estrangement is due to Martin's, the father's, sexual orientation, which I think Rob may have his suspicions about. Rob is quite bigoted, very anti-gay. I don't have the courage to reveal myself to him, let alone my relationship with his father. He keeps pressuring me about his sister. You might think I could go out with her once anyway to get him off my case, but she lives at home. Imagine calling for her and being greeted at the door by her father, my lover."

"Why don't you try this?" said Kellog. "You say Rob knows you haven't got a regular girl. But I'm sure you could get a date with one of your female friends. Take her out with Rob and his fiancée. You don't have to pretend you and she are that closely involved as yet, but you could let Rob think you're sufficiently interested in her not to want to see anyone else romantically at this time. That would take care of the matter of the sister."

"I suppose I could do that," said David. "I'm on good terms with the divorced lady in the next apartment, but then I've got all kinds of female friends."

"I wouldn't advise much real lying, though, David," Dr. Kellog said. "Asking your date to say she knows you better than she does and so on. Such misrepresentations can be embarrassing when you least expect it. Now, as to your lover, Martin. Why in the world couldn't you tell him about your friendship with his son Rob? Tell him just as you've told me. There's nothing shameful or dishonest about your friendship with his son, who is your colleague at work. By the way, isn't he at least aware that you work at the same place as Rob?"

"No," David said quickly. "He doesn't have any idea of even what kind of work I do. I happen to love Martin, but he's terribly self-concerned. All he really wants me for is his own gratification. Despite his age, he's sex-crazed. That's all he cares about, not me really. Yet I love him. Isn't it weird, with me the young and attractive one? Yes, it's true. I would put my hand in the fire for him. In return, he'd just jump into bed with someone else. He's cold, ruthless. Martin's cruel. He —" David sounded ready to weep, and Kellog couldn't let that happen.

"All right, then. I think your best course of action would be to tell Martin about knowing Rob. If Martin's interest in you, as you say, is mostly physical, then why would he care much about your friendship with his son, since it is furthermore nonerotic?"

"Oh," said David, gasping, "you don't know how malicious he can be. He'll immediately call up Rob and taunt him. 'Your best friend is one of those faggots you so detest!' He wouldn't pass up a God-given opportunity of that sort."

"And Rob would be outraged with you . . ." Kellog really had nothing against the sexually inverted as long as their problems were routine, but when complexities appeared, one's instinctive though unspoken reaction could too easily be, even in an oversophisticated era: *Why in the name of God don't you just go straight?*

As it was, the doctor took an extended breath. "Rob sounds like the better man, not because he's heterosexual but because, at least as you present him, his friendly affection for you seems genuine. In return, you know, you haven't been genuine with him. I'd take the chance if I were you and make a clean breast of it. If he can stay bigoted after knowing you all this while, and thinking you a fine enough human being to have as his close friend, then he's not worth bothering about."

"You see," David said sadly, "the reason Rob's so anti-gay is a serious one. I can't find it in my heart to condemn him. He was raped by a male teacher when he was only five years old."

"He told you that?"

"His father told me — not being aware, you remember, that I knew his son." David was silent for a moment. "And there's more: that teacher was a lover of Martin's. Maybe Rob even knows that. Furthermore, Martin says this man was the only person he has ever really loved his life long, that since their breakup he has had no feeling left for anyone else."

Kellog was claimed by a probably quixotic stubbornness, but it was suddenly a matter of pride for him not to dispose of this ever more complex matter by recommending application to a therapist. "All right, but I'll stick by my guns. Unless you are yourself a violator of little children, and somehow I doubt that you are —"

"I'm certainly not!"

"Then the point stands. You're a decent man, who happens to be homosexual. A *friend* should be able to accept that."

David reported back several weeks later. With all the calls Kellog had received in the interim, it was necessary that most of the story be retold before it was remembered by the doctor, not to mention those listeners who had forgotten it or had missed it first time around.

"Yes, David," said Kellog eventually. "And what has happened?"

"You won't believe this," David said. "I told him everything, and Rob's reaction was to *proposition* me! Right then and there, in my car! 'But you're not gay,' I said — I always *know*. 'Why are you doing this? To make fun of me?' 'It's quite true that I'm not queer,' said he. 'But apparently everyone else in the world is, so maybe I ought to try it.'"

"And?" asked Kellog.

"I've never been a whore," David said. "I've got morals. If he wants to be a thrill-seeker, he can try someone else."

"So you said no. How did he respond to that?"

David spoke flatly, with no audible emotion. "Rob hasn't spoken to me since, and I have good reason to believe he's slandering me around the office. Also he called Martin immediately and said *I* had been the one to make a pass at *him*. Ordinarily Martin, alley cat that he is, couldn't care less if I had other lovers, but now he's used this thing to break off relations with me altogether. I realize that he was just looking for an excuse: I'm not as young as I once was."

Of course this debacle could have been interpreted as the result of a grievous error on the part of Dr. Kellog, and after David hung up there were several callers who wanted to chide the radio psychologist, but his producer diverted them from the air. Kellog himself felt no guilt: he had been honest in giving what after a reasonable amount of thought had seemed the best advice. Nothing more could be asked of a practitioner to whom an unseen patient spoke for three minutes.

And in fact David had no complaint. "Doctor, after all is said and done, and after quite a bit of intense pain — I'll admit that — I'm beginning to feel nothing but a profound sense of relief. These are terrible people! I'm glad to be free of them both. The atmosphere at work has become too poisoned, and I'm going to have to quit. But I've been stuck in that dead-end job for too long anyhow! It's as if I've been imprisoned both personally and professionally, and now the jail doors have sprung open. I'm ready to spread my wings and fly on my own! And I owe it most of all to you, Dr. Kellog. My profound gratitude!"

This was always Kellog's favorite moment. "David, you owe me nothing. You've done it yourself. All you needed was a very little push, and you proceeded in the right direction. If I or anyone else had tried to *tell* you what to do, it wouldn't have worked. Now you can see what your basic strengths are. You're going to be all right from here on."

"Don't I know it!" David said. "And I'm in love again. This time it's for real."

Kellog would have shown a wry moue to his producer behind the glass partition, had the veteran Pat still held that job, Pat having been Lesbian since puberty and thus secure enough to be ironic about quick infatuations. But she had risen to an executive post at the station and been replaced by Jill, an emotional young woman who regularly fell in love with men who treated her like dirt: Jill would identify absolutely with David.

As to Kellog's personal life, since the brief and unsuccessful marriage with the daughter of his boss in an earlier job, he had made it a rule never to have a relationship beyond the professional with any of his colleagues or employees. It was unthinkable to have any association with someone who had called him for advice. Emotionally troubled women were hard enough to endure at the end of a telephone line. He was only made uncomfortable by learning there were those who found his voice aphrodisiac. If rebuffed on the phone (in exchanges that never reached the air), some would apply by mail, a few indecently, enclosing nude photos and perfumed underwear.

What he sought for himself by way of female friend was a woman remote as possible from the milieu in which he made a living — and a very good living it was indeed, for every month new stations signed on somewhere across the country, and despite constantly rising rates, the advertisers obsequiously waited in queues to place commercials on Dr. Kellog's program. With such success came a certain celebrity, not of the sort experienced by movie actors or television personalities, but of a more comfortable kind. One could attend to the business of life unobtrusively, serenely eat meals in public, attend sporting events or go to the theater without fear of being accosted, perhaps even attacked, by importunate fans. Yet privileges could be claimed: a radio psychologist with a transcontinental audience could obtain hard-to-get tickets to almost any spectacle, well-placed tables in fashionable restaurants, seats on fully booked flights, and the best suites in major hotels.

Kellog was also the recipient of many proposals to write works of popular psychology, and sent complimentary copies of most of the books written by others in this area: it was by means of the latter that he continued to educate himself in the field into which he had strayed by accident. As to producing a book of his own, or even the articles he was asked to do for mass-circulation Sunday supplements and supermarket-checkout magazines, he cautiously abstained. Nor for a long time would he appear on TV talk shows, though invited to do so after a prominent news magazine had taken note of the latest phenomenon of American culture, therapists of the microphone, and identified him as being preeminent amongst the practitioners thereof. For many years he remained in awe of the fate that had directed him into a trade for which he had had no training whatever, but practiced so easily, with such a generous reward.

All he required now for a balanced existence was someone with whom to share that time when he was off the air, but not only was he determined for reasons of personal pride never to have another failed marriage: as America's adviser on relations between the sexes, he could not afford to make a mistake in his choice of spouse, for it would be widely and derisively publicized. It was a matter for careful procedure —

but neither could he delay to the degree that the audience would begin to question how effectual he was in his own life while being so glib about the lives of others.

It took a while to find her, but his third wife was perfection: a lawyer, whom he had met when his second spouse, about to remarry, had her attorney seek his cooperation in legitimizing their Mexican divorce. As it happened, Annabelle had never listened to his show; she had never even heard of it. But Kellog found her ignorance in that regard a challenge. Immediately attracted to her, he welcomed the opportunity to win her attention when starting out from scratch as simply another client. Annabelle was herself unmarried at thirty-five. For a while he worried about her sexuality, for she seemed to persist in overlooking his attempts to be personal. But when he finally came out and asked her to dinner, she accepted with a sudden and unprecedented display of warmth.

Afterwards, at her apartment, now aware of his profession, Annabelle told him of her doomed love affair with a prominent judge, a man married to a hopeless invalid, a woman who had lived on interminably after suffering the stroke that left her a vegetable. When she finally died, her husband followed her to the grave within two months. By this time Kellog had listened to so many sad stories that while he had not become callous, he had, like physicians, cops, priests, developed a means of distancing himself from such catastrophes lest he be drawn vicariously into them and so be rendered as helpless as the victims. But he could not keep himself aloof from Annabelle's trouble — and that was strange, for it would not have come about without her passion for another man, indeed a man who was her senior by three decades, father of two children who were her contemporaries.

Kellog's feeling for Annabelle was such that he felt only

kinship with and never jealousy for the man she had so worshiped. He was reluctant to call this feeling love, associating that word as he did with the emotion that had claimed him each time he had previously got married, though with the first wife it had not been very passionate and with the second it had been little else. Not to mention that his callers overused the word as an all-purpose term for anything but outright hatred, even professing "basically" to love those who had betrayed them, blighted their lives, destroyed everything they held dear. No doubt this reflected the social-betterment agenda of the makers of TV and movies, in which not only those related by blood or law but also persons whose connections were only casual embraced one another regularly while assuring Mom or Son or Anonymous Passerby that he or she was loved.

But he cherished her, and apparently he in turn was of some value to Annabelle. They had much to share at the end of each working day, trading stories from two vivid areas of human conflict, over dinner in one of their many favorite restaurants. On weekends they retreated to their country house, which over the years had become more luxurious as the address was changed to successively more fashionable areas, as their friends and neighbors became more powerful and in some cases even famous. In the early years of their marriage the only time they used a home kitchen was for a pickup lunch on Saturdays and at Sunday supper, and the weekends were also the time for a moderate sort of sex.

Annabelle was almost forty when they decided they simply must make a place in their lives for children, but given her age and the demands of her profession — she had by now expanded her practice, in a feminist era, to include any legal action a woman might take against men, specializing in the catch-all that had come to be known as sexual harassment — they adopted an infant and named him, for Annabelle's late father, Neil. Now the weekends became their time with the baby, and though their privacy was compromised by so doing, they hired a kindly Hispanic nursemaid to deal with feeding, diapers, and wails in the night. They soon became so devoted to the idea of a family that in the following year they acquired an adopted daughter whom they called Phoebe.

Annabelle had become well known in her field, and when eventually she told Kellog she had decided to try her hand at politics, he asked her why she had waited so long. He could not have admired her more; she had proved to be the perfect partner. He was not reluctant to admit that she was his superior in intellect and ambition. Why not, then, in her situation in life as well?

As a member of Congress belonging to the party in power and furthermore to a sex with whom the Chief Executive wished to ingratiate himself strategically, she took Kellog to several social functions at the White House during her first two years. She was easily reelected but before her term was over the president called her to the cabinet as attorney general, a controversial appointment in view of her little experience in government but one very popular with women, for she proceeded to specialize, as she had in private legal practice, in matters of peculiar concern to them.

Annabelle's party took a whipping in the next national elections, and she returned briefly to private life only to run for the Senate next time a seat was contestable. Her victory over an old incumbent was narrow, but once in power she became quite popular with her constituents. She succeeded usually in identifying herself with forward-looking legislation while managing to avoid being labeled as one of the big spenders by consistently demanding that the fat be ruthlessly trimmed even from her favorite programs and that the administrators thereof be carefully policed. Thus the bureaucrats were not overly fond of her and sometimes vengefully arranged for damaging news leaks regarding program failures which they had arranged — making common cause, and not for the first time, with the reactionaries who opposed her on every matter without noticing that her rhetoric, generally of the liberal-pietistic sort well received by the press, was often not matched by her votes: e.g., judged only by her votes on military projects that brought jobs to her state, she might justifiedly have been called a warmonger.

Meanwhile Kellog remained at his weekday microphone in New York. Once the children were old enough for boarding school, off they went. It became his regular practice to have as mistress his current secretary, usually a divorced woman in her early-to-middle thirties, efficient, quietly attractive, and emotionally balanced. These persons remained with him only a year or two before going on to better things: one even to Washington to work as legislative assistant to his wife, a post for which he had recommended her. He was as ready to see them depart when the time came as they were to go.

Over the years Annabelle became an ever more commanding presence. Though fine-boned and of no more than average height, and of course slender, she was one of the first to be identified at a distance amongst a crowd of political and show-business notables. Her once raven hair had turned a premature white that was even more striking. Her eyes and chin projected that combination of strength and compassion that distinguished successful male statesmen from the herd, while her full mouth represented elements of both sensuality and, yes, the maternal, sororal, uxorial loving-kindness so prized by men in the most dynamic of women, so little resented by fellow females. She was once named Mother of the Year after a twelvemonth in which she had seen her own children only on the major holidays, but her voting record on child care and related issues was seen by the honoring organization as worthy of reward. No hint of scandal had been associated with her since the death of the married judge in what, for a politician, was her earliest youth, and throughout the years in the Senate she became, as befitted a woman of her age, more bluenosed as to sexual issues, if possible quietly avoiding taking provocative positions on homosexual issues but conspicuously attacking printed and videoed smut, obscene rock lyrics, and the peep shows at which men masturbated while female performers writhed behind a window of plate glass. Thus she found herself for the first time the recipient of praise from the religious Right.

Kellog himself took a comparably conservative turn as to sex, much of which was not hypocritical. He had by now had his fill of the deviates to whom he had listened sympathetically in earlier times. While some were no doubt pitiful, many were simply self-indulgent, and those who called radio psychologists were too often tiresome exhibitionists. Eventually he asked his producer not to put through to him any caller with a sexual problem. If one did penetrate the screen, he was forestalled, by the seven-second delay, from reaching the air.

Kellog had made good money over the years and invested it wisely, with the help of his colleague Seymour Channing, the popular adviser on monetary matters whose radio show came, in a mercenary era, to outdraw his own. Annabelle, with her senator's salary and earnings from speaking engagements, was self-supporting. It was he who had always paid the rents and borne the expense of the children, with their governesses and special schools and, at a very early date in each case, psychiatrists. Neil was an addict for almost a year before Kellog knew about it and, having spent on his insatiable habit a large allowance plus a fortune in extra sums given him by a generous father for a car, a trip to Europe, a new wardrobe, he turned to crime as a source of funds, stealing and selling a power boat, burglarizing the home of a friend's parents, and eventually becoming a dealer in the substances to which he was enslaved. Kellog was successful in keeping these matters out of the news, no small achievement in view of the public recognition enjoyed by himself and his wife. Fortunately, Neil's criminal activities while a juvenile had been pursued in small-town venues in and around the schools he attended, where underpaid law-enforcement officials could be discreetly corrupted.

How early in life Phoebe began to have sexual experiences, and with whom, Kellog never wanted to know, but her first abortion came when she was scarcely fourteen. A story of rape by an unknown invader of her school dormitory was accepted by all concerned, even the press, who concealed her identity as a minor, though some law-and-order elements were responsible for vague leaks to the effect that a family member of a soft-on-crime senator had been the victim of one of the animals that she would coddle. Phoebe herself, at various moments of high self-centered emotion, identified, for her friends and father, a succession of partners — the janitor, the man who serviced the school's Coke machine, a black townie younger than she — and once even spoke of artificial insemination by an old Frankenstein sort of scientist who had taken her in hand. She had run away from school several times throughout the years and when recaptured had committed violence towards property, which had always been interpreted as childish revenge. But when now without provocation she attacked her roommate with a scissors, it was no longer practicable to continue to ignore the symptoms of mental illness she had displayed so consistently and for so long. A canvass of her schoolmates revealed that some incidents had gone unreported. She was institutionalized, but again not even the gutter press made the fact known to any public, despite her parents' celebrity.

Annabelle had long since gone well beyond the so-called women's issues. By her third term she was a member of several of the most powerful committees dealing with the most fundamental concerns of government, the defense of the nation and the economy, and known for her eloquent statements of position, which were strong, sometimes even ringing. Even the other side had to admit she could legitimately qualify as a statesman. In her own party she had come to be admired even by the most mossbacked male elements, who were not necessarily the oldest in years. There was still, however, some resistance against nominating her as presidential candidate over a popular wonder-boy governor who had revitalized a major state in decay when he had taken office, and she did not prevail at the convention until the third ballot. When the governor loyally agreed to run for the vice-presidency, they had a ticket that electrified first the party and then, were the polls to be believed, the country.

Kellog had at last been conclusively eclipsed by his wife, and nobody was more pleased than he. For some time now, weary with many years of the emotional problems of strangers, he had been looking forward to retirement but had never before found the proper pretext. He had been reluctant to quit simply because he was old enough, sufficiently prosperous, and bored with his work: any public confession as to those negative motives would repudiate the advice he had consistently, over the decades, given his callers. Though in many incidentals the proper response was No, a winner always said Yes to the big question posed by life, namely, was it worth the effort? A man, and nowadays a woman as well, should not be without a purpose so long as he could breathe.

With Annabelle's nomination, Kellog had a new job. He would play an active role in supporting her in whichever ways he could best be used. Over the years he had acquired a devoted following that was perhaps even large enough to make a difference in a very close election. FCC regulations would of course prohibit him from injecting political exhortations into his own program, but if he retired as psychologist to reemerge as the eloquent partner of his wife and drumbeater for her in airtime paid for by her party, most of his flock could probably be counted on to favor the presidential nominee of his choice. After the election (which it was realistic to assume Annabelle would win, the other side having haplessly chosen an old man who had in fact already once been defeated in a run for the same office), Kellog could certainly make himself useful around the White House and also write the book for which he had long been begged by leading publishers.

But as the campaign heated up and each poll gave Annabelle a greater lead than the last, the other side, desperate, resorted to the smear. The son's failings no longer remained unknown to the world at large. Nor could Neil keep his nose clean even for these few months: stopped for drunk driving on the New Jersey Turnpike, he took an ineffectual swing at the trooper and thereby provided the top item on the nightly news. Kellog's own background was revealed as though it were shameful, with his pre-radio occupations and his previous marriages now presented as verging on the sleazy, as respectable as they had been: somehow wholesale hardware was made to sound like selling stolen merchandise from the tailgate of a station wagon. Next the hyenas got hold of the story of Annabelle's affair with the judge, and did their best to imply that it was she who had in effect invalided, then killed, his wife.

Cruelest of all were the revelations about poor tormented Phoebe, who had seemingly made progress during her early course of treatment, but then, not long after her mother received the nomination, slashed her wrists with a broken water glass and bled to death before she was found. But the extraordinary fact remained that after weeks of mudslinging Annabelle continued to widen her lead in the polls. And by 11:30 P.M. on the night of Election Day the networks projected her as the clear winner. She had been elected to be the first woman president of the United States. That a man whose humble beginnings had been in wholesale hardware could go on to acquire celebrity in a field of which he had known nothing at the outset and learned on the job, and finally to become First Gentleman of the land could happen only in America — a point he made many times in public between November and January, for he was everywhere in demand as a speaker.

Snow fell in Washington on the fifteenth of January, but by the twentieth the weather was unseasonably warm. Annabelle took the oath of office in a navy blue silk suit with a white blouse and a single string of pearls. Owing to the rise in temperature, she wore no outer coat. Erect with pride, Kellog stood just behind her as she put her hand on the Bible extended by the chief justice of the Supreme Court.

As if to furnish a punctuation point, a single shot was heard just as the new leader of the free world completed the oath. Annabelle fell to the floor of the platform, shot through the heart. She died in the ambulance.

The assassin, who had somehow inserted himself amongst the television cameramen by the use of forged credentials, seemed in a coma when first questioned by the Secret Service, but in time he came around to state that his intended target had not been the first female president. He was simply inexperienced in aiming a powerful handgun. He readily revealed his motive: he had made twenty-seven telephone calls to Dr. Kellog's program with a purpose of discussing his lifelong impotence, but had never succeeded in getting through. He now expressed great regret for killing the new Chief Executive, for whom he had in fact voted, but he had no remorse for aiming at Kellog.

Kellog was benumbed. That the course of history might be changed by some nut with a gun and a personal grievance was not without precedent, but the bystander is not likely to have anticipated his own role in such an event. After years of providing free and public counsel to anybody who called him (and could get through), he rarely encountered any applicant with a strong sense of individual responsibility. They all expected someone else to look after them: if not an agency of government, then at least a radio psychologist. This was more than a national problem.

But what was peculiarly American was that the person who started out in wholesale hardware, went on to become a star on the airwaves, and married a woman who would be elected president, could have his life changed as dramatically in the negative way, but much more quickly.

Now that he would never live in the White House, Kellog decided to conclude another life.

V

"**B**Y NOW I should no longer be amazed, but I am," said Walter Hunsicker. "Kellog showed no emotion but self-pity when his wife was shot down in cold blood."

"I thought she was the president," the little man said sourly. "Here as elsewhere you persistently confuse personality with publicity. No wonder none of your alternative lives has been satisfactory, though all were successful enough, bringing you money, celebrity, excitement, even a certain power or anyway access to it. But I find it significant that you did not make *yourself* president, nor as a writer did you present yourself with the Nobel Prize, and as a performer you did not become a Dean of American Comedy, acquiring a fortune in real estate and playing golf with successive Chief Executives. . . . There was always something about you in each life that was not quite what it should have been. Perhaps it was a basic lack of imagination. But then you never had much enterprise in your original existence."

Hunsicker rallied. "At least I never was ashamed of myself! Of course, I didn't take many chances. We always waited till we could see our way clear financially to take the trip to Europe, buy a house, have a child. . . . We even did them in that order." He was, after all, a rational man who relied on cause-and-effect, a moral man who could not dispense with principles. "What was wrong with the alternative lives is that they were essentially false. I wasn't any of those people, for the reason that at any time I had the power to quit being each of them and become someone else or return to the original me. That's not life. Life is taking your medicine. That's not reality."

The other leaned forward, the overhead light reflected through the strands of hair on his yellow crown. "Reality was what you wanted to escape from."

"I was being a coward," Hunsicker said. "I wasn't protecting anybody. I was denying life."

The little man shrugged. "You have to admit you got everything you asked for, without condition, without fee, and you haven't had to accept the consequences of any of your choices. And you can carry away what you came with. Not a bad deal."

No doubt a contemporary personage of this sort *would* talk like a used-car salesman, but what precisely had the "deal" been?

"You really don't want anything from me?"

"We've already had it," said the little man. "You gave it a go, not once but four times. You've certainly strived. You've been an excellent participant."

"The implication is that there are others to whom I can be compared."

"Of course."

"But," said Hunsicker, "you aren't going to tell me who they are."

"It's the only way to keep it honest." The little man frowned. "But I can tell you this: you haven't disgraced yourself." He pushed the chair back and stood up, extending a hand, smiling incongruously. "Sorry I had to be so sour while the process was under way. But you understand, anything else would have hardly been professional."

Hunsicker did not really understand, but he was nevertheless moved. "Thank you," he said, shaking the small hand warmly but being careful not to apply too much pressure, for it seemed frail. Now that he thought about the matter, he considered whether the little man was in the best of health, with that poor color and watery eye. "Thank you for giving me the strength to accept my lot."

The little man frowned again. "Oh, no, you were given nothing! You may have lived a modest life, but you're affirmative." He then freed his hand to gesture towards the shabby shop beyond the squalid office. "I feel I should explain why this place is perhaps overly grim. It's not just the budget, stingy as that is . . ." He showed embarrassment. "Perhaps it's foolish of us, but we simply could not bear being called vulgar."

Enlightened, Hunsicker returned to the fate that, at too high a cost, he could have evaded.

HE SAT in his car, in the home garage. It was dawn now, judging by the daylight that entered through the window over the work bench against the forward wall. Hunsicker had a certain gift for carpentry. He employed it only practically, for home repairs, but once had toyed with the idea of installing power tools and embarking on some more ambitious projects, handmade bedsteads and the like. As with most of his impulses, this one was the product of a book he had copy-edited, the last word on home workshops, written by a surprisingly articulate craftsman whose prose was superior to that of many foreign-policy pundits and biographers. All in all, Hunsicker held those who could *do things* in greater esteem than the commentators thereupon, among which latter company he had himself been a lifelong member — except for his modest talent at "shop," which had first made itself known in his high-school freshman year, when he executed one of the earliest assignments, a simple wrenhouse, four sides and a slanted roof, with a proficiency that earned the instructor's commendation.

Had Elliot been at all attracted to woodworking, the garage would have been equipped with lathe, jigsaw, and whatever else was wanted — and it went without saying that the boy would have been no mere carpenter, but rather a cabinetmaker. Having never, even as a small boy, set limits for himself, Elliot naturally rejected those which others tried to impose upon him even if well intentioned. His father had learned that early on and never afterwards offended. Those who did were deftly set straight, but with such grace that they thereby almost always became close friends: e.g., Ralph Troutman, Elliot's first college roommate, who, taller and wider, was initially something of a bully with respect to the closets, lights-out time, and the rest, but came off second-best in the inevitable showdown, for Elliot had boxed with distinction in preparatory school. From then on, Ralph was a hearty friend, though he finally fell out of touch in later years when he was married and became a father. . . . Was that defection due to . . . ? Hardly. Elliot had all sorts of married friends, and in the case of many if not most, he was much closer to the wives than to the husbands. Hunsicker could remember worrying about whether Elliot might be going too far as a pal of Jim Randolph's wife, with whom he was for a while inseparable, with or without Jim, escorting Sally alone to horse shows, German opera, artists' retrospectives, especially when Jim was out of town on business, and driving away up through the country on antiquing excursions while Jim stayed home and napped on Sundays. In other words, Jim knew.

No doubt everyone did. Hunsicker of course lied to himself for years. After all, Elliot had had a series of supposed fiancées, all of them eminently qualified for the role, attractive, often extravagantly so, bright, charming, sometimes well-born, but also there were those young women who had risen beyond their origins, and indeed Elliot confessed he preferred that sort, perhaps with the implication that they shared his own experience. If so, Hunsicker could agree. Was it not the right thing that a child should exceed his progenitors? Elliot always did the right thing. He would do so now. He would die as well as anyone could. Extraordinarily, Hunsicker felt a sense of a kind of triumph, too private even for him to name it as such to himself. But it was there, within the anguish.

He left the car and for the first time, because, trailing him, it impeded the closing of the door, he realized that he had been under a blanket. Feeling a sudden chill now, he drew it around his shoulders and walked to the house.

He stayed in the kitchen and started to make the coffee, the lone exercise in this area that he did better than Martha, for he had remained that old-fashioned sort of husband who was ritualistically awkward when it came to the preparation of food. The secret with coffee was warming the pot before adding the water — if you could believe that. He doubted whether a blind taste test would have established any difference whatever, but it was one of those matters accepted as established principles in a family, and when you're a kid and visit elsewhere you are always at first taken aback when your friend's family displays a heresy: puts powdered sugar on French toast instead of syrup or calls a faucet a tap. Such houses always had an odd smell, not necessarily unpleasant, but notably different from that of your own, at first alien but, if you were a frequent visitor, eventually that of a friendly power, a kind of England where things are different from home but at least they spoke your language. He never had, in all these years, got that comfortable under the roofs of any of his relatives-in-law. It had been socially a step up for him to marry Martha, and none of her people ever forgot it.

As a child Hunsicker had a pal named Bobby Marsh, in whose company he spent every moment of life that could be so employed: sat beside him in the same schoolroom, lunched with him in the cafeteria, often suppered with him at either of their homes, and each slept over at the other's house most Friday nights. These were the years from ten to twelve or thirteen. This friendship was probably physically closer than any he had ever known except the very different kind with Martha, but the idea of touching Bobby (or Bob, as he demanded to be called on turning twelve) in any manner but with boxing gloves or in a football tackle would have been unthinkable. Staying over at Bob's house, Hunsicker slept beside him in a double bed, but they never collided, something that frequently happened in the early days with Martha, whose body, even more ample in bed, had a way, an affectionate way, of encroaching on his side during the night. When the time came that he often awakened in the morning with an erection, he and Bob gradually abandoned the sleep-overs. Very likely Bob experienced the same phenomenon, but close as they were, they would have been incapable of comparing notes on such intimate matters though they sometimes discussed sex, in generic terms when the references were personal, in frank particulars only when referring to other boys who boasted of masturbation, sex with animals, peeping through bathroom windows, and one, a precocious rake or more likely just a liar, who at fourteen was never without an account of another erotic adventure, most of them with older women: the lady next door, the prettiest teacher, even the Negress who cleaned the female lavatories at school. Hunsicker's own erotic life at this period consisted exclusively of manipulating himself to fantasies concerning the breasts of Bob Marsh's sixteen-year-old sister, whose laundered brassiere he had seen, and caressed, as it hung dripping down the shower curtain.

Obviously, growing up had been otherwise with Elliot, though his father never suspected it at the time. And what would he have done if he had? Taken the boy to a whorehouse — when he had never been to one himself? Anyway, in an era much different from that of his father's youth, Elliot had soon enough had sex with women. As he was to assure his father, later on when the revelation came, he simply did not care for it. There could be no answer to this, and Hunsicker had not insulted either of their sensibilities by trying to find one. As with all else of life, he had made the best of existing conditions, adjusting himself when necessary.

Steam gushed from the spout of the kettle. Hunsicker dampened the ground coffee with a generous splash, then waited the requisite minute before adding the rest of the water. Drops of amber-colored liquid began to fall into the glass receptacle from the point of the inverted cone that held the paper filter. When Hunsicker was himself a child, the baby brother of a friend of his, reaching from a nearby highchair, tipped over one of those stacked-globe coffee pots, new in that era, and was scalded horribly to death by the boiling water. At least Elliot had lived to manhood. No doubt that was the sort of thought that would be habitual from now on.

He took his filled mug to the table. Martha was seated in her usual place, having entered, in soft slippers, while he waited, staring at the wall, for the water to boil. He was surprised but not startled. She wore pajamas and robe, a costume in which she had hitherto seldom appeared on the ground floor. Martha had always had a foible regarding appropriate attire. After she put on extra weight in early middle age, Hunsicker had never again seen her nude, except when, in the closest quarters, it was impossible to see all of her, or in abbreviated costume, not bathing suit nor underwear — even though, as he repeatedly asseverated, he found her body more sexually appealing than ever. He had never had a taste for women with the chests and hips of boys. . . . God Almighty, what could attract a man in a body exactly like his own? Immediately he was contritely sensitive to the cruelty of the question, though it had been asked only to himself.

He added milk and sugar to Martha's coffee and joined her at the table. Only on sitting down did he remember he had, all this while, been wearing the blue blanket as shawl. He must look like a man considerably older than he was, or perhaps even like an old woman.

"Thanks," he said, "for thinking I might be cold."

She touched his fingers with her own, which were warm from the sides of the mug: he had never known why she often avoided the handle nor how she could endure the heat.

He covered her hand. Because he loved her, he wished there were a means by which he could share his alternative lives with her at least as entertaining narrative, but it was also because he loved her that that could never be done: he could not alter her sense of him at this late date.

But he could ask, "Have you ever thought about what

might have happened in your life if you hadn't met and married me?"

"Only when I was considerably younger," Martha said. "There was a time when I did it a lot. Oddly enough, it was right after having Elliot. You might not think that would occur to a new mother, but it did to me. I had moments of sheer panic: I thought, God, I'm really trapped and forever!"

Hunsicker was warmed now and stood up to take the covering from his shoulders. Martha rose with him, reaching for the blanket. "You *never* fold it right. I can't stand it when the corners don't square up."

"Yet you never make a bed good and true at the corners."

"*I* wasn't in the army. And I've told you throughout the years that I hate to get in between tightly stretched sheets and have to fight my way down inside with my toes."

"We agree on a lot though," Hunsicker said uncertainly. He withstood an urge to embrace her, for it would have been physically awkward with the blanket clasped to her body, and he was too morally fastidious so to beg his case.

"As a child I wanted to be a dancer," said she. "Then later on, in college, I wrote what I thought was poetry. Does anyone still want to be another Edna St. Vincent Millay?"

Hunsicker tenderly assured her, "You could have been either."

"No, I couldn't have," she said with spirit. "I fell over my own feet as a young girl. And it took no great courage when I got only slightly older to see that my poetry was silly stuff." She looked at him with her fine eyes and said proudly, "I have no regrets. I did what I should have done, am what I should have been."

"So did I," stated Walter Hunsicker, "so am I." But something still remained to be said, and he said it. "I couldn't even imagine another life."

FOR THE BEST IN PAPERBACKS, LOOK FOR THE

In every corner of the world, on every subject under the sun, Penguin represents quality and variety—the very best in publishing today.

For complete information about books available from Penguin—including Pelicans, Puffins, Peregrines, and Penguin Classics—and how to order them, write to us at the appropriate address below. Please note that for copyright reasons the selection of books varies from country to country.

In the United Kingdom: For a complete list of books available from Penguin in the U.K., please write to *Dept E.P., Penguin Books Ltd, Harmondsworth, Middlesex, UB7 0DA.*

In the United States: For a complete list of books available from Penguin in the U.S., please write to *Dept BA, Penguin*, Box 120, Bergenfield, New Jersey 07621-0120.

In Canada: For a complete list of books available from Penguin in Canada, please write to *Penguin Books Ltd, 2801 John Street, Markham, Ontario L3R 1B4.*

In Australia: For a complete list of books available from Penguin in Australia, please write to the *Marketing Department, Penguin Books Ltd, P.O. Box 257, Ringwood, Victoria 3134.*

In New Zealand: For a complete list of books available from Penguin in New Zealand, please write to the *Marketing Department, Penguin Books (NZ) Ltd, Private Bag, Takapuna, Auckland 9.*

In India: For a complete list of books available from Penguin, please write to *Penguin Overseas Ltd, 706 Eros Apartments, 56 Nehru Place, New Delhi, 110019.*

In Holland: For a complete list of books available from Penguin in Holland, please write to *Penguin Books Nederland B.V., Postbus 195, NL-1380AD Weesp, Netherlands.*

In Germany: For a complete list of books available from Penguin, please write to *Penguin Books Ltd, Friedrichstrasse 10-12, D-6000 Frankfurt Main 1, Federal Republic of Germany.*

In Spain: For a complete list of books available from Penguin in Spain, please write to *Longman, Penguin España, Calle San Nicolas 15, E-28013 Madrid, Spain.*

In Japan: For a complete list of books available from Penguin in Japan, please write to *Longman Penguin Japan Co Ltd, Yamaguchi Building, 2-12-9 Kanda Jimbocho, Chiyoda-Ku, Tokyo 101, Japan.*

☐ **THE WOMEN OF BREWSTER PLACE**
A Novel in Seven Stories
Gloria Naylor

Winner of the American Book Award, this is the story of seven survivors of an urban housing project — a blind alley feeding into a dead end. From a variety of backgrounds, they experience, fight against, and sometimes transcend the fate of black women in America today.

192 pages   ISBN: 0-14-006690-X   **$5.95**

☐ **STONES FOR IBARRA**
Harriet Doerr

An American couple comes to the small Mexican village of Ibarra to reopen a copper mine, learning much about life and death from the deeply faithful villagers.   *214 pages   ISBN: 0-14-007562-3*   **$5.95**

☐ **WORLD'S END**
T. Coraghessan Boyle

"Boyle has emerged as one of the most inventive and verbally exuberant writers of his generation," writes *The New York Times*. Here he tells the story of Walter Van Brunt, who collides with early American history while searching for his lost father.   *456 pages   ISBN: 0-14-009760-0*   **$8.95**

☐ **THE WHISPER OF THE RIVER**
Ferrol Sams

The story of Porter Osborn, Jr., who, in 1938, leaves his rural Georgia home to face the world at Willingham University, *The Whisper of the River* is peppered with memorable characters and resonates with the details of place and time. Ferrol Sams's writing is regional fiction at its best.

528 pages   ISBN: 0-14-008387-1   **$6.95**

☐ **ENGLISH CREEK**
Ivan Doig

Drawing on the same heritage he celebrated in *This House of Sky,* Ivan Doig creates a rich and varied tapestry of northern Montana and of our country in the late 1930s.   *338 pages   ISBN: 0-14-008442-8*   **$6.95**

☐ **THE YEAR OF SILENCE**
Madison Smartt Bell

A penetrating look at the varied reactions to a young woman's suicide exactly one year later, *The Year of Silence* "captures vividly and poignantly the chancy dance of life." (*The New York Times Book Review*)

208 pages   ISBN: 0-14-011533-1   **$6.95**

FOR THE BEST IN CONTEMPORARY AMERICAN FICTION

☐ **IN THE COUNTRY OF LAST THINGS**
Paul Auster

Death, joggers, leapers, and Object Hunters are just some of the realities of future city life in this spare, powerful, visionary novel about one woman's struggle to live and love in a frightening post-apocalyptic world.

208 pages   *ISBN: 0-14-009705-8*   **$5.95**

☐ **BETWEEN C&D**
New Writing from the Lower East Side Fiction Magazine
Joel Rose and Catherine Texier, Editors

A startling collection of stories by Tama Janowitz, Gary Indiana, Kathy Acker, Barry Yourgrau, and others, *Between C&D* is devoted to short fiction that ignores preconceptions — fiction not found in conventional literary magazines.

194 pages   *ISBN: 0-14-010570-0*   **$7.95**

☐ **LEAVING CHEYENNE**
Larry McMurtry

The story of a love triangle unlike any other, *Leaving Cheyenne* follows the three protagonists — Gideon, Johnny, and Molly — over a span of forty years, until all have finally "left Cheyenne."

254 pages   *ISBN: 0-14-005221-6*   **$6.95**

FOR THE BEST LITERATURE, LOOK FOR THE

☐ THE BOOK AND THE BROTHERHOOD
Iris Murdoch

Many years ago Gerard Hernshaw and his friends banded together to finance a political and philosophical book by a monomaniacal Marxist genius. Now opinions have changed, and support for the book comes at the price of moral indignation; the resulting disagreements lead to passion, hatred, a duel, murder, and a suicide pact.   *602 pages*   *ISBN: 0-14-010470-4*   **$8.95**

☐ GRAVITY'S RAINBOW
Thomas Pynchon

Thomas Pynchon's classic antihero is Tyrone Slothrop, an American lieutenant in London whose body anticipates German rocket launchings. Surely one of the most important works of fiction produced in the twentieth century, *Gravity's Rainbow* is a complex and awesome novel in the great tradition of James Joyce's *Ulysses*.   *768 pages*   *ISBN: 0-14-010661-8*   **$10.95**

☐ FIFTH BUSINESS
Robertson Davies

The first novel in the celebrated "Deptford Trilogy," which also includes *The Manticore* and *World of Wonders*, *Fifth Business* stands alone as the story of a rational man who discovers that the marvelous is only another aspect of the real.   *266 pages*   *ISBN: 0-14-004387-X*   **$4.95**

☐ WHITE NOISE
Don DeLillo

Jack Gladney, a professor of Hitler Studies in Middle America, and his fourth wife, Babette, navigate the usual rocky passages of family life in the television age. Then, their lives are threatened by an "airborne toxic event"—a more urgent and menacing version of the "white noise" of transmissions that typically engulfs them.   *326 pages*   *ISBN: 0-14-007702-2*   **$7.95**

FOR THE BEST LITERATURE, LOOK FOR THE

☐ A SPORT OF NATURE
Nadine Gordimer

Hillela, Nadine Gordimer's "sport of nature," is seductive and intuitively gifted at life. Casting herself adrift from her family at seventeen, she lives among political exiles on an East African beach, marries a black revolutionary, and ultimately plays a heroic role in the overthrow of apartheid.

354 pages   ISBN: 0-14-008470-3   **$7.95**

☐ THE COUNTERLIFE
Philip Roth

By far Philip Roth's most radical work of fiction, *The Counterlife* is a book of conflicting perspectives and points of view about people living out dreams of renewal and escape. Illuminating these lives is the skeptical, enveloping intelligence of the novelist Nathan Zuckerman, who calculates the price and examines the results of his characters' struggles for a change of personal fortune.

372 pages   ISBN: 0-14-009769-4   **$4.95**

☐ THE MONKEY'S WRENCH
Primo Levi

Through the mesmerizing tales told by two characters—one, a construction worker/philosopher who has built towers and bridges in India and Alaska; the other, a writer/chemist, rigger of words and molecules—Primo Levi celebrates the joys of work and the art of storytelling.

174 pages   ISBN: 0-14-010357-0   **$6.95**

☐ IRONWEED
William Kennedy

"Riding up the winding road of Saint Agnes Cemetery in the back of the rattling old truck, Francis Phelan became aware that the dead, even more than the living, settled down in neighborhoods." So begins William Kennedy's Pulitzer-Prize winning novel about an ex-ballplayer, part-time gravedigger, and full-time drunk, whose return to the haunts of his youth arouses the ghosts of his past and present.   *228 pages   ISBN: 0-14-007020-6*   **$6.95**

☐ THE COMEDIANS
Graham Greene

Set in Haiti under Duvalier's dictatorship, *The Comedians* is a story about the committed and the uncommitted. Actors with no control over their destiny, they play their parts in the foreground; experience love affairs rather than love; have enthusiasms but not faith; and if they die, they die like Mr. Jones, by accident.

288 pages   ISBN: 0-14-002766-1   **$4.95**

FOR THE BEST LITERATURE, LOOK FOR THE

☐ **HERZOG**
Saul Bellow

Winner of the National Book Award, *Herzog* is the imaginative and critically acclaimed story of Moses Herzog: joker, moaner, cuckhold, charmer, and truly an Everyman for our time.

342 pages   ISBN: 0-14-007270-5   **$6.95**

☐ **FOOLS OF FORTUNE**
William Trevor

The deeply affecting story of two cousins—one English, one Irish—brought together and then torn apart by the tide of Anglo-Irish hatred, *Fools of Fortune* presents a profound symbol of the tragic entanglements of England and Ireland in this century.   240 pages   ISBN: 0-14-006982-8   **$6.95**

☐ **THE SONGLINES**
Bruce Chatwin

Venturing into the desolate land of Outback Australia—along timeless paths, and among fortune hunters, redneck Australians, racist policemen, and mysterious Aboriginal holy men—Bruce Chatwin discovers a wondrous vision of man's place in the world.   296 pages   ISBN: 0-14-009429-6   **$7.95**

☐ **THE GUIDE: A NOVEL**
R. K. Narayan

Raju was once India's most corrupt tourist guide; now, after a peasant mistakes him for a holy man, he gradually begins to play the part. His succeeds so well that God himself intervenes to put Raju's new holiness to the test.

220 pages   ISBN: 0-14-009657-4   **$5.95**

You can find all these books at your local bookstore, or use this handy coupon for ordering:
Penguin Books By Mail
Dept. BA Box 999
Bergenfield, NJ 07621-0999
Please send me the above title(s). I am enclosing _____
(please add sales tax if appropriate and $1.50 to cover postage and handling). Send check or money order—no CODs. Please allow four weeks for shipping. We cannot ship to post office boxes or addresses outside the USA. *Prices subject to change without notice.*

Ms./Mrs./Mr. _____

Address _____

City/State _____ Zip _____

Sales tax: CA: 6.5%   NY: 8.25%   NJ: 6%   PA: 6%   TN: 5.5%

FOR THE BEST LITERATURE, LOOK FOR THE

☐ **THE LAST SONG OF MANUEL SENDERO**
Ariel Dorfman

In an unnamed country, in a time that might be now, the son of Manuel Sendero refuses to be born, beginning a revolution where generations of the future wait for a world without victims or oppressors.

464 pages   *ISBN: 0-14-008896-2*   **$7.95**

☐ **THE BOOK OF LAUGHTER AND FORGETTING**
Milan Kundera

In this collection of stories and sketches, Kundera addresses themes including sex and love, poetry and music, sadness and the power of laughter. "*The Book of Laughter and Forgetting* calls itself a novel," writes John Leonard of *The New York Times*, "although it is part fairly tale, part literary criticism, part political tract, part musicology, part autobiography. It can call itself whatever it wants to, because the whole is genius."

240 pages   *ISBN: 0-14-009693-0*   **$6.95**

☐ **TIRRA LIRRA BY THE RIVER**
Jessica Anderson

Winner of the Miles Franklin Award, Australia's most prestigious literary prize, *Tirra Lirra by the River* is the story of a woman's seventy-year search for the place where she truly belongs. Nora Porteous's series of escapes takes her from a small Australia town to the suburbs of Sydney to London, where she seems finally to become the woman she always wanted to be.

142 pages   *ISBN: 0-14-006945-3*   **$4.95**

☐ **LOVE UNKNOWN**
A. N. Wilson

In their sweetly wild youth, Monica, Belinda, and Richeldis shared a bachelor-girl flat and became friends for life. Now, twenty years later, A. N. Wilson charts the intersecting lives of the three women through the perilous waters of love, marriage, and adultery in this wry and moving modern comedy of manners.

202 pages   *ISBN: 0-14-010190-X*   **$6.95**

☐ **THE WELL**
Elizabeth Jolley

Against the stark beauty of the Australian farmlands, Elizabeth Jolley portrays an eccentric, affectionate relationship between the two women—Hester, a lonely spinster, and Katherine, a young orphan. Their pleasant, satisfyingly simple life is nearly perfect until a dark stranger invades their world in a most horrifying way.

176 pages   *ISBN: 0-14-008901-2*   **$6.95**